Critical acclaim for *Remembrance Day*

'The best book of its kind I've read since *The Day of the Jackal*. When thrillers get better than this, I'd like to read them'   Jack Higgins

'Relished without pause. An extraordinary tour de force about terrorist exploitation of highly sophisticated technology. Porter avoids explanatory clutter by the use of quite brilliant dialogue which keeps everything on a very human level: fast-flowing but sure, neat even in complexity, and eschewing grotesqueries that might suspend our belief in a series of events which are all too credible'   *Glasgow Herald*

'*Remembrance Day* is an ultra-modern thriller, using state-of-the-art technology. Porter reveals himself to be a master of the form'   *Sunday Telegraph*

'A canny thriller ... it starts with a bang when a bus blows up in a London street ... Impressive high-tech research. Porter works hard at the mechanics of plot assembly and it pays off'   *Guardian*

'Henry Porter takes the familiar ingredients of maverick police officer, sociopathic killer and heroic innocent and adds a dollop of technology to produce a creditable thriller. Porter's handling of fascinating material sets it above run-of-the-mill'   *Daily Express*

'A captivating first novel ... Pacy and well-researched and culminates in an explosive finale'   *Tatler*

Henry Porter was born in 1953. He is married to Liz Elliot and has two children. He lives in London. His latest novel, *A Spy's Life*, is also published by Orion.

By Henry Porter

Remembrance Day
A Spy's Life

HENRY PORTER

REMEMBRANCE DAY

An Orion paperback
First published in Great Britain by Orion in 1999
This paperback edition published in 2000 by
Orion Books Ltd,
Orion House, 5 Upper St Martin's Lane,
London WC2H 9EA

Copyright © 1999 Henry Porter

A CIP catalogue record for this book
is available from the British Library.

Printed and bound in Great Britain by
Clays Ltd, St Ives plc

www.orionbooks.co.uk

To my parents and brother

Author's Note

I would not have written this book without the help of Liz Elliot and Gilbert Adair, both of whom devoted much time to encouraging me. My editor, Jane Wood, and agent, Georgina Capel, are also owed debts of gratitude for having confidence in the book and – in the most delicate way possible – telling me where I was going wrong. I was lucky to meet Joseph I. Mulligan III, my tireless guide in Boston, and Kenny Young of the Ritz Carlton Hotel, Boston, whose conversation inspired a crucial idea in the plot. Professor Roy Anderson, Dr Alison Snape, Ed Ross, Manish Somani and Tom Standage were all generous with their expertise.

Finally, thanks to Riva Mantis who knows everything.

Chapter One

He knew where he had been standing. He knew what he had been thinking before that moment. He had been thinking that he'd like to speak to the girl in the short dress and tunic, a few yards from him on the pavement. She was swinging a small backpack against her thigh impatiently. She was waiting for someone too. He smiled at her but only managed a smirk, not the look of solidarity that he'd intended, which said, 'We've both been stood up.' She ignored him and moved towards the entrance of the tube station and made a great show of peering down the stairs. A breeze came up from the underground and lifted her dress. This seemed to annoy her. She slapped it down, brushing it as if it were covered in dust, then retreated out of the draught to stand by a curved glass recess at the front of an airline office.

Con Lindow remembered thinking that the evening was warm for October, like a late summer day in Boston. He strolled away to show that he was not trying to pick her up. He went twenty paces or so, then wheeled round back towards the station. There was a lull in the traffic and he began wondering why Eamonn was late, and exactly how they would spend the evening when he arrived. Eamonn had been vague on the phone. Said they'd have a few drinks and then go on to a Latin-American place somewhere north of Oxford Street. It hadn't sounded promising, but Lindow would be pleased to see him again. He imagined Eamonn shambling up from the tube station, a book and a newspaper under his arm, laughing ruefully at his lateness and then turning it so that Lindow would feel a prick for being so punctual. It was two years since their mother had been overwhelmed by cancer and taken before any of them had realised she was ill. That was the last time they had met. Lindow saw the funeral – Eamonn's wounded face in the procession of mourners that signifies a great Irish occasion.

A bus turned into Clarence Street and slowed to negotiate a traffic island. Lindow looked at it and idly wondered if his brother was on board. He guessed not because Eamonn had said he'd be coming straight from work by underground so he wouldn't have to worry about the traffic. He'd be there by seven fifteen for sure. He was definite about that, but you never knew. He might meet someone and forget the arrangement. No, Lindow reassured himself, he would come because they hadn't seen each other for so long, and it had been Eamonn who'd been pressing for them to get together. He'd be there soon enough. Lindow looked at the bus and glanced down at his watch. He remembered doing that.

It was seven thirty-five when the street exploded.

Lindow was lifted clean off his feet and hurled into a metal bollard, which smacked him on the back of his neck. He was knocked out, but only for a few seconds, and came to to find that his world had been extinguished. He couldn't see. He lay utterly still, hearing the sounds that fill the first moments after an explosion. Glass loosened by the shockwave was crashing around him, stabbing his legs, and somewhere along the street there was a terrifying roar, as if a furnace door had been opened. Alarms shrieked. People cried out with the awful recognition of what had happened to them. Lindow had one thought: he must shield himself from the glass still falling from the buildings above. He tried to move his right hand, but it was held by something heavy. He shifted a little and freed his left arm, which was locked behind his back in a half-nelson, then wrapped it across his face. But it wasn't his face. Then he understood. He hadn't been blinded at all, but something – some cloth – had fallen over his face and covered his eyes. He pulled at the material and found himself looking up. It was dark and the air was filled with smoke and dust. In the night sky quantities of paper flew on the thermals from the fire. He understood now that it had been a bomb and somehow knew it was the bus that had exploded, although he hadn't actually seen the explosion and couldn't see the bus because he was facing the other way. Then the pain came, coursing from the back of his skull to his forehead and down into his eyes. He squeezed them tight and felt his stomach heave. He was going to be sick. He had to get up, had to get away. He turned his head from the bollard and checked through an inventory of his senses. He wiggled his toes: they moved. He felt his chest gingerly with his fingertips, like a blind man reading Braille, and progressed down to his stomach and groin where there was a horrible sensation of dampness. He reached the belt of his trousers, and touched a viscous mess. Christ, he thought, the explosion had opened his stomach. He knew injuries like this confused the nervous system, knew that his brain would not make sense of the wounds for a few moments: people got out of car crashes with injuries like this, walked a few paces, then fell down dead. These would be his last conscious seconds. This was it – everything he so desperately wanted to do, the things that he thought only he could do, would never be accomplished. He readied himself for the final convulsions. Nothing came. Then he dabbed again at his stomach, probing a little deeper into the mess. There was no pain at all and – bafflingly – no wound either.

He heard a groan, a thick, guttural word he couldn't make out. It was a woman's voice. She had fallen across him, pinning his right side to the ground. Her tunic had flown up and covered his face, which was why he had the smell of perfume in his nostrils. Her head was very close to his, and very still.

'You hurt?' he said, and shifted his body so that she slid from him on to the stone and let out another groan.

'You hurt?' he repeated stupidly. He knew then that the blood pooled on his stomach was not his but the woman's, and that she must be very badly injured indeed.

He moved again, lifted his head and strained to look at her. It was the girl he had been watching by the tube entrance. He sat up, propping himself against the bollard, and with his right hand reached over to draw back the hair glued to her face. There was an earphone, which had come detached from the tape-player. He pulled away and looked at her face, saw a mass of blood on the right side with white flecks glinting in it. He thought he'd wipe it for her – then he understood that there was nothing behind the blood. No face. What he was seeing were her teeth, moving as the girl tried to cry out. Further down her body the dress was stained and shone wet in the light that still came from far inside the airline office. Beneath her ribcage was a very dark patch. He squirmed and tried to call out, but his voice had gone. He coughed and then shouted again, hoarsely. No one came.

He looked about him. Down the street, about seventy yards from where he lay, the bus was on fire. He could feel the heat on his face. Flames shot from the engine and heavy black smoke spilled from the windows. Between the billows of smoke he could make out a rupture along the flank of the bus. The rear of the vehicle had slewed round at the moment of explosion and mounted the traffic island in the centre of the road. Other cars had simply stopped in their tracks and a black cab, which had been following the bus, stood with its bonnet blown open and its front tyres on fire. Around the bus there were smaller fires. Wastebins and the plastic fittings of traffic-lights had ignited from the heat; bits of panelling, blown from the sides of the bus and now edged with ribbons of flame, lay in the road. He watched with astonishment as a figure ran towards the bus, vanished into the smoke at the front, then reappeared dragging something.

He couldn't remember how crowded the street had been before the bus came on the scene. He knew that a party of tourists had been filing through the stone arcade that straddled the pavement up to the corner where the bus was. Maybe they cleared it in time. He couldn't tell because of the curtain of smoke. Nearer to him – just beyond the station – what he had taken for a pile of rubbish moved. An arm emerged from the debris and waved in the smoke; a cyclist, whom Lindow had passed as he walked away from the girl minutes before, was standing up and straightening his helmet. Nearer still a man, whom Lindow recognised as the news vendor from outside the tube station, was crawling towards them. He stopped to rest on his elbows, looked down at his hands, then felt in his jacket for something.

Lindow shouted, 'Don't go any further, you'll cut yourself.' He was having difficulty finding his voice.

The man took no notice. He reached over to one of the bundles of newspapers and with a pocket knife slashed at the string that held it together, letting the newspapers sprawl over the pavement. Then, chucking the newspapers ahead of him, he made a path over the glass to where Lindow and the girl lay.

'Is she hurt bad?' he cried, as he shuffled towards them.

'Yes, I think so.' Lindow had cupped his right hand to hold her head so as to avoid touching her wounded face. The girl was moving in and out of consciousness, her jaw working in a slow, chewing motion.

'It's her head and stomach.'

'Oh, God, look at the state of her,' said the man, collapsing beside them. 'Where are the ambulances?'

Lindow saw the man's leg was sticking out at an odd

angle just below the knee. He guessed it was dislocated, or that the tibia had been shattered. The man rolled over on his back. Then he did something extraordinary. He slid a hand inside his trousers and worked away at something, revolving his hips as he did so. Finally he shook his leg and it came off. It took Lindow several seconds to understand that this was an artificial limb.

The news vendor pushed himself up a little and looked down at his good leg. Lindow saw that the trousers had been shredded. There was a lot of blood.

'Jesus, I can't lose that one too. Bastard, bastard bomb!' he said, choking in a little tide of smoke that had crept to where they lay.

Minutes passed. No one came. But people were moving about, shouting for help and trying to find each other. Lindow decided that it was no use trying to move the girl. Better to sit there with her. He leaned back on the bollard and put his left hand down to give himself support. He felt something soft and warm in his palm. Without thinking, he picked it up. It was a bird, a starling that had fallen stone dead from its perch above them, killed instantly by the shockwave or a splinter of glass. As he dropped it on the pavement, a line he'd once read came to him. 'So easy and swift is the passage between life and death in wild nature.'

He wondered if the girl would make that passage. He looked at her again. She probably wouldn't. With her face like that, maybe it was better that she didn't.

Someone ran up to them. It was a cycle messenger, speaking into a radio strapped to him in a shoulder holster. He was radioing details of the injured and dying to his control.

'There are three here,' he shouted. 'Three, yes. That makes at least five seriously injured that I've seen. Yeah, they'll need blood . . . I'm looking at a woman. She's very badly hurt. And a man with a broken leg. Everyone's cut and bleeding. It's a fucking mess, I tell you.'

He said nothing to them and ran off across the street. Then a policewoman came and crouched between the news vendor and the girl. She was white-faced and on the edge of panic. She touched the girl's clotted hair with the back of her hand.

'Do you know her? What's her name?' she asked, her voice high and uneven.

'No,' replied Lindow.

'I don't know her name,' said the news vendor. 'But mine's Harry Ribb. Can someone phone my wife and say I'm all right? She'll know I'm here right in the middle of it when she sees the news. She knows where my stand is, see.'

The policewoman did not hear him. She said to Lindow, 'Stay here with her. Try to keep her conscious. Have you got something to cover her with? I've left my coat with a man over there.'

Lindow said that she could have his jacket. The policewoman held his shoulders as he leaned forward and helped him pull it off.

'You've got a nasty gash there,' she said, looking at the blood on his collar.

They placed his jacket over the girl. The policewoman got up and glanced at Lindow. Her lower lip was trembling. She turned her head away and sucked in air, frowning with effort. The sinews in her neck were working furiously. She was fighting to control herself. 'There's help coming,' she said, and hurried away with one hand clutching her belt to stop her night stick and radio flapping.

The alarms in the street seemed to have synchronised into a single pulse. Now that Lindow knew he wasn't badly hurt, he focused on the girl, leaned down and talked to her about anything that came into his head. He told her about Boston and the campus at MIT, about skiing in Vermont and how in the summer his laboratory became so hot that he had once opened one of the lab

7

fridges and moved a desk into the doorway. He ran on, not knowing whether she heard any of it. At one stage she became totally still and he thought she had died. Then a fuel tank exploded down the street and he felt her stiffen. He bent down to her face and asked her name. A murmur came but he couldn't make out what she said. Harry Ribb looked up and drubbed a fist slowly on the pavement.

Some way behind them Lindow could hear the first ambulance make its way through the stalled traffic. He strained round to see it pull up in the middle of the road and two men get out. They ran over to a policeman, who gesticulated rapidly, showing them where the injured lay. Other people were staggering about the street now, all of them streaming with blood. Lindow shouted and waved to them, but they took no notice. At length one of the ambulancemen came to them, sliding and crunching on the scree of glass.

'You must help this woman!' demanded Lindow. 'She needs help now.'

The man ran a flashlight up and down the girl's body, then scribbled something on a clipboard. 'I'm sorry, sir. You're just going to have to bear with us. We're the first here, you see. We have to report back to Headquarters. Give them an idea of the scale of this thing.'

Lindow's temper snapped. 'Look, while you're making your goddam lists she could die. She's bleeding inside. Look at her. Look at her, man!'

'I hear you,' said the crewman coolly. 'But we have to do it this way. She'll be the first to be seen when the other crews arrive, I promise you that. They won't be long now. Stay here and keep her calm. It won't be long.'

He hurried away to another group where a woman was rocking over a body in the street, sending screams to the sky. Lindow was aware of a bright light tacking across the pavement. He looked round to his right to see a news cameraman who'd come from somewhere behind

8

and was panning his camera from the wreck of the bus on to him and the girl.

'Get the fuck out of here!' Lindow screamed. 'Can't you see what's happened to her?'

He raised his arm to protect the girl's eyes from the camera's light. But he knew in an instant that the pictures could never be shown. The light spilled across her face and body and left nothing to the imagination. No station would use it because somewhere out there her parents would see it before they even knew she was hurt.

The light dimmed and the cameraman jerked back, unplugging himself from the eyepiece. 'I'm sorry,' he said, swinging the camera down from his shoulder. He walked away, shaking his head.

'Jackal – fucking jackal,' growled Harry, from the pavement.

Lindow decided that he must do something for the girl. They might wait all night before anyone came. He pushed himself against the bollard. His legs were stiff and cold, and they hurt like hell.

'Can you support her?' he said to Harry. 'I'm going to get help. She won't last otherwise.'

Harry moved around a little, dragging his artificial limb with him. Then Lindow eased the girl's weight slowly on to Harry's big belly. Her head flopped sideways. As Harry looked down at her, Lindow saw that his eyes had watered up and that tiny fragments of glass shrapnel glinted from the cuts in his forehead.

He stood up shakily and looked about. There were several ambulances now. A white Volvo estate car with a green flashing light had just pulled up at the front rank of emergency vehicles and was disgorging what he knew must be a medical team. The street had become cold. It was beginning to rain and the team were hurriedly putting on waterproofs. He tried to run to them but something stopped him. He looked down at his left leg and saw a piece of glass protruding from the outside of his thigh. Each time he put his leg forward the material of his corduroys snagged on it, causing it to work itself deeper into the wound. Without thinking, he reached down and pulled it from his leg like a thorn and flung it into the gutter. Then he ran to the Volvo.

'Are you a doctor?' he shouted, over the noise of the sirens and alarms.

'Yes,' the nearest man shouted back. 'Is it for you?'

'No, for a woman over here,' said Lindow. 'She's in a very bad state.'

The doctor saw Lindow's face in the flashing light and understood that he had to go. He told one of the nurses to accompany him and signalled to the others that they should follow with the ambulances moving up the street towards the bus and the victims lying on the opposite side.

'We shouldn't be here,' he said, as they clattered over the glass to Harry and the girl. 'The area isn't secured yet. The police say there could be other bombs. They don't know – no warnings.'

When they reached Harry, he was talking to the girl with a slow insistence about his garden and how the rain that was now falling had come too late to do any good. But there was always next year, he said, and he'd have another crack at the flower show, which he hadn't entered because of the drought.

The doctor handed Lindow a torch and told him to hold it high up so that he could see the girl as well as his bag. He was in his early thirties – Lindow's age, but with a heavier build, like a rugby player.

'Now let's have a look here, shall we?' He peered at her face then lifted Lindow's jacket to look at her stomach.

'What's her name?' he said, moving his head from side to side. 'Hold the torch over here, man. Here!' He pointed to the place with the finger of his surgical glove.

Then he lifted the dress and got very close to the gash below her ribcage. 'What did you say her name was?'

The girl tried to speak.

'I think it's Kay,' said Harry. 'She was saying something like that just now.'

'Right, Kay. We're going to have you in hospital in no time at all. I want to examine you a little more and then I'm going to give you something to ease the pain. Okeydokey? Good. You're going to be fine.' His expression said otherwise. 'Hold on there, Kay.'

A nurse arrived and set up a light, then a fragile stand on which she hung a container of fluid.

'We need to get a line into her,' said the doctor, 'and we'll give her a shot of morphine straight away.'

The nurse held a syringe up to the light, pressed the plunger until the liquid spurted out and gave it to the doctor. Still squatting, he manoeuvred to the girl's left side, felt for her buttock and rubbed it vigorously. He eased the syringe into the flesh and waited for a few seconds while it emptied. His eyes met Lindow's.

'What *do* they think they are doing?' he said quietly. 'What's she ever done?'

Almost immediately the girl relaxed and her head fell back into the crook of Harry's arm. Harry braced it with his free hand and looked away. He couldn't take the sight of her face.

The nurse inserted the drip of Hartman's blood substitute into the girl's right arm, then attached leads from the ECG to an area clear of laceration just above her right breast. The girl was breathing regularly, but the doctor looked worried. He leaned down close to her face. 'Kay, we're going to move you very soon. Hang on there.'

He stepped away and spoke to the nurse. 'Her liver may be pretty badly damaged. She's bleeding inside and there's a lot of glass in her. Get David Peretz on the phone and tell him I'm sending her to him. Explain her injuries. I'm going to get one of those ambulances.'

The nurse pulled the hood of her waterproof over her head and stood up. The rain was coming down hard now. Lindow shivered. She jabbed the number of the hospital on the mobile phone and put it to her ear inside the hood.

'Can you do this for me?' she shouted to Lindow. 'You don't need the number. Just keep pressing redial. I'll get these bandages on her.'

Lindow tried several times but failed to get through. 'I'm doing something wrong here,' he said. 'I can't seem to get a line.'

'There probably aren't any lines. The cell antennae will be blocked with people phoning to say they're okay, and calls from journalists. They keep the lines open and no one else can get on the network. It's always the same. We'll have to patch a message through the ambulance radio.' While she spoke, she ripped surgical pads from their wrappers and pressed them lightly to the girl's stomach and face. She unravelled a bandage around her head to hold one of the pads in place.

The doctor came running back with two ambulance crews, one for the girl and the other for Harry. Lindow wondered why they hadn't brought their vehicles up to the spot and then realised that they couldn't because of the certainty of punctures from the mass of glass.

Kay was lifted on to a stretcher and moved swiftly to an ambulance. The doctor and nurse went with her, he to use the radio and she to carry the bottle of fluid. The second ambulance crew began working on Harry, whose face was now covered in a mask. They wrapped his leg in a suction cast. As they prepared to carry him away, he pulled the mask from his face and told them drunkenly not to forget his artificial limb, which had been moved to one side by the crew and was now lying incongruously on

12

the pavement. Lindow picked it up together with his own jacket and followed them to the ambulance.

Before climbing in to sit by Harry, he looked towards the wreck of the bus, which was crackling and steaming under the firemen's water jets. He hadn't seen them arrive – they must have approached from the other direction, but now five or six hoses arced over the bus and filled the street with a spray that was pooling in a great orange lake. The bus's superstructure had almost completely burned away, although odd bits of metal remained sticking up like antlers. The back of the vehicle had collapsed as the tyres burst and it squatted down, still burning, on the traffic island.

Lindow looked at his watch. It was eight thirty, near enough an hour since the bus had turned the corner into Clarence Street.

Commander Kenneth Foyle, head of the Metropolitan Police's Anti-terrorist Unit, had taken his first day off in nearly three weeks to watch the appearance of his daughter at a magistrates' court in the West Country. Along with thirteen others, she faced charges ranging from obstruction to criminal damage. Katherine Foyle was part of a group protesting against the building of an agricultural research centre. At dawn on the previous day the police, and security men employed by the local authority, had moved in on the camp around the new laboratories and Katherine had been hauled from the scene by two security guards. He knew this much because he had seen his daughter's picture in the following day's tabloids. He telephoned the Somerset police to discover that she had been charged with obstruction and threaten-ing behaviour, and locked up overnight. Katherine! Threatening behaviour! He knew her better.

Foyle rang New Scotland Yard to tell his assistant, Graham Forbes, that he had family business to attend to and would not be in that day. He hadn't been any more explicit than that and hoped that no one at the Yard would recognise Katherine in the newspaper. Then he had dismissed his police driver and made the 150-mile journey to Somerset in his own car, reaching the court in time for Katherine's hearing. He asked if he could speak for his daughter, then assured the magistrates that she would not break the law again. The bench nodded in unison, not without some sympathy, and imposed a fifty-pound fine for each offence. Foyle paid by cheque on the way out of the court.

He minded about it all terribly, but driving back to Katherine's digs in Bristol he tried to avoid mention of the protest and her first night in police custody. He'd forgive Katherine anything because he held himself responsible for so much of her turbulent nature. There was a lot of him in her. When she was growing up, he had been away, running undercover operations for the Drugs Squad and then a succession of investigations into organised crime in the capital. But now that he had got where he wanted – heading SO 13 – his family seemed to have disintegrated around him. June had decided to make her own life: as Katherine was preparing to leave for Bristol University a year ago, his wife had told him over an anniversary dinner that she would now be spending much of her time away from home researching her doctoral thesis. When she was not bottom up in some desert burial ground, she'd be writing and lecturing at a university in the Midlands. She told him she'd finance herself with money left in her father's will, then added crisply that she was not ending their marriage but suspending it. Foyle didn't quite know what that meant. He was less certain in these matters than he was about police work and had decided to put up with the arrangement and get himself a housekeeper.

'Heard from Mum?' he asked Katherine.

'No, you?'

'Not for a while. When does she get back from Jordan?'

'Mid-November, or when it starts raining there.' Katherine looked out of her window at the bank of black cloud that smothered the last light in the west. A silence ensued while she picked at some mud on her jeans.

'Did you really threaten that police officer, Katherine?'

'Kate! I'm called Kate now, Dad. I just prefer it, if that's all right.'

'Okay, sorry . . . *Kate*! Did you take a swing at him, like he said in court?'

'No, course not. I didn't touch him.'

'But you got your picture in the paper with those two officers.'

'I know, they showed it to us in the cells. I'm glad Mum didn't see it,' she said, looking conspiratorially at her father.

'It's not funny. You've got a criminal record now. That could count against you. It matters, Katherine . . . Kate.'

She laughed. It didn't seem to worry her remotely.

'Tell me something,' said Foyle, 'what have you got against this agricultural centre, and why now, for goodness' sake? There's nothing growing at this time of year.'

'Dad, you know nothing about the subject – I mean, about the release of rogue genes into the natural world. It's very serious. They're sowing a new variety of genetically engineered winter cereal for next year's harvest. That's why we were there.'

Ten miles from Bristol they stopped at a steak house, where Foyle insisted that she have a proper meal because he thought she looked undernourished. He studied her as she read the menu. She had inherited his big-boned frame and dark looks, which came from his Cornish grandfather. But her hair was less wavy and happily she had not been endowed with his weathered complexion, nor his nose, which in profile looked a little like the old Duke of

Wellington's. He also knew that she had taken on some of his mannerisms. June often remarked that they made the same quick, expressive movements with their hands.

After a glass of red wine, Katherine became chatty and asked him about work, something he never encouraged – partly because there was so much he couldn't talk about, but mostly because he didn't trust the company she kept. To his mind, the fringe that included road protesters, animal-rights activists and crop burners, of which Katherine was now apparently a member, were not too many degrees saner than the terrorists whose profiles filled his computers at New Scotland Yard.

'I hope you don't talk about my job to your friends,' he said.

'Course not, Dad. I'm not very likely to admit there's filth in the family.' She saw that he'd been stung. 'It's a joke, Dad. Seriously, how's it going?'

'It's not too bad, but we have to keep on our toes. I could show you faces of a hundred men – and women – who desire nothing more than to spray London commuters in the face with anthrax. And there's still plenty of potential in Ireland – the guns and explosives, the men. It's a way of life for some. It gave people a living and a sense of purpose.'

'Not unlike you, Dad,' she said, looking up slyly from her salad.

Foyle rose to the bait. 'The difference, if you really need me to spell it out, Kate,' he couldn't get used to the name, it made him feel as if he was talking to someone else, 'is that I'm appointed by a public body, and what we try to do is save lives and enforce the laws, which have been made by democratically elected representatives. And second, if it was all to stop suddenly, I'd be more than content to go back to catching your run-of-the-mill villain. I really miss the neatness of a straightforward murder.'

'Dad, don't be so serious. I was teasing.'

He smiled. They passed the rest of the meal talking about Katherine's hope of changing courses. She was fed up with drama and wanted to do law.

At eight p.m. Foyle glanced at his watch. He had to drop Katherine at her flat in Bristol then drive on to London. It would be three hours before he was home. He signalled for the bill to the three waitresses, who were talking over by the bar. They were engrossed and didn't notice him. He began to rise, at which point the woman who'd served them came over with apologies. 'I'm sorry, sir, they were just telling me about that bomb. It's terrible – when we thought that was all over.'

'What bomb?'

'The bomb that's gone off in London, sir. Some people are dead, they think. It was on a bus.'

'Where's the phone?' He cursed himself for not taking one of the office mobiles or a pager. Why hadn't he called in to the office? He dialled his assistant's direct line. Forbes picked up on the second ring and gave him the details. Foyle wrote hurriedly on the back of his cheque book, then asked the waitress to arrange a cab to take Katherine back to Bristol, paid the bill and gave Katherine a cheque for three hundred pounds.

She hugged him as he left. 'Dad. Thanks. Love you.'

Unaccountably Foyle blushed. He looked at her hard. 'Keep in touch, Katherine – and out of trouble.'

'Kate!' she said.

'Where do you come from, sir? You sound American.'

Lindow had given his name to the man in the hospital but didn't feel like answering the rest of the questions. He shifted sideways on the stretcher and collapsed his left arm over his face. The strip lighting of the emergency department at St Luke's hurt his eyes, and the back of his head was pounding. A little while before, he had felt faint and asked a nurse if he could lie down. Now he was grateful for the pillow.

'I've been in the States for a long time,' he said groggily. 'That's why I've got an accent.'

'So you're on holiday in London, sir?' his interrogator asked. He was a young man, but stout for his age, with fleshy cheeks and small, greedy eyes. His hair was damp and fell over his forehead in oily wet locks.

'No, no, I've come to work here. What do you need to know for?'

The man ignored him. 'So, if you're not American, where do you come from?'

'I'm Irish,' said Lindow.

The man looked down at him hungrily, as though he was some kind of quarry. Lindow sensed that he was waiting for him to expand, but he didn't feel like obliging him. Anyway, who the hell was he, asking these personal questions?

'So you're Irish and you're working here,' said the man. 'What do you do, sir?'

'I'm a molecular biologist. I've just come here to do research at Imperial College.'

'Genes and that sort of thing?'

'Yes, but it's a little more complicated than that,' said Lindow wearily.

'You're a researcher in genetics?'

Lindow began to explain that this wouldn't be strictly accurate and then stopped. 'Who are you, anyway? Why does the hospital need this sort of information now? Surely it can wait.'

'Oh, didn't I mention it?' said the man, straightening to go. 'Richard Abbott-Tring – *Evening Herald*.' He touched Lindow's hand with four chubby fingers. 'You've been most helpful, sir. Now, take it easy – you've been through a terrible ordeal.'

He departed with a hasty, self-important waddle. A clipboard that he had been holding behind him was now pressed to his chest.

*

Half an hour passed before Lindow was seen by a woman doctor. She peered into his eyes and examined the wound on his head. Then she kneaded his stomach with expert fingers and took a cursory look at the cuts on his legs.

'You've been very lucky,' she said, feeling the rest of his head. 'We'll X-ray this head of yours just to be on the safe side then get the cuts stitched and give you a painkiller. The nurse says you've been feeling faint, so I think it's best if we keep you in overnight. How are you feeling otherwise? Any shock?'

'I don't think so. Just tired.'

'That's understandable. You rest here and somebody'll be along shortly to take more details.'

He didn't rest. The noise and light of the emergency department reverberated in his head. He couldn't think straight, which was an unpleasant novelty. He struggled to order the last couple of hours in his mind, but all he could do was replay a stream of images from the street. After the bomb exploded he'd been plunged into a limbo, lodged between earth and hell. He remembered the brush-fire heat of the burning vehicles and the coldness of the paving stones. He remembered the smell of burning rubber and fuel, and before that a bitter odour, which he assumed was the explosives.

Yes, he'd been looking at his watch and waiting for Eamonn when the bomb had gone off, and then he'd been with Kay and Harry and the medical team had arrived and then Kay was taken away half dead. Now he was here in hospital and pretty much in one piece. Shaky, but nothing like that poor girl with her face. He couldn't stop seeing the moment when he'd lifted her hair that first time. God, he thought suddenly, where the hell was Eamonn? What had he been thinking of? He must get up and telephone him. He dropped his legs from the gurney.

A nurse came scurrying up to him. 'Not so fast, Mr Lindow, we're going to take you to X-ray now and then we'll deal with these cuts.' She held his head with both hands and peered at the gash. 'Goodness, you need this seen to, don't you? So pop your legs back up there and we'll wheel you in now.'

'Yes, but you don't understand. I must call my brother.' He was surprised at how loud and panicky he sounded.

'Look. I'll see if one of the girls on Reception can telephone him and let him know where you are. Then you can talk to him yourself a little later.'

Lindow fished in his wallet and gave her the piece of paper with Eamonn's number on it. She signalled to a porter to wheel him away. X-ray took a matter of minutes, then he was moved to have his cuts stitched and dressed. He watched with interest as his trousers were cut off by another nurse, leaving a patch of material that had dried into an open wound on his leg. While the material was being soaked off with warm water, the nurse who'd taken Eamonn's number returned with the piece of paper and said no one had answered. There was a machine on, and the woman had thought he'd prefer to leave the message himself so she'd hung up.

'There'll be a telephone upstairs in the ward,' she said brightly. 'You're being sent to the Liskeard wing. That's where the private rooms are so you'll have everything you need. Liskeard is the lap of luxury.'

Within a quarter of an hour he was lying in a private double room with a young black man, whose hands and right eye were bandaged. The ward sister said he had been thrown into a window by the explosion. He raised a bandage in greeting and introduced himself as Clovis Cox.

'Fuckin' mess this. Fuckin' mess!' said Cox, after mumbling to himself. 'Know what I mean? They got no fuckin' right.'

He turned his head through a complete right angle to

look at Lindow with his left eye. 'You straight? You not a policeman, nor nothing?'

'No,' Lindow said. 'I'm not a policeman.'

'Not a policeman?'

'*No*, I said.'

Cox relaxed. 'Okay. Will you do somethin' for me? See the jacket over there? That's my jacket and in the linin' you'll find Charlie. Take the bag out and make me a line on this tray here. Then you throw the stuff out of the window.'

Lindow considered Cox's face. 'Is Charlie what I think it is?'

'You know, Charlie! Cocaine! Coke, powder, snow, blow. Get the bag and gimme some. I can't get into the linin' nor nothing with these.' He held up his hands for inspection like a heavyweight boxer before a fight.

'You mean you're going to snort that stuff without the slightest idea what other drugs are in your system?' asked Lindow.

'That's exactly what I'm going to do.'

'No.'

'Come on, man. It's pure stuff. I missed my connection tonight and there's no other use for it. See what I'm saying?'

'No.'

'Okay, okay. Just get the stuff and throw it away – out of the window. Now, please, man, I'm asking you. If the nurses find it, I'll be doing time again.' He gurgled a laugh.

Lindow thought for a moment. Without a word he got off the bed and went over to the jacket. He felt around the hem then retrieved the bag through the ripped inside pocket. Without looking at it, he opened the window and shook out the powder before letting the bag go in the draught gusting up the side of the building. As he closed the window, a nurse came in and asked what he was doing.

'Just getting some air, Nurse.' Lindow smiled at her. 'Do you have a phone I could use? I need to speak to my brother.'

As he left with her, Clovis Cox winked at him with his good eye.

He read Eamonn's number from the piece of paper, dialled, then heard a message. 'If that's you, Mary, we'll be at the Lancaster Arms until about eight thirty. Then we'll go to a restaurant called Sam Samosa's in Kellet Street. See you there. Anyone else who's calling, leave a message with your number.'

Lindow spoke into the telephone. 'Eamonn, it's Con. Had a bit of trouble with the bomb in the West End. Nothing to worry about. A few cuts and bruises, that's all. I'm in the Liskeard wing at St Luke's, but I'll be out tomorrow and I'll call you then. Hope you're having fun there. By the way, who the hell is Mary?'

He hung up. He wondered why Eamonn wasn't in. He'd probably gone to the pub, knowing he'd never find Con in the chaos of the West End. Perhaps he had met this Mary and was already lying in her arms. But surely even Eamonn was not capable of being so unconcerned. After all, they had arranged to meet right where the bomb had gone off. Lindow turned back down the corridor.

On the way, he stopped by the nurses' station where the television news was on. An agitated woman reporter was talking to a studio interviewer, brushing her hair aside and tripping over her words. She looked down at her notes. 'The latest figures we've been given are that seven people have lost their lives in this explosion and forty-five people have been injured, eleven of them seriously. Police say that no warning was received and that the bomb exploded on the bus as it was moving. In the light of the Irish Peace Agreement, they're not prepared to speculate about the origin of the bomb or which group planted it. Police say that as yet no organisation has claimed responsibility. It is understood that the Prime Minister has already spoken to the Irish premier and all sides of the Northern Ireland Assembly. All parties, including Sinn Fein, have agreed to await the outcome of the investigation.'

Lindow returned to the room where Cox lay asleep, propped up on the pillows. Some sandwiches had been left on a tray with a glass of orange juice. He drank the juice – an unchilled soup of vaguely citrus origin – then peeled back the bread of the sandwiches to inspect the tuna filling. He decided against them and climbed into bed. He switched off the reading light and lay in the dark with his eyes open. Tomorrow he'd go back to his new laboratory at Imperial: life would begin again and he'd resume his inquiries into the discreet messages transmitted between bacteria. The bomb would become yesterday's disorder and soon it would be folded up in the past like the other explosion – the one that rumbled, long ago, through an Irish summer dawn, blowing a crater in a church graveyard. He'd left that behind and he'd do the same this time.

His last thought before slipping into a fitful sleep was to wonder where the hell Eamonn was. Odd that he wasn't home by now, odd that he hadn't tried to contact the hospital. God, he hoped he was all right.

Chapter Two

Lindow was in the street again, making love to the girl. He cradled her head as they rocked together; his hands were filled with bunches of her hair. He could smell the perfume rising from her and feel the undulating movement of her body. Then he slid from her, appalled. He looked down at the blood that swelled in her midriff, an unstoppable flow that came from the wound. There were other people in the street, standing just behind him. He heard them cluck with disapproval. He wanted to say that he hadn't done this thing, but then he couldn't be sure that he had not driven the wound into the girl. He began to hear other noises, noises that made him turn from her and concentrate hard. He left her in the cold wet street and groped towards the noises. Then he woke.

There was just one sound left in the hospital room – the whisper of a nurse's uniform, receding towards the door. Lindow opened his eyes as the door closed. He hadn't imagined it. Someone had been there because a smell of perfume – a clean, young scent – lingered in the room. He raised his head and looked over to the other bed. It had gone, and all trace of Clovis Cox with it. He concluded that his companion must have felt ill in the night and had called the nurse with the bell push. He'd find out in the morning. Then he sank back into sleep.

He woke again at 7 a.m. There were voices in the room, but he decided not to open his eyes. Two or three men were by the door and nearer to him was a woman.

He smelt her scent again. It must be the nurse who had come in the middle of the night to wheel Cox away.

'He's still asleep,' she said. 'You can't talk to him until the doctor has seen him.'

The voices left the room. Lindow opened his eyes. 'What's going on?' he asked. 'Where's the guy who was in the next bed?'

The nurse didn't answer but busied herself straightening the bedclothes and moving away the bedside table.

'What's happening?'

'I'm sorry. I'm afraid I've been told not to talk to you. The doctor will be along shortly to look at your head.' Her manner was brisk and formal.

'Who are those men out there? Why are they here?'

She looked at him without smiling, and repeated that she couldn't talk to him. He lay back on the pillows with a rising sense of alarm. When the doctor came to see him a few minutes later, Lindow caught sight of a uniformed police officer in the doorway. Perhaps the other men were police officers too. That might explain why Cox had disappeared during the night – a drugs bust?

'Is this about Cox?' Lindow asked the doctor, as a light was shone into his eyes.

'No. I believe they want to talk to you.'

'What about?'

'About the bomb, I expect.' He paused to get Lindow's full attention. 'Your X-ray results were good. No sign of a fracture, or anything like that. Have you experienced any more dizziness?'

'No, it seems fine. My leg hurts a little, but that's all.'

'Good. Well, I expect you'll experience a little shakiness today, but that should be all. You ought to take things easy for a while and come back to us in ten days' time to have those stitches out of your head and leg. In the meantime I'll leave you with these.' He handed Lindow a bottle of pills. 'You may need them over the next few days. They're to stop your head hurting.'

The doctor was barely out of the room before two men came in. Beyond them stood an armed police officer.

'What do you want?' asked Lindow.

'Good morning, Mr Lindow. I take it you *are* Con Lindow – Constantine Lindow,' said the shorter of the two men abrasively. 'This is Detective Inspector Bostock and I'm Superintendent Simmonds. We want to talk to you about last night's explosion in Clarence Street.'

'I don't know much about it,' said Lindow. 'I saw the bus explode. That was all, but I'll tell you as much as I can.'

Simmonds smiled. 'We know you saw the bus explode, Mr Lindow. But what we don't know is what you were doing there at the time.'

'I was meeting my brother.'

'You can tell us all about that later. For the present you may consider yourself detained under Section 12 of the Prevention of Terrorism Act. You will be taken from here to a police station by Inspector Bostock and myself. Then we'll have our chat and you can tell us about your brother.'

Lindow gaped at them. 'What about my brother?'

Neither answered.

'You think *I* had something to do with it! For Chrissake, I don't blow people up.'

'Please get dressed as quickly as you can, Mr Lindow. The nurse has laid out some clothes for you. The trousers should be about the right size and she's sponged down your jacket and sweater.'

'This is absurd. I want a lawyer.'

'Not in the provisions of the Act. Please hurry, sir. We don't want to get caught up in the rush-hour traffic. As it is, it will be snarled up after last night.'

Dressing shakily, Lindow slipped the bottle of pills into his trouser pocket. Bostock took his arm and marched him along the corridor past the nurses' station to the service lift. There, another policeman with body armour

26

and a machine-pistol waited, holding the doors open. They took the lift to the basement. As the doors opened, Bostock tightened his grip and pulled Lindow out into a corridor that was heavy with the smell of laundry and disinfectant. They reached a set of doors opening out on to a service yard. Four police vehicles were waiting there. Lindow was put in a van with Bostock and the armed policeman. The doors closed, someone banged on the van's roof and the convoy took off up a ramp to join the early morning traffic. Lindow could see a blue light flashing through the van's windscreen. There was no siren. He looked across at Bostock. 'You're making a big mistake here. I'll sue every one of you for this.'

Bostock leaned forward, swaying in and out of Lindow's face with the motion of the van. 'No, you won't. You won't sue anyone, you fucking terrorist cunt.'

The police vehicles crossed the river, passed through Parliament Square and headed up Birdcage Walk towards Hyde Park Corner. From there it was a matter of minutes to Paddington Green police station. Lindow was aware only of the car park as he was pulled from the van and hurried into a waiting area where he was regarded with indifference by two uniformed police officers. One of them held a white board on which was written in red felt-tip pen: 'Irish Suspect: Lindow.'

'Full name and address,' he demanded.

'I'm not saying anything until I have a lawyer. Not a thing. Do you hear me?'

'Under the provisions of the Prevention of Terrorism Act you are not entitled to see a solicitor for forty-eight hours,' said the officer.

'You mean I can't have a lawyer here?'

'Not for two days. Then, and only then, do you get legal representation, but that decision is taken with our advice. Now, get used to things here, Lindow. Full name and address!'

Lindow didn't answer.

'That's all right, Sergeant,' said Simmonds. 'He'll give us all we need. Won't you, Mr Lindow? Get him fingerprinted and photographed.'

Lindow stood against a wall, holding up a numbered board. The way he looked now – unwashed, unshaven, hair uncombed, crumpled shirt – he'd be convicted by any jury. There's another Irish suspect, they'd think. There's another murdering bastard sent here to blow our people apart and kill our children. But that was over now. What the hell were they doing arresting him just because he was Irish?

A uniformed officer with close-cropped hair took hold of his hands and scraped at his fingernails with a little instrument, dropping the dirt into a glass phial. He smelt of the night shift and, as he rolled Lindow's fingertips and palms in the ink, he looked up into his face and smiled.

'What was that business with my fingernails for?' Even as he asked, Lindow knew the answer. They were taking samples to be tested for explosives residues.

'Makes you nervous, does it? Well, you shouldn't play around with explosives. You people, you never think, do you?' the officer concluded, with mock exasperation. Then he demanded Lindow's watch, shoelaces and keys. He checked the trousers for a belt and put everything but the keys into a plastic bag and sealed it. He flipped the keys through the air to his sergeant.

Lindow was patting his pockets for his wallet. 'You've taken my wallet.'

'Yes, that's right,' said the policeman. 'It was removed by police officers at the hospital. You'll get it all back when you leave.'

At the far end of the corridor Simmonds, Bostock and three other plain-clothes officers stood in a huddle. The group dispersed as Lindow emerged to be led down the corridor. One of the policemen punched some numbers on a key-pad and they passed through a metal door.

Bostock and Simmonds followed. The door shut with a hydraulic wheeze. Then they moved to a cell, where he was left with a man who introduced himself as the duty doctor. He checked Lindow's head and eyes, his back and arms.

'Look,' said Lindow, 'I was examined half an hour ago.'

'Yes, but this is to make sure you don't claim we gave you these,' the doctor said, thumbing the bruise on Lindow's bicep.

He left the cell and nodded to the policemen, who came in and took hold of Lindow. They marched him to an interview room where Simmonds and Bostock were waiting with another man, who sat some distance from the table and didn't look up when they entered.

Lindow was put in a chair opposite Simmonds. Bostock was sitting beside him. He had removed his jacket and sat stroking his brawny, fair-haired forearms.

'Right, Mr Lindow,' Simmonds began contemptuously.

'If you're going to be accurate,' said Lindow, 'it's Dr Lindow.'

Simmonds raised his eyebrows with theatrical admiration. 'So – Dr Lindow, when were you born?'

'November the fifteenth, 1965.'

'And you are a citizen of the Irish Republic?'

'Yes.'

'You still carry an Irish passport?'

'Yes.'

'And you were meeting your brother last night? What time would that have been?'

'Look, if I answer your questions, will you let me phone someone? I need to speak to my brother or my father. They'll be worried.'

Simmonds nodded. 'The sooner you answer our questions, the sooner we'll be finished with you.'

'I arranged to meet Eamonn at seven fifteen outside the

tube station in Clarence Street. You can check with him. He said he was coming straight from work.'

'And did you?'

'What?'

'Go straight from work?'

'No, I went home first and changed.'

'Where is that exactly, Dr Lindow – your home?'

'You want the address?'

'Yes.'

Lindow thought for a moment. 'Flat two, forty-six Homer Road. It's in Notting Hill Gate – a rented place.'

There was a silence in the room. None of the officers made a move. Lindow searched their faces. They had desperately needed his address, but they didn't seem to be doing anything about it. Then he understood: someone was listening to this interview elsewhere. He looked up to a small dark glass bubble on the far wall. They were filming him too.

'That wasn't difficult, was it – giving your address?' said Simmonds eventually. 'Why didn't you give it to the hospital last night? The staff told us you gave your brother's telephone number and that was all.'

'I don't expect to be in the flat long. I'm looking for a place to buy, or somewhere to rent nearer Imperial College. I gave my brother's telephone number because I had it in my hand and I knew they'd be able to contact me through him when I moved. That's all there is to it. I suppose I could've given my direct line at Imperial, but it didn't occur to me and I'm not sure I can remember it.'

'So you went straight from your home to see your brother? Were you going to meet anyone else?'

'Yes, a woman was coming later – Mary someone. I'd never met her before.'

'This Mary, would that be Eamonn's girlfriend?'

'I don't know. Ask him.'

'Yes, we will . . . when we can,' said Simmonds. 'Now, tell me, what sort of work is it that you do, Dr Lindow?'

'I'm a molecular biologist.'

'Yes?' Simmonds revolved his hand for more information.

'I'm a researcher. If you need to know exactly, I'm researching what are called message chemicals. It's related to my original genetic studies.'

'And does this involve much laboratory work?'

'Naturally. It's mostly done in the laboratory.'

'So you come into contact with chemicals?'

Lindow saw where Simmonds was heading. 'If you think I've been making bombs in my laboratory, you're mad. Besides, I've barely been inside the place. I've only just got here – only just settled in.'

'From America? How long ago did you move?'

'Until three weeks ago I was working at MIT – that's the Massachusetts Institute of Technology. Imperial College made me an offer I couldn't turn down.'

'Are you telling me that you decided to leave a job in the States to come to London? Is that what they call the Irish brain drain?'

Bostock sniggered. Lindow ignored him. 'Nowadays, it's quite common for people to come from the US to Britain.'

'Was there another reason for your return. Was it part of a plan, Dr Lindow?'

'Of course not. It wasn't my idea to come back. They made me the offer out of the blue a year ago. There were negotiations to be completed about facilities, research funds, people. Check with Imperial, if you want. Check with Professor Sharma. That's Sethe Sharma.'

'You've quite an accent there. How long were you in the United States?'

'It's nearly fifteen years now.'

'And how many times have you been back to visit the Irish Republic in that time?'

'Four or five times. The last time was two years ago when I attended my mother's funeral.'

31

'But you kept in touch with your family there – kept in touch with Eamonn in London, kept in touch with the political situation in Ireland.' Simmonds was pushing now, leaning forward. Bostock had stopped scratching his arms.

'Of course I kept in touch with my family. But I don't know what you mean about the political situation. I know a little about the peace process – what I've read in the papers.'

'I mean "the struggle to throw off the British yoke".'

'I don't see it in those terms, certainly not now. There's a peace agreement, an assembly.'

'But you once did see it in those terms and you still share the views of your lot now?'

'I don't have a *lot*, if by that you mean the IRA. And, anyway, they abandoned their struggle a long time ago.'

'Still, you knew about them and their strategy, knew about the Real IRA.'

'Yes, I read about it in the Boston papers. There are a lot of Irish people there and the papers tend to cover the story well.' Lindow instantly regretted saying that.

'Yes, a big community of Irish folk, a big community that has sent money and guns to the IRA – some of those folk are still pouring money into the republican groups. They said they were griefstricken about the Omagh bomb, but they went on collecting, didn't they? You must have met many of those kind of people there. They're your people, aren't they? Did they urge you to come here and work for them? Who were your contacts in the Boston area?'

'I didn't have any *contacts*! I had friends and colleagues, but not contacts in the way you're using the word.'

'Did you have a girlfriend there? Some nice Irish-American lass?'

'No, I didn't.' Simmonds looked at him knowingly.

32

'I've had relationships in the past, but there's no one special at the moment.'

'No ties. That's always the best way, isn't it? Are you a homosexual by any chance, Dr Lindow?'

'No, I'm not, for God's sake. I just don't happen to have a girlfriend. My work consumes all my time.'

'Forgive me, Doctor, these are sometimes delicate matters.' He spoke with sarcastic formality.

'Look, I don't know what you want me to say. I was going to meet my brother last night and I was blown up. Then you haul me from my hospital bed, you bring me here against my will and you ask me if I'm gay. I mean – it's – it's – ridiculous. When are you going to let me speak to my family?'

Simmonds paused, which was evidently the signal for Bostock to take over. 'Where do you keep the explosives?' he asked.

'Oh, for God's sake!'

'In a garage? A warehouse? A safe house somewhere? Where do you keep them, Con?'

'I don't know what you're talking about.' Damn, that was always the phrase the guilty used. He'd have to watch what he was saying and how he was saying it. He eyed the new interrogator carefully.

'Who makes the bombs? Is it you who makes them? With all that technical expertise of yours, that shouldn't be a problem.'

'I don't make bombs. I study bacteria and human cells and a process called protein biosynthesis, but I don't suppose you'd know what that is.'

'No, I don't. But I'll tell you what I do know. I know I've got a bloody liar sitting in front of me – and a fucking terrorist to boot.'

Lindow didn't reply. It was useless. They weren't going to listen. They were going to lock him up. He'd have to be on his guard. Whatever they did to him, he wouldn't budge. He'd refuse to talk, refuse to give them anything –

33

and then the time would come when they'd have to charge him or let him go. Until then he would retreat into himself, just as he had before when the RUC had questioned him about the explosion in Ireland. They had been rough. At times he'd thought they were going to kill him there and then, right in the interview room. But they hadn't and then one morning they'd let him go.

'I want a glass of water,' said Lindow. 'I haven't had anything to eat. I won't answer any more questions until you get me something to drink.'

That was the only way, Lindow thought. Fight back. Every small victory counts.

'Okay,' said Simmonds. 'I'll get you some tea. Milk and two?'

'No sugar.'

The tea arrived very soon, as if someone had known it would be called for. Lindow felt in his trouser pocket for the bottle of pills, which had eluded the policeman when he was being processed. He shook one into his hand under the table and was preparing to swallow it when Bostock reached over and grabbed his arm.

'What's this, then? Drugs as well? I just said tea. I didn't say we'd have a tea *and* drugs break, did I? I'll take those. Don't want any overdoses, do we, Dr fucking-Irish-cunt Lindow?' Bostock wrested the bottle from Lindow's hand.

'They're prescribed painkillers,' he protested. 'I was given them at the hospital for this.' He turned to show the back of his head to Simmonds.

'Very impressive,' said Bostock, 'but not half as impressive as Miss Gould's face, eh?'

'Miss Gould?'

'Yes, Kay Gould. Surely you remember her. The girl who was blown up in the bomb. They say you were with her. You must have seen her face – shredded by flying glass. Imagine being Kay Gould this morning, waking up with half her frigging face gone. Imagine that! Imagine

34

that poor girl's life now. Months of plastic surgery. I mean, they're going to have to start rebuilding her face from scratch, aren't they? From the bone upwards, using skin from her arse and anywhere else they can find it. But it's not face skin, is it? Not the same – and she'll never be the same. No more nights out in the West End for Kay Gould, no candlelit dinners for Kay Gould. That's what you've done, Con. Destroyed a young girl's life. So now you're going to tell me what went wrong last night. You weren't aiming for the bus, were you? You were going to plant that bomb somewhere else, weren't you? What was the real target?'

'I'm not going to say anything. I have no comment. This is ludicrous!'

'No, it isn't. It's dead serious. You see, we can't ask anyone else about last night because the other suspect is unconscious. So it's you we have to ask, Con.'

Bostock looked at Simmonds. Something passed between them.

'What other suspect? What are you talking about?'

'The other bomber, you cunt! Eamonn, your brother – your accomplice.'

Bostock had moved round the table and was gripping Lindow's thigh just above the stitches. Lindow didn't feel the pain.

'What are you saying?'

'Oh, come on, now. You must've known Eamonn was on that bus. Blew himself up with the bomb, didn't he? Not dead – just unconscious. You see, we knew it was him when we found his wallet in his clothes early this morning. Then all we did was check through the casualty lists – and guess what we find? We find you in the same hospital. Another fucking Lindow, right under our noses. Wasn't that a coincidence, now?'

Lindow averted his eyes from Bostock's leering features and looked first at Simmonds, then at the other man who had been sitting silently at the back of the interview room. He knew it was true. 'Has Eamonn been hurt? Is that what you're telling me?'

Simmonds nodded.

'How badly? Tell me!'

Simmonds spoke. 'Eamonn was on the bus when it exploded. He's still alive, but he hasn't come round yet.'

Lindow lunged at Simmonds, but his mind clouded and the ground disappeared beneath him.

Foyle had risen early. Too early. He needed six hours' sleep and had had only three. It wasn't yet light, but from his kitchen window he could see his driver, Alex, waiting in the street in the unmarked green police Rover. He scribbled a note to the housekeeper about the shopping and the laundry, then left the house with little regret. He never minded leaving now.

'When are you going to move from Wimbledon, sir?' Alex asked gloomily, as Foyle sank into the back seat. 'The bridge is closed again so I'll have to take the long route.'

'Leave off, Alex, I'm not in the mood. Just get me there quick as you can.' He caught a petulant look from Alex in the driver's mirror and glowered back at him.

Foyle had got back to London by eleven fifteen on the previous evening, in time to see the bus still smouldering in Clarence Street. God, he hated bomb scenes – hated the smell and chaos and the sense of utter waste. But he had spent a long time there, tramping through the glass and water trying to envisage exactly what it had been like, asking himself why the bus exploded there. He found two explosives officers he knew who told him that the bomb had been placed on the lower deck at the rear of the bus. This was fortunate because it meant that the survivors were able to scramble down the stairs and leave by the exit at the front, although the doors had jammed for a few crucial seconds and the driver had had to use the emergency lever. He had dragged the injured from their seats, returning to the bus three times to bring people out. The two officers had estimated that twelve to fifteen pounds of explosive had been used, two or three times the amount usually deployed as the core of a car bomb. It had all the signs of a Semtex device which, because of its innate stability, was unlikely to have triggered itself unless given a severe shock. They thought the bomb was the work of a professional, and that, too, argued against self-detonation. As yet, little had been found in the wreckage and, as they had waited for teams of white-suited forensics officers to comb the street, they had both made the point that it didn't seem to add up. If someone wanted to cause serious damage in Clarence Street, it would have been easier to load a fertiliser bomb into a car and leave it in the street. That way much less Semtex would have been needed.

Since there was nothing Foyle could do in the middle of the night at New Scotland Yard, he called Forbes and told him he was going home. He knew that he would have to snatch as much sleep as he could. The next few days would be punishing. He got home at two a.m. and was soon in bed asleep. At five he was woken by a call from a detective constable in his department, who told him that two Irishmen, both named Lindow, might be involved. Both had been injured and subsequently taken to St Luke's. Eamonn Lindow was on the bus when it exploded. He had been badly hurt and was still unconscious. His brother, Constantine Lindow, was standing in the street near by when the bomb went off. He had suffered only minor injuries and would be well enough to be questioned that morning. Both brothers had been carrying ID. One had given his name freely at the hospital but when asked for his address had given his brother's telephone number. Police officers and forensics teams were already on their way to search Eamonn Lindow's flat in Peckham.

'Are you saying that one brother didn't know of the other's injury?' Foyle asked.

'Yes, sir. It seems he tried to call him from Casualty.'

'Has anyone informed him of his brother's condition?'

'No, sir.'

'Okay, keep it that way. Meanwhile, send my driver. I'll be ready in half an hour. Oh, by the way, did you get the address for the second suspect?'

'Not yet, sir, but we should have it soon.'

'Make it a priority.'

On the way to New Scotland Yard, Foyle considered what he had been told by the young officer and wrote a series of questions on a pad he kept in the car. When he arrived at the Yard he would rip the piece of paper from the pad and transfer the notes and questions into a big hardback accounting book that was laid out in columns. Foyle was convinced he had to guard against a disorganised streak in his character. Since his first murder inquiry twenty years before, when he had neglected a crucial piece of evidence at an early stage, he'd made it a rule to note down all the questions that had to be answered. He kept a smaller pad by his bed because his most creative period came in his first conscious moments of the day. These inspirational seconds had stopped about the time June left and nowadays he found he had to work harder at a problem.

He turned on the car reading light and wrote: 'If accidental detonation, what was intended target? If not, why blow up bus? Why *this* bus? Why large amount of explosives? Why both brothers at scene? Why carrying ID?' He then wrote, 'Who – Real IRA or other group?' and underlined the words so that the ballpoint broke through the paper.

He looked out of the window as the car crossed Wandsworth Common. The first overnight flights from America had turned over Essex and were now making their final approach to Heathrow, their lights dancing in the mauve-grey dawn. In a matter of minutes south London would be rudely dragged from sleep.

He returned to his notes and began to tease out the inconsistencies in what he knew so far. There had been no warning before the explosion and no admission of responsibility. It could be anyone – a renegade IRA group, the INLA, Ulster loyalists, Iraqis – bloody well anyone. And yet they were holding two Catholic Irishmen. But those were not grounds any longer. Besides, their behaviour didn't suggest that they were trying to conceal their presence. The ID on both of them gave the lie to that. So perhaps the bomb had gone off accidentally while being transferred from one brother to the other for use at a later date? But that didn't make sense either: if the slightly injured man had expected to take delivery of a bomb and an explosion occurred, the first person he would assume to have been hurt was the carrier – in other words, his brother. Moreover, the explosives section said they thought it was a professionally made bomb and was unlikely to have detonated by itself. He wrote again: 'Trigger mechanism? Origin of explosives? Background of brothers? Intelligence re R-IRA and OTHER groups.'

They were approaching Chelsea Bridge when Alex slowed down. 'Do you fancy some coffee and a sandwich from the cab stand, sir? It won't take more than a few minutes.'

'Good idea,' said Foyle, laying down the pad beside him.

Alex scampered over the road, holding his jacket together with one hand, and jumped the line of cab drivers who were waiting at the hatch. Foyle smiled as he saw him put up his hands in mock surrender and shout over their heads. He returned with a bacon sandwich and a Styrofoam beaker of coffee. 'A few late nights this week, I expect, sir?' he said. 'Unless those two were the ones that did it. But that seems too simple, doesn't it, sir? Too easy, if you know what I mean.'

'Yes, it does,' said Foyle, sinking his teeth into the sandwich. Alex had been on the beat himself once and had worked in various capacities for the Met for thirty-five years. As a driver, he picked up a good deal over the course of a day and acted as an information exchange between senior officers. Foyle had learned long ago not to talk detail with him, but it never deterred Alex, who'd already heard that a suspect was about to be lifted and taken to Paddington Green nick.

'Is that so?' said Foyle between mouthfuls. 'Promise to tell me when you've got the rest of the case sewn up.'

At the front entrance to New Scotland Yard, Foyle marched through the security barrier, took the lift to the eighth floor where the Anti-terrorist Unit was quartered, and presented himself impatiently at the security door where his credentials were checked. From there he moved swiftly to the general office, which acted as a kind of traffic control, communications post and secretariat for SO 13. Seven officers were there, including two women. Three were dressed shabbily and had obviously been on a surveillance operation. They had come in at the end of their shift to make their reports and hear about the Clarence Street explosion. The other four were manning computers and telephones.

'Forbes?' shouted Foyle. 'Where's Forbes?'

'He's just having a wash and shave, sir. He hasn't been home,' replied one of the women officers.

'Fine. Tell him I want him now. There'll be a briefing at seven thirty sharp. I want everyone there. I want reports on the suspects, their backgrounds, explosives and any intelligence we've got – the lot.'

He set off down the corridor towards his office, but before reaching it caught sight of two officers sitting with their door open. 'Kepple, Hardwood, what are you doing? Has anyone checked the cars in the area of the bomb? No? Right, well, let's start with the most inconspicuous models, blue or grey mid-range saloon cars, made from 1989 onwards. See if there were any parked in the vicinity of Clarence Street last night. Check the area around Eamonn Lindow's address. Ask about lock-ups in the area. And while you're about it, get me a plan of the bus route with a list of the places where the bus would have stopped before the explosion and where it would have gone on to. We also need to know the places where different bus routes intersect with ours. Got it?'

Foyle turned and saw Forbes standing by the open door of his office, tucking the excess material of a crisp white shirt into his waistband. 'There's something very reassuring about you, Graham,' said Foyle. 'How do you do it?'

'Army training, sir, as you well know, and a spare set of clothes in my locker.'

Foyle looked down at the gleam of Forbes's black shoes, shook his head and let out a whistle of admiration. 'What have you got for me?'

'I've set up the video next door. We've got some footage from the street. And there's a slim chance there may be something from the bus.'

'There was a camera on board?'

'Three. One at the back of the bus above the bomb, which was totally destroyed, but there were another two – one just in front of the stairway to the upper deck and another above the driver's head. The lab say it will be some time before they get the film. Possibly Friday. They have no idea what state it's in. There may be nothing at all.'

'Good. Let's see the other footage, shall we?'

Foyle threw his raincoat on to the sofa, skimmed his message book, placed his notes from the car journey under a glass paperweight and moved to the adjoining room where three officers stood waiting for him. He grunted a good morning.

The officer with the video remote control spoke first. 'This film comes from a camera belonging to Reeves and Cuddy, the store that occupies the building on the south side of Clarence Street, sir.'

'Which way was it pointing?' asked Foyle.

'It was positioned on the apex of the outer arch of the arcade, facing westwards. It was very close to the explosion, but was sheltered from the main force of the blast by the arches. We've got as much tape as we want up until that moment. The relevant material comes in the last fifteen minutes or so, but we'll be going over the rest again more thoroughly.'

The tape was played. At the bottom of the screen a digital clock gave the date and counted the minutes and seconds. It read 23.10 – 19:17:23. Foyle saw a smudged grey street scene that could have been anywhere in London, except that it was identified as CLAR ST at the top of the screen. On the left-hand side, about a third of the way up, he could make out the entrance to a tube station and a newspaper stand. People walked briskly in and out of the camera's field. Opposite the newspaper stand a cab pulled up and a man got out.

'That's one of the Lindows,' said Forbes, freezing the image. 'Inspector Bostock, who's at St Luke's now, identified him about twenty minutes ago. He says the jacket that Lindow has with him at the hospital is a match. There's a good shot of his face coming up.'

Foyle watched as the man walked a few paces to the tube station then withdrew to look into a shop window. A girl came on the scene. Other people passed. The lights of the oncoming traffic flared in the right of the camera's lens. A group of tourists emerged from the tube station, gathered round a tour leader and set off in the direction of the camera. It was 19:25. Three people ran to the tube entrance, a man chained his mountain bike to the railings on the left-hand corner of the screen and began fiddling with the rear wheel. Nothing happened for a minute or so. Lindow looked up and down the street then towards the tube station. It was obvious he was waiting for someone. He glanced at the girl who was standing by the entrance. Foyle noted how good her figure was and wondered if they'd talk, but then she moved away. Lindow kept watching her until her dress billowed upwards, then he averted his eyes and strolled in the direction of the camera. Now Foyle saw him clearly – a good-looking, slender man just under six feet tall. He wore trousers, not jeans, a V-neck sweater and an expensive-looking jacket. He paused, spun on his heels and walked back towards the tube station.

It was 19:35. Nothing moved in the camera's field. The street waited. The man looked to his right for a few seconds then down to his watch. That's when it happened. The picture shook, objects and people were propelled out of the top of the screen as it filled with a cloud of dense smoke. Foyle gasped. It reminded him of a film he'd once seen of an atomic test, which had been shot from a military bunker. There was the same ferocious blast wind. In Clarence Street the girl and Lindow had disappeared instantly, as if they'd been vaporised. Then the picture went blank.

'The cables from the camera were cut by falling masonry, sir,' said one of the officers. 'But it's a helluva picture up till then, sir.'

Foyle sat in silence for a few moments, his mind running through the evidence in the film. It told him several things about Lindow. The first was that he took care of his appearance. If he *was* a terrorist, he was a damned well-dressed one. More important, the man he'd seen wasn't acting at all suspiciously and hadn't tried to hide his face from the camera. This was in contrast to the usual behaviour of terrorist bombers, who were alert to the threat of security cameras and went about their

43

business hooded and wearing sunglasses. Plainly, this man hadn't expected a bomb to go off. Furthermore, when he was taken to hospital it seemed that he had not even considered the possibility that his brother might have been one of the injured. This suggested to Foyle one of two things: innocence or a superb acting ability. But what did it say about the injured man?

Obviously, Eamonn Lindow hadn't planned to blow himself up. Perhaps he had stowed the bomb on the bus, setting a short time fuse in preparation for getting off at the next stop. But the danger of something going wrong was too great. A terrorist never took that sort of risk, not when even a basic alarm clock could be adapted to give him twelve hours to get away.

There was something else that Foyle noticed. Lindow spent most of the time with his back to the traffic, watching the entrance to the tube. Only once did he look at the road in the direction of the bus. Foyle was certain that he had been expecting his brother to come by underground.

'Where are the brothers now?' he asked.

'Eamonn Lindow is still unconscious, but Constantine – Con – is being processed at Paddington Green,' said Forbes, looking at his watch.

'What about the search of Eamonn's place?'

'Nothing yet – no lists of targets, no trace of any bomb manufacture, no signs of any operational paraphernalia. Just a lot of books and videos. They're going through them at the moment. An officer is coming back with a tape, but that's all.'

'What sort of tape?'

'An audio-cassette, sir. From Eamonn Lindow's answering-machine.' Foyle got up. 'Bring the video from the street to the briefing. I want them all to see it. I'll be along in a couple of minutes.'

He returned to his office, took a notebook from his desk and revised the questions he had asked himself in

44

the car and added those that had just occurred to him. He reached for the phone to call Martin Scarratt, assistant commissioner in charge of Specialist Operations, whose duties included overall responsibility for counter-terrorism. Then he thought better of it. He'd prefer to conduct this particular briefing without Scarratt breathing down his neck. For one thing, the assistant commissioner always had fixed ideas about the way an inquiry ought to proceed; for another, his looming presence at the back of the room tended to inhibit the flow of ideas.

Foyle gathered the reports of the explosion from his desk and made his way along the green-tiled corridor to the briefing room where some forty officers had gathered. There was a low murmur when he entered – none of the usual banter. At one end of the room was a map of the Metropolitan area, a large white Nobo board, a screen that could be pulled down from the ceiling and a TV and video player. Foyle glanced out of the windows: they were coated with one-way reflective material and hung with Venetian blinds in the belief that the slats confused the vibrations that are picked up by bouncing a laser beam from a window.

The officers sat about in groups, more or less reflecting the different disciplines of the Anti-terrorist Unit – surveillance, computing, explosives, weapons, intelligence and records. Special Branch was there in force, as well as two forensics officers.

He went to a map of the Clarence Street area drawn on the board and spoke without preamble.

'We've had a bomb in Clarence Street – here.' He pointed to the map. 'It was detonated on a 147 bus travelling on a north–south route, between Peckham and Kilburn, at seven thirty-five p.m. last night. There were forty-seven casualties. Seven were killed immediately, three died overnight and twelve are in a serious condition. As you know, two of the injured are brothers. Constantine Lindow was standing outside the tube station – here – and was slightly hurt. We have film of him from a security camera trained up Clarence Street, away from the explosion. You'll see it at the end of the briefing.

'Then there's Eamonn Lindow, who was on the bus. We assume he was on the lower deck. His injuries tell us that the bomb exploded behind him, but we cannot as yet gauge how far behind him. He may have been dragged off by the driver, so we need to interview the driver at the earliest possible opportunity. We also need to pay particular attention to the people who were hurt on the bus and who are in a condition to talk to us, especially those sitting on the lower deck. Trace anyone who got on or off the 147 about forty-five minutes before the explosion – you'll need to talk to the press about that. Put out an appeal.

'This is a very serious incident indeed. But we can't assume anything. Now, Colin, if you'd like to tell us about this bomb, we'll move on to the intelligence reports and suspects.'

Foyle nodded at Inspector Colin Lafferty, the senior explosives officer of the Anti-terrorist Unit, who was standing at the side of the room. He was as tall as Foyle – well over six foot – but he moved with much greater agility, like a man who worked hard to keep himself fit. He'd told Foyle on more than one occasion that he owed his life not to his technical acumen, his safe-breaker's fingers, or his knowledge of timing mechanisms and explosives, but to his legs. If all else failed when he was dealing with a carload of explosives, he dropped everything and ran like hell. During his time as an ammunition technical officer in the Army he had acquired the name Legs. It had survived his transfer to the headquarters of the Met's bomb-disposal team near Cannon Row police station and was now so widely used that no one could remember his rank. That suited Lafferty just fine.

Lafferty made a sketch on the board of an oblong box

46

then gave it a pair of wheels. At the lower right-hand corner of the vehicle he placed a cross. 'This is where the bomb was left – under the back row of seats, which probably means that at some time during the journey the bomber had occupied a seat in either of the two back rows on the near side of the vehicle. We believe that the device was contained in a canvas-type hold-all, something similar to a services kitbag, but of better-quality material. At that time in the evening such a bag wouldn't have remained unnoticed for very long. Sooner or later it would've been detected and the bomber must have known this. So, there are two possibilities. The first is that the bomb exploded and blew the pants off the bomber before he could get out. The second is that it was intentionally detonated – which must mean that Lindow isn't our man. There's no way of telling between the two possibilities because we haven't got a timing device yet. In fact, very little of that nature – circuitry, batteries, clocks or anything like that – survived the blast. What we do have are bits of the bag. Forensics will no doubt have things to say about that.'

Lafferty put his hands in his pockets and stepped towards the front row of officers. 'At first we thought the explosive used was a plaster gelatine, a very powerful high explosive that has a nitro-glycerine base. This might have accounted for an accidental detonation. But we're certain now that Semtex was used, about five or six kilograms – well over twelve pounds of the stuff. That's a lot more than it took to blow up the Grand Hotel in Brighton, which accounts for the considerable damage in Clarence Street. So this was a very compact, powerful bomb indeed. It's too soon to say what batch of Semtex it comes from, but the labs are working on the chemical traces that are placed in the material by the Czech manufacturers as a form of production date. This may help us with lines of supply and so forth.' He folded his arms. 'That's about all we've got so far.'

He looked at Foyle, then his audience, and waited for questions. None came.

Then Foyle called out, 'Intelligence, what do we have?' He knew there was nothing, but he asked nevertheless.

A detective sergeant from Special Branch, who was sitting at the back of the room, summarised the situation. There had been nothing to suggest that the Real IRA, or any other splinter group in Ireland, was planning an offensive. Sources in Dublin and Belfast were baffled. The men and women currently under surveillance by Special Branch could not have had anything to do with the explosion, and none had had any contact with either of the brothers. As to the Middle East, it was difficult to tell. Several groups were being watched in the London area, particularly one led by a Syrian named Emad. But these were thought to be involved in plotting explosions abroad.

'And what about the brothers?' asked Foyle. 'Let's hear about them, since they're the only thing we've got.'

'Yes, boss.' An eager young sergeant named Pennel stood up. 'They've both got a history. We've just had word that they were questioned in 1983 about an explosion in Northern Ireland, seven miles from the border. An arms and explosives cache blew up, killing two soldiers and wounding two others. The Lindow brothers were arrested by the RUC and given a going-over. Pictures from eighty-three have been wired and I've got some copies here.'

Pennel handed out the photostats of two young men, both with long hair and sideburns. They wore the fashion of the time. Big collars and tight-fitting sweaters. Eamonn Lindow, the older of the two, was thicker-set than his brother and had a bruise to his left eye. Constantine was a good-looking young man with no sign of a beard, and light eyes that glanced away from the camera.

'At the times these were taken the brothers were twenty-four and seventeen years of age. This is Eamonn

48

Cardell Lindow, born January the eleventh, 1959,' he said, holding up one of the photographs. 'He's the one injured on the bus. The other is Constantine Cardell Lindow, born November the fifteenth, 1965. Both were born in the Irish Republic and are Irish citizens, but they were brought up in Fermanagh in the North, where their father was a teacher. In 1986 the parents moved back to the Republic – Ballyhanna in Monaghan – after their mother came into some property. Marie Lindow is part of the Cardell family, an old republican clan, and is related to Jimmy Cardell, who was tried and convicted of killing an off-duty RUC constable in 1975. We don't know if the parents are still alive.'

Pennel stopped as the door opened and Assistant Commissioner Scarratt entered. He acknowledged Foyle, then turned towards Pennel. 'Don't mind me. Please continue.' A study of intelligent interest, thought Foyle.

'I was hoping someone could find you a chair, sir,' said Pennel helpfully. Foyle smiled. 'The circumstances of the incident in Droy cemetery', continued Pennel, 'are still a bit hazy. It seems Eamonn Lindow may have been watching the dump over a period of three and a half weeks. The place was also staked out by a group of soldiers who observed his comings and goings. They were hoping to pick up half the Fermanagh brigade of the IRA when the stuff was moved. It's not clear exactly what happened, but in the early hours of July the twelfth the cache blew up. Neither of the brothers was near the cemetery at the time, but they were taken in for questioning and held for thirty-six hours each. They weren't charged. Since then they've kept their noses clean. Some time in eighty-eight Eamonn Lindow moved to London and began working at a local library. We'll have someone round there when they open up this morning, but we've already talked to his neighbours. He's a quiet sort of fellow. Few visitors, goes out a lot.'

'We don't know what happened to Constantine – or

Con, as he appears on his credit cards – except that he went to university in Dublin and then seems to have emigrated to the States. We'll check with the police and the FBI as soon as we can, and with the university authorities at MIT.'

'Well, we have two Irish suspects,' said Foyle, 'but it goes against everything we know about the intentions of the republican movement. These two could belong to one of the breakaway factions. Let's not make too many judgements at this stage. I want more information about this couple – friends, girlfriends, political affiliations, financial circumstances, bank accounts, who they talk to on the phone, how much contact they have had with each other and with people on both sides of the border in Ireland. I want a complete picture by the end of the day. Somebody should talk to the officer who investigated that explosion in 1983. He may know something that isn't in the reports.'

He looked around the room. An officer nodded to indicate that this was in hand.

'Have we got Con Lindow's address in London?' asked Foyle. 'Can we check through the credit-card companies? There must be something in his wallet.'

'No, sir,' replied Forbes. 'Everything refers back to addresses in America, which will be useful in itself because it'll give us a start there. But we expect to get his address here within the hour from the officers at Paddington Green.'

'Good, I want a forensics team ready to leave for Con Lindow's place as soon as we hear where it is. Now, what about the tape?' Foyle had seen a WPC hand something to Pennel, who stood up.

'This is the ansaphone message. It's been copied on to a standard-size tape so the quality may not be too good. There's a transcript coming.'

Pennel played the tape. First there was Eamonn's message, telling a girl called Mary to meet him at a pub

50

called the Lancaster Arms. Then a woman came on the line. She was American and there was a smile in her voice. 'Hi, it's Mary. I guess I'll see you before you get this! You better be there, Lindow – byeee.'

There were two bleeps as callers hung up without speaking. Finally, there was Con Lindow's message. 'Eamonn, it's Con. Had a bit of trouble with the bomb in the West End. Nothing to worry about. A few cuts and bruises, that's all. I'm in the Liskeard wing at St Luke's, but I'll be out tomorrow and I'll call you then. Hope you're having fun there. By the way, who the hell is Mary?'

'That's what *I* want to know,' said Foyle. 'There may just be some kind of an American angle here.'

This was for Scarratt's consumption. Privately, Foyle was forming the opinion that Con Lindow was innocent, but he'd learned enough during the last year to know that it would be best to keep this to himself. The assistant commissioner's mind would already be resolutely closed to anything but the most obvious solution. Foyle imagined him preening at the press conference that would announce the detention of two men in connection with the Clarence Street bomb.

After the video from the street was shown, Foyle rattled off a stream of instructions and announced that there would be a briefing at five thirty that afternoon. Then he left the room, beckoning Lafferty to follow him.

'What do you think, Colin?' he asked Lafferty, once they were in his office.

'I'm not a detective.'

'I know that, but what do you think?'

'Well . . . I think it's odd, to say the least, that we've got what seems to be a very professional device, but two suspects who are rank amateurs.'

'Yes. But isn't it a possibility that this Con Lindow is an exceptionally cool customer and that he's putting on an act?'

'It's a possibility, I grant you. But it seems peculiar that he went to the hospital with those minor injuries and *then* agreed to stay overnight, risking detection and arrest. Terrorists don't do that – do they?'

Both men turned to see Scarratt standing in the doorway. 'Not disturbing you, am I, Commander?' He walked around the office, hands clasped behind him, looking at Foyle's pictures, which weren't the standard studies of police rugby teams, but watercolour landscapes. Scarratt sniffed and turned to Foyle. 'Well, that seems a very good start. I need hardly tell you we're looking for quick results on this one. With ten dead and that number of injuries the press isn't going to leave us alone. When can we expect charges, Commander?'

'When we've got a case, sir.' Foyle tried his damnedest to look co-operative.

'Come along now. You've got a case already. Two Irishmen known to the authorities placed at the scene of the bomb. You can't get luckier than that. It's plain to me that Con Lindow was a sleeper, sent to the United States of America to get himself a cover, while his brother dug himself in over here. What's the problem with that?'

'None, sir, except that I want to get the right people and we must consider the possibility that these two brothers are innocent. Unless I've been missing something, a peace agreement has been signed. They're all sitting down together behaving themselves.'

'Consider all possibilities. That is your job. But never forget the obvious, Commander. That would be a mistake.'

He left the room, flashing a swift, thin-lipped smile at Lafferty.

Chapter Three

Three or four hours passed after Lindow was taken to the cells and examined again by the doctor. Without his watch, he didn't know exactly how long it was. The doctor gave him a tranquilliser and murmured that he should get some rest. Lindow looked at him incredulously, but tried to sleep after he'd left. Each time he dropped off he was woken by someone opening the metal observation hatch in the cell door, waiting for a minute then closing it with a ringing clank. They were keeping him awake. He lay on the bed with his knees raised so that they couldn't see his face, and looked up at the squares of bottle glass in the ceiling. He could just make out the daylight. If they kept him there, at least he'd be able to tell the difference between night and day. That was important. He had to hold on – keep track of time, not lose himself in worry about Eamonn. They wanted that.

They'd told him about Eamonn to throw him into a blind panic and then they'd put him in the cells to dwell on it. Soon they'd be thrusting statements in his face, demanding that he sign. He'd read something about that once – a woman from Belfast who signed a piece of paper after three days without sleep. She'd thought she was giving them a handwriting sample. Then they told her she'd confessed to being part of some plot or other. He would sign nothing. He'd say nothing until they let him speak to the hospital.

No sooner had he made these resolutions than he was

overwhelmed by a sense of hopelessness and – more puzzling – guilt. What the hell did he have to be guilty about? He was as innocent as anyone else in the street last night, a bystander, like Harry Ribb and Kay Gould. He thought of her again and shuddered. If she'd got those injuries so far away from the bus, what would Eamonn look like? He was overwhelmed by a sudden cold certainty that the police weren't telling him everything. Eamonn was going to die. He wondered if his father and sister had any idea how bad he was. They must've heard by now. Tag would have taken a call from the hospital or opened the door to a sheepish young officer from the Garda. He hoped she would keep her head and stay in Ireland. If she came over to England, she was bound to be arrested and held, like him, in a cell with no daylight to speak of and a bed that smelt of someone else's fear.

He looked around for something to distract him. There was nothing – just the aluminium toilet, the bed and the white prison-gloss walls, etched with graffiti beneath the last coat of paint. They wanted him to turn in on himself, to feel wretched and unwashed. But now he understood that, he'd be able to fight them. He'd fight like the last time, and he'd win again. He closed his eyes and tried to nap but within a few minutes the observation hatch was wrenched open. He peered round his knees. There was no face this time, just three fingers that twitched before drawing the plate back again.

He looked up at the daylight and thought of his father. If Eamonn died, it would destroy him. They were so alike in everything, right down to the same expressions of anxiety and pleasure; they had given the same sudden, downcast look when sensing disappointment in the only audience each of them had cared about, his mother. She had swooped on them with affection that could suddenly change into raging frustration. In her worst moments she had said outright that neither was quite man enough for her. Then they had slunk away, still hopelessly in her thrall. Father and son had bonded as victims of the same love, and when the cancer had sprung from her liver to kill her in a matter of weeks they had been equally stricken. Con never experienced the sharpness of grief, yet a void opened in his life and he was gripped by a puzzling sense of loss and also release.

The guilt returned like a stitch in his side. Fuck them! They wouldn't make him feel like this. He'd done nothing. 'I'm a doctor,' he muttered to himself, 'a doctor of science, a professional, legitimate person.' But the police didn't want to see that. They needed a terrorist bomber and he was it. He'd be held here for days. Then they'd bring him out, charge him and put him in prison. With each remorseless step the system would drench him in guilt. He'd become the shifty, banged-up Irish suspect.

Some time later the two uniformed policemen who had delivered him to the cell returned and beckoned him from the open door. One stood smiling and twirling a key in his hand.

'I want to phone the hospital where my brother is,' Lindow demanded.

They didn't respond, but came forward and hauled him to his feet.

'Don't want you falling down, do we, sir?' said one, taking hold of the waistband of his trousers and wrenching it upwards so his balls were crushed.

Lindow yelled, 'I can walk without your help.'

They pushed him into the bright light of the interview room, which made him shield his eyes for a second. Bostock and Simmonds were still there but Bostock's place at the table had been taken by a new officer, a man with a gaunt face and old-fashioned horn-rimmed spectacles.

'Sit down, please, Dr Lindow,' said the man, gesturing to the chair opposite him. He smiled, and the corners of his mouth turned downwards in a curious grimace.

Lindow eased himself into the chair, holding the

material of his trousers away from the cut on his thigh. He wasn't much to look at, this officer. He was small and sat so that his back formed into a rounded hunch. He was also seedily dressed – knitted tie, checked shirt and dark grey suit that was shiny at the cuffs. His grey hair was plastered to his skull with some sort of lacquer.

Lindow studied the man's eyes, which were moving rapidly over a document, held up so that Lindow could not read it. He glanced to see what time it was on the man's watch, but it was hidden by a slightly frayed shirt cuff. That was one thing he could do for himself. He'd make sure he got the time before he left that room again.

'Good morning, Dr Lindow, I'm Superintendent Phipps,' the man began. 'Sam Phipps is my name. Now, perhaps we can get this over quickly. I know that you've had some distressing news.'

His manner was soothing, almost apologetic, like that of a bureaucrat commencing a wearisome formality that he knew would be trying yet which, none the less, was necessary. But in his behaviour there was also something hard: the deadly patience of a man who expected to be lied to.

'I don't care who you are or what you want from me. But I do know that you're holding me against my will and that these officers deliberately concealed information about my brother's condition. I won't answer your questions until I am allowed to speak to the hospital. I've done nothing to justify this treatment.'

Simmonds and Bostock smiled.

'I understand your concern, Dr Lindow,' returned Phipps, looking down at his papers. 'But you must try to see it from where we stand. Both you and Eamonn were in the vicinity of the bomb last night and this naturally gives rise to suspicion.'

'Why?'

'Because you have been questioned before, haven't

you? That business at Droy cemetery in Ireland. I take it you know what I am referring to.'

Lindow wasn't surprised that they had found out about the cemetery. He could handle it. He'd say exactly the same as he had to the RUC Special Branch.

'We were nowhere near the place when the explosion happened,' he said. 'I told that to the police at the time. They accepted it. They let us go so they must have believed us.'

'Yes, they let you go and both of you went on to make fine careers for yourselves, particularly you. But it all looks too pat, if you don't mind my saying so. It looks to us as if you were working to a plan, a plan that involved your going to the United States of America and gaining a respectable cover while your brother, Eamonn, merged into the background here in London. During that time the developments in Ireland meant that you were cut off from the original cause. People who you believed were solid republicans joined the peace process so you sought out the hardliners associated with the Thirty-two County Sovereignty Movement. Then you returned to the British Isles and almost the moment you got to London a bomb went off. You must see that it doesn't look good – that it looks very much as if you were working to a plan.'

'Maybe that's the way you see things, but you're making a mistake. My brother and I are innocent.'

'As you say . . . but let's go through these questions and see if you can demonstrate that you are indeed innocent in this matter, Dr Lindow.'

'I want to speak to the hospital. I want to call my father.'

'We'll see about that later. Perhaps it would help if Simmonds here gave you the latest bulletin from the hospital.' He turned to Simmonds, revealing to Lindow an oddly hooked nose. He could also see his eyes better. They were pale and watery and the lids were reddened as if afflicted by conjunctivitis.

Phipps dabbed his right eye as Simmonds referred to the back of an envelope and began to read. 'Your brother was operated on last night. He lost a lot of blood and suffered some burns to his back and legs. He will need further surgery, but the hospital say he is in a "comfortable condition".'

'I want to hear that from them myself, not from you. This is my brother we're talking about. I demand that you let me phone the hospital.'

'Yes, as I say, we'll see how things go,' said Phipps. 'Then you may be allowed to speak to the doctor. Now let's talk about you, Dr Lindow. Tell me about this episode at Droy church. Why did the police think you had anything to do with it?'

'I don't *know* why they thought we had anything to do with it. We were miles away when the explosion happened – at home in bed. There were some soldiers involved. I can't remember much about it now, but they wanted to prove that the soldiers hadn't set off the explosives by mistake. They arrested a lot of people – not just us, you know.'

'Yes. But they arrested you because you had both been seen at the churchyard on several occasions before the explosion.'

'We stopped there a couple of times on our way back from fishing. I don't think I even got out of the car. Both times Eamonn pulled over by the church and relieved himself. He liked stopping there – it was part of the crack. He drank a lot while we fished and by the time we got to the church he needed to stop.'

'Pure coincidence, then, that enough explosive material and weaponry was hidden there to keep the Irish Republican Army supplied for four or five years.'

'We didn't know that. We wouldn't have stopped the car there if we'd thought the place was crawling with British soldiers.'

'Yes, British soldiers. You say that as if you loathed the

security forces. Is that right? Did you loathe the British presence? After all, they were only trying to protect people like you – law-abiding citizens.'

'No, I didn't hate the British, you're twisting what I said. Besides, all that stuff is over, isn't it?'

'But you *are* a republican?'

'Not in an active sense. I am a republican but I don't believe that anything except evil could come from the Real IRA, the IRA or from the loyalists, for that matter. All of them are detestable. Apart from that basic conviction, I don't give much thought to these things. Politics is not my interest.'

'But your mother is a republican, is she not – a fervent republican?'

'My mother died two years ago.'

'Ah, I'm sorry . . . but the fact remains that you were brought up in a fiercely republican household and that this hatred of the British was part of – how shall I put it? – the domestic culture in which you grew up.'

'That's not true. It *is* true that my mother was nationalist. I don't deny it, but there was no question of us imbibing it with her milk.' Lindow felt himself colouring. Phipps looked at him closely and seemed to murmur to himself with a private understanding.

'So, the RUC accepted this story of yours and you were allowed to go. Then the following October you went to Dublin to begin your studies. You became a biologist and graduated with a first-class degree. You began to specialise in an area of molecular biology and you were offered a post in America, which combined teaching and research. Is that more or less how things developed?'

'Yes.'

'While you were living in the United States, did you have much to do with your countrymen? Boston has a famously large Irish community, does it not? Did you perhaps see the Irish situation more clearly while you were there? Were you radicalised during those years?'

'One of the reasons I leaped at the chance to go to the States was because I found home oppressive.' He paused. 'I don't know how much you know about research – it leaves little time for anything else. It's very demanding and very competitive. I was part of a team working to identify chemicals that are used in the communication between cells. This was not just science, but big business. We were up against it because we knew that a group of scientists was working on the same problems on the West Coast. We were chasing patents, working all hours God gave us. I didn't have time to think of Ireland, let alone to be radicalised, as you put it. In fact I came to care about Ireland less and less. I expected to spend the rest of my life in the United States.'

'So why did you come to Britain? Was it the case that you were woken from your status as an IRA sleeper?' Phipps put the question as a harmless inquiry about Lindow's career, as though it was a matter of unsurprising possibility that, during all that time abroad, he might have been preparing himself to detonate bombs in central London.

'Look, for Chrissake,' Lindow exploded. He paused to collect himself. 'I explained it all this morning. I came because of the opportunities open to me here. Imperial College offered me a good salary and an excellent team of people to work with. I wanted my own set-up and they gave it to me.'

Phipps looked away to a corner of the room and revolved his tongue in his mouth. Lindow followed his gaze. He remembered being told by an American attorney that the best way of unsettling a too-confident witness on the stand was to turn away and look bored. Lindow waited for Phipps's eyes to return. He was determined to show the man that he could remain every bit as controlled as he was.

'Why are you smiling, Dr Lindow?'

'Oh, it was just something a lawyer friend told me about the art of cross-examination.'

'Yes, well, no doubt you will soon be able to make further acquaintance with the legal profession. But, to return to the matter in hand, you won't deny that you're a man of considerable ability, Dr Lindow? I mean, you are a person who works both theoretically and practically – you excel at both.'

'I don't know what you're driving at, but I guess I must be good at something – yes.'

'It's therefore within the bounds of possibility that a man like you could rig an arms dump so that it would explode. There would be no problem at all with that, would there?'

'In theory, I suppose, no, there wouldn't be. But if you're asking whether I rigged that particular booby trap, no, I didn't.'

'Which booby trap?'

'The one at Droy cemetery. That's presumably what you're talking about.'

Phipps was at him like a terrier. 'I didn't say there was a booby trap at Droy. You did – because you knew the dump was fitted with a device and that you made one or two adjustments so that it would blow up the soldiers who put it there. You've all but admitted to something which, until now, you've insisted you knew nothing about. Now we're getting somewhere, aren't we, Lindow? What were you doing in Clarence Street last night?'

'That's crazy and you know it. I did know that the police suspected that the dump had been rewired, or whatever, because they told me when they questioned me. So I knew you must be talking about Droy cemetery. And anyway, for the record, I'm not admitting to anything.'

'What were you doing in Clarence Street last night?'

'I went there to meet Eamonn. I've told you. I have told

these gentlemen a dozen times that we were going for a drink, then a meal. That was all there was to it.'

'Who else were you going to meet?'

'Some friend of Eamonn's. Her name was Mary. I've never met her before.'

'Not even in the United States? Mary is, apparently, an American. You knew that.'

'No, I knew nothing about her.'

'So you were going to meet up and go for a meal. Are you sure about that? Weren't you in fact about to take delivery of the explosives in order to plant them at a predetermined target chosen by Eamonn? That's why you were meeting Eamonn, wasn't it? Eamonn was carrying the bomb, or at least the components of a bomb, and that's why he used the bus. He knew he could take it right across London without the slightest risk of being stopped.'

Lindow shook his head. 'No, no, no.'

Phipps ignored him. 'But when the bomb blew up, you knew that Eamonn would be hurt, if not killed . . . By God, you kept your cool. I mean, all that business about ringing your brother from the hospital when you knew that he must have been dead – or damned near it . . . You see, we know all about it. So it will be much better for you to come clean. Tell us what you both planned, Con. Tell us where Eamonn keeps the stuff. Tell us who else was involved. Was Mary part of it? Was she the link between the two of you? We need to know and put a stop to this mess. You saw what happened last night. You saw what an explosion of that force does to people.'

Then Phipps stopped, leaned over the table and spoke very quietly. 'Con, I know you did it. I know you're guilty. I've seen people like you before – a college lecturer just like you from Queen's University, Belfast. He thought I'd never tumble him. But I did because I could taste his guilt, just like I can yours.'

'That's ridiculous.'

Phipps shook his head. 'I know you, Con. I know about the murdering fanaticism that brought you here. I've been seeing it for twenty-five years now and I've learned to recognise the signs.'

'Believe what you like, but you must let me speak to the hospital.'

'Not until you start giving us what we want, Lindow. Not until you start facing up to what you have to tell us and what you did to those people last night.'

'I didn't do anything. You know it, I know it, and these people here know it. I DIDN'T DO ANYTHING.'

'We're not getting anywhere,' said Phipps, nodding to Bostock and folding his notes. 'Perhaps you need some time to reflect on the seriousness of your position.'

'I don't need any time. But I am begging you to let me phone the hospital. I must hear from them myself.'

'I am sorry. That won't be possible for the time being,' said Phipps. 'Right, take him away, please.'

Bostock knocked on the door. The two uniformed officers returned.

Lindow looked down quickly at Phipps's watch. It was four twenty p.m.

'Who did this?' Foyle demanded, holding the front page of the *Evening Herald* on which was emblazoned the words BOMBERS SNARED. 'I didn't authorise this. They've got the whole damned story – names, pictures. There's even a bloody interview with one of them. What the hell's been going on?'

'I don't know, sir,' said Forbes. 'I've had a word with the press department and they assure me that they didn't give out any of this material.' He proffered the single page of that morning's press release, which bore two deftly unspecific paragraphs saying that two men had been detained.

'Who's this Abbott-Tring?' Foyle asked, rapping the

paper with the back of his hand. 'What kind of name is that? Is he a crime reporter?'

'No. Apparently they've never heard of him at the press department. It's significant that he didn't feel the need to check with them before running the story. That's because he knew it all. Must've been tipped off.'

'Where'd he get it from?'

Forbes shrugged.

Foyle put the paper down and planted a fist either side of the photograph of Con Lindow being marched from the hospital's service entrance. 'How did they get this?'

'The photographers were there all night. One of them must have spotted our vehicles at the service entrance and decided to wait and see what happened.'

Foyle picked up the paper and began to read.

One of the two Irish brothers who were taken into police custody after last night's West End bomb was interviewed by the *Evening Herald* before his arrest.

Con Lindow, a genetics engineer, who is the younger of the two men, spoke while waiting to be treated in St Luke's emergency department. He suffered minor cuts and bruises. His brother, Eamonn Lindow, who was on the bus when it exploded at 7.35 p.m. last night, is believed to be in a serious condition and is under guard in hospital.

Lindow described how he had just arrived from the United States to take up a job at Imperial College, London. Clearly shocked by his experience, he went on to talk about his work in genetics. At the time he was unaware that Eamonn was being treated in the same hospital for burns and blast wounds. It is understood that Eamonn Lindow, a librarian, was travelling on the bus when the bomb exploded in the early evening, killing 10 people and injuring 47.

Lindow was arrested early this morning by officers

from New Scotland Yard's Anti-Terrorist Branch and taken to Paddington Green police station. He is being held under the Prevention of Terrorism Act. His brother remains under armed guard and is expected to be informed of his arrest when he regains consciousness.

Before anti-terrorist officers realised that the brothers were being treated at the same hospital, the *Herald* interviewed Lindow among the many injured at St Luke's. He told how he had spent the last decade living and working near Boston where there is a large Irish community recognised by American and British authorities as a major source of funding for republican hardliners.

A spokesperson for Imperial College confirmed that Dr Lindow had recently joined the college. She said: 'We cannot make any comment about last night's bomb. We are very sorry to hear that Dr Lindow was injured. He is a scientist of world standing and holds several patents for medically important proteins.'

Meanwhile Eamonn Lindow was thought to be still unconscious following surgery in the early hours of this morning. A hospital spokesman said that he was under guard and that Con Lindow had been discharged into police custody.

Earlier today the Metropolitan Police issued a short statement, which confirmed that they were interested in the two men and that one of these was being held. They appealed for witnesses who may have used the 147 bus last night to come forward

So far little is known of the brothers' background, except that they were both born in the Irish Republic and were brought up in Northern Ireland.

Foyle straightened up. The reporter had plainly got into the hospital the night before, but someone must have leaked the names for him to have made the connection between the suspect and the man he talked to in Casualty. The picture snatched by the paper's photographer in the morning must have confirmed that the person the reporter had interviewed was the suspect Lindow.

'Who's pushing this stuff?'

Forbes's eyes rolled to the ceiling.

'Upstairs? I wonder why. Anyway, whatever the reason, that smart-alec journalist had better watch it. If the Lindows turn out to be innocent, they'll both have excellent grounds to sue. I mean, "Bombers Snared" – you couldn't get less ambiguous.'

Privately he had an idea who might be briefing the press so hard that the editor had taken that sort of risk, but decided to keep it to himself.

Forbes flipped a sheet on his clipboard. 'I don't mean to hurry you, sir, but your meeting at the Cabinet Office is due to start in twenty-five minutes. Shall I get Sergeant Taylor to send for a car?'

'No, I'll walk. I need the exercise. What's it about? I mean, precisely what do they want to know?'

'Seems that the Cabinet Secretary has been asked by the Prime Minister to get together everyone involved in this inquiry. It replaces the Joint Intelligence Committee meeting, which is normally held today, and will include people from the current intelligence committees on Ireland and the Middle East. They're pooling all knowledge on this one for a quick assessment. The PM wants to be brought up to speed before his appearance on the television news tonight. He's due to meet the Irish premier and needs to know exactly what the position is. The unionists are getting hot under the collar, saying that the peace process has been blown apart by the republicans. No one can see a way out of it.'

'They don't normally ask us to meetings like this. Isn't the commissioner going?'

'No, sir. The official I spoke to said the Prime Minister wanted it from the horse's mouth. Assistant Commissioner Scarratt will also be there, along with representatives from MI5 and MI6. It will be chaired by the Cabinet Secretary, Sir Derek Crystal, who's reporting to the Prime Minister immediately afterwards. It should be interesting for you – it's *the* Whitehall powerhouse.'

Foyle rubbed his nose with a knuckle. 'Yes, well, it means that the five thirty briefing will have to be postponed. Make it six thirty. Okay.'

From New Scotland Yard Foyle walked through Queen Anne's Gate, leaving the fortress of the Home Office to his left. The weather had brightened and he decided to sit for a few minutes in St James's Park to gather his thoughts. He chose a bench under the drooping yellow leaves of a catalpa tree, picked a newspaper with thumb and forefinger from an adjacent bin, spread it on the bench and sat down carefully.

He was nervous about his appearance at the Cabinet Office. At this stage of the investigation, less than twenty-four hours after the explosion, he couldn't hope to provide anything but the haziest outline. What these people wanted from him was certainty, not doubts and conjecture. This he didn't possess, still less did he know the answers to the questions that had stacked up in his mind since watching the film of Con Lindow in Clarence Street. He rose from the bench, walked to the gravel expanse of Horse Guards Parade then passed through the archway to turn right down Whitehall. His last thought before presenting himself at the security door of the Cabinet Office was that he should confine himself to the facts of the case and leave it at that. A detailed, neutral description – that was all they would get.

Foyle was ushered into a large room decorated in formal green and hung with portraits of long-deceased

men of affairs. Twenty or so of their modern counter-
parts sat around a long mahogany table, helping themselves to coffee from two white Thermos jugs. Foyle
noted that Scarratt was already there and had positioned
himself at the far end of the room next to the director
general of the security service, David Cantor. It was only
the second time that he had seen the now legendary
Whitehall operator and he watched closely as Cantor
nodded at Scarratt with flattering interest. His face was
well made and exuded a sense of polish and mild good
humour. He smiled easily, the corners of his mouth
spreading out, rather than upwards, to reveal a set of
neat, even teeth. It was in the eyes that Foyle imagined he
saw Cantor's strength of purpose. Hooded and grey, they
seemed to perform a mute calculation, quite independently of the expressions that played about the lower part
of his face.

'Ah, Commander,' said the man sitting at the centre of
the table, whom Foyle recognised as Sir Derek Crystal.
'We'll get straight on with it, shall we? I expect you know
most of the people here, but probably not Robin
Teckman, the director of MI6, and Adam Durie, who
runs the Joint Intelligence Committee.' He indicated a tall
man by his side and a younger official opposite him.
They looked up and nodded. For a moment Foyle had the
idea that he was about to be examined by the member-
ship committee of a grand gentlemen's club. There was a
lull while Crystal sorted through his files and consulted
another official. Nobody said anything to Foyle, so he sat
looking at the portraits and feeling he ought to have
something with him – some papers to show that he'd
come prepared and knew what he was about. Then he
looked round the table. Forbes was right. This was where
the power lay, the arena in which MI5 had scored
innumerable victories over the years, wresting primary
responsibility for counter-terrorism in Northern Ireland
from Special Branch and MI6, then moving into the

Met's preserve of criminal intelligence, offering to integrate knowledge about surveillance and secret sources into the judicial process. Foyle had heard from Forbes, a keen observer of these things, how MI5 had consolidated its position by pointing out to a grateful Civil Service that the security of government computers was dangerously lax. In one move it gained access to all government data banks, including the police national computer. There wasn't a file that the people at Millbank could not read. Millbank was unquestioned and pre-eminent and now there were even suggestions that it would be shadowing certain Met operations in a drive against police corruption.

Sir Derek whispered a few words to the young man, then called the meeting to order with a businesslike smile. 'Perhaps you'd care to bring us up to date with your investigation, Commander.'

Foyle began with the basics: the positions of the bus and the Lindow brothers when the bomb went off. He described the way the bomb was contained in a canvas bag and how it had been carried on to the bus some time between six forty-five and seven thirty-five p.m. He said there were still a large number of unknowns. The police did not know whether the bomb had gone off of its own accord, or whether it had been intentionally detonated. No timer or trigger device had been found in the wreckage, and this was due to the damage caused by the large amount of explosive used. Debris was distributed over a wide area and it was difficult to distinguish between what might have been part of a bomb and what was not.

He moved on to the film from the security cameras showing Con Lindow, and told them how the younger brother had been interviewed twice that day but that nothing had come of it. Both the brothers' flats were being examined by forensics teams, but so far nothing had come of this either. Foyle presented it all in a scrupulous matter-of-fact tone. At each pause he stressed that the evidence could be read either way.

'But what do *you* think, Commander?' asked Sir Derek Crystal. 'An informed guess, if that's all you can manage. Are these two men members of a republican splinter group? Or are we dealing with some hitherto unappreciated menace from the loyalists, in which case these are clearly not your men? Is this a one-off, or are we in for a long campaign? I need your ideas on these questions.'

'It's difficult to say. There has been no admission of responsibility, but that is to be expected since it's been announced that we are holding two suspects. In these circumstances terrorist groups never confirm their men's involvement. Still, from an intelligence point of view, the attack was surprising. There may still be dormant active-service units here, which have become renegade, but there was no indication that they were about to start bombing London again. As to the loyalist solution – the idea that the protestant paramilitaries bombed the heart of the capital in the hope that the republicans would be blamed – well, there's nothing to suggest that they have been considering such a drastic step.'

'Are these the men who did it?' asked Sir Derek, the perpendicular cleft in his forehead deepening with impatience.

'To be candid,' said Foyle, looking up the table to Scarratt and Cantor, 'I am not yet convinced of it. If we accept that the explosion was an accident, and that they had planned to use the explosive material at a later stage, it's still difficult to know why both brothers were carrying identification. The IRA, like other terrorist organisations, has learned a lot in the last twenty years. We know that they have procedures and that one of these is to check that their people go out stripped of identity – of anything that helps us trace them. It means that if something does go wrong it gives the others time to escape. But, of course, other groups would have the same procedure.'

'But surely,' said David Cantor, from the other end of the table, 'we're not going to ignore the fact that one of these Irishmen had his rear blown off by the bomb and the other had just conveniently arrived in this country after a long period in Boston. These things *do* seem to add up.'

'Yes, on the face of it they're persuasive.' Foyle addressed his remarks solely to Cantor. 'Nevertheless, I believe we should keep an open mind.'

'Well, is there anyone else we suspect of blowing up Clarence Street?' asked Sir Derek.

'Not at present, sir, but—'

'Then we cannot rule out that this was a renegade IRA action. I take it, from what you are saying, that there will be no charges tonight.'

'Yes, sir. That's correct.'

'Will the police be applying to the Home Secretary for an extension of Lindow's detention under the Prevention of Terrorism Act?' asked Cantor.

'We have another twenty-four hours before that will be necessary, sir. But it is perfectly possible that we will. We may still have his brother to question,' said Foyle.

'And what state is he in?' asked Sir Derek.

'Not good. He's back on life-support this afternoon,' said Foyle.

Sir Derek made a note, then looked round the table with his eyebrows raised, inviting other contributions. Cantor darted to press home his point. 'I don't want to anticipate anything that you were planning to say, Sir Derek, but I think it would be useful for the Prime Minister to know that both these men have been interviewed before. Is that not the case, Commander? As I understand it, they were arrested in Ulster in connection with an explosion in a churchyard in the early eighties.' There was an implied question mark after the word

71

'churchyard', as if he couldn't quite remember the details. He looked for help from Scarratt, who obliged him with a nod.

'Yes,' said Foyle. 'There was an incident, but neither of these two men was charged. We're going over the papers from that time to gain a clearer picture of their involvement.'

'Our information is that Eamonn Lindow may be more than he seems,' Cantor continued. 'We have little in terms of hard evidence. As you will know, we've recently received much useful instruction from the police on the distinction between intelligence and evidence. I would place this firmly in the category of intelligence. But let me just say that Eamonn Lindow was not unknown to us. Before the ceasefire and the Stormont Agreement, he was mainstream IRA, a valued operator. After the settlement, many of the IRA's men here were stood down or simply receded into the woodwork. However, in his case there was a feeling that he was still effectively operational. We made it our business to find out what he was doing and we were watching him. After some months we concluded that he had been activated, but for what purpose eluded us. The important point is that our information adds to the significance of his presence on that bus and of his brother's at the scene. You may wish to keep an open mind, but I think you'll agree that we should not ignore what is staring us in the face.'

The room caught the note of menace in Cantor's voice. Foyle was beginning to feel a sense of doom when the head of MI6, Robin Teckman, leaned forward and spoke. His manner was deliberate and precise, each point emphasised by small sweeping motions of his right hand. Cantor's features remained impassive but Foyle noticed a concentrated look enter his eyes.

'Commander, I wonder if there is another point that we are ignoring here. This is not my area, but am I right in thinking that this bomb was unusually large? I believe it contained over twelve pounds of Semtex, whereas one or two pounds would have been easily enough to destroy the bus – enough to make the point, if you see what I mean.'

'You mean the size of the bomb has a bearing on the sort of target it was made for,' said Foyle, 'and therefore we might conclude that it was destined for another much larger target?'

'Yes, as you say, a larger target – a public building, a motorway flyover, an installation of some sort.' He removed his glasses to reveal two exceptionally large dark eyebrows, which had been masked by the frame. 'But there have been occasions when the opposite was true, when a large bomb was used to disguise the fact that the target was rather modest. There were two such devices used in Eastern Europe recently. These appeared to be aimed at a train and a large building, but were in fact targeted at specific individuals. In neither case did the relevant authorities appreciate that they were dealing with assassination devices. I mention this because if the bomb was not an accident, it may just conform to this pattern. We'll furnish your department with the relevant material by the end of the afternoon.'

Foyle thanked him.

'So I take it,' said Sir Derek, 'that I should tell the Prime Minister things are at an early stage, and that you will let us know if there are any developments, particularly if charges are to be made. Assistant Commissioner Scarratt, can I rely on you to liaise with my office? I don't have to stress how important this is in the current circumstances.' He paused and looked up with another bleak smile. 'If you'll forgive us, we just have a little more business to attend to. Thank you both for joining us.'

With that, Foyle and Scarratt were dismissed from the meeting.

Outside, Scarratt stood on the pavement looking at the traffic and slapping his black leather gloves against the palm of his hand. 'That, Commander, was a bloody disaster. We've got to get our act together on this one. We're in the front line, you know. Our performance is being scrutinised.' Then he turned to his car, swept off his cap and climbed into the back seat.

Foyle watched as he was driven off down Whitehall. Scarratt was an officious fool, but Foyle knew he was right: his performance had been woefully unconvincing. Still, the meeting had not been a complete waste of time. He walked slowly towards Parliament Square with Teckman's words playing through his mind. The more he thought about it, the odder Teckman's intervention seemed. It was plain that the director of MI6 was steering him, or at least trying to open the investigation to other possibilities.

It was just past six thirty when he arrived at New Scotland Yard. He went straight to the briefing room, where SO 13 and Special Branch officers were already assembled. He called for silence and asked Sergeant Pennel to read out what his team had learned about the Lindows' movements.

'I'll begin with Eamonn Lindow,' said Pennel. 'He left the library at five forty-five, which is his usual time, and walked to a pub with a colleague, where they had a pint. The colleague said he seemed relaxed until he realised that he was running late. She said that she told him the bus would be quicker because it would be going against the traffic flow into the West End. There were problems with the tube line and she was quite sure that she recommended the bus.'

'That's interesting. Was he carrying anything?'

'No. She was sure about that too.'

'What time was this?'

'She thinks it was about six forty-five. The pub is a ten-minute walk from the library. She reckons they were there for about half an hour.'

'And they didn't meet anyone else?'

74

'No.'

'When had they arranged to have a drink?'

'She said that it was a spur-of-the-moment thing to discuss some problem at the library. She suggested it.'

'Would Eamonn have had time to go back to his flat?'

'No, it's in the opposite direction, sir. And if he had, he would have travelled by another bus route into town. Of course, he may have picked up the bag along the route.'

'What about Con Lindow?'

'Much the same story, sir, except he seems to have gone back to his place to change before going out. The people at the university said that he had been wearing a suit when he left. There had been a meeting with a group from industry. He needed to make a good impression. But he wasn't in his flat long.'

'When did he leave Imperial College?'

'At five forty, sir. The department secretary remembers exactly because she wanted to leave early herself and felt she couldn't go before he did.'

'So what we are saying here is that there is nothing out of the ordinary in their behaviour?'

'That seems about right – yes.'

'Have we got anything on the woman they were going to meet – the woman on the message tape from Eamonn's flat?'

'Nobody at the library knew of her. Their impression was that Eamonn didn't have a girl. He never mentioned anyone. Apparently he has a lot of interests – poetry, old films, real ale – but nothing in the way of a permanent relationship.'

'So what do we have from the two flats?'

The officer in charge of the searches, Inspector Lockyer, rose and held up his thumb and index finger to form a zero.

'It's the same story, sir,' he said. 'Absolutely sweet FA. Both places clean as a bishop's bed. There's a lot of junk in Eamonn's flat, which we're going through. His clothing is being submitted to the standard tests for explosives and we're examining all the bed linen, soft furnishings, kitchen utensils but it doesn't look very hopeful. The brother's flat in Notting Hill is interesting. It's a service place on a short let. The sort of flat a wealthy businessman would rent for a couple of months. Not a lot of his personal possessions, apart from a few books connected with his work and his clothes. They're being tested too. There's a woman downstairs who looks after the place for the owners. Lindow told her he was looking for a bigger flat. He said he would move when he got his stuff out of storage. He had asked her to put out feelers and he was talking to estate agents. He didn't seem to want to buy, just rent.'

'How long's he been here?'

'Close to three weeks. The woman says that he's out most of the time. No sign of him ever cooking anything; goes early, returns late. No visitors that she knows of.'

'That ties in with the people at the university,' said Sergeant Pennel. 'They say he eats in the canteen and rarely leaves his office before nine p.m. The department secretary keeps his diary. She made two previous arrangements for him to see Eamonn, but they were cancelled.'

'Any reasons?'

'She remembers Dr Lindow saying that his brother had been ill. Nothing serious. And then the second time he had to attend a welcoming party that had been sprung on him by his head of department.'

Foyle turned to Lockyer. 'You say his things are in storage. Any idea where that might be?'

'Yes, sir, we found the shipping forms. The container should be at Tilbury by the end of the week and they'll go into storage then.'

'Good, I want it searched as soon as it hits the dockside. Forbes, can you keep that in hand?'

Forbes nodded.

'Okay,' said Foyle, addressing the room. 'What we need to do this evening is to work on building up the profiles of these two fellows. I want to know everything about Eamonn Lindow. Millbank say they've had him under surveillance and that he seems to have republican connections. I'll get the relevant material from them this evening. We also need to trace anyone who knew Con Lindow in the United States. Start hitting the phones.'

'We already have, sir,' said Sergeant Pennel. Foyle smiled. Pennel had turned out well since he'd been brought in from a liaison job between Customs and Excise and the Drugs Squad. 'One of his referees for the new post was a Dr Peter Varrone. He also figures in Lindow's address book. We rang him earlier today and taped the interview. He had nothing but good things to say about Lindow. Said he was one of the smartest people to come his way in years. Lindow is the owner of patents that will make him a wealthy man. We're talking to other people in the address book. So far the picture we're getting is of a very dedicated person – brilliant in his field.'

'And what is that exactly?' asked Foyle.

'Originally he was involved in work on the human-genome project and then he moved on to studying bacteria and the way they communicate with each other. As I have had it explained to me, it's about the behaviour of human cells and bacteria. He dives in and out of different areas. Apparently he's smart enough to do that.'

'Good, we need more of that sort of thing. Find out where he lived. Talk to his friends, girlfriends, associates – I want to know about his political convictions and any contacts he had with Irish groups. Run it all past the FBI.'

The briefing continued with inconclusive reports from Irish intelligence and then routine updates from the Special Branch surveillance of other suspects. There were no obvious connections with the Lindows.

Foyle began to wrap up the briefing. 'While we'll be

doing a lot of work on the Lindows tonight and tomorrow, I want you to try to think of this inquiry without them. Think what we would be doing if two Irishmen hadn't been handed to us on a plate. Where would we be looking? Who would we be talking to? It may turn out that the Lindows aren't our men, after all.' He turned to leave the room, then pulled up by the door. 'Oh, by the way . . . we can't have any more coverage like this morning's. I don't want the press creating an atmosphere in which it becomes impossible for us to see our way through this thing. Just thought I'd mention it, although I'm certain none of it came from this department.'

Back in his office, Foyle found Sam Phipps waiting. 'What do you think, Sam? Guilty, or what?' He realised at once he should have known better with Phipps, who was famously noncommittal, particularly when in the middle of an interrogation – or examination, as he preferred to call it. In his view, interrogation smacked of beatings and intimidation.

'Hard to say,' he said morosely. 'It's difficult when one hasn't been in on it from the outset.'

Foyle knew that Phipps hated the fact that Simmonds and Bostock had been let loose on the first session with Lindow. Phipps liked to feel his way like a blind clock-maker working out the mechanism by touch and instinct. When he found a part he didn't understand, he never forced it, but left it alone until gradually the thing made sense to him. Only then would he allow himself to fit it tentatively into the whole.

'How long have I got?' he asked.

'Well, we can go for an extension until tomorrow afternoon, at which point we will have had him in custody for thirty-six hours. There won't be any problem with that. The Home Office will let us have him for the maximum seven-day period. Do you feel you're going to need that?'

Phipps sucked at his teeth. 'I'm not sure. Something's there, but I'm not certain whether it's relevant. It's that business in Northern Ireland. When I press him on it, he's easily rattled and becomes inconsistent. Yet when I ask him about last night and the circumstances that led him to come to Britain, I sense he's much more relaxed. I'll be in a better position to give you an opinion tomorrow morning.'

Phipps left. Foyle picked up the phone and asked to be put through to Peter Speerman, the deputy director of MI5. He knew Speerman, a thin, cautious bureaucrat with slightly sunken cheeks and an ill-disguised bald patch. They had met during Home Office sessions designed to increase co-operation between the police and the security service.

Speerman came on the line. 'Hello, Commander. Hope you're well. I've got some material for you.'

'Good. Is there anything in it?'

'The main point is that Eamonn Lindow has had some dealings with a character called Rudi MacMahon. You may have heard of him. He was a member of the IRA's army council. He went legitimate nine years ago and got himself elected as a Sinn Fein councillor. He has played a big part in the Stormont peace agreement. He's quite a player, and at root he's still a hard man. Lindow and MacMahon have met at least twice in the last five years. In fact, we have pictures of them talking in the street. They were at the same school.'

'You'll send the file over, then?'

'Certainly, and if there's anything else, please call me. We are here to help.'

Foyle hung up.

Later that evening Con Lindow was roused and taken from the cells. His eyes ached and his mouth tasted stale. Phipps did not look up when Lindow was put in the chair opposite him.

'Right, Dr Lindow. We need a few more answers from you. Then you can have a wash and shave.'

'You mean you're going to ask me to sign some damned stupid confession, then you'll let me have a wash. You know I'm innocent and you know that you're abusing my rights – my right to exercise, to sleep without being disturbed, to know the time of day, to take meals at the normal times, to telephone my family. And what about the right to visit my brother? You're abusing my rights, Phipps, and when I leave here I'll pursue every course open to me to expose you for what you are.'

Phipps looked up at him with the expression of a man waiting for a rain shower to pass. 'We have no further information about your brother. But we will let you know as soon as we do.'

'Then I will say nothing,' Lindow said, feeling his face flush.

'In which case we will have to take it that you have something to hide – and in these circumstances, Dr Lindow, a judge and jury are liable to draw an adverse inference from your silence. Even if you do get out of here, that silence may prompt the Home Secretary to make you the subject of an exclusion order – which, despite the advances of recent years, is still an option open to him. Now, just answer these few questions for us. Then we'll see about the other things. What do you know about a man named Rudi MacMahon?'

Christ, when the hell were they going to let up?

'I don't know anyone of that name.'

'Oh, come along. He's a friend of your brother's. They were school pals and they kept in touch.'

'Look, I can't answer for my brother. I don't know what he does. I'm here to answer questions about myself, not my brother.'

Lindow jumped as Phipps barked with surprising volume. 'Under section eleven of the Prevention of Terrorism Act you are required to answer questions about anyone we suspect of terrorism. If you withhold information you may be charged with a criminal offence. So please *do* answer our questions about your brother and MacMahon, Dr Lindow.'

'I don't know him. Eamonn never mentioned him to me.' Then he paused, remembering. 'Oh, of course, yes, I *do* know who you mean. Isn't he the Sinn Fein man? Yes, Eamonn was at school with him. But I've never met him and I'm sure Eamonn didn't kept in touch with him. They didn't like each other much.'

'It's very interesting you say that,' said Phipps. 'You referred to him as the "Sinn Fein man". Rudi MacMahon only became an official Sinn Fein candidate nine years ago. Before that he was the brigade leader in Fermanagh. How would you know that he was an official Sinn Fein candidate if you had not talked to your brother about him? By your own account you didn't keep abreast of the events in Northern Ireland so there's no other way you would know.'

Lindow sighed. 'Really, you are desperate, aren't you? I knew he was a Sinn Fein politician because I saw his picture some time ago in Boston. It was the St Patrick's Day parade and MacMahon was on the front of the local paper. I remember it because there were some stories about him getting a visa. The picture showed him holding up a little girl to the camera, like a politician would. At the time I wondered if the girl's parents had any idea about the things he had done in his life.' The room was hot and airless, and Phipps was so close to him that Lindow could smell his breath.

Phipps grimaced a smile. 'So MacMahon visited Boston. Did you happen to meet him while he was there, Dr Lindow?'

'No, of course not. I told you, I just saw his face in the paper. Nothing else.'

'But you agree that your brother was consorting with senior members of the IRA, men who posed as politicians but were still at the time deeply involved in the armed struggle. You agree that he was a friend of your brother's.'

'He was a contemporary of Eamonn's at school. That's all. You can't help who you're at school with. I mean, Eamonn and I . . . we didn't know that he was definitely a Provisional.'

'Oh, please, Dr Lindow,' exhaled Phipps. 'You just said that you wondered if the girl's parents had any idea what Rudi MacMahon had done in his life – meaning, of course, that you wondered if they had any idea about the bombs and murders and beatings he was responsible for. That's what you said and everyone in this room heard it – I'll play it back on the tape for you, if you require. And yet now you say you didn't know he was a member of the IRA.'

'You know what I meant. I didn't know for certain. That's all I was saying. You have suspicions about people, but you don't know for sure.'

Lindow felt the fight draining from him and, in his head, he heard his voice rise in a panicky falsetto. Collect yourself, he thought. Lower your voice and cool it.

'Yes. We all have suspicions about people, don't we?' Phipps continued. 'For instance, I have my suspicions about you. I don't know exactly what happened last night, but my guess is that bomb was not primed to go off. Indeed, I think it likely that you were meeting your brother to take delivery of a consignment of Semtex, which would be used in several different devices that you were going to construct in your flat in Notting Hill. That would explain the unusually large amount of explosive in the suitcase. I'm right, aren't I? When you had finished your work, you'd leave the flat and bugger off back to America.'

'No, no, that's not right. Can't you see? What do I have to do to convince you, for Chrissake?'

'But then the Semtex blew up of its own accord, nearly

killing Eamonn. Perhaps there was more in that suitcase than just Semtex – primer-charge material, detonators, batteries, tilt switches, timers. Who knows, a whole bomb-making kit? At any rate the case was subject to a sudden shock and the whole lot went up with a bloody great BANG.' Phipps crashed both fists down on the table. Lindow recoiled. 'You had a pretty good idea that Eamonn was injured but you knew that you had to pretend otherwise, which explains the pantomime at the hospital and all that acting in here today when you were told that Eamonn had been hurt.'

'No. None of this is true. You're wrong. You don't know how wrong you are. I am not a terrorist, for God's sake!'

'You're not listening properly, Lindow. We know what happened, so why not make a clean breast of it? Maybe we can fix something up. It'll be hard for us to prove that you had an intention to cause explosions and a good lawyer might even get you off altogether. Talk to me, Con. Tell me what Eamonn planned. Tell me where the rest of the explosives are hidden. Talk to me now, Con, then you can take your shower, have something to eat and get some kip ... Tomorrow you'll speak to the hospital and see a lawyer. We'll fix it. It'll be all right for you. You'll see.'

Phipps's face had tilted very close to the table. He was looking up into Lindow's eyes. Then he placed a hand on Lindow's shoulder and squeezed a little. Lindow felt the hand draw the tension from his neck. It made him yearn to sleep. He'd never felt so tired and he knew he was about to succumb to Phipps. He had to keep fighting him.

Minutes seemed to pass without anyone speaking. Then Phipps said, very quietly, 'You're going to talk to us properly now, aren't you? You all right, Con?'

'Yes, I am all right, thank you,' said Lindow, looking up to face the others. 'I won't bother with the shower, or any of the rest of it. I've done nothing. I am saying nothing more and I am going back to my cell. You can keep me here as long as you like, but I'm not confessing to something I haven't done.'

He got up, and before anyone could stop him, pinned Phipps's left arm to the table and snatched at the sleeve on his jacket to reveal his watch. It was eleven twenty p.m. Bostock leaped forward and cuffed him to the ground.

'That's enough,' shouted Phipps. 'Take him back to the cells and give him something to eat.'

Chapter Four

'Can I give you some advice, Kenneth?'

Foyle had learned to be wary when Scarratt used his first name. Moreover, he knew the assistant commissioner had just returned from lunch at MI5's Millbank headquarters, a piece of intelligence gleaned by Forbes that morning.

'Yes, sir, if you like. I'd be happy to hear your thoughts on the case.'

'It's not so much the case, Commander, it's more your general approach. At this level you can't work in isolation. You must learn to see the bigger picture and understand the way the different parts interlock and depend on each other. We have to work with those different interests and take into account their requirements.'

'What are you saying, sir?' asked Foyle, although he was pretty sure what was coming.

'If you release Con Lindow, you will give out certain signals to those interests. To lock up a man and then let him go within a day or two looks as if we're not trying hard enough. It will tell the other agencies concerned that we do not respect the information and help that they have offered us over the past twenty-four hours. For instance, the director general of the security service has informed us that he knows of contacts between Eamonn Lindow and a well-known republican figure. It would be wrong to ignore that, Kenneth, very wrong indeed.'

Scarratt took a turn around Foyle's office while waiting for his reply, then suddenly said, 'How's the family?'

Foyle raised his eyes to the ceiling. 'Away, sir.'

'Perhaps you should spend more time with them, when you can.' He was feeling the brush of his cropped hair. 'I saw my daughter on Tuesday.'

Scarratt swivelled round. 'Yes, I heard about that, Kenneth. Most unfortunate for you. Let's hope she stays out of trouble from now on. You don't want that sort of worry as well.'

Foyle had wondered how long it would be before Scarratt found out about Katherine. No doubt he had learned about it over lunch. MI5 kept files on various groups of troublemakers. Katherine's name must have been picked up on Tuesday.

'To return to this business about Lindow. It would be wrong – profoundly wrong – and impolitic not to hold him a little longer. You have to give Phipps more time with him, a day or two more and he'll have everything we need to know.'

'But on what grounds do I continue to hold him? Everything suggests that the brothers are innocent. The phone logs from both flats, their movements over the last two weeks, the forensic tests, their behaviour on the evening of the bomb – everything produces a negative reading. I can't hold a man without evidence. If there *is* more to him than meets the eye, he'll be just as useful to us on the outside. We're not going to get anything now.'

Scarratt's expression changed. 'Think about the man you're returning to the streets of this city, Commander. What if he gets away scot-free? Have you thought of that? You're on a fixed-term contract. I can't see it being renewed if you seek to defy the collective desire that Con Lindow's interrogation should be allowed to run its full course.'

So that was the threat: if Foyle didn't do the bidding of the 'collective', that is to say Scarratt's new friends at

Millbank, he'd be out. Scarratt had been primed by Cantor or one of his creatures and plainly someone at Paddington Green was keeping him informed about the Lindow interrogation. It wouldn't be Phipps, who made no secret of his dislike of Scarratt. Maybe Simmonds or Bostock, or the spook who had been allowed in as part of his department's co-operation with the security service. At any rate, the fact that Millbank, Special Branch and his squad all knew that nothing had come from the interrogation was no bad thing. It helped his case to release Lindow.

Still, if a few more hours might placate Scarratt, it would be stupid to go against him and release Lindow now. He was on the point of agreeing to hold Lindow through the weekend when there was a rapid knock at the door and Forbes entered with his clipboard. 'Yes?' said Foyle.

'I am sorry to interrupt, sir. Eamonn Lindow's dead – died twenty minutes ago in surgery.'

Foyle looked at Scarratt. 'That changes things, doesn't it, sir? Has he been told yet, Forbes?'

'No, sir.'

'I think you'll agree', said Foyle, turning back to Scarratt, 'that it makes it difficult to hold him under these circumstances. We'll keep close to him. If you're right about him, he'll make a mistake and then we'll have him.'

Scarratt marched from the office without a word.

Foyle sat down. 'I want round-the-clock surveillance on Lindow. We mustn't lose track of him for a moment. I guess he'll fly home to Ireland some time next week with the body. It seems the natural thing to do. Ask the coroner's office to hurry along with the inquest and then brief the RUC and the Garda. We're going to need their help to watch him once he's out of the country. Right, I'm going to see Lindow to break the news.'

Forbes lingered in the doorway.

'Yes?' said Foyle.

'Well, I was wondering if it was strictly necessary – if it was advisable – for you to go to Paddington Green yourself. It might seem odd now.'

'Thank you, but I know what I'm doing,' Foyle snapped. Forbes should have known that Lindow was all he had got. He had to get close to him.

Forbes nodded.

Half an hour later Foyle was shown into the secure section of Paddington Green. He found Phipps in an ill-lit office looking at winter-holiday brochures. In the next-door room he could hear Simmonds and some others talking.

'Someone else's,' said Phipps drily, letting a brochure slip from his hands to the desk. 'But I could do with the break. What brings you here, Commander?'

'Eamonn Lindow's dead. I've come to tell his brother and after that I'm going to let him go, Sam. Have you had any more thoughts on him?'

'It's difficult to be precise at this stage. He's not one of your usual IRA nuts. I don't have a sense that he's acting and I'm sure he hasn't been trained to resist this kind of examination. I would have spotted it. As I said to you yesterday, there's an area I'm not happy about and that's the period in the eighties. He's all over the shop about that. But when it comes to the evening of the bomb, his story stands up. If you want a definite view, I really need more time.'

'I'm afraid that's not possible, Sam. But with Lindow out we might get something else. You never know.'

Phipps led Foyle down to the cells. On the way he told him that he'd kept Lindow locked up for the best part of the day because he thought the extension would be granted as a matter of course. That always did a lot to break a man's resistance and Phipps had kept him in the cells waiting for that moment. Except for a short time first thing that morning when he had been allowed to wash, and five minutes' statutory exercise, during which Lindow had been marched round the station car park handcuffed to an officer, he'd been in his cell for nearly sixteen hours.

They found him sitting on his bed with his head bowed. He didn't look up when they entered.

'Dr Lindow,' said Foyle, 'I am Commander Foyle. We are going to let you go in a little while, but first I'm afraid I have some bad news for you. It's about your brother, Eamonn.'

Lindow looked up slowly and searched his face. Foyle was impressed by the intelligence in his eyes.

'He died while undergoing surgery this morning. The injuries he sustained were very severe indeed. The hospital say that he never regained consciousness after the bomb.' He paused to let it sink in. 'Do you understand what I have said to you, Dr Lindow?'

Lindow nodded. Then he said flatly, 'I understand what you're saying . . . Eamonn is dead.'

'I'm very sorry,' said Foyle, clasping his hands awkwardly in front of him. He hated this. He'd done it too many times before as a young officer. 'Believe me, Dr Lindow, I know how tough this is for you. I'm sorry that you've been held here at such a distressing time.'

Lindow opened his mouth, as if to cry out, but no sound came.

'Do you want to leave straight away or would you like to sit here for a while? There are just a few formalities to complete, then you'll be free to go.'

'Now!' said Lindow. 'I'd like to go now.'

A uniformed officer appeared with a sealed bag of Lindow's possessions and asked him to sign for them. Lindow checked through the bag.

'Where're my keys? They're not here.'

'They must be with us,' said Foyle. 'I'll get them to you this afternoon.'

'There's another set with the woman who looks after the place, but I'll need them tomorrow.'

Foyle led the way up out of the back of the station and towards his car, where Lindow stopped and looked up at the overcast sky. He blinked back tears and shook his head.

'I'm afraid they need you at the hospital to identify your brother's body,' said Foyle. 'Of course, there was identity on your brother and we're pretty certain it was him. Still, we would prefer it in these circumstances . . . It isn't going to be easy for you. Would you like a cup of coffee beforehand? I'll take you to a place round the corner.'

Lindow inhaled deeply and shook his head. His tears had gone. 'What for? More questions? No. I've answered enough of your questions. I won't forget the way I've been treated here. Not once was I allowed to call the hospital about Eamonn. I'd have liked to have seen him before he died, or perhaps you don't understand that.'

'Yes, I understand very well, but you must see why we had to detain you. When so many people have lost their lives and been injured, we would have been failing in our duty not to talk to you. Ten people were killed. Now the toll is eleven – the largest count over here for years. We owe it to them to find the men who did this. I know it's been rough but I am afraid there simply wasn't an option. Look, why don't you let me run you to the hospital? It won't be any bother.'

Reluctantly Lindow climbed into the back of Foyle's car. Alex pulled into the traffic and began to retrace the route taken by the police van the day before. Foyle said that when they arrived at the hospital he'd better go in with him to ease the way.

'There was some publicity yesterday,' he said. 'Your picture was in the papers and they may wonder what you're doing out.'

'Are you saying that I may have a case against the press as well?' asked Lindow.

'In due course you may feel you have. I'm not a lawyer, but I would guess that you might want to press for some sort of retraction. We've no idea where they got it from. Only a short statement was released yesterday.' Foyle watched Lindow's reaction very carefully.

'But today you'll make another statement exonerating my brother and myself,' said Lindow.

'Yes, we'll make it clear that you have been released after helping with our inquiries.'

As they came to a halt in the jam around Marble Arch, Foyle examined Lindow properly for the first time. He was taller than he'd gauged from the security film and had finer features: a long aquiline nose, well-defined cheekbones and jaw, blue-grey eyes with lids that slanted down sharply at the corner. His light brown hair was thinning at the front, which exaggerated his brow. Foyle was struck by his composure. He did not look about him or fidget. His hands rested on his thighs, palms down, long thin fingers splayed out evenly. When he spoke, he did not turn to face Foyle. This wasn't a man who wasted energy on unnecessary movement. If he had something to hide, Foyle thought, it would take a long time to find it. And yet he also seemed open and human in his responses.

At the hospital Foyle took Lindow to the main reception, and told a receptionist there that they had come to identify his brother's body. While they waited Foyle gave Lindow his card and told him to expect that his flat and also his brother's place would look disturbed as they had both been searched. If there were any problems he wanted Lindow to call him.

Foyle shrugged his shoulders in apology then said goodbye, and went to a nearby phone to call Forbes. 'I have left him at the front desk of St Luke's. He's going to identify Eamonn Lindow's body. Tell them to pick him up as he leaves the hospital. He shouldn't be more than half an hour, unless he goes to Casualty and has his cuts dressed again. Impress upon the surveillance teams that they must not lose him. He's all we have at the moment . . . And, Forbes, get a press release sent out immediately saying that we've let him go.'

Lindow was shown to the mortuary by a man from the hospital administration, which had been warned by New Scotland Yard to expect him. At the back of his mind he knew that he was doing the wrong thing in seeing Eamonn's body. Eamonn had seen their mother in hospital after she died and he had written to Con to say the memory wasn't easily shaken from his mind. His lasting image of her was of her corpse.

In the long, tiled room a police officer was waiting with two other attendants, who looked on with sympathetic interest. Lindow was led to a spot in the centre of the room, where Eamonn's body lay on a trolley under a sheet. The administrator nodded to one of the attendants, who drew back the sheet.

'Is this your brother, sir? Is this Eamonn Lindow?' said the police officer quietly.

Lindow looked down at the body for several seconds. The only evidence of the monstrous trauma suffered by Eamonn was a large bruise that had coloured the skin on his jaw and neck a sickly ochre. But this wasn't the reason why he barely recognised him. Even in repose, Eamonn was never sombre. The gravity of his final expression seemed to have altered the whole structure of his face. Lindow had the uncomfortable impression that he was intruding on his brother, that he might wake suddenly and produce a vivid stream of invective, just as he had once when Lindow had barged into the bathroom and caught him sitting on the lavatory. He imagined his blue eyes flashing open. 'What are you about, Con? Can't a man get any rest without his brother sneaking up and peering at him like some sort of specimen in his laboratory?' He heard Eamonn drawing out each syllable for comic effect – 'spe-ci-men', he would have said.

Lindow held the side of the trolley. 'Sorry . . . I haven't seen him for two years. What I mean to say is that he's changed.' He looked at Eamonn again. 'You see, he's lost weight and his hair has receded more. At first I didn't think it was him . . . But it is . . . Yes, this is my brother, Eamonn Lindow.'

'Thank you, sir. I am sorry,' said the policeman. 'Would you like a few moments here alone, sir? It's perfectly in order. We'll be outside.'

'No, that's all right.' He shook his head. He could feel himself losing control, but he knew that he couldn't – not in this place. He composed himself and turned to the policeman. 'Is that all you need?'

The officer nodded, then followed Lindow and the administrator out of the mortuary. At the door he asked for Lindow's telephone number so that the coroner's office could let him know about the inquest.

'Don't you have it already?' he asked.

'No, sir, I'm from the local police station, but I can get it from New Scotland Yard, if it's difficult for you now.'

'Isn't it on a list somewhere? I gave it to the people in Accident and Emergency Reception before.'

'Ah, yes, I didn't think of that. I'll get it from them, if you like.'

Lindow relented and gave him the number. Then he asked for directions to the outpatients department. He wanted his stitches checked and dressed again. His leg was bothering him. The doctor gave him a local anaesthetic, removed another piece of glass that had come to the surface, then stitched the wound.

In less than half an hour Lindow left the hospital via the Casualty exit and walked down the ramp to hail a cab for Notting Hill. It was rush hour and the ride back to his flat was agonisingly slow. He longed for a bath and his bed. When he reached Homer Road he got out, felt for his keys, then, remembering that the police still had them, rang the bell of the ground-floor flat where he retrieved another set from the housekeeper. She looked at him suspiciously but wished him a good evening. Finally he dragged himself up the steps to the main entrance of the building and let himself in.

It was exactly forty-eight hours since he had been home. During that time the flat had been subject to a kind of hostile occupation. The carpets in all three rooms were curled up at the edges where they had been wrenched from the floor and, as he moved about, Lindow could feel the floorboards creak beneath him. They'd been pulled up then hastily nailed back. Everywhere there were signs of furious search and botched repair. The skirting-boards and panelling of the long window-seat in the sitting room appeared to have sprung free of their own accord. Most of the light fittings and electrical sockets were loose. The drawers in the bedroom had been rifled and upturned and the few books that he had kept out of storage thumbed then tossed aside. Even the back of the television lay broken on the floor. In the bedroom the ceiling of the fitted wardrobe was hanging down and the drawers from the unit inside piled high beside the bed, their contents heaped in a midden of clothes and linen. They'd been sure he wasn't coming back.

He went to the kitchen, where he found all the cooking utensils coated in fingerprint dust and smelling of a pungent chemical. He opened the fridge and withdrew a bottle of white wine. He poured a glass and drank it at a gulp, more from thirst than a need for alcohol. He poured another and returned to the sitting room where he pressed the flashing button on his answering-machine. There was a message from the letting agent whom he'd been due to meet the day before.

He picked up the phone and dialled his father in Ireland. Tag answered. Suddenly he found he couldn't speak. He was lost in the memory of the day that

Eamonn had christened their little sister. She would follow them everywhere, never let them be alone, so he called her Tag Along. It was shortened to Tag and stuck. 'I'm sorry,' Lindow said eventually. 'I had to gather my thoughts.'

'Oh, Con! It's you. It's so good to hear you. We were worried sick. When did they let you go?'

'This afternoon . . . Look, Tag, I've been to identify Eamonn in the hospital. That's why I didn't ring before.'

'Oh, God . . . poor Con.'

Lindow heard her control a sob. Then she told him about their father who had had an attack of angina during the day and been given some pills and something to calm him down by the doctor. He was too upset to speak on the phone.

'I would come over to help,' she said, 'only Dad has taken it very bad. I can't leave him now.'

'It really isn't necessary. I can manage it all.' Lindow tried to soften his voice, but it was difficult because he was certain that someone would be listening. He had a lot to say to her, but it would have to keep until they saw each other.

'Tag, I don't want to talk now. Do you mind?'

'I know, we'll talk when you're here.'

'I don't know when that'll be. I'll phone the coroner tomorrow and see when they're prepared to release the body. Then I'll ring you and we'll talk about the arrangements.'

He rang off then dialled the number on Foyle's card. A woman answered and told him that the commander was in a meeting. He said he'd call back but would like to register a complaint now about the state of his home. He would be suing the police.

He didn't care much about the flat: it wasn't his place and he could easily settle the bill with the landlord. The money wasn't the point: the abuse of him and his home was. The next day he'd see a lawyer about his arrest.

There was also the newspaper coverage to think about. He must get copies of Wednesday's papers.

The wine began to take effect. He walked unsteadily towards the bay window in the sitting room to let down the blinds. It was dark outside, but he could see two men sitting in a parked car across the road. The street lighting made the passenger's spectacles glint. A little way up the road was another car. A man wearing a motorcycle helmet was leaning down to the nearside window. They'd all be there the next morning, he was sure.

He pulled at the blind cords and began to strip off his clothes. Then he carried them into the kitchen and dumped them into the waste-bin. He'd never use the clothes he'd worn in prison again, nor the bloodied jacket that he'd used to cover the girl in the street.

He was hungry. He searched around for food and found some cheese crackers, a wedge of processed Cheddar and a packet of salami. Clutching the wine and the food, he padded into the bedroom, where he caught sight of himself in the full-length mirror. He stopped for a moment and regarded the white, bandaged figure framed under the light. While gazing at himself he munched a cracker and swilled it down with wine. He looked a full ten years older.

A few minutes later he had swept the mess from his bed and was asleep.

It was late. Foyle toyed with the idea of leaving New Scotland Yard for La Bourriche, a French bistro he'd taken to using once or twice a week because he'd become friendly with the owner, a woman named Carla Pryn. Their relationship had never quite developed into an affair, but Foyle had relied increasingly on her company after June left. He wanted to see her that evening but knew he needed to go over the files and reports that had accumulated on his desk during the day. Everything would have to be read again, absorbed, sifted and considered so that next morning he'd be able to supply new lines of attack and new inspiration, both of which were badly needed. Scarratt was on his back about Con Lindow and had formally requested that he set down his reasons for not using the full interrogation time provided under law. There was no doubt in his mind that Scarratt was preparing the ground to get rid of him, but Foyle was sure he couldn't move against him yet and he estimated that he had between ten days and a fortnight to produce some results.

He unlocked his hands from behind his head, rose and walked to the coffee and snack machines at the far end of the corridor. They'd been his idea, although – as the memo from Scarratt's office had pointed out – they needed to be stocked and serviced every day, which entailed a loss of police man hours. Each time the service man came he was accompanied by an officer to make sure there were no security implications. That was the phrase in Scarratt's memo: 'The coffee machine presents security implications for the department.' Foyle wrote back, facetiously telling him that the machines would be regularly swept for listening devices and checked for explosives. Scarratt solemnly replied that, after reviewing the matter, he would allow Foyle's department to keep its machines. In memory of his victory he patted the coffee vendor as it spewed a watery version of cappuccino.

Way down the corridor Foyle could hear keyboards at work and officers murmuring into phones. He returned to his desk and pulled over the folder sent that morning by Robin Teckman. It contained reports about two explosions, one in Prague and the other in Budapest, both apparently caused by portable devices. The Prague bomb had gone off at eight thirty in the morning of 10 December 1994 as a commuter train travelling from Konopiste in the south drew out of its last stop before the capital. The rear carriages had been blown off the track. Three people were killed, one of whom was a journalist named Jan Nosecky, who'd exposed the illegal export of arms from Russia to the Middle East through the Czech Republic. Nosecky had traced the individuals responsible for the trade through a number of shelf companies in the Czech Republic and their trading partners in the former Soviet Union. At first the local police refused to believe that such a large bomb had been deployed against one man. Besides, that day Nosecky had changed his routine by boarding a train. Nobody could possibly have known that his car would break down ten miles from the city and that he would have to resort to using the train on one of its innumerable stops northwards. At length they got round to examining his car and found that the fan-belt had been sawn part of the way through so that it would snap soon after the engine began to heat up. Somebody had wanted Jan Nosecky to take the train. But still, the police remained unconvinced and tried to persuade Nosecky's colleagues in the press that if someone had wanted to kill the journalist they had had only to fix a device to his car. Clearly they had access to it.

Foyle read on and noted that no timing or command device had been found in the debris of the carriages. It was a mystery as to how the bomb had been detonated. At one stage the Czech police had been tempted to view it as an accident, wondering for a time whether Nosecky had been carrying the explosives himself. Not until the Hungarian police researched the background of the victims in the Budapest bomb did the Czechs grasp that Jan Nosecky must have been the principal target in the train bombing.

On the face of it, the lunch-time bombing of the headquarters of the old state-enterprise organisation appeared to be a motiveless attack. The device had exploded in the foyer of the building, killing five people, on 9 March 1995. Among them was one Bela Namany, the chief executive of an agro-chemical company that traded with the Russians. It turned out that Namany had also been part of a smuggling operation and used his trucks to transport contraband cigarettes into the former Soviet Union and bring artefacts and drugs back to the West. At first it seemed he had been the victim of turf war between rival gangs in Budapest where bombing was considered the best way of eliminating a rival. But then the criminal intelligence branch of the Budapest police contacted the Czechs and they eventually concluded that Nosecky and Namany had separately offended some serious figures in the Russian Mafia, and that the same hitman had been hired to kill them. He'd used the ploy of deliberately killing more than one person to hide the nature of his contract.

The bombs themselves were remarkably similar, both in the amount and type of explosive used, as well as in the way they were disguised. Both were hidden in large sample cases, often used by travelling salesmen. The bomber had come and gone leaving not a trace of himself and no hint of how the bombs had been detonated at the right moment to kill their targets. The authorities in Budapest ruled out a timing device because it would have been impossible for the bomber to calculate the precise instant when the target would pass the case. The hitman must have seen Namany and detonated the bomb by remote control. The problem with this was that nothing like a radio receiver had survived the blast, although they had found some of Namany's personal belongings intact – a briefcase with a lap-top computer and a mobile phone, which, according to the injured receptionist, he'd used to make a call as he left the building. She knew that because she had handed him an urgent message as he passed, and he had acted on it immediately.

In the case of the train, the bomber was thought to have planted the device close to his target then alighted at the previous station. A short time fuse might have been used, but again it seemed more likely that the detonation was caused by a radio transmitter, probably an adapted model-aircraft control of the type utilised by terrorists from Bogotá to Belfast. But again, nothing was found – and none of the survivors could remember anything suspicious either. Even when they were shown a diagram that pinpointed their position in relation to where the bomber must have been, they remembered nothing unusual. That, Foyle noted, was the response they had got from passengers who used the 147 route on Tuesday evening. No one had seen a man getting on to the bus with a canvas bag between Peckham and the West End. Foyle made a note in his book to remind himself to get the copies of the film printed up and sent to the Hungarian and Czech police forces. There might just be a face that someone remembered. In return he would ask for the chemical analyses of the explosive used there – he was particularly interested in the batch of Semtex. It seemed improbable that the same stock was being used in London as in Prague and Budapest, but there might be an inference to be drawn about the bomber's supply line and his connections.

All of this, he admitted, was groping at the margins of the case. He reminded himself that he mustn't close his mind to any possibilities. The Lindows *might* have been involved, after all, and they were still the best thing that he had to go on. He must cast the net wider, but at the same time he should not appear to exclude the Lindows. To this end he'd ordered copies to be made of the papers that arrived by special courier from Thames House. They included the file on Eamonn Lindow, a much larger document than he had expected, which included photographs of Eamonn and Rudi MacMahon. The pictures had been taken on two different occasions and showed Eamonn talking animatedly with MacMahon in the street.

More interesting to Foyle were the reports from the mid-eighties that fleshed out the incident at Droy cemetery. The cache of arms and explosives was of crucial strategic importance to the Provisional IRA, but they'd never been aware that a small transmitter placed in one of the cases had allowed the shipment to be tracked by satellite on its meandering voyage from North Africa. The security forces knew exactly when the material was transferred from one ship to another in the Atlantic, 150 miles north of the Azores; where and when it was landed in the Republic; and how it had been transported over the border. The entire supply line run by the southern command of the IRA had been exposed by the electronic tracker: every stage of the journey had been lit up like a board in a railway signal box. The churchyard was put under surveillance by a team from a shadowy Army group called 14 Intelligence Company; the back-up was provided by a heavily armed special support unit from the RUC, which had set up base five miles away in a sewage-processing plant. The operation – codenamed CUDGEL – lasted four weeks, during which time there was little activity. At one stage the operation commander thought the Provisionals knew that the churchyard was being watched and considered removing the explosives and guns. Then Eamonn Lindow stumbled on the scene. He was sighted three times, although there was a lot that was ambiguous about his behaviour. He never entered the churchyard and only fleetingly looked over to the far side of the church where the cache was hidden in a large Victorian vault that housed the remains of an extinct line of flax merchants. All he did was pull up his car and relieve himself. When he was taken in by the RUC after the explosion he had seemed a rather hopeless character, too attached to his drink to be trusted with one of the IRA's largest ever consignments to have been brought into Ireland. The younger brother was reported as brighter and more resilient under questioning. But the RUC hadn't suspected him of having a role in the affair and had questioned him chiefly to get a better idea of Eamonn's movements and character.

The papers were vague as to why the dump had blown up. Foyle surmised that the IRA would certainly not have sacrificed their precious supplies to kill and injure four soldiers, so there was no question of them having booby-trapped the cemetery. Besides, the Provisionals appeared not to have known that the place was being watched. Something was missing. Foyle circled the passage in the report and made a note to call the RUC to ask how the explosion had come about.

He leafed through the folder again and stopped at the description of Eamonn Lindow's life in Peckham, a fairly humdrum existence led between the library and a first-floor flat in Jasmine Road. Still, MI5 had done consider-able work on him, especially in the last year, when they were in receipt of exceptionally detailed information. There were minute records of his social life, the dates on which he attended the Yeats Society and a regular Irish folk-music evening in Croydon. The summary included the facts that Eamonn Lindow had been to confession at a nearby church three times during Lent and had occasionally attended a meeting of the local constituency Labour Party. Outwardly he did not fit well into the role of IRA master-bomber, or even intelligence officer. Foyle was intrigued by the profile, particularly at the effort mounted by MI5 since the Stormont talks. He began to form a synthesis of two opposing solutions. What if Eamonn Lindow was, in fact, a republican sympathiser with IRA connections, but had not been responsible for this bomb? It seemed crazy, but it satisfied his doubts about the way the Lindows had behaved that night and it embraced MI5's surveillance and background material. What if Eamonn had been, in fact, the primary target?

Foyle had no idea why it seemed right to him. He must get more of a feel for Eamonn Lindow, and talk to his interrogators at the RUC. It was then that he remem-bered there were still some calls waiting to be returned. He pulled over his message book. There were six messages, three from Scarratt's office and three from outside the building. The press office had called with a request from the BBC for an interview; his housekeeper had passed on the depressing news that his washing-machine had broken down; and a Superintendent Black-ett from the RUC had got in touch late that afternoon. The message said that he was on holiday in the north of England and asked Foyle to ring if he needed background on the Lindows. There was a mobile number.

Foyle thought he remembered the name but couldn't put a face to it. He looked at his watch. It was ten five p.m. – not too late to call. If Blackett didn't want to be disturbed, he'd have turned off his phone. He dialled the number and waited for the line to connect. Ten seconds passed. The number responded with a single ring, then it went dead. The connection was broken. Blackett must have switched off the phone when he heard it ring.

Foyle replaced the receiver. A long, dull crump sounded in the distance. He looked up in time to see his reflection vibrate in the windows of his office, then turned to find Forbes at the door. 'Is that what I think it is?'

'Yes, that's a bomb,' said Forbes.

Foyle snatched up the phone again. 'Put me through to the surveillance team outside Lindow's flat.' He waited for a few seconds then asked the voice on the mobile phone in Homer Street, 'Has he moved?'

'No. He's asleep,' came the reply. 'There's not a sound in the flat.'

He replaced the receiver. 'If that was a bomb, Lindow's not the bomber. Find out where it is and get a car for me.'

Chapter Five

Kirsty Laing did not hear the bomb from her flat in Maida Vale, but ten minutes later there was a television news flash, saying that a device had exploded in Floodgate Street, to the north of the City of London. Then the deputy director, Peter Speerman, was on the phone, calling her back for an urgent meeting with the director general and relevant section heads. She was more than a little surprised to be included and spent the twenty-minute drive to Millbank wondering exactly why Speerman had summoned her. True, he had appointed himself her mentor and indeed her new position as head of government liaison had been largely won on the deputy director's recommendation, but it was difficult to see how she would be needed in the immediate aftermath of the bomb.

She steered the Golf hatchback into the deserted car park and hurried across the road to gate six at the rear of the building. As she took the short flight of steps to the night entrance, she noticed David Cantor's car sweep under the huge fortified door that protected the building's basement car park. Cantor sat in the front, wearing a dinner jacket, looking impassively ahead of him. A few minutes later he followed her into the special-conference area, a glass capsule set within a much larger room on the seventh floor. As she entered there were one or two looks of surprise. Angus Grove, in charge of D-Branch (counter-terrorism), cocked an eyebrow at Keith Craven-

Elms, his counterpart at A-Branch (domestic surveillance). Then Rory Fuller, head of Domestic Terrorism, made an overly solicitous fuss about where she would sit, which caused Grove and Craven-Elms to smirk like schoolboys.

During the last eighteen months both had made overtures to her. In each case there was nothing so overt as a pass, but they'd enthused about her talent and indicated their availability over lunch. She had little difficulty in resisting them. Such manoeuvres were more about power and dominance than sexual attraction and, anyway, her interest lay elsewhere.

David Cantor coughed and ran his hands over the frosted-glass surface of the table, then looked expectantly at Speerman who took his cue.

'Scotland Yard have confirmed that a device went off at ten seven p.m. It appears to have been placed in the foyer of a building named Black Lion Court, a medium-sized office block in Floodgate Street. About three-quarters of the block is leased by Interwaste, a company specialising in the disposal of hazardous material. At this stage there appears to be nothing to link it with the bomb on Tuesday, except that approximately the same amount of explosive appears to have been used. We will have reports from the Met's forensic team in the morning. They will be as anxious as we are to establish whether there are further connections to be made.'

'Yes, connections,' mused Cantor. 'What possible connections exist between a 147 bus and this unprepossessing building, I wonder? Has anyone got any ideas? Angus, Keith, what do you make of this?'

Angus Grove, the counter-terrorism specialist, answered first. 'There may be no connection between the two incidents. If it is our chap, he could be working through some sort of contract list, which would explain the disparity in the nature of the targets.'

This did not seem to satisfy Cantor, whose eyes flicked

to Keith Craven-Elms, head of the 'watchers' section, who leaned forward and stared at his notes. 'Well, there's nothing to suggest that Interwaste is the kind of target that would appeal to the IRA or any of their lunatic subsets unless, of course, it's some kind of diversionary tactic. The report says that the bomb was placed inside the building, rather than in the street, which means that the bomber was aiming at Interwaste. That might argue for an ecological implication. If the explosive residues tie this with the first incident I would guess that we would have to look very closely at the motive for the Clarence Street bomb, because, of course, that has no ecological connotations, as far as we understand. I have to say that this doesn't look very Irish to me. Nor do I think it's a loyalist attempt to destroy the peace agreement. They'd make more of a job of it by blowing up a well-known target and admitting responsibility on the Real IRA's behalf.'

'What about these sightings your department has had?' said Cantor, placing his fingertips together and pressing the ends so that they went white. 'Have we made any progress on them?'

'We're still checking through Weegee's data from this evening, but as yet there's nothing. Floodgate Street is just outside the area covered by the cameras.'

Laing remembered learning about the Weegee project when Speerman undertook to give her a personal induction to the highest level of the security service by summarising the various technical innovations being used. Weegee consisted of a vast computer, in the basement of the building, linked to cameras positioned all over the West End and the City of London. Known officially as the Automatic Recognition and Tracking System, it was referred to by its acronym ARTS or the nickname Weegee, an obscure reference to the omnipresent New York crime photographer of the 1940s. Weegee was programmed to pick out a gallery of known faces from the crowds of pedestrians that thronged the centre of the capital. She recalled the vertiginous numbers involved. One camera working at forty frames per second produced nearly 3.5 million images a day. With thirty-five cameras operational, 120 million images had to be scanned and matched against the gallery of suspects in the computer's memory. Speerman had produced the statistics with a kind of pride, and Laing had taken care to remember them because she assumed that she would be called upon to defend Weegee to Whitehall when the inevitable civil-liberties fuss was kicked up in Parliament. For the present Weegee was still a secret.

While Rory Fuller reviewed the terrorist groups operating in Britain, Laing's gaze drifted briefly to her reflection in the glass of the special-conference room. She looked at herself dispassionately. Her hair was still its natural light brown and her skin was unlined – not bad for forty-three and a regular twelve-hour day. But when Fuller said something about 'our fellow', her mind snapped back to the proceedings around the table. It was a similar phrase to Grove's. And now it struck her as odd. Plainly the only suspect was under observation. How could they hope to be using Weegee to track a man whom they knew to be at his home in Notting Hill?

Grove stopped talking as Cantor raised his hand. 'I assume we all know what is being discussed here,' he said, looking directly at Laing. His eyes were grey marble, unreadable and without passion. 'I assume that we know *who* we are talking about.'

The table was silent as the four men nodded in unison. Grove and Craven-Elms looked towards Laing and waited for her reaction. 'I'm sorry,' she said, 'but I'm not sure. Are we discussing Lindow or someone else?'

Cantor's eyes glinted with irritation. Laing knew she'd made a big error. At this level you had to find out things for yourself. Knowledge didn't just fall into your lap: you had to acquire it and make use of it. There were no training manuals. She could imagine what was going through the minds of Grove and Craven-Elms. No field experience, they'd say; not one of us, not one of the boys.

'Well,' said Cantor, 'I had assumed that Peter would have given you an outline of this matter by now. Can I take it that this will occur tomorrow, Peter? In the meantime we must step up our efforts to eliminate him from these two incidents. But I also want to know exactly what he has been doing these past few years, where he's been. No rumours. Hard facts – a complete chronology.'

Laing was reeling with the implications of what was being said. Who was 'our fellow'? And if, indeed, there was some other suspect, why hadn't the police been informed?

'I don't understand,' she blurted out. 'Who else can be involved, if not Con Lindow? Do we have a name?' Out of the corner of her eye she could see that Speerman was shifting uneasily in his chair.

Cantor's eyes returned to her. 'As I said, Peter will explain things to you tomorrow. But clearly the police can be expected to take the point that Con Lindow was not involved in tonight's incident because they have had him under observation since he was released this afternoon. So if the two bombs are linked forensically, this will serve to exonerate Lindow in the police's eyes. Thus they will be looking for other suspects.'

'What the director general is saying', said Rory Fuller, plucking the air with his forefinger and thumb, 'is that for the moment it would be helpful if the police continued to believe in at least a tangential involvement of the Lindow brothers. A legitimate suspicion hangs over them, and it is not difficult to imagine a scenario that ties them into this latest device. For instance, their colleagues in a renegade IRA unit might well have arranged for the explosion this evening in order to remove the blame from Con Lindow.'

'But why—' started Laing, before she was silenced by Cantor's hand.

'I think that is all that can be usefully said this evening,' he said. 'We'll await the outcome of the police investigations tomorrow. Peter, Keith, I wonder if we could have a word now. There's something I need to discuss with you.'

He rose and left the room, quickly followed by Peter Speerman and Keith Craven-Elms. Fuller and Grove swept up their papers and left also, saying goodnight to Laing with elaborate politeness.

She drove back to Maida Vale very slowly, wondering why on earth she had been involved in the meeting by Speerman when he knew she was not in full possession of the facts. As a result, she had made an absolute fool of herself and she didn't like it one bit, particularly as it had been in front of two enemies. But the offence to her self-esteem was quickly forgotten as she considered the alarming implication of the second, undisclosed suspect.

A voice came from Lindow's sitting room. He raised his head from the pillow and strained to hear. It was a man's voice and he was speaking rapidly. Someone was leaving a message on the ansaphone. He leaped from his bed, hopped into the grey light of the sitting room and lunged for the phone. The caller had gone.

Lindow cursed, then played back the message. 'Dr Lindow, this is Mr Lustig from the letting agency. My colleague Mr Robertson, with whom you were dealing last week, has found just the place you're looking for. I wonder if you'd be so kind as to give me a call between nine and ten this morning, or at the same time on Monday? The number is 08052 289476. Thanks.'

Lindow listened, wiping the sleep from his eyes. He looked at his watch. The hands stood at ten minutes to eight – too damned early to call. He shivered and ran back to bed. He would try Lustig in an hour or so. Better not oversleep.

He woke again at nine, called, but got no answer. He showered, dressed and phoned Professor Sharma, who told him to take as much time off as he needed. Then he called a civil-liberties group and asked their advice about a lawyer. The woman gave him the name of Casper Crisp & Co., a firm of young solicitors who specialised in civil-rights issues. They agreed immediately to act for him. They would get in touch with the coroner about the release of Eamonn's body and look into the possibility of a libel suit against the *Evening Herald*. They also said that they would help wind up Eamonn's affairs. The senior partner asked him to get copies of any insurance policies Eamonn held, the mortgage agreement on his home and, if possible, a will. Lindow was doubtful about finding any of these in Eamonn's flat. His brother, though organised in practically every department of his life, had never been strong on money.

Eventually he set off for Eamonn's, but first he went to Oxford Street to buy a new jacket.

Foyle strolled down Victoria Street towards Scotland Yard, carrying a bag containing a new shirt, socks and underwear that he had just bought at the Army and Navy Stores. Considering he had not been to bed for a full day he felt pretty well, unusually light-hearted.

Although no one had been injured by the bomb in Floodgate Street, there had been a hell of a mess when he reached the scene with Forbes twenty minutes after they heard the explosion. The force of the blast had ripped off the front of the building and deposited it in the street, crushing two vehicles. The windows of three residential tower blocks had been blown out and a car had been up-ended and tossed into the front of an electrical suppliers.

Foyle was intrigued by the nature of the target. Overnight, Sergeant Pennel had dug up some information about Interwaste and found that two years earlier the company, a subsidiary of a sprawling American combine called Fallon Group International, had been at the centre of controversy when it had been contracted to transport and dispose of thousands of gallons of chemical waste from Eastern Europe. The chemicals were moved by train through Poland and Germany, loaded on to ships and taken to a point in the Western Atlantic over the Milwaukee Deep and lowered into the trench. The operation had been accompanied by protests along the train's route through Germany and it seemed a distinct possibility that an extremist ecological group had now taken it into its head to blow up the anonymous little building where the disposal had been planned.

What did that say about the bomb on the bus? Almost nothing. In the early hours Foyle had instructed officers to return to the list of passengers and go through their backgrounds again to see if any of them was likely to have incurred the ire of such a group. He also had the bus route checked for other targets that might have attracted extremist eco-warriors. Nothing came of either search.

Foyle turned off Victoria Street, looked at his watch and hastened to the bank of lifts in New Scotland Yard. He had only twenty minutes before he was due at the Cabinet Office to update Sir Derek Crystal's committee. Once in his own office he pressed the speaker button on his phone and dialled the number that Superintendent Blackett had left the day before.

'It has not been possible to connect your call,' intoned the recorded voice. 'Please try again later.'

While taking off his shirt, Foyle called the operations desk.

'A few things, Nancy,' he said, recognising the voice of WPC Longmore. 'I've just tried to call Superintendent Blackett of the RUC on his mobile. He left a message with a number yesterday. See if you can track him down for me and arrange a time for us to talk later this morning. Can you also see that Con Lindow's flat keys are on my desk this afternoon – the ones that were taken from him at the hospital on Wednesday morning?'

He replaced the receiver and retreated behind a filing cabinet to remove his trousers and underwear. Forbes knocked and entered just as Foyle was pulling up the new pair of shorts.

'Sorry, sir, I'll come back in a little while,' he said.

'What the hell's so funny, Forbes? Something wrong with these boxers?'

'Well, to be honest, they look a little large, sir, and it seems odd to change in here.'

'Yes, well, I've got to be over at the Cabinet Office in a few minutes. Any news?'

'There's a match on the explosives, sir. Exactly the same batch.'

'Christ. That's interesting. What do you make of it?'

'For one thing it puts Lindow in the clear. But don't ask me who the hell is doing this. It doesn't add up.'

'No, it doesn't. But I'm not sure about Lindow. There's something nagging me and I cannot for the life of me work out what it is. I'm going to have a word with him this afternoon.'

He emerged from behind the cabinet, placed his laundry in a drawer, put on his jacket and swept up the folder that was waiting on his desk. 'Do not go naked into the conference chamber,' he said, clasping it to his chest.

By the time he arrived at the Cabinet Office, Scarratt was already speaking about the second bomb. Foyle nodded an apology to Sir Derek and settled into the same position he had occupied two days before. Scarratt concluded his outline and gestured to Foyle, saying, 'But I am certain Commander Foyle will be able to give you a clearer picture of what has been discovered overnight.'

'Yes,' said Sir Derek. 'Perhaps. What's the latest

information, Commander? Were these devices planted by the same group?'

Foyle rose. Although it was not the practice in this committee to do so, he felt easier addressing it on his feet. 'Yes, they were. We've just had the tests back. The explosives residues match. We also know how and when the bomb was planted. At five fifteen p.m. yesterday afternoon a man telephoned Reception at Interwaste to say that he would be delivering two fire extinguishers. Fifteen minutes later he arrived with them and left them in the lobby. He called out to the receptionist – who also acts as the company's switchboard operator – that he would return early the next day to fit them. Then he was gone. The receptionist thought nothing of it until this morning when she heard that the building had been blown up. She remembers little about his appearance, apart from his overalls and cap. She detected no Irish accent, either on the phone or when he spoke to her in the lobby.

'In the four hours between the office closing and the explosion at a few minutes past ten p.m., the extinguishers lay undisturbed in their packing cases. The force of the explosion was considerable. Sixteen pounds of Semtex were packed into two nine-litre extinguishers and linked to a central firing mechanism.

'As for the implications this has for investigations into Tuesday's bomb, well, it's rather puzzling. As you know, Dr Lindow was released yesterday following his brother's death. We can account for his whereabouts for all last night and we know he made no significant telephone calls after his release. We are looking into the suggestion that Interwaste was blown up because of its work in dismantling a chemical plant in Eastern Europe. There have been no calls admitting responsibility and, as with the earlier explosion, there was no warning. We are at a loss to explain why these two incidents appear to be on one level consistent with each other but on another totally different.'

Sir Derek looked up at Foyle and removed his glasses. 'That doesn't really advance things much, does it, Commander? We have to know whether these bombs are being planted by an Irish group or whether we face some new threat. I don't have to tell you that things are very delicate politically. It won't take much more for Ulster to blow up again.'

Foyle opened his hands in a gesture of frustration and sat down. He watched as Sir Derek's gaze travelled the length of the table and settled on Scarratt. 'Mr Scarratt, what are we to do in these circumstances?' boomed Sir Derek.

Scarratt opened his mouth to answer but was cut short by David Cantor's hand. 'These are very difficult matters to investigate, Sir Derek. I admit I couldn't see the wisdom of letting our only suspect go yesterday, but leaving that aside, it is my belief that the government should proceed on the basis that these two explosions were caused by an Irish group. Last night's attack may well have been designed to put us off the scent – in other words, to exonerate Con Lindow and his brother. We still believe that we are dealing with some kind of extremist republican element.'

Foyle made to object, but a look from Sir Derek silenced him.

'If this scenario of the rogue active-service unit were to be accepted,' continued Cantor, 'it would mean that the Prime Minister would be able to continue talking to Sinn Fein and the IRA – a head-on confrontation would be avoided. At the same time, we would look at these explosions entirely within the context of Irish terrorism and use all the methods built up over the last few years to track these men down. That is why it would be a distraction to cast around in search of an ecologically inspired terrorist group. There is no evidence whatsoever for that.'

Foyle saw that the room was beginning to relax and that Cantor had won over his audience. Sir Derek sat back in his chair and nodded to Adam Durie, head of the Joint Intelligence Committee, who then turned to the two men from the Northern Ireland Office and silently sought their reaction. Foyle reflected that intervention had been a virtuoso display of Cantor's skill, which satisfied everyone's immediate needs for a solution yet committed Cantor to nothing. There were no facts that he could challenge, nothing for him to disprove, so he remained silent.

'Very well,' said Sir Derek. 'I believe this will help matters over the weekend, but we cannot use it indefinitely. We must see an advance by next week. No doubt Scotland Yard and the security service will redouble their efforts to catch these people. Thank you all very much for coming.'

Sir Derek got up and moved past Foyle without looking at him. The other officials followed, the rear of the procession taken up by Scarratt and Cantor. As they neared him, Cantor squeezed Scarratt's upper arm, then slipped away. Foyle and Scarratt stood looking at each other while two junior civil servants scurried about the room clearing notepads left on the conference table.

'We need results, Commander,' Scarratt hissed. 'I'm meeting with the commissioner this afternoon. He will want to talk to you too, so please make yourself available.' He moved to the door. 'And, Commander, I would like to see your explanation in writing about the release of Lindow before that meeting takes place.'

Jasmine Road, Peckham, had known better times. The houses were large and set back from the street, a cut above the rows of dark artisans' cottages that Lindow had noticed, with a sinking feeling, on the train ride from

Victoria Station. For the most part, though, they were shabby, the small front gardens untended and filled with rubbish. There were a few children playing in the street and a group of men leaning into the bonnet of a car, watching an individual in overalls pumping at a spanner in the engine.

Lindow found number fifty-six a little way up the street behind a large cherry tree, which had turned a mustard yellow. Much of the ground floor was hidden from view by an overgrown vine and a climbing rose, which reached up the façade of peeling plasterwork. He climbed five steps up to the front door and slipped into the lock the first of the three keys he had been given at the hospital. The hallway was surprisingly light and clean. There were plants, and mail had been stacked neatly on a polished side table. The entrance to his flat was on the first floor, a dark green door with two locks. Lindow hesitated before opening it, listening for any other sound in the house. He wondered if he should explain to Eamonn's neighbours who he was. But the house seemed empty. The only noise came from the children outside.

At first sight Eamonn's flat seemed undisturbed, but as Lindow looked closer he saw that it had been subject to exactly the same treatment as his own. This police team, however, had taken more care to restore what they had wrenched and stripped from the floors and walls. Lindow bent down, picked up half a dozen books that had been left in a pile on the floor, all volumes of Irish history, and replaced them on the shelf. As he did so he suddenly remembered his brother's surprising passion for order. When they were boys, Eamonn had spent all his time sorting and labelling boxes of fishing flies, cigarette cards, records – anything that could be subjected to different principles of classification. It had been his obsessive taxonomy that first stirred Lindow's interest in biology. Eamonn had once produced two trout from a wicker creel, one that he'd caught from a lake in the hills and another from a stream, and showed Lindow how they varied minutely in nearly every respect – colouring, shape of mouth, size of dorsal fin and tail. It was the first time he'd heard the word gene.

He walked around the flat, then poked about in the kitchen. It occurred to him that he should throw out the old food. He found a plastic bag and tipped the contents of Eamonn's vegetable tray into it, then emptied the fridge. Having left the bag outside the flat, he went to look in the bedroom. There was an old flat-topped partner's desk standing to the right of the window. Its leather surface had been ripped and he could see that it had been glued recently. He pulled open the right-hand drawer and found a folder of photographs, mostly snaps from family holidays in Donegal back in the early seventies. Eamonn wore long hair and looked sheepishly from under his eyebrows. Their father was brandishing a walking-stick. He looked at himself, aged eight, presenting a bucket of crabs to the camera.

Lindow picked up a small rucksack that was lying by the desk and put the folder of photographs in it. He found a letter he'd sent to Eamonn the year before their mother died. It was a quick, cold, casual letter. He grimaced and dropped it into the wastepaper bin. In the lowest left-hand drawer he found what he was looking for: a plastic file containing the papers relating to the ownership of the flat, the mortgage and Eamonn's life-insurance policy. There was also a clip of bank statements and a building society savings book, which revealed that Eamonn had £1,200 in his account. He put all the documents on top of the desk. Then he tried to push the drawer home. It was stuck. He pushed again, putting all his weight behind it, but the drawer wouldn't move. He crouched down to see if something was catching it underneath. He couldn't see anything. He looked inside the drawer to see if the bottom had come loose at the back. Again, there seemed to be nothing amiss. Finally he fetched a knife from the kitchen and slid it between the bottom of the drawer and the desk. By using it as a lever he was able to release the drawer inch by inch. At length he pulled it free and peered into the aperture. He could see that a panel of wood had sprung out from the side of the desk and trapped the drawer. As he tried to press it back into place, his hand felt something. A package was wedged behind the panel.

He pulled it out into the light to find that he was holding a thick brown envelope about the size of a paperback book. Inside was an American passport and a smaller envelope containing between forty and fifty hundred-dollar bills. He rose slowly to his feet and opened the passport. There was a picture of Eamonn, dressed in a dark suit jacket and a tie, looking much younger and slimmer. Lindow barely recognised him. Further on there were four US immigration stamps recording arrivals at Boston and Shannon where, Lindow remembered, it was possible to clear US immigration before boarding the flight. He flipped through the pages but found no other stamps. At the back a scrap of paper was lodged in the spine. He unfolded it and read, '– RHODES = 8 degrees – LIMERICK; 342 degrees – BELFAST. (Av Declination – 20 degrees) AXIOM DAY'. They were obviously compass bearings, but the relationship between Limerick, Belfast and the island of Rhodes escaped him. And what the hell did Axiom Day mean? This was all most unlike Eamonn, yet the deliberate handwriting was certainly his.

He replaced the piece of paper and returned to the front of the passport. Suddenly he sank back on the desk, winded. There was no mistaking it: the passport was held not in Eamonn's name but in *his*. For reasons that he couldn't possibly fathom, his brother had travelled four times to the States under the name Dr Constantine Cardell Lindow, born in Monaghan, Irish Republic, 1965.

*

118

Foyle crashed the telephone receiver down, breaking the plastic of the cradle. Lack of sleep was beginning to tell. Half an hour before, he had come close to resigning in a meeting with Sir Roy Urquhart, commissioner of the Metropolitan Police. Although Urquhart was clearly not yet prepared to go the whole way and fire him, a transfer from SO 13 seemed inevitable.

'What finally appears to be the problem, Commander,' Urquhart had said, at the end of the meeting, 'is that you have nothing else to go on. In the face of this onslaught from a highly organised terrorist group you have got *nothing* to offer – not even a theory. NOTHING! We will speak again next week. In the meantime, Assistant Commissioner Scarratt will use the weekend to carry out a complete review of the inquiry and your supervision of it, Commander.'

Foyle unplugged the phone set at the wall and stormed to the next-door office where, without a word to the three officers in the room, he dumped it in a bin and snatched up a spare set. On the way back to his office he met Forbes. 'I take it you've acquainted yourself with the latest developments,' he said, motioning his head to the ceiling.

'More or less, sir,' said Forbes regretfully.

'Yes, well, there's not much I can do. I saw it coming this morning. There's something about that man Cantor that makes my flesh crawl. For the life of me I can't see what he's up to, except that he's used Scarratt to get at the commissioner and have me thrown off this inquiry – and probably off the force. But for the moment I'm still here. What have you got for me?'

Forbes reeled off the results of investigations into the second bomb but trailed off when he saw that Foyle wasn't listening. 'I'm sure this can wait. Is there anything you want me to do, sir?'

'I want the keys to Lindow's flat. I asked for them to be put on my desk but they're not here. Oh, yes, there was something else. I was trying to get hold of Blackett at the RUC. Has anyone tracked him down?'

'Yes, they have. It's rather strange. He was always in Belfast, never on holiday – never in the north of England. And he doesn't have a mobile number either.'

Foyle looked down at his message book. 'Am I going mad? It's here, see for yourself.' He spun the book round to Forbes and busied himself plugging in the new phone set. Then he dialled the front desk and summoned WPC Nancy Longmore.

She arrived a few seconds after Foyle had replaced the receiver.

'Nancy, did you write this?'

She looked down at the message marked by Foyle's forefinger. 'Yes, sir. Superintendent Blackett phoned yesterday afternoon. He was anxious to see if there was any help he could give. He said he knew the Lindows and wanted to talk to you personally about their involvement.'

'But how come he's in Belfast, not in the north of England? And he doesn't own a mobile phone and, according to Inspector Forbes, who has spoken to him, he made no attempt to call me in the first place.' Foyle's irritation was aimed at the mystery, not Nancy Longmore, but she flushed none the less. Forbes coughed to tell Foyle that he was getting the thing out of proportion.

'It's not your fault, Nancy,' Foyle said evenly. 'Someone is playing silly buggers here. Get Blackett on the phone for me now and we'll see what the hell's going on.'

She retreated hastily. Within a few minutes Superintendent Blackett had been located in his Belfast office and was put through to Foyle's extension.

'What's this phantom message about? Inspector Forbes here tells me that you didn't ring me and yet I have a very specific message saying that you did. What's going on?'

'You tell me,' said the Ulsterman. 'All I can say is that I didn't call you. To be candid, it hadn't occurred to me to call you. But I've got all these messages here from you, so I'm very happy to help in any way I can.'

'Hold on!' said Foyle, tugging his ear. 'What messages have you got from me?'

'Well, I talked to your Inspector Forbes, and then there's this message to ring a mobile number. I've got it here now. I didn't get around to it because we've a lot on at the moment. I was going to give you a bell this evening when there was time to talk properly.' He repeated the number.

'I don't understand,' said Foyle. 'I never sent such a message and I don't recognise the number. No, hold on, it's the same number as I've got.' He paused and shook his head silently at Forbes. 'Well, since you're on, what do you know about Con and Eamonn Lindow?'

Blackett replied that he knew a lot about Droy cemetery because he had been involved with some of the undercover work and had had a hand in Operation CUDGEL. He remembered less about the brothers, although he recalled that under interrogation Con Lindow had been, as he put it, a canny young fellow. Foyle ended the conversation by saying that he was sorry for the confusion and that he would be in touch if he thought of anything else. He replaced the receiver and let his weight drop into the chair, causing the fake leather cushion to gasp under the impact. 'Well, what do you make of that?'

'About what?'

'About all these messages. It's a bit odd, isn't it? Blackett said he'd got a message to call me on the same number I was given. I mean, I never even thought of calling him.'

'It *is* odd, I agree. But don't take it the wrong way, sir, if I say that I think it's the least of our problems at the moment.'

'You're probably right. Can you see to it that I get those keys? I'm going to pay a visit to Lindow after the briefing. The surveillance team will need to inform me when he reaches home – if he does.'

Chapter Six

Lindow slipped his hand inside the desk again and found that the panel could be pressed back and locked into place by a strip of wood that acted as a runner for the drawer. He moved the drawer in and out and saw that he could release the panel only when the drawer was pulled out to its maximum extent. Otherwise there was no hint of the tiny cavity hidden in the side of the desk. He reasoned that the catch must have come loose while the police were searching the desk and sprung out of its own accord when he opened the drawer. It was an ingenious design and he wondered who had made it. Eamonn certainly hadn't possessed that sort of skill. Then a more worrying thought occurred to him. What if the police had found the package and left it there for him to pick up? It'd be difficult to explain the fake passport in his name, even if it wasn't his photograph inside.

He jumped. A loud buzzing noise was coming from somewhere. Christ, the doorbell. He rammed the drawer shut and stuffed the package, with Eamonn's mortgage papers, into the bag, then went into the sitting room to pick up the entryphone.

'Can I come up?' asked a woman's voice. 'It's Mary Menihan – Eamonn's friend.'

He pressed the button to open the front door, walked out on to the landing and leaned over the stair rail.

'Hello,' said the voice. 'Is that Eamonn's brother?'

'Yes, it is.'

'Oh, good. I thought it was the damned police.'

'No, it's just me here. No police.' He watched the woman's head bob round the corner of the stairs.

She reached him, smiling, with her hand out. 'Hi. I'm Mary. I was a good friend of Eamonn's. Forgive me, I thought you'd come here after they let you go. I know it's kind of crass of me. It's just that I wanted to see you and had no idea how to get in touch. Look, tell me if it's a bad time.' She gazed at him with her head slightly cocked.

'No, no, no. Come in, please. Hi – Con Lindow.' He gave her his hand.

They stood awkwardly in the doorway.

'The last time I came up those stairs, Eamonn met me here at the door with some lines of poetry. Do you know them? "From the going-down of the sun, I have dreamed that women laughing or timid or wild, in rustle of lace or silken stuff, climbed up my creaking stair. They had read all I had rhymed of that monstrous thing – returned and yet unrequited love."'

'Yeats,' said Lindow. 'I haven't heard it for twenty years.'

'Yep – Eamonn and Yeats,' said the woman, sighing. 'A lifelong love affair, wasn't it? He sent it to me on a postcard later. That's how I came to learn it by heart.'

Lindow looked at her. She was very striking: about five feet four inches, with thick dark hair worn short and brushed backwards. Her complexion was dark too, and when she smiled her mouth turned downwards and her eyes glistened with intelligent understanding. She held herself well, and even though she wasn't dressed for show – blue jeans, a grey V-neck sweater with a white shirt underneath and a short black leather jacket – he would certainly have noticed her in the street.

'I was just going through Eamonn's stuff,' he said, moving into the middle of the room and placing a hand on the back of the sofa. 'There's a lot to do. You never think of the bureaucratic side of death, do you? All the damned insurance and things. Look, would you like some coffee? I noticed there's some ground stuff in a jar – no milk, though.'

'I take it black anyway. Yes, I'd love some.'

'So, you're Mary and you're from the States,' Lindow called, from the kitchen.

'Yep. Half Irish, half Jewish and all American.' She wandered into the kitchen. 'It's strange us meeting here without Eamonn, isn't it? I'm truly very sorry for you. It was a terrible, terrible thing that happened to you – the police thinking that Eamonn and you had been planning it all along. It's crazy. I saw in the newspapers you'd been arrested. That must have been some ordeal when you knew Eamonn was so badly hurt.' She touched Lindow's arm. In his three weeks in London he had forgotten about Americans, how warm and natural they could be.

'At first they didn't tell me that Eamonn was injured,' he said. 'I didn't even know he was involved.'

'My God, that's awful.'

'Yes. It was. I still haven't got used to the idea of him being dead. It takes time.'

'But at least with the explosion last night, they can't possibly still suspect you.'

'That's what I'm hoping.'

'Hey! Why don't I make the coffee and you get on with what you were doing?'

'No, it's fine. I've found what I came for.'

'So what happens now?'

'The first thing is to take Eamonn back to Ireland. There'll be the funeral. Then I'm going back to work at Imperial. It'll be a relief to get back to it.'

'When will the funeral be held?'

'As early as possible, once the body has been released for burial. It will be good for my father to get it over with quickly – probably Tuesday or Wednesday.'

'Would you mind if I came?'

'Of course not. I can let you know all the details by

phone. There are plenty of hotels near by so that won't be a problem.' He hesitated. 'Can I ask you something? Were you . . .?'

'No I wasn't Eamonn's girl – "returned, but unrequited", I s'pose. He helped me through a rough time and we became very close. But you know how it is – that part of it didn't work out. I loved being with him, though. He was so interesting and well read,' she said, gesturing to the bookshelves with her mug of coffee.

They talked on for a little while, until Lindow said he should leave for his lawyer in South Kensington. Mary jumped up and suggested they travel together since she lived one stop from Kensington. He looked confused. He decided he wouldn't have time to replace the package in the compartment in the desk, and he certainly didn't want to do it while Mary was in the flat. He would take it to the solicitors instead and they could include the money in Eamonn's estate. He collected the bag from the bedroom then left the flat with her, locking both doors behind him and removing the rubbish to the bin outside.

It was just past three by the time they reached the station. Lindow noticed a tall man in his forties and a younger woman on the platform, watching the electronic display. It was something about the woman's body language that told him they weren't a couple. Between them was the discreet and almost imperceptible distance that a woman maintains before she's been to bed with a man. His gaze stayed with them for a few moments. The man noticed him looking, reached over to the woman and kissed her ear. As he did so she jerked back with a tiny recoil of surprise. They were police officers, Lindow was certain of it.

'He's left the brother's flat with a woman,' said Forbes, through Foyle's open door. 'They split up at Sloane Square and she walked to a house in Pimlico. We've got pictures, but Special Branch is already sure that she is

Mary Menihan, the same Mary referred to on Eamonn Lindow's message tape. They're running a check on the owner and tenants of the Pimlico address.'

Foyle beckoned to Forbes to sit down, then fell into a brooding silence.

'That's interesting,' he said at length, 'because it tells us that neither of them minds if they're seen together. If they were members of an IRA cell they would be sure that we were following them – she'd have fled by now and he'd be keeping his head down.'

'Unless it's some kind of bluff.'

'That's hardly likely when you think of the risks involved. But you're right to keep on about Lindow. I'm becoming intrigued by him.' Foyle waved some papers in the air. 'I had these sent over from Blackett's office. I felt I owed him an explanation for this morning. In the end he was very helpful about the business at Droy cemetery.'

A look of mild exasperation passed over Forbes's usually composed features.

'I know you think I am becoming obsessive about it, but wait until you read this. It was a hell of a story at the time – Operation CUDGEL was a complete disaster. They had followed the supplies all the way from the mid-Atlantic by satellite. Then, somewhere in the Republic, the shipment was divided and part of the consignment was lost. The part that contained the tracking device ended up buried in a vault at the back of a disused country church at Droy in Fermanagh. The Army had rigged the dump so it would blow up the boys from the local IRA brigade when they came to collect it. Instead they blew themselves up, but in the oddest circumstances – nobody knows how it happened. The papers here refer to some sort of internal Army inquiry, but of course this has never been published. We don't even know the names of the men involved. All we do know is that the cache blew up after being visited three times by the Lindow brothers.'

'But we knew all this, sir,' said Forbes quietly. 'I can't see the relevance to what we're doing.'

'Don't you see that even if the sightings of the Lindow brothers had nothing to do with the explosion at Droy, a lot of people must have been left with the impression that they had?'

'So you're saying there is some sort of revenge motive?'

'Could be.'

Forbes looked down. 'It doesn't sound right to me, sir. Nobody kills ten innocent people and injures God knows how many others to get even with one person a decade and a half after the event.'

'Have a read of this, then,' said Foyle, chucking the MI6 file on the Prague and Budapest bombings across the desk. 'You'll see it's not such an outlandish theory.'

'Say your theory is right, sir. How do you then link in the explosion last night? We know that the same explosives were used and therefore must assume it's the same person – or persons – responsible for the manufacture and planting of the bombs.'

'I don't know how they're connected, but I'd like you to read this stuff over the weekend and see if any of your Army pals can help. I want the names of the soldiers involved in the original crew watching that arms cache. If you can't get them, see if Lafferty has any contacts from his time in Ulster. Try Blackett also.' Foyle stopped, ran his hand through his hair then leaned forward on to the desk. 'Have you got anything more on Floodgate Street? Anything turned up on Interwaste? Do we know how these devices are being let off?'

'Not much advance on any of those fronts. Lafferty's people will know more about the construction of the second device by this evening. There's one other thing I forgot to mention. The laboratory recovering the films from the bus has been in touch. It's taking longer than they expected. They hope to send the film by Monday.'

'Good, let's hope there's something on them.'

*

By the time Lindow tramped up Homer Road it was dark and the street lights wore orange haloes of moisture. It had turned cold – not the honest, harsh cold of a New England winter, which he liked in a way, but the cloying dampness of the British Isles. He stopped before mounting the steps to his front door and looked up and down the street. There didn't seem to be anyone watching him, but he was certain that they must be there, sitting in parked cars or in a rented room observing his flat. He didn't much care. He had left the envelope containing the passport and money at Casper Crisp and now felt less nervous. Jane Casper had placed it in the firm's safe, while telling him that Eamonn's body would be released for burial on Monday. She didn't ask about the envelope. Lindow said he would collect it after the weekend. As yet he had no idea what he was going to do with it. One option would be to hand it over to the police, but that would only risk further condemning Eamonn's reputation, and would almost certainly reinforce their suspicions of him.

But he'd kept the piece of paper from the passport because it intrigued him. It also worried him. He felt he'd stumbled on a nasty little secret, a secret that he'd rather not know about. After all, nobody hides that amount of money and a false passport innocently. He also felt hurt – abused. What had Eamonn been doing, assuming his identity like that?

Once in the flat he took the paper from his wallet and scrutinised it. Even without a compass or map to hand, he knew there was no obvious answer to it, for both bearings were northerly and he estimated that the island of Rhodes in the Aegean Sea would be at a south-easterly bearing of about 100 to 115 degrees from the two Irish cities. It was nonsensical. He returned it to his wallet, collapsed on the sofa and idled through a couple of scientific journals. Then he switched on the satellite sports channel and watched ten minutes of an ice-hockey game. But he couldn't keep his mind from turning over the discoveries he'd made. What the hell was Eamonn up to with all this cloak-and-dagger stuff? Why did a librarian need a fake passport and nearly five thousand dollars in cash?

For the second time that day he was disturbed from thinking about the package by a doorbell. It sounded right at the back of his head like a fire alarm and he shot up from his position on the couch. On the way down to the door he told himself that he had to get a grip.

A profile was cast by the street light on to the frosted glass of the door. He opened it to find the policeman who'd taken him to the hospital the day before – the big man with watchful eyes.

'Yes?' said Lindow, certain that he was going to be rearrested.

'Good evening, Dr Lindow,' said Foyle.

Lindow looked out into the street, left and right, then back to the policeman.

'It's just me. I'm here unofficially. Well, not quite. I came to return your keys.'

'Yesterday I'm sure you told me you were a commander,' said Lindow aggressively. 'Haven't you got constables to do that sort of thing for you?'

'Yes, I have. It's really an excuse. I wanted a few words with you. To be honest, I hoped you'd be able to help out.'

'Is this a formal interview, Commander Foyle? Should I consider myself to be helping police with their inquiries again, or are you trying to make up for the mess your officers made of this place?'

'Neither.'

'Then presumably I don't have to talk to you.'

'No, you don't,' said Foyle, his frustration beginning to show. 'But I'd be grateful if you'd spare a few moments, since I was the person who decided that you should be released. I may well pay for that decision with my job.'

'Are you serious? They still think I had something to do with the bombs? They must be crazy. I couldn't possibly have had anything to do with either of them.'

'All I'll say is this, Dr Lindow. It's in your interest as well as mine that we talk. I think you're involved in some way, although I don't believe you know how or why, but it has something to do with your brother. Maybe something to do with the past.'

Lindow studied Foyle. He was shrewder than he looked, and he thought he'd better find out exactly what he wanted. 'Look, my apartment's still a mess and I don't have much food or drink here. Do you mind if we do this in public? There's a wine bar round the corner that serves food.'

'Good idea.'

Lindow fetched his wallet and a jacket, then they left together in silence.

They were given a table in the corner of the bar, away from the heaving Friday-night crowd, and ordered straight away.

'What is it that you do, Dr Lindow?' asked Foyle, when the waitress had departed. 'No one in my department has quite pinned it down.'

'I came here to lead a project on bacteria. It is related to my work in the States, which was to do with the way that human cells communicate with each other by minute secretions of messenger chemicals. It's pretty dull stuff to the uninitiated.'

'Go on,' said Foyle, waving a knife covered in butter, his mouth already full of bread. 'I'm genuinely interested.'

Lindow was sceptical but continued. 'The difference between a bacterium cell and a human cell is that the bacterium cell doesn't have a nucleus. It's like a little bubble of genetic material. In a human cell the strands of DNA are mostly contained within a membrane at the centre of the cell. But the way both bacteria and human cells talk to each other is essentially the same. Bacteria send out messages that instruct other single-cell organisms to go and do things.'

'What things?'

'Well, to reproduce, to die, to defend themselves against viruses. In some cases they cluster together into little tree-like structures. In others they light up. I'll give you an example. There's a species of squid which hunts by night, but it can only do this because it's specially equipped with an organ that collects a particular type of bacteria in the sea. When the bacteria crowd into the organ they release a chemical which travels between them and causes the production of a protein in each cell that gives off a burst of light. So with the help of the bacteria the squid can see its prey. In return, the bacteria receive a safe, nourishing haven and are able to reproduce. Without each other, the squid and the bacteria would not do so well.'

'It makes you wonder how they got together in the first place. Which came first – the nocturnally feeding squid or the bacteria?'

'Both,' said Lindow. 'They adapted to each other gradually, natural selection causing the squid with better bacteria collectors to do better and pass on their particular characteristics to future generations.'

'But you're not researching squid, are you?' asked Foyle.

'No, I'm interested in tracking down other substances that bacteria use to talk to each other. They may be very useful to us, particularly in the control of disease.'

'And that's how you've made your money.'

'You *are* well informed! It's not as much as you'd think. I share in a few patents. That's all. I do okay,' said Lindow. 'What about you? Are you married – children?'

'Wife and daughter, both away on academic studies. My wife has taken up archaeology and is in the Middle

East. My girl, Katherine, is at university, at the moment doing drama but she hopes to change to law.'

'So you live alone. That must be hard with your job.'

'No, it just means I work all the time.'

The wine and the first course arrived. Lindow poured the wine. 'After this week, I never thought I'd have dinner with a cop. I'm still not sure that I should be. The system here, which allows you to hold people without trial or without being charged, is completely wrong. Just because we're sitting here exchanging pleasantries doesn't mean that I've forgotten about it.'

Foyle shrugged. 'It'd be impossible to do my job without it. Remember, we're dealing with well-organised people, seriously bad people who don't mind killing mothers and children in the street.'

'Yes, I've heard the argument, but it doesn't make it any better when you've been in my position.' He paused and drank some wine. 'What do you want to talk about?'

'I want to know about Eamonn. Above all, I want to know if someone would go to those lengths to kill him. You see, there's evidence that he was involved with the IRA up until his death.'

'What evidence?'

'The first thing is this relationship with Rudi Mac-Mahon. What was he doing mixing with someone like that? I've seen the surveillance photographs. There's no doubt about it. They were filmed in Ireland twice together, which probably means they met much more frequently.'

'Look, my brother wasn't a Provo. You didn't know him – he was incapable of hurting anybody.'

'But why did he see MacMahon? Did you know MacMahon was suspected of carrying out three or four assassinations in cold blood before he became a Sinn Fein politician? He was charged twice with murder but both times the witnesses simply faded away. He may be part of the peace process but this man is a very bad guy indeed. He has blood on his hands and none of the fine words of

Stormont will wash it off. Why would your brother spend time with him if he wasn't somehow involved?'

'I can't tell you.'

'What about this business at Droy? Was he working for the IRA then?'

'No.'

'You seem very certain of that, but I believe you knew that the IRA got their hooks into Eamonn pretty early on and that Droy was the first job he did for them. You know, watching that cache of weapons and explosives.'

Lindow said nothing.

'That's what the security services think. They've been watching him in London. I've seen the file. They were convinced he was an important link man and they think he was part of a group continuing the armed struggle.'

'Your logic's all up the spout, Commander. On the one hand you say my brother was suspected of being a member of the IRA but on the other you suggest that he was a target of what looks very much like an IRA attack. That is almost the definition of a contradictory position. It seems to me that the police just change the story to fit each piece of evidence as it comes along.'

'Look,' said Foyle, 'I don't pretend to understand this thing, but it's in your best interests that I begin to. If I lose control over the inquiry, the first action my replacement will take is to rearrest you. They could come for you next week.'

'I'll be in Ireland for Eamonn's funeral.'

'Yes, but you won't stay. There's no future for you there.'

Lindow watched as Foyle ate his steak greedily, swilling it down with gulps of red wine. The policeman was boorish, but he was obviously good at his job and he possessed an agile mind. He had locked on to the one area that Lindow found it difficult to talk about. He couldn't be certain any longer about Eamonn, and he was

134

aware that every time Foyle mentioned his brother it showed in his face.

'Tell me about Mary Menihan – sounds like a good Irish name,' said Foyle.

He knew he was being tested. 'I met her today, as you are no doubt aware. She was a friend of Eamonn's. She's American, from the East Coast, just south of Boston. She works here in publishing as a part-time editor. I'd guess she has money of her own because she only does a couple of days for the company and then some manuscript reading for another publishing house. She said Eamonn and she became friends after he'd helped her through a bad patch. That's all I know about her.'

'So you don't think she's got anything to do with all this?'

'No, I don't. She's a clever, good-looking, middle-class girl – frankly she was a cut above most of Eamonn's girlfriends. She's classy. Not the type to run around with Semtex in her purse.'

'What type is that?'

'Isn't that rather a dumb question? You know I know nothing about these things. It's just that this woman has other things going for her. Anyway, there's less Irish in her than you'd think by her name. Her mother is Jewish.'

'The IRA get their people from anywhere. Just because we've had this period of peace, it doesn't mean that the basic organisation isn't there and the more extreme people, the Real IRA, aren't still recruiting and setting up cells in Britain. By the way, these aren't your type of cells because they don't communicate with each other. In fact, they're the opposite. They have no knowledge of each other whatsoever. They just communicate with the lead man in the hierarchy in Ireland.'

'Oh, come on, Commander. You're not seriously suggesting that Eamonn was the link between a cell involving me and Mary and that we're under the direct control of Rudi MacMahon? That's fantasy-land. For a start, MacMahon is part of the political process now. He's respectable. Wears a tie and kisses babies.'

'Maybe, but that theory looks good to my superiors. MacMahon may have been an old contact who was lost when the IRA started to talk.'

'Yes, but you don't believe their theory. Otherwise you wouldn't be sitting here with me. You know there's something else going on and you don't understand it.'

'Yes, and I have admitted that to you.'

'But what makes you think it?' Lindow was pleased to be driving the conversation at last. 'What else could be going on?'

'I shouldn't be talking to you about it, but I suppose, in these circumstances, I don't see why I shouldn't. There's not much to lose.' Foyle folded his napkin and began to probe his teeth with a toothpick that he'd taken from a pot in the centre of the table. Lindow waited for him to finish without saying anything.

Presently Foyle disposed of the toothpick and poured himself another glass of wine. 'To answer your question, I don't understand what's going on at all. There is a good reason for questioning you, but equally now there seem to be very good reasons for removing you and your brother from direct suspicion. And yet all the pressure from above has been to focus on you two. Possibly there's a political motive, I don't know. So much of it doesn't add up – the two targets this week are inconsistent in nearly every respect. The other thing is that the bombs are different from what we've seen before.'

'How?'

'They've got the same arrangements, explosive and detonator, but we don't know how they're being triggered. If we knew how they were being set off and we could prove that the bomb on the bus was triggered from a distance we'd be halfway to putting you and your brother in the clear. Look, this is sensitive stuff, I really shouldn't be talking about it. So I'd rather you keep it to yourself.'

'Why's it so difficult to work out how the bombs are being detonated? Your forensics people must have found clues at the scenes. Something must have shown up.'

'Nothing of that nature. Still, I don't expect you to help me with that. What I am asking you to do is to keep me informed of anything you discover about Eamonn which is relevant to this investigation. It may be painful, but in the long run it will be better. If you're going to Ireland, keep your eyes open. There may be some kind of republican presence at the funeral, which might tell us something, and I guess they may approach you.'

'I doubt it,' said Lindow. 'What would they want to say to me?'

'Who knows? But the main thing is that I've got your agreement to help me, if you can. That's right, isn't it?'

Lindow nodded. Foyle took out a card, wrote his home number on the back and gave it to him. 'If anything occurs to you over the weekend, call me. I don't have a cellphone but you can get hold of me at any time through my office.'

Foyle paid the bill and they made their way to his car. Foyle turned to Lindow. 'It's been good to talk to you, Dr Lindow.' He looked away up the street. 'You realise that you and I are like the squid and the bacteria at the bottom of the sea – we need each other.'

'Which of us is the bacteria?'

'I'm afraid it's got to be you,' said Foyle. 'I'm the one who needs to find his way in the dark.'

It was nearing midnight. Lindow did not go to bed immediately but returned to the sofa and flicked through the satellite channels – sport, soft porn and movies with bad plots. He ended up watching a programme about the history of telecommunications made for the Discovery Channel, but it held his interest for only a few minutes.

He thought about Foyle's visit and wondered whether he should have told him about the things he'd found in Eamonn's flat. No, he had been right not to tell him. Despite Foyle's likeable nature and apparent openness, there wasn't anything to be gained from it, particularly if he was about to be kicked off the investigation. Better to keep it to himself. It did occur to him that Foyle might have known the package was there all along and was testing him, but somehow that didn't work. The contents would be too important to the investigation to be left there as bait on the off-chance that he would roll up and find them.

Eventually he turned in and fell into a deep, troubled sleep. He woke at five, then again at six, this time with a jolt that propelled him from the pillow. He'd been dreaming. He was in some kind of laboratory, but the equipment was unfamiliar. There were batteries and clocks and tangles of wire and telephones, lots of them from every age, like he'd seen in the TV programme. Now that he was awake he was quite certain he'd found the solution to one part of Foyle's problem. He knew how the two bombs had been detonated.

He got up and made himself coffee, fixing it in his mind. He left his flat and walked to the phone booth around the corner where he dialled the number written on the back of Foyle's card.

Foyle's voice came on the line, drugged with sleep. When he heard Lindow's name he said groggily, 'I'm sorry after all that I forgot to give you your keys last night.'

'I didn't ring about that. I've got a spare set now,' said Lindow, with impatience. 'Something occurred to me in the middle of the night. I think your bomber is using cellphones to trigger the explosions.'

At the end of the line Foyle was silent. Then he whispered, 'By God, I think you're right.'

His mind focused and he began to recall the report

from MI6 about the Budapest bombing. Hadn't the victim received a phone message from the receptionist as he was leaving? Yes, and he'd pulled out his mobile phone and dialled a number. The call could easily have triggered the bomb that was lying, like the Floodgate Street device, in the foyer of the building. The explosion on the train near Prague could also have been set off by a phone call made by the bomber once he'd got off at the station. Lindow's theory certainly worked.

'Are you there?'

'Hold on. I'm thinking,' said Foyle.

Then he had a more chilling thought. No, it couldn't be! Foyle fumbled in his mind to get it absolutely straight. What had he been doing when that second bomb went off? Yes, he'd been trying to get hold of Blackett in the north of England – but Blackett hadn't been in the north of England. He had been in Belfast all the time. When he'd made the call on Thursday, the line went dead after the first ring. Then he had heard the bomb.

'Were any phone parts found in the bus?' asked Lindow, interrupting Foyle's train of thought. Foyle made an instant decision not to tell Lindow about the Blackett business.

'Yes.' He paused. 'I'm sure there were, but Forensic must've assumed they came from one of the passengers. Anyway, not much would be left if a mobile was attached to that amount of explosive. What in heaven's name made you think of this, anyway?'

'You remember I was explaining my work about the messages transmitted between cells by chemicals. Then you made a remark about the way IRA cells didn't communicate with each other. That, and a TV programme I watched about telephone technology, must have set my mind thinking about the relationships between different types of cells and the way they communicate with each other – or don't, as the case may be. One system of cells that do communicate with each other is the honeycomb network of the cellular phone system. When a phone call is made to a cellphone it is transmitted to anywhere in the cell from the antennae, which is the equivalent of the nucleus in a human cell. That's more or less an exact parallel to the way human cells work. Messages move from the centre to the outside. But when a call is made from the phone somewhere in the cell, the signal goes to the antennae at the centre, which is the opposite process.'

'Yes, yes,' said Foyle, anxious to stem Lindow's flow. 'Your theory only works if a phone can be connected up to a bomb. Are the electronics feasible?'

'I don't see why not. The phone would simply act as a switch – like a radio transmitter, an altimeter or a mercury tilt device.'

'You know an awful lot about this, Dr Lindow.'

'Oh, come on! This stuff is all common knowledge. It's posted in a hundred places on the Internet. Look, I'd hardly be telling you if I had anything to do with this, would I? Anyway, it's only a possibility.'

'Yes, but if it's true, the potential is terrifying. You could plant twenty bombs then set them off at will from anywhere in the world.'

'The battery life must be a factor.'

'Course,' said Foyle, 'if you're right it means a lot for you, doesn't it? For one thing it puts you both in the clear. Yet it also means that you've got to acknowledge that Eamonn was the target that night. The other casualties were incidental to that one aim. It means someone followed your brother on to that bus and placed that bomb right behind him. Who wanted to kill him so much that they were prepared to slaughter ten other people in the process?'

'I don't have any idea. Believe me, I'd tell you if I knew.'

'Right, I'll talk to you later today. Stay in touch and

don't leave for Ireland without telling me. In the meanwhile, thanks. I believe you've helped us a great deal.'

Lindow hung up. He felt sick and deflated. Sooner or later he would have to tell Foyle about the envelope and what really happened in the churchyard.

Chapter Seven

A couple of hours after receiving Lindow's call, Foyle left his house with clothes for three days and drove to New Scotland Yard. By midday he'd assembled a small group of officers who were prepared to work through the weekend on the implications of Lindow's idea about telephone detonation. There were nine in the room when he outlined the theory, which he did without crediting the author because he wanted it to be given an unbiased hearing. Foyle's mood was upbeat, although he knew well that by the end of Monday he would probably have been relieved of his command. This was his last throw and he sensed that the nine officers perched around his room were pretty much trying to make it work for him.

They had little problem accepting Lindow's idea in principle. Lafferty nodded and said it had been only a matter of time before somebody thought of using the cellphone networks. Inspector Lockyer chimed in by reporting that tiny fragments of circuitry, consistent with the insides of a cellphone, had been found at the scenes of both explosions. There was no reason why these could not have been part of the devices.

Then Foyle told them about the call he had made on Thursday evening in response to a message left by Superintendent Blackett in Belfast and how it turned out that Blackett had also received a message to ring him. What was downright puzzling was that neither had phoned and yet both had been asked to call each other on the same number. It was possible that the bomber had set them up to ring each other, knowing that the first to make the call would detonate the bomb. It was just a second or two after he had dialled the number written in his message book that he had heard the explosion in Floodgate Street.

'Forbes will tell you. He was with me.' He glanced at Forbes, who was looking less than convinced. There was a silence. 'Yes, I know you all think I've lost it, but hear me out just this once because, if my suspicions are correct, it means that we're dealing with a very different type of terrorist altogether – someone who is playing with us, someone so confident that he's prepared to give us a massive clue like this and still know he's going to get away with it. If, for a moment, you accept the theory, several compelling questions present themselves. Why was Blackett linked with me in the bomber's little joke to get one of us to finish the work at Floodgate Street? Were we inadvertently responsible for detonating the Clarence Street bomb also? What point was the bomber making? Why was he making it?'

Foyle paused to look down at the notes in his book. Then he raised his head and revolved his index finger in the air as though he was conducting a very slow piece of music. 'You see, Blackett hasn't been chosen at random. There is a connection. In the early eighties Superintendent Blackett was one of the investigating officers after the explosion at Droy. He was the man who interviewed Eamonn and Con Lindow. If you draw this thing out, there are links between the two bombs, which go way beyond the similarity in design of the bomb and the batch of explosives. I'll show you what I mean.'

He turned to a board behind him and made two crosses, which he labelled 'Clarence Street' and 'Floodgate Street'. Then he drew a line downwards from 'Clarence Street' to a circle where he wrote 'Lindow'. He followed this with another line from 'Floodgate Street' to a circle in which he wrote 'Blackett/Foyle'.

'It's like this,' he said, sketching wildly between the two crosses and the two circles. 'We have a square in which everything is connected. We don't know the exact nature of all the relationships between these points, but there are hints. I believe there's a logical answer to this diagram and it's our job to solve the riddle before another bomb is exploded.'

'But this is all based on supposition, unproved theory,' said Lockyer, voicing the scepticism of the room. The forensics specialist had made it clear with a series of sideways glances to Lafferty that he doubted Foyle's sanity. 'I accept there's some good reasoning behind it, Commander, but you've no evidence for any of this whatsoever. Nothing.'

'Yes, you're right. I admit it. However, this theory at least explains the inconsistencies *and* the consistencies between the two bombs. Of course, if you've got a better idea about it all, I'm happy to give it a go.'

'There could be something in what you say,' said Lafferty. 'It's just that I feel uncomfortable when we're dealing with theories, not evidence.'

'Then we shall have to find that evidence,' said Foyle, 'and that is what I plan to do now.'

He divided the four junior officers into pairs: Kepple and Hardwood to go back over the Droy cemetery explosion and extract more records from the RUC, and Sergeant Pennel and WPC Tina Wei to research the cellular networks and the feasibility of cellphone detonation. Lockyer and Lafferty disappeared with their sergeants to review the forensic evidence gleaned from the two bomb scenes, while Forbes made himself useful, trying to find out the names of the Army officers involved in Operation CUDGEL.

The team did not meet again until early Monday morning, by which time Foyle's theory had established itself in each officer's mind as at least being feasible, although there was still no conclusive proof from either of the two bomb scenes. On another front, however, there was better news. The laboratory handling the film from the two remaining cameras on the bus had finally unpicked a two-hour tape from the forward-facing camera, situated halfway along the lower deck. The technicians had hoped to be able to take something from the camera above the driver's head, but everything had been lost when the electrical wiring in the cab caught fire.

On the inside of the salvaged spool they'd found a section of tape where the magnetic signal had not been melted. These fifteen and a half minutes from the beginning of the journey were in working order, except for a regular interruption lasting a second or two. The laboratory had transferred the film frame by frame to another tape and sent it round first thing on Monday. Forbes brought the envelope, still sealed, and gave it to Foyle as if it was a Christmas present.

They watched the film immediately. Eleven minutes passed during which the bus stopped five times. Then suddenly Eamonn Lindow appeared, clear as day, hurrying on to the bus with a book under his arm. He showed the driver a travel pass and moved through the camera's field, smiling, perhaps with the afterglow of the exchange with the driver or perhaps because he'd seen someone he recognised. There was a pause while an elderly woman paid her fare, and then two men got on. The first was using a walking-stick and took some time to haul himself up through the doors. He paid the driver and turned away from the camera to receive something from the man behind. It was obviously something heavy. At that point a party of four women crowded on board and the individual disappeared behind them. Because of the damage to the tape, the picture faded for a few seconds then returned in time to catch the man with the stick moving to the back of the bus.

'That's him,' murmured Foyle. 'That's got to be the bomber.'

145

He pressed the replay button then froze the image of the top of the man's head, but he had missed the moment he wanted. He moved it on a few frames, then back again and stopped the film on the man's face. Much of it was hidden, but beneath the cap you could make out the left eye, an ear and a very well-defined young jaw.

'Well, I think that's something, don't you?' Foyle was relieved at last to be dealing with some concrete evidence. 'The first thing that this film proves is that Eamonn Lindow carried nothing more than a book on to that bus. He could've been given the package later, but it seems unlikely since he was the one who was blown up. And look at his manner – all smiles, no concern in the world.'

'We should certainly trace that man with the stick,' said Forbes. 'I'm pretty certain that he's not among the people who've come forward and I know he wasn't among the victims. I wonder if any of those women remember him.'

'Right.' Foyle sprang from his chair. 'I think we're due at the briefing. Have the tape copied and stills made of the relevant frames, but first let's show it to the others.'

The film was played several times and the mood of SO 13 picked up. But when Foyle introduced the business of his phone call on the night of the Floodgate Street bomb, despairing glances were exchanged. The news that an inner group had been working over the weekend on this crackpot theory didn't help either. Foyle sensed the mood, and briskly asked Pennel to tell the briefing what he'd discovered about phone technology.

'In theory this might be an extremely useful method to a sophisticated terrorist. The maximum battery life of a standard phone can be as much as ninety to a hundred hours – nearly four days. Some advanced phones have as much as one week's standby time. The terrorist could plant his bomb, fly back to Libya or Belfast or wherever and then, at his leisure, phone the number. That's the first advantage. The second is that you can't jam the signal as was done in Ulster when the IRA used model-aircraft radio controls to detonate their culvert bombs. The security forces got on to the frequency and blocked it, at which point the Provisionals returned to using the old-fashioned command wire. But a phone cannot be jammed, unless you have the subscriber's number or you lay a curtain over a whole area. That's only been done a few times. We discovered that the Italians blacked out their parliament building to stop MPs using their phones during debates. That was a permanent arrangement. At short notice it would be difficult to screen off parts of London. You have six networks operating in Britain – four digital and two analog – and then there are several separate cells in central London with hundreds of local area networks, which are like micro-cells. You might be able to shut down one but you'd have to be sure that you'd got the right one. There are areas of overlap, which means a signal might still get through.

'The third advantage is that unless a phone is linked up to the GPS system – Global Positioning by Satellite – you cannot track a subscriber's phone even if it is switched on. Only when the subscriber makes a call can the set be traced because it sends out an individual code. However, in receive mode its signal to the cell antennae will not include an individual code. There's no way of telling which phones are switched on or where they are.' He looked across to Tina Wei, the Chinese detective with whom he'd been teamed up over the weekend. 'Is there anything I've forgotten?' he asked.

'No,' she said, 'except that there is another advantage and that is the sheer number of cellphones in circulation. There are about twelve million subscribers in Britain and the number increases annually by nearly half a million. Most of the phone companies insist on the production of proof of identity and address. But at least one doesn't, which means that any individual can buy a phone and a service on a credit or charge card that's held in a false name. There's also services in which you buy your talk-time in advance, so no references or credit cards are required. Once they're out there, there's no way of tracing these phones.'

'What about cloned phones?' asked Foyle. 'Is there any possibility that he is using them?'

'A cloned phone has no relevance in these circumstances,' replied Pennel. 'First of all you can only clone a phone by picking up a signal from an analog set and copying it. Of course, there'd be no point because the terrorist needs his bomb to have a unique number. If he has cloned a phone there will always be a risk that someone makes a call to the number while he is handling the bomb. Cloning is only useful to someone who wants to steal airtime – to make calls on the subscriber's bill. The purpose of a device attached to a bomb would be to receive calls only.'

After the briefing Foyle and Forbes adjourned as usual to Foyle's office. Foyle walked over to the window and looked down on Victoria Street. A few people were struggling along in the wind, which was wrenching their umbrellas from their hands.

'Jesus, what the hell do they want?' he said, crashing both hands down on the radiator casing. 'I gave them hard facts, direction and not a bad theory – all of which are advances on Friday evening – and yet the whole lot of them sat there nonplussed. What's going on, Forbes?'

'Well, you know how it is. If things aren't going well for us they get frustrated and they're beginning to wonder where the break's going to come from.'

'And what else are they saying?'

'They're wondering if you're going to be here next week.' Forbes looked down.

'Well, you can bloody well tell them I'm not going yet,' Foyle said, without conviction. 'This is my investigation and I'm going to complete it.'

*

After his call Lindow did not hear from Foyle and spent the weekend trying edgily to get back into his routine. But he couldn't settle to work. He went to a couple of movies and took solitary meals in his local Greek restaurant. Monday came as a relief. He started the day by calling Lustig, the letting agent. It was odd. The phone didn't respond at all. No message service – nothing.

He tried again, checking the number from his ansaphone, then rang Mary Menihan to tell her that the funeral had been fixed for Wednesday at eleven thirty a.m., which would mean that she would have to fly to Ireland on Tuesday. 'There's something else,' he said. 'I haven't asked my father yet, but I know he'll agree. Will you read something at the service? A piece of Yeats, maybe, or something else that you know Eamonn would've liked.'

She thought for a moment. 'Yes, I'd be pleased to do that. I'll think of it as an honour – so long as your father likes the idea too.'

'He will,' said Lindow definitely. 'So, I'll see you tomorrow. Come over for a drink and meet what's left of the Lindows. It'll be just me, Tag and Dad.' He gave her the address and telephone number, and replaced the receiver, registering the pleasure he'd felt in talking to her.

It was nine thirty a.m. – two hours before the inquest opened on the victims of the Clarence Street explosion. He thought about Harry Ribb, who'd died of a heart attack after being sent home from the hospital on Saturday afternoon. His son had been quoted saying that it was the shock of the explosion, and the Sunday papers had no hesitation in including him in the toll.

Lindow decided not to go to the inquest and made a call from another phone box near his flat to ask the solicitors to represent him. Then he walked up to WH Smith on Notting Hill, where he selected some magazines and a child's geometry set, which he placed between the magazines as he approached the sales counter. He didn't know if he was being watched, but he certainly didn't want anyone to see him buy the instruments, nor did he want them to know what he planned to use them for. As the woman gave him his change, he asked her where the nearest library was. She told him there was one just off Kensington High Street.

He left and walked quickly along the pavement, trying to give no hint that he was looking for a taxi with its light on. It was still raining and there were few about. When one eventually came along he shot his arm into the street and climbed in. He pulled back the partition window, handed the driver a ten-pound note and asked him to drive to a large store in Oxford Street. He had a vague idea that it would be a good place to elude any pursuers he might have. The cab set off eastwards, passing the drenched landscape of Kensington Gardens. Lindow turned round a few times but stopped when he noticed the driver examining him in his mirror.

'Are you being followed?' the driver said, as they idled at some lights at Lancaster Gate.

'What makes you think that?'

'You keep looking out of the back. If you are being followed, there's an idea I've always wanted to try out. Do you want to give it a go?'

'Sure, why not?'

A little way down Oxford Street the driver took a left turn without indicating, then made another left so that they ended up in a car park attached to the back of a department store.

'I'll drive you in,' said the driver as he took a ticket at the barrier. 'Then you get yourself into the shop pronto and vanish. I'll wait in the car park a bit before leaving. That should do the trick for you.'

Lindow thanked him and gave him another ten-pound note. He entered the store through a door marked Furnishings and Kitchenware and moved through the more or less deserted floor to the escalators. He took a quick turn through Women's Fashion on the first floor then went down to the ground floor and left the store by one of the main exits. Out in Oxford Street, he hailed another cab and told the driver to take him to Kensington Library.

Once inside, he walked straight to the reference section, where he withdrew the largest atlas and opened it at the full map of Ireland. Realising he couldn't draw on it he made a colour copy on the library's machine and carried it back with the atlas to an unoccupied desk at the far end of the reading room. He then removed the protractor from its case and aligned it over the centre of the city of Belfast. To get a bearing of 342 degrees by using a schoolboy's protractor – not a compass – would be a simple matter of subtracting 18 degrees from the 90-degree vertical on the protractor. He made a mark at the edge of the protractor at 72 degrees, the equivalent on the compass of 342 degrees. He repeated the procedure for Limerick, but this time made the mark on the paper at 8 degrees, a little to the right of the vertical line on the protractor. Then he took out the ruler and traced the two bearings on to the photocopy. The lines intersected about 140 miles north of the coast of Ireland.

Lindow sat back and thought. Some way from him a woman with a shoulder-bag was browsing through the science and technology reference section. Then she went over to look at the set of the *Dictionary of National Biography*. He waited, making no secret of following her progress around the shelves. She knew he was watching her. Suddenly she looked at her watch and walked with haste to the entrance.

He returned to the copy of the map. Perhaps the bearings indicated the presence of a boat. It seemed unlikely. He was sure he was making a mistake with the figures, but he couldn't think how. Then he remembered that Eamonn's scrap of paper included another piece of information. He took it from his wallet and read the words 'Av Declination – 20 degrees'. This must have referred to the magnetic variation, the difference between magnetic and true north, which anyone using a map and compass in the field must allow for. There was no note in the atlas about the magnetic variation for Ireland, nor in any of the other atlases, so he asked at the desk where he could find out about declination for different parts of the world. The attractive woman librarian suggested he ring the Royal Geographical Society's map room and, with a smile, offered him the use of the library's telephone.

'Be my guest.' He noticed a glint in her eyes. 'It's library business, after all.'

The woman in the map room was equally helpful. She looked up an airline chart and came back on the line.

'No, no,' she said. 'Twenty degrees would be far too much. The declination for Belfast is eight and a half degrees west and for Limerick it's seven and a half. So to be accurate in Ireland you would need to set your compass at an average declination of eight degrees west of true north.'

'Is there anywhere in the world where the westerly declination is as much as twenty degrees?' asked Lindow.

'Oh, yes,' she said. 'From memory, I'd say parts of Canada and America have a twenty-degree declination.'

Lindow snapped his fingers, thanked her profusely and hurried back to the reference section, where he took down an atlas of North America. He ran his finger down the index. He knew there was another Belfast, some way up the coast from Boston, in the state of Maine. Was there another Limerick? His instinct was absolutely right. There was, and it was also in Maine. He turned to the map and found the tiny town of Limerick about twenty-five miles due west of Portland. He knew straight away that the two compass bearings would intersect somewhere in the north of the state. But he decided to be certain and wandered over to the library's large travel section where he scanned the shelves for anything on the east coast of America. He pulled down a large paperback called *Fifty Hikes in the Maine Mountains*, which confirmed in the introduction that 'Maine's declination varies from seventeen to twenty degrees, usually around twenty degrees for hikes in this book.'

He made a photocopy of the map of Maine from the atlas and traced out the bearings from Limerick. As he had predicted, the lines met in the north of the state, a little to the left of an area called the Allagash Wilderness. Lindow had heard of it, but knew nothing of the area; still less did he understand why Eamonn had pinpointed a spot that contained nothing but forests and lakes. However, he was certain he'd found the solution to the slip of paper. After all, it had been hidden in the passport that contained entry stamps for Boston, which was only a few hundred miles south. Something was there, something Eamonn had been anxious to keep secret. He wondered if he could learn anything from the dates of the entry stamps in Eamonn's fake passport.

He folded the copies of the two maps, placed them in his inside pocket and left the room with a nod of thanks to the pretty librarian. He couldn't help feeling a little exalted at his discovery.

Kirsty Laing nursed a large cappuccino and waited for Peter Speerman, who'd said he would drop by to give her the briefing. He had not found time on Friday and, when pressed by her, agreed to an early meeting on Monday. At nine o'clock. Speerman put his head round the door and gave her a conspiratorial smile. He was carrying a file under his arm and a National Trust mug, filled with strong tea.

'So, Kirsty, we must have our little chat.' His manner made Laing feel she was about to be told the facts of life. She sat back in her chair and waited.

'Some years ago we became involved with a man

named Ian Rhodes – Major Ian Valentine Rhodes – one of the most remarkable soldiers ever to have served in the British Army. When he left in the late eighties the people at the top of the service believed he could be very useful to us. They were proved right. He was highly intelligent, and physically without parallel. There seemed to be nothing he couldn't do. He became attached to the service in an unofficial capacity and carried out a number of important tasks – on one occasion he single-handedly managed to release an informant from interrogation by the Provisionals that would have ended in certain death. He also undertook a number of missions abroad for us, which I won't enlarge on. Suffice to say they were all expedited with the minimum fuss and the maximum speed. But Rhodes came with problems that no one appreciated at the time. There was an imbalance – a nervous breakdown of some form, which was said to have been the delayed reaction to a skirmish in Ireland when his men were wiped out in an incident near the border. His trouble did not surface until the early nineties and he was hospitalised for treatment. When he recovered he went into business for himself, first as a contract agent to the private security firms that have sprung up in Victoria over the last ten years, then on his own behalf. We remained on reasonable terms with him and used him once or twice more, but it became clear that his own business took priority. Besides, there was no telling who else he was working for. Rhodes was an extremely capable individual, but he was also addicted to risk. There was evidence that he'd sold knowledge of our arrangements and *modus operandi* to the other side, by which I mean the IRA. This was before the first ceasefire. We weren't certain but we had our suspicions, and we knew the republicans were interested in doing business with him. Incidentally, so was every other terrorist group in the northern hemisphere. We began to think of Major Rhodes as someone whose movements it was prudent to track, which is why the watchers included him in the gallery of faces that Weegee was programmed to look out for.'

'And Weegee spotted him on the night of the first bomb.'

'*May* have spotted him.' He gave a matronly look of reproach. 'We're not absolutely certain it was him.'

'But surely we should have told the police.'

'That is not an option at the moment. When you read the file, I think you will agree about that.' Speerman picked up his mug. She felt him studying her.

'You're probably right, but surely the downside of sharing this information with the police is almost negligible. After all, the director general can't be held responsible for decisions taken by his predecessors. And if this man, who was never a member of the service anyway, caused the bombings, it would be only wise to bring in the police at the earliest possible opportunity.'

'It may come to that, but we would prefer to solve the problem using our own resources. That way our security is maintained and there's no danger of our association with Rhodes leaking to the press. But there may be a time when we need you to help explain this problem in certain government quarters, which is why I asked you to come along last week. That moment, however, has not yet arrived.' He slid the file across her desk and got up to leave. 'Return it to me before the end of this morning. It needs to go back into the safe. Oh, I hardly need tell you that no copies should be made.'

She read through the file and found that Speerman had covered most of the ground. The thing that absorbed her was the colour headshot of a man with a chiselled face and receding hairline, which was clipped to the inside of the file. At the bottom of the picture, time and date were recorded – 19.22:23.10. There were some other figures, which she presumed identified the camera and the subject's exact location on a grid of the street.

She examined the face. It wasn't possible to see the man's eyes, for he was glancing down to the right, but she had the strong impression that he was someone to be reckoned with. There was a composed, brutal intelligence about the face that Weegee had plucked from the street six days before. As she stared at the picture, she realised that she couldn't simply return it to Speerman's safe. It might never see the light of day. And, given the apparent determination of the service to save its own skin by pursuing Lindow, there was a very large principle at stake here. This was the moment she had always suspected would come. She argued with herself for some minutes, then got up and moved quickly to a small flat box by her filing cabinet – the scanner she used for copying newspaper clippings and documents on to her computer's memory. She placed the picture face down on the glass surface, closed the lid and set the machine to run. Some minutes later she brought up the picture on her screen. But instead of storing it in the computer, she printed off a copy. It was a laborious process but it meant that she had avoided having to use the photocopier down the corridor, which was too public and, anyway, was reputed to be fitted with a device that made a record of all copies taken. She examined the print, checking that the date/time line had been reproduced, then slipped it in a folder of old memos. Finally she deleted the file from her computer.

On the way back to Speerman's office to deliver the Rhodes file she kept reassuring herself that the picture would be used only if circumstances demanded. So, in a sense, she had not yet done anything against the service but was merely reserving the right to stand by a principle.

Speerman ushered her in, took the file and gestured to a chair. 'There's been an interesting development. Lindow's been acting very suspiciously this morning. He made an amateurish attempt to give us the slip in Oxford Street. Our people might have fallen for it had they not been lagging behind the police. Quite by chance they saw him run from a department store. I believe the police lost him some time before.'

'Perhaps he knew he was being followed and didn't like it.'

'Maybe, but then he went to a library and spent a long time in the reference section using the atlases. Obviously it had nothing to do with his work. He was observed making some sort of measurements by one of Keith's people, who couldn't get close to him. She thought he spotted her. Later we found out that he was making inquiries about magnetic declination with the Royal Geographical Society. We don't know what he was up to but the police have been informed. They will be none too happy, particularly as I gather that Foyle had more or less eliminated Lindow from his inquiry. This behaviour would suggest that he has something to hide.'

'Good,' she said. 'That sounds very promising indeed.'

Foyle read the MI5 report with a sense of mounting despair. The story of Lindow giving the police surveillance team the slip spread quickly through SO 13. Morale was not helped by the news that Millbank's watchers had kept in touch with their target and tailed Lindow to a library where they had observed him working on some maps. It was not clear what he had been doing, but the fact that he had used the ploy in Oxford Street so that he could be alone in the library was enough to convince practically every member of the Anti-terrorist Unit that Lindow was guilty. It was well known that terrorists used public libraries to research such things as targets, which was why Eamonn Lindow's job as a librarian had been regarded as being far less innocent than it seemed. In the mid-nineties, members of an IRA active-service unit had been observed thumbing through manuals on the national electricity grid. Lindow would not be the first bomber to curl up in the reference section with a good book.

Foyle knew now that his hours in the department were numbered. He chucked the report aside and asked Forbes with ill-concealed exasperation if Lindow had been located again.

'Yes, sir, we picked him up at his solicitor's office about an hour ago. We believe he has been settling his brother's affairs. The lawyer was at the inquest this morning and is apparently helping him with the arrangements for the transportation of Eamonn's body to Ireland.'

'Permission for burial has been given?'

'Yes, you said that you had no objections so I let the coroner's office know on Friday that it would be all right by us.'

'Do we know when he's going to Ireland?'

'It seems likely that he'll leave today or tomorrow morning.'

Foyle thought for a few moments.

'Should we have him arrested again?' Forbes asked.

'On what grounds? For giving our surveillance team the slip in Ladies' Hosiery?'

'On the grounds that he has been acting as if he has something to hide. That's reason enough, in these circumstances.'

'It would be pointless to arrest him,' said Foyle. 'He's not the man behind this. In fact, it was Lindow who gave me the idea about the telephones. It still seems the only workable solution we've got.'

Forbes raised an eyebrow. 'He gave you that idea? But don't you see that it helps his case if he can make us believe that someone outside that bus detonated the bomb? It's a very clever idea, but in his case it could be seen as self-serving.'

'Yes, that's what Lockyer said when I told him.'

'You told Lockyer? Lockyer and Scarratt are very

158

tight. They're members of the same Lodge. It won't be long before Scarratt hears.'

'Oh, fuck,' said Foyle. 'Look, find out where Lindow is and let me know.'

At that moment Lindow was stepping out of a cab at Heathrow Airport. He had booked a flight to Dublin from Jane Casper's phone, having taken the passport and money from her safe. Instead of examining the US immigration stamps at the lawyers', he decided to wait until he got to Ireland where he'd have time to think through Eamonn's double life. He also wanted to ask Tag her opinion. She'd seen a lot of Eamonn over the last few years and would have a better notion of what he had been doing in the States. Tag had been the one member of his family to whom he had spoken regularly while he had been away. He had left Ireland while she was still young and had only properly come to know her two summers before when she stayed with him in Boston for three months, working at a restaurant on the waterfront. She had made a similar effort with Eamonn and visited him several times in London. They had got on well, although there were seventeen years between them, and Tag, like Lindow, had veered to the sciences, in her case chemistry.

Back at his flat, Lindow slipped the passport, money and the copies of the maps into the breast pocket of the suit he intended to wear for the funeral. Then he packed it, with clothes and some books, and left for the airport. All the arrangements had been made. The body was to be picked up by a firm of undertakers and would be flown to Dublin, there to be met by a hearse from Desmond Quorny, Ballyhanna's funeral director.

He had about an hour to wait at the airport, which didn't bother him. His mood was lightening somewhat at the thought of leaving London and spending some time at home. Over the weekend he'd resolved to put more effort into his family. That was what was in his mind when, on his way to the departure gate, he was approached by two men who asked if they could have a word. They assured him that he would not be delayed and that there was nothing to worry about. He followed them down a corridor to a suite of anonymous offices, without windows, where he was offered a chair and a cup of tea. 'Are you arresting me?' he asked.

'No, sir,' said one, a stout man with shiny hair. 'We're just interested in your travel plans. We thought you'd prefer it that we talk to you here, rather than when you're about to board the aircraft. Commander Foyle would like to have an idea of when you plan to return to the United Kingdom, sir.'

'I haven't decided yet,' said Lindow. 'I've been given compassionate leave by the university and it's possible that I'll choose to spend some time with my family. I may be away for a couple of weeks.'

'You can't be more specific than that?'

'No, I can't.'

'Are you travelling with your passport, sir?' asked the older man, a military type of about fifty.

'Yes, as a matter of fact I am, but that's out of habit. You don't need it to travel from Britain to Ireland.'

'That's right. Would you mind if I looked at it?'

Lindow felt inside his jacket and handed it to him. The man leafed through the passport while his companion studied Lindow.

'You see,' he said, still examining its pages, 'Commander Foyle wants to be certain of your return.'

'There's no question of me not coming back. Tell Commander Foyle that I'll be back by the first week of November, if not sooner. That's a promise. I've got a job to come back for.'

'Yes, well, just to be on the safe side, he wonders if you'd have a problem leaving this with us – to be collected on your return.' He presented it as a request, but Lindow had little doubt that the passport would be taken whichever way he answered.

'Have I got any option?'

'Not really, sir, unless you want to delay your departure and sort this out here in England. But if you're not planning to use it, there isn't any reason why you should mind, is there, sir?'

'That's not the point! The point is that you're taking my passport – an Irish passport – when you haven't any right to do so. I'm not under arrest.'

'You're very welcome to appeal against the decision, sir. As I say, this is a request made by Commander Foyle personally, in a spirit of trust. He hopes you will see it that way because he has already placed considerable trust in you.'

Lindow saw that it was no use arguing. He shrugged his shoulders and said that he would be willing to oblige the commander as long as he was guaranteed the return of the passport when he set foot back in England.

'That's understood,' said the other officer. 'If you hold on a moment there, sir, I'll go and get you a written receipt, which will enable you to collect your passport from New Scotland Yard when you come back.'

He disappeared for ten minutes, then returned waving a flimsy bit of paper, which he presented to Lindow with great ceremony. 'Thank you for being so understanding, Dr Lindow. We appreciate it, don't we?' he said, nudging his colleague.

'Oh, yes, we appreciate it, Dr Lindow. Now, have a good trip, sir.'

'Yes, sir. Have a good trip,' said the other.

Lindow left the Laurel and Hardy of the British Special Branch and made his way to the boarding-gate.

Chapter Eight

Lindow hired a car at Dublin airport and drove north-wards. In the fading light, Ireland came flooding back – its louring skies and the sweet, earthy fumes of occasional peat fires.

He was reminded that Ireland was still a country where people walked because they had no means of transport. He picked up a couple of hitch-hikers, first a young boy lugging his schoolbooks home, then a middle-aged woman with her shopping. She got into the car and began talking about Irish politics and some scandal or other involving a minister and his mistress. He let her out at a crossroads where a telegraph pole was festooned with election posters. She said goodbye and strode away, muttering that each one of the faces that flapped in the breeze was exactly the same. He got out of the car, went over to the posters and examined them. She was wrong. The topmost poster showed Rudi MacMahon bursting from the Sinn Fein colours with a family-man grin. 'Vote MacMahon – A Better Chance for Peace', it declared.

He returned to the car and drove on to Ballyhanna, the market town ten miles south of the border where the Lindows had moved when his mother inherited some land and a comfortable house on the edge of the town. The White House, as it was still known, although painted a pale terracotta by Marie Lindow several years ago, was set back from the road at the end of a short gravel drive, which announced Lindow's arrival with a crunching sound that reverberated around the walls of the house.

As he pulled up the light over the front door came on and Tag bounded out to meet him. His father followed, stooped and smiling. 'Ah, that's good,' he said, gripping his son's arms. 'You look fine, Con. It's good to have you home.'

Lindow felt his eyes pricking with tears. He turned round abruptly, hauled his bags from the car, then walked to the front door between Tag and his father.

Not long afterwards they sat round the kitchen table eating a stew made by Tag and talking over the arrangements for the funeral – an agonising process for the old man, who fell into long silences during which he stared at the glass door of the wood-burner.

'The thing I don't understand, Con,' he said quietly, 'is why Eamonn? Why the bus with all those people on it? What's been gained by their deaths?'

Lindow and his sister looked at each other. Tag shook her head and placed a hand on her father's arm. Lindow waited a moment, then told them about Eamonn's friend, Mary, and how he'd asked her to read at the funeral. His father nodded to say that it would be fine, then he looked directly into his son's eyes with a kind of fierce bewilderment. 'I don't know what's been going on, Con.' He said it in a tone Lindow had never heard him use before. 'I don't understand it, but you must promise that you won't try to hide anything from me. You mustn't keep anything from me, Con. You must promise me that. Whatever it is, I want to have the truth. It's not knowing that is the painful thing. Just because we're to bury Eamonn on Wednesday doesn't mean that it's an end of it. I want to know everything. You understand that, Con?'

Lindow found himself unable to speak. He understood exactly what his father was saying, because he felt the same. 'I promise you, Dad,' he said. 'I'll tell you if I hear anything – promise.'

At that Gerard Lindow rose from the table and bade his children goodnight. As he left the kitchen to fetch his book from the living room he seemed to his son not so much older as smaller. Lindow and Tag waited until they heard the water running in the bathroom above before they began to speak again.

'Is there anything you're not telling us?' Tag asked.

'I was going to ask you the same thing. You saw him in London, Tag. You went over there and stayed with him. Was he doing something he shouldn't have been? Was he working for the IRA?'

'No, of course not. What makes you think that?' said Tag, with a flash of their mother's anger. 'You know Eamonn! Anyone could see that he wasn't a Provo. This is *our* brother we're talking about, Con, not one of those killers from Tyrone!'

'Yes, I know. I know, Tag,' he said, pacifying her with his hands. 'But there are things that I just can't explain. I mean, the police told me that the security services had been watching him for a long time. How do you explain that?'

'Because they still think every Irishman who sets foot on the mainland is a fucking terrorist. They don't see that it's all finished. The Provos will never go back to bombing.'

'But, Tag, Eamonn did have a secret.'

He got up, went to one of the bags in the hall then returned to the kitchen and placed the envelope on the table without saying anything. She picked it up and took out the passport and the money.

'I don't understand. This is an American passport!'

'Look at the name, Tag! It's my name, but Eamonn's picture. I found it at his flat on Friday, hidden in a desk with all that money. I'd have missed it if the damned drawer hadn't jammed.'

'But what's it mean?' she asked. 'What was he doing with this? Why was he using your name?'

Lindow shrugged his shoulders.

'So what does it mean?' she repeated.

'There was something else in the passport,' he said, placing the two photostats on the table and taking the slip of paper from his wallet. 'It took me some time to work out what it meant. The bearings from Limerick and Belfast appear to give you a position in Ireland, but if you draw them out on the map they meet each other in the Atlantic. The clue is the magnetic variation, which Eamonn put at twenty degrees. That's impossible in Ireland, but it isn't in Maine, USA, which has a town called Belfast and another called Limerick. Eamonn had obviously been up there but I don't know what for.'

Tag stared down at the maps while Lindow took the passport from her and looked silently at the US immigration stamps. At the end of the book there was one for 21 September that year – a little over a month before Eamonn was killed. He hadn't noticed it before, but it made complete sense. Eamonn had known he was leaving America to live in London so he had had to make use of his identity while he was still working at MIT. Why? What was so important to him there?

'He used this passport to travel to America four times in the last two years. Each time he landed in Boston. It doesn't say how long he stayed, but the point is that it ties in with the location in Maine, which is only a few hundred miles north of Boston – a stone's throw, in American terms. I was the perfect cover for him. What could be more normal than Lindow travelling from the British Isles to Boston where he worked at the Massachusetts Institute of Technology? Whatever Eamonn was doing, he was being damned cunning about it. You can see he lost weight before being photographed so he looked a little more like me. When I went to identify him, I noticed he'd got thinner.'

'Oh, don't say that. How could you?'

'I'm sorry, Tag. I just know there was something going on. When Dad asked me, I felt I couldn't explain it properly so I didn't try.'

'What are you going to do? Give it all to the police?'

'I considered that. But then I thought they'd use it against me. They already suspect me of complicity and you can just imagine what interpretation they would place on me finding this and not handing it over immediately. They'd probably use it to arrest me again. Have you any idea what it all means?'

'No. I was sure Eamonn had never been to the States. He never mentioned it, and you know that's the sort of thing he would talk about. For months we'd be hearing stories of his trip to the States.'

'Who did he see in London? Did you meet any of his friends?'

'Yes, a few men in the pub, but they were English. There wasn't anything odd about them. They talked football and films and made passes at me. Christ, they were just normal, harmless, boring Brits!'

'Did he ever mention Rudi MacMahon to you?'

'The Sinn Fein man?'

'The gunman.'

'No,' she said, flaring up again. 'He said nothing about Rudi MacMahon or any other terrorist – all right? For Christ's sake, it's as if you're talking about someone else, not Eamonn. What's going on with you, Con? It wasn't Eamonn's fault you were arrested.'

'You're right, it wasn't, but since I found the passport with all this money I've been turning it around in my head and I cannot think of an explanation that doesn't include the IRA. You know he had some kind of friendship – association, I don't know what you'd call it – with MacMahon. I want to find out what's been going on. But first we've got to get through this funeral.'

The next day passed uneventfully. Lindow walked into town to check the funeral arrangements with the priest, then retraced his steps down the high street to Desmond Quorny's Lounge Bar, next door to Quorny's Funeral

Parlour. It was said in Ballyhanna that one half of Quorny's enterprise always kept the other supplied.

Quorny greeted Lindow with a little bow and ushered him away from the huddle of morning drinkers at the front of the bar. 'May I say how sorry I am for the great misfortune suffered by your family – and so soon after Mrs Lindow's passing away. It's a very tragic business to be sure, Dr Lindow. Very sad indeed.' He rubbed his hands together.

'Thank you,' said Lindow tersely, not wishing to encourage Quorny in his well-practised condolences. 'I came to see that everything would be all right for tomorrow.'

'Everything is in hand, Dr Lindow. The car will be outside the White House at half past nine, which will give us plenty of time to be at the church by ten. There'll be a good many people who wish to show their respects, given all the good friends Eamonn made here in Ballyhanna. He never forgot them when he was away in London. Some of them have offered to be pall-bearers and I've chosen six. In actual fact, they're mostly the lads I use when the family can't supply them.'

'It was my impression that Eamonn didn't come back that often.'

'Oh, no, that would be quite wrong, Dr Lindow. Your brother was still closely involved in the community here and popular too. He was many a time in this very bar, sitting at that table over there.' Quorny pointed to a table hidden by a screen at the back of the room. 'He liked to talk to his political friends there,' he added, with a knowing cock of one eyebrow.

'Political friends? Who were they?'

'Oh, I couldn't tell you who they were,' said Quorny shiftily. 'But I'm sure they'll all be along to pay their respects to Eamonn tomorrow.'

'But you must have some idea who they were. Were they nationalists?'

'I expect they might have been, sir, but I couldn't say for certain. I try to respect my customers' privacy.'

'Was Rudi MacMahon here with Eamonn?'

'I wouldn't know, sir. I wouldn't know who the gentlemen were, I'm sure.'

Lindow left the stale atmosphere of Quorny's and went to find Tag, who was arranging food for the mourners at the church hall.

Foyle took the call from the commissioner's office at one ten on Tuesday 30 October. He was required to see Urquhart at two thirty, at which hour, he had no doubt, the command of SO 13 would pass to Assistant Commissioner Martin Scarratt.

He put down the receiver gently. His anger had long evaporated and was replaced by an odd sense of liberation. He knew it wouldn't last but for the moment he enjoyed it. He settled down over the *Guardian* and consumed a chicken baguette, brought up from the Italian sandwich bar by Nancy Longmore. He rang Katherine – she was out – then Carla Pryn, to book a table at her restaurant in the evening. At least he'd be free to enjoy her company and maybe . . . well, he'd see. He put the thought of her out of his mind.

Forbes walked in without knocking. Foyle motioned him to a chair.

'I'm being put to sleep at two thirty,' said Foyle, without emotion. 'By close of play Scarratt will be running things.'

'It's a great pity,' sighed Forbes. 'He won't be particularly pleased to have me on the team because I'm your man. So I imagine I'll be following you pretty soon, sir.'

'Nonsense, you're invaluable. Even Scarratt can't miss that.'

Foyle rose and stretched as if he was limbering up to take some exercise. He swung one arm in the air, then the other. 'It's all such a damned fuck-up. I feel I owe you some sort of apology, but for the life of me I'm not sure why. Perhaps I did become obsessive about linking the business in Ireland with all of this.' He swept a hand at a map of Inner London, on which the two explosions were marked with red stickers. 'The problem is, I can't believe I'm wrong. There's something in it, I'm sure of that. And the phone thing is looking even more feasible.'

'Oh, by the way,' said Forbes, changing the subject, 'I found out about that close-observation group involved in the Droy operation. Had a bite with a friend of mine at the Ministry. Somebody doesn't want us to know who was at Droy. They received specific instructions yesterday, but my friend had already written down the details so he gave them to me. Anyway, he said that if we looked hard enough we'd find all the names on record somewhere – regimental newsletters, that sort of thing – so he didn't mind giving them to me.'

Foyle's interest picked up. 'Don't keep me waiting. What did you find out?'

'They're an *ad hoc* group of soldiers who came together for special jobs as a close-observation platoon. They'd done a couple in Ulster and some of them had served together in the Falklands War. There were six men in the group. The key figures were a young major called Ian Rhodes and his second in command Robert Lasseur.'

'Lasseur?'

'Yes,' replied Forbes. 'Seems he was brought up in Quebec, but he's a British national, his English mother having moved back after a divorce. The other men involved were Sergeant James Pascoe, Corporal Robert McGurk, Private Vincent Creech and Gunner Christy Calvert. McGurk and Creech were killed in the churchyard and Pascoe and Lasseur were injured. Pascoe lost his eyesight and Lasseur was badly scarred. Only Calvert and Rhodes were unharmed. None of the men is still in the Army. Calvert and Rhodes left quite soon after Droy – a couple of years or something like that.'

'So Droy finished all their careers. Do we know what happened to them afterwards?'

'There's very little on record, just gossip. But it seems that Lasseur left the country, Calvert went into personal protection and Pascoe lives up north on a disability pension. Nothing is known of Rhodes's whereabouts, or his occupation.'

'But at least it shouldn't be too difficult to trace Calvert and Pascoe. Might be worth someone having a word with them,' said Foyle.

'That rather depends on your meeting, doesn't it, sir?'

'Yes, I suppose it does, but in the meantime I'd like you to get someone started on it.'

Then Foyle went upstairs and waited outside the commissioner's office. Ten minutes later he was shown in. Scarratt and the commissioner were both in uniform. Foyle was not offered a seat.

'As you know, we have been concerned about the progress of your inquiry, Commander,' began the commissioner, 'and after a thorough review I've decided it would be best for you and the force if you relinquished your command of SO 13.'

He waited for Foyle's reaction, but nothing came.

'By my estimate you are owed three and a half weeks' holiday. I want you to take that leave starting from tomorrow and to return to work towards the end of November. Given the current circumstances, I do not think a return to SO 13 is either desirable or practical, so I'd like your thoughts on how you wish to develop your career. On reflection, you may feel that things have come to a natural end, in which eventuality we'll make the necessary arrangements.'

Foyle had heard all of it before in his imagination and knew exactly how this little speech would end, with the commissioner moderating his tone, which he did right on cue.

'For the moment, Commander, I want you to have a

good break. Take some time for yourself and your wife, Kenneth. She's still abroad, isn't she?'

Foyle nodded.

'Why don't you go and see her? Surprise her.'

'I want to know why you're doing this, sir.'

'Oh, come on, man,' said the commissioner. 'The department's in a shambles and your judgement has been wide of the mark on practically every issue these past seven days. You let our only suspect go, then you deploy your department's resources investigating a theory, supplied by that very same suspect, for which there is not a shred of evidence. This is beginning to affect your men. I don't have to tell an officer with your exemplary record about the importance of morale in a department. Once a commanding officer has lost his men's confidence it rarely, if ever, returns. That's the stage we've reached with you. I'd be failing in my duty, failing in my responsibility to you too, Commander, if I did not take steps to resolve the situation.'

'What will you do, sir, if I turn out to be right about Lindow's innocence and if I'm right about the use of cellphones to set off these bombs?'

'We'll have to consider that, but I must deal with the situation as it stands today. What I have is a rudderless department, bogged down, demoralised, frustrated, failing. That's the only thing which concerns me now. I am certain, Commander, that you'll have valuable insights to offer Assistant Commissioner Scarratt and that he will be able to build on some of the work that you have already done. But to be brutally candid, Commander, I don't envisage that there's the slightest chance of you being right. I mean ... the idea that you were tricked by the bomber to ring a number connected to one of the devices is madness. Imagine the coverage in the newspapers if they heard about it.' He paused again, moved some paper on his desk, and said, 'I want you to hand over to Assistant Commissioner Scarratt formally tomorrow morning. You'll need time to go through things. Is that all right with you, Martin?'

'Yes, sir.' Scarratt turned to Foyle. 'We'll meet at midday tomorrow, or shortly afterwards.'

'And we'll talk in a month's time when you've thought things over,' said the commissioner.

He extended his hand in a gesture of farewell. It was then that Foyle realised that his career was over and that there would be no meeting in a month's time. He was out and he'd have to get used to it – get used to the idea of no longer being a police officer.

For him that was an unimaginable condition.

The following morning Foyle found Forbes waiting for him at the lift doors. The moment he saw his face he could see something was up.

'We've got another one,' Forbes said. 'Nothing certain yet. We've just had a report in a few minutes ago. There's a car with a suspicious package in it near King's Cross station. It's parked behind an office building on a piece of land due for development. Lafferty's on his way now. I've got a car waiting.'

They left immediately. The roads around King's Cross had seized up with the rush-hour traffic. In the back of the car, voice raised against the wail of sirens, Forbes filled him in. Earlier that morning a young policeman had become suspicious of a blue Audi estate, which had been parked in the same spot since Friday. He knew it hadn't been moved because leaves had collected along the bottom of the windscreen. His attention was drawn to a metallic suitcase, hidden under a rug in the back of the car. He made some inquiries about the car, which was found to belong to a Dr Richard Brett from Maidenhead. The Audi had not been reported stolen, but Dr Brett's daughter explained that her parents were away for a three-week holiday in Kenya and had left the vehicle in the long-stay car park at the airport.

'So whoever removed it knew it wouldn't be reported missing,' said Foyle.

'Yes, but that's not all. The officer noticed there were wires running from the case to the lighter socket.'

'A phone charger.'

'Exactly – and he got the desk sergeant to telephone the daughter again to find out if her father possessed a mobile phone and also whether he was likely to have left it on charge in the car. She replied that his mobile was sitting on his desk. She was looking at it as they spoke.'

'And the case?'

'As far as she knew, her father didn't own a case of that description.'

'Smart lad that constable, we ought to have him in the department.'

They came to a halt about two hundred yards from Euston Road. Foyle and Forbes got out and made for the spot where two Explosives Unit vans were parked. As they approached, Lafferty's face appeared from the back of the van. He hailed Foyle. 'You could be right about these bombs, Ken. The robot camera shows the package is connected to a telephone charger. That may be just acting as the supply but it could be attached to a phone in the case. We're going to get the barrow to break the rear window. If the bomb isn't hooked up to the car alarm we'll get it to stick its snout in and have a closer look.'

They went over to the second expo van. Foyle picked up a pair of binoculars and trained them on the Audi. He saw the robot edge to the right rear window behind the driver's seat, extend an arm and fire a punch at the glass. There was a barely audible phut as the window pulverised. The robot's arm extended further, allowing its sensors to sniff the air inside the car for explosives. At the same time a second low-light camera fixed to the end of the probe swept the interior of the car. The images and sniffer readings began to flow down a fibreoptic cable to a lap-top in the back of the van.

'There's definitely something in there,' said Lafferty, looking at a panel on the screen. 'Probably Semtex. If it was Co-op explosive we'd smell it from here.'

'What's Co-op?' asked Forbes.

'Nitrobenzine and sodium chlorate.' Lafferty was watching the screen intently. 'Smells like hell. The IRA used it to blow up a Co-op store in Belfast.'

Lafferty told the man operating the joystick controlling the robot to see if the camera could trace the exact route of the wire leading to the back of the vehicle. Nothing came up on the screen. The wire seemed to disappear into a crack just behind the rear seat.

'It could be a detonating cord,' Lafferty explained, 'which would transmit a detonating wave from the main charge in the suitcase to the bulk of the explosive in the boot. The stuff may be hidden in the spare-wheel well or under the rear seat.' He paused to concentrate on the screen. 'Still, my instinct tells me that the real business is confined to that suitcase and that there are no other explosives. We'll have to take a closer look.'

'Are you sure?' said Foyle. 'Can't you use the robot to blow it up?'

'Yes,' said Lafferty, looking down the alley. 'That thing's got every conceivable gadget – water disrupters, sidewinder shotguns, explosives sniffers. They say it can smell the difference between Pepsi and Coke. But that won't help us learn how these bombs are being made. We need to know how this guy is putting them together. My guess is that this device has malfunctioned in some way. We know it's been there for over five days, which means it was probably planted with that other bomb last week. If it's gone wrong it may be easier to deal with.' He paused, then said grimly, 'On the other hand he may have built in one or two surprises.'

They walked to the other van, where Lafferty checked a low trolley on which lay a portable X-ray machine, the metal pipe and explosive cartridge of another water disrupter, a roll of roofing lead and an attaché toolcase. He cut a dozen four-inch strips of insulating tape and hung them on the left-hand side of the trolley. Then he opened the tool case and ran his hands along the implements, an array of clamps, knives, electrical bypasses and tools adapted or fashioned by Lafferty during his time as an ammunition technical officer in Belfast.

He selected some wire-cutters and a pair of pliers, closed the case and put them on top. Then he turned to the uniformed officer from the Explosives Unit who stood holding the black body of a BBS-3 bomb suit. 'I still can't get used to these things,' he said. 'You can't move in them.'

The officer trussed Lafferty into the suit. When all the straps were secure, he picked up the pliers and wire-cutters and fixed each with a single piece of tape to Lafferty's left arm. Lafferty told Foyle that if he wanted to hear what was going on he should use one of the headsets over at the other van. Then he disappeared into the huge turret-like armoured helmet and made for the Audi, towing his trolley behind him. One of the expos explained to Foyle that Inspector Lafferty was moving slowly because he didn't want to be all sweated up inside the suit by the time he reached the car.

Foyle didn't need the explanation. Late one night over a tumbler of rare twelve-year-old malt, Lafferty had told him about the Long Walk from the police cordon to an Improvised Explosive Device. It was never more than 150 yards at most, but with each step taken, the expo would be calculating his chances of survival. He'd move from the maiming zone to the killing range, a place where a bomb suit afforded only a little more protection than a plastic mackintosh. And then he'd be right up close to the device, staring into the eyes of the beast and wondering about its electrical circuits. How much time did he have before the circuits closed and the detonator began to generate its lethal heat? Was there an anti-handling mechanism that would complete the circuit and trip the bomb ahead of the timer? Lafferty spoke as if each device had a personality, a crude projection of the bomber's own character. Some were easily understood, others sophisticated and devious. To Lafferty the business was very personal indeed, a test of his nerve and ingenuity against the terrorist's cunning. It was a game that was weighted in favour of the terrorist. While the expo risked everything, the bomber could never lose. Even when a device was defused he still chalked up a draw.

For what seemed like an age Lafferty, moving like a deep-sea diver, circled the car, bending down to peer inside at the roof. At length he spoke over the radio. 'It's no good,' he said. 'I think he's wired up the interior light to the bomb and I can't get at it without climbing through a window. I'm coming back to take this bloody suit off. Meantime, get the robot to break the front passenger window. Do you read? Front passenger window.'

Lafferty walked back to meet an officer, who helped him out of the suit and helmet and gave him a new earpiece. Visibly relieved, he jogged back to the car and hauled himself expertly through the newly broken window.

'Yes!' he said softly over the radio. 'The old trick: he's connected the detonator to the door light.'

The effect of the binoculars, combined with the sound of Lafferty's exertions over the headset, made Foyle feel that he was almost in the car with him. He saw Lafferty lift his arm and smash the light with one short well-aimed blow.

'Now for the main course,' Lafferty said, getting out of the driver's door and swinging round to open the door behind it. He pulled the rug from the suitcase and dropped it on the road with the sweeping motion of a matador. Then he squatted down and began to speak again. 'There are two holes bored in the case. At the hole nearest to me I've got what looks like the rubberised aerial of a mobile phone. Two wires exit the other hole, one to the light I've just smashed, and the second goes to the cigarette lighter. I won't touch them until I've X-rayed the case. I'm still pretty certain that the explosives are confined to the case. I can't see anything under the seat and there's no detonating cord going back to the boot.'

He stepped back into the road and removed the X-ray unit and the roll of lead from the trolley. He positioned the unit in the car, unrolled the lead and dropped behind it to lessen his exposure to the rays. A few seconds later he removed the machine. While he waited for the positive X-ray image to develop, he fashioned the lead into a crude three-sided shield then cut a square and placed it on the top.

'What's he doing?' asked Forbes, in Foyle's ear.

'He's making a screen so that a call can't get through to that phone,' replied Foyle, covering his microphone.

'That's right.' Lafferty had overheard. 'Ah, here's the X-ray. It's not as bad as I thought, but there's a shit-load of wiring in there. I'm going to cut the wire to the charger cable from the lighter.'

Lafferty was silent for a long while. The explosives officer standing next to Foyle exhaled. 'That wire may be connected to a relay – an electromagnetic switch – which means that when it's cut the power holding the switch open closes. The current goes straight to the detonator.'

Lafferty's voice came again. 'That's good. Now I'm going to try to open the case.'

Another long silence ensued while Lafferty placed his crude lead screen in the car and went to work on the case. At length he itemised the contents of the case over the radio. 'Three or four pounds of Semtex, a standard detonator, a cellphone and a video timer. The timer is a fall-back mechanism. If the phone doesn't receive a call, the video timer is here to make sure that the bomb detonates. The bad news is that the whole lot is still working on the phone's battery. The phone's display shows that it is fully charged. But it also shows that the reception is non-existent here. It's funny he didn't notice that.'

Another pause. 'Damn,' said Lafferty. 'What time is it? I can't turn my wrist to see my watch.'

One of the officers with a headset replied. 'It's eight fifty-five, sir.'

'I've got an hour then,' said Lafferty. 'This timer seems to be set for ten a.m. today, Wednesday October the thirty-first. Oh, Jesus. There's a tilt switch fixed to the bottom of the timer and it's wired into the detonator. I can't move it. So I'm going to confine my attention to the phone.

'Take this down carefully,' he continued. 'The back section of the phone has been cut away to expose the contacts of the ringer. Wires lead from the ringer to the detonator. When the ringer is activated by a call, it completes the circuit. By my count that makes four separate mechanisms connected up to the detonator – the phone, the doorlight, the timer and the mercury tilt switch. He certainly didn't want his little baby examined. Are you sure about the time? The display says it's nearly ten.'

'Yes, sir,' said the officer.

Foyle listened intently. Con Lindow's inspiration about the telephone had been spot on. What was especially interesting was that the bomber had done everything to ensure that the phone would not be retrieved. But something was stabbing at the back of his mind, a sharp anxiety that would not form into coherent thought.

He concentrated. The idea took shape and, as it did so, he rose and bellowed, 'Get out of there, Lafferty! It's going to blow! The clocks went back on Sunday!'

Forbes and the other police officers gaped at Foyle.

Lafferty hadn't taken it in. 'For fuck's sake stop shouting in my ear,' he said.

'The clocks went back on Sunday!' repeated Foyle. 'The timer is on British Summer Time and is set for ten a.m. That means it's going to blow at nine a.m. You've got two minutes, Lafferty. Maybe less.'

'I'm coming. I'll bring this phone with me, though.'

'No!' shouted Foyle. 'Bring the card and get out of there!' He had remembered Pennel's lecture about cellphones. Every cellphone possessed a removable chip known as the subscriber identity module – or SIM card. This transmitted a unique number to the cell antennae when the phone was used. The card was the phone's brains. You could move it from one phone to another and transfer the subscriber number, and also the phone's memory. There was nothing you couldn't find out, once you got the SIM card.

'What card?' asked Lafferty.

'It's plastic, about two centimetres long with a serial number printed on the back. They're usually purple or yellow. It slides out. On the other side you'll find a printed circuit.'

'Got it.'

Foyle watched him turn from the car, dodge the trolley and run towards them with his arms outstretched. He reached the end of the alley and was crossing the road to the vans when the video timer switched on, causing current to flow into the detonator and fire the explosive charge. The Audi levitated and disintegrated in a violent white flash. The blast thundered up the alley, bringing a storm of bricks and metal fragments. Lafferty was flattened. The officers by the vans threw themselves on the ground, covering their heads against the flying debris. Then came a second roar as the scaffolding by the Audi collapsed in slow motion down the length of the alley, ripping masonry from the surrounding buildings and plunging it into the brew of smoke and dust below.

Foyle was the first on his feet. He shouted to Lafferty who had raised his face from the ground and was looking at Foyle with an odd, rueful expression. Together, they ran back to the cordon, where the other officers were picking themselves up.

'That', said Lafferty, 'was the exact same device used on the bus, give or take a few nasty surprises.'

'Have you still got that card?' asked Foyle.

He held it up. The sunlight streaming down the Marylebone Road glinted on the oval of gold circuitry. Foyle slipped it into his wallet, patted Lafferty roughly on the back and went to his car with Forbes.

Out of the corner of his eye, Lindow saw three men climb from a parked car and head towards the procession. He strained round from holding his father's arm, peering above the heads of the crowd to see if they joined the mourners. He couldn't be sure but he thought they had. He bent down to his father and Tag, and told them he was going back to check on something. Then he said to Mary Menihan, who was walking behind Tag, 'I think that bastard MacMahon's come. There're some TV people up at the church. I don't want them filming him here.'

He slipped from the procession and stood on a small rise at the side of the road, watching the faces pass. Most of the mourners were local, but there was also a big contingent from the North, which included a dozen or so Cardells – stout, wily people from his mother's family, who arrived outside the gates of the White House and waited for the hearse, shuffling and murmuring to each other in the early morning mist.

As the end of the procession approached, Lindow spotted Rudi MacMahon, flanked by two thickset men. He hadn't changed in twenty years: his hair was still dark and thick, there was no spare flesh on his face and very few lines. The only change Lindow noticed were the round gold-rimmed spectacles that MacMahon had acquired as a prop to his political legitimacy. He pushed into the crowd towards MacMahon, but one of the minders caught sight of him and placed himself squarely in the way before he could confront him.

'That's all right,' said MacMahon. 'This is Con Lindow, Eamonn's brother.'

'What the hell are you doing here?' Lindow demanded. The mourners around them looked at Lindow apprehensively. 'You're not taking over this funeral, do you hear? Eamonn wasn't one of yours. Now, please leave before I ask the Garda to remove you.'

'That's not possible,' said MacMahon, nodding at someone who had turned to see what was going on. 'Your brother was a friend of mine from school. I have as much right to be here as any of these folk.'

'You know damn well you're here to parade in front of the camera, not to mourn Eamonn.'

'Untrue.' MacMahon's eyes grew cold behind his glasses. 'I knew Eamonn for twenty-five years and I've come to pay my respects. That's all there is to it.'

The procession came to a halt as the coffin and first mourners passed through a pair of iron gates to file up the avenue of lime trees that led to the church.

'You knew him, all right, and you tried to use him,' said Lindow. 'If you'd any respect for Eamonn at all you wouldn't be here. Your presence means that the people in London will think that Eamonn was blown up by his own bomb. They'll believe that he was guilty – because you're here, making it look like every other fucking republican funeral.'

MacMahon's eyes narrowed and his lips formed into a slit. He kept his eyes fixed on the gates ahead and leaned very close to Lindow's face. 'The point', he said quietly, 'is that we know Eamonn didn't plant that bomb. That's why I'm here. And the people in London will know that *because* I am here. Do you understand what I'm saying, Con? We know Eamonn had nothing to do with it.'

They stood in silence, forced shoulder to shoulder by the crush of mourners. The slow toll of the church bell reverberated around the buildings either side of the churchyard. A stiff breeze came up from the direction of the town and whipped at the lime trees. Suddenly Lindow felt sickened by the contact with MacMahon. 'I don't want a killer at Eamonn's funeral,' he said, losing his temper. 'That's the bottom line, MacMahon. I don't want a killer here.' Then he grabbed hold of Mac-Mahon's sleeve and tried to pull him to the edge of the crowd. Instantly the bodyguards were either side of Lindow, wrenching his arms downwards and holding them fast.

'That's okay,' said MacMahon calmly. He closed in on Lindow's face again. 'If I *was* a killer, Con, I wouldn't be the only one here with blood on his hands, would I now?'

Lindow recoiled as if he'd been slapped in the face, but he had no time to answer. Tag had struggled back through the gates and was snatching at his arm. 'Con, you're holding everything up,' she implored. 'For God's sake, leave him. Don't make a scene now.'

MacMahon withdrew, tugging the lapels of his jacket downwards. He walked through the gates and the mourners parted to let him through. Halfway up the avenue the cameramen switched on their lights and followed him to the church door.

'That'll be on every news programme tonight,' said Lindow. 'He's got what he wanted – a republican funeral.'

Tag took hold of him and didn't let go until they reached the front row of the pews where their father sat, looking mildly about him. A few minutes later the service began. Lindow's mind strayed to think about the night of the bomb and Kay Gould's injuries. His attention returned when Mary Menihan walked to the lectern to read 'The Second Coming' by Yeats. She stood for a moment and let her gaze travel over the congregation. Light streamed through the stained-glass window and fell across her, dappling her skin mauve and green. She recited the poem without referring to the book she held.

'"Things fall apart",' she said, her eyes moving to where MacMahon sat, ' "the centre cannot hold; mere anarchy is loosed upon the world. The blood-dimmed tide is loosed, and everywhere the ceremony of innocence is drowned. The best lack all conviction, while the worst are full of passionate intensity." '

Then Eamonn's coffin was borne a little way from the church to the cemetery and there lowered into the ground. A flight of rooks spilled from the trees as the priest began to speak. Lindow held his forehead and placed an arm on his father's shoulder. Tag wept, emitting short, girlish sobs. They left the graveside and moved slowly through the heavy autumn dew back to the church. Lindow noticed that MacMahon and his bodyguards were already making for their car, walking briskly down the avenue through the fallen leaves. One of the bodyguards stopped to answer his phone, placing a finger in one ear against the tolling of the church bell. Then he handed the phone to MacMahon. Lindow could just see MacMahon's features tighten as he answered. What the hell was going on?

Chapter Nine

After they'd escaped from the wake, they went back to the White House where Mary changed from a skirt into jeans, an old leather jacket, and wrapped a soft, green scarf around her neck. Lindow suggested they drive out into the countryside and take some air. They set off with no particular aim and drove through the empty border country, passing one or two sullen towns with their still-fortified police stations. Presently they came to an iron bridge, slung across a narrow part of Lough Erne. They parked and walked to the point at the centre of the bridge through which passed the border between North and South and looked out across the choppy expanse of the lake. The water was dark and streaked with rivulets of white foam.

'We used to come fishing here, Eamonn and I,' said Lindow, following her gaze. 'But it was only ever good in the spring, lousy for the rest of the season. See those frothy white trails on the surface? Eamonn always used to cast his fly near one of them. He said the fish waited for flies to get caught in the foam.' He paused, swamped by the memory. 'Christ, that seems a long time ago.'

Lindow felt that she was looking at him. Something had happened between them since they'd stood side by side at Eamonn's wake, both desperate to leave, but trapped by the excruciating solicitude of the mourners. They now had a kind of pact, he felt.

'What are those islands?' she said, pointing to the east. 'They look as if they had been put there.'

'They were,' replied Lindow. 'They're called crannogs. Some were built thousands of years ago. Each one supported three or four houses. Only the people who lived on the islands knew the route through the shallows to get out there.'

'So they didn't trust their neighbours in those days either.'

They walked along the side of the lake to a stand of Scots pines where a squat brick boathouse had fallen into ruin. Lindow explained that Eamonn and he used to moor up there, when the sun was too bright to fish, and drink themselves into a comfortable stupor, Eamonn's stories getting progressively wilder and more bizarre.

'You'll miss him, won't you?' Mary said.

'Yes,' said Lindow thoughtfully. 'I'll miss getting to know him again, which is what I sort of had at the back of my mind when I went to London. I'll miss finding out what the hell he's been doing these past ten years.'

'Didn't you ever talk?'

'Not much. I really wish we had now, wish I'd bothered to find out what was going on.'

'How do you mean?'

'There were things in his life that I don't understand. I can't explain them.'

'Things you disapprove of?'

'Maybe – I'm not sure. And that's the problem. I can't make a judgement because I don't understand them.'

'So, he's left you not knowing what to think of him. That *is* a problem for you. If you found out something that you didn't like, how would it affect your feelings towards him?'

'I can't say. You can never really know what goes into other people's decisions.'

'My, what an impeccable liberal you are! Do you know those lines from Swift?'

'Please go ahead,' said Lindow, gesturing with both

hands. 'I'm endlessly impressed by your ability to remember verse.'

She looked out over the lake and spoke the lines. '"To guide his steps afford your kindest aid, and gently pity whom ye can't persuade. Leave to avenging heaven his stubborn will; For, O, remember he's your brother still."'

'Very good. But, of course, none of us believe in heaven any longer so we do our avenging down here.'

'You mean that you don't believe in heaven?'

'Nope. Do you?'

She shook her head.

Out of an old habit, and perhaps as an act of remembrance, Lindow heaped some pine cones together, broke a couple of fallen boughs into pieces and built a fire at the end of the dock. The resin in the cones made the fire flame quickly. They sat down with their legs swinging from the dock, mesmerised by the snapping of the fire and the slap of water against the old timbers.

He didn't hear them coming across the field from the lane that passed near the boathouse. Not until the last moment did Lindow turn to see five men bearing down on them, moving quickly and silently. One was holding a gun and coming straight for him.

The man placed the pistol against Lindow's ear and motioned him to get up. Mary was simply lifted to her feet by two of the others. Lindow saw the blood drain from her face.

'What do you want?' He heard his voice crack.

'A talk, that's all, so don't be getting yourself into a panic, Con,' said a short man in his sixties, who had followed the others up the old jetty. Lindow stared at him. He looked like any character you'd find on a racecourse – a small-brimmed trilby on the back of his head, dark green waterproof jacket, newspaper rolled up and stuffed in his pocket.

'A chat – that's all we want with you, Con.' The man came close. Lindow saw that the lid of his left eye drooped a little and that his cheeks were scrubbed shiny and patterned with burst veins. His eyes were full of purpose and he spoke with a soft Southern Irish accent.

'But if you want more than that we can certainly give it you, can't we, boys? Okay,' he said, gesturing with his chin, 'take her down there and keep her quiet until we've finished our business with the doctor.'

The two men pulled Mary away. She threw an imploring look over her shoulder but Lindow was concentrating on the man in front of him. He understood quickly that this was the most dangerous person he had ever met. This man would kill without the slightest qualm.

'It's a pleasant spot here to be sure. Wouldn't be bad for fishing, if you'd a mind to. No patience for the sport myself. So, Doctor, you heard about the bomb this morning. A nasty piece of work, by all accounts, and a professional job too.' He removed his hat and inspected the inside, revolving it in his hands and looking past Lindow at the lake.

Lindow didn't know how to answer. When they'd heard during the wake about the controlled explosion, the only thought that had occurred to him was that it would help to remove suspicion from him.

'Yes, I did, but I don't know any details.'

The men relaxed their grip on Lindow, but he could still feel the pistol pressed into his back under his left kidney.

'Sad business, your brother being killed. A good man was Eamonn. Carried the family's honour, there's no mistaking that.' He replaced his hat and looked at Lindow hard. 'How much did you know about your brother's work for us?'

'Nothing. I didn't know he worked for you,' said Lindow.

'Well, he did. He was never what you'd call an obvious candidate, but that was his advantage. No one suspected him, not until the end at any rate. I don't mind telling you that Eamonn was very important to us and we're going to miss him.' He paused to gauge the reaction he was having on Lindow. 'When he was killed he was looking for some men. They were people we once had business with. They went rotten on us and now they're giving us a bucketload of problems over in England. It's them that we think have been letting off these bombs in London. It's them that we need to find before the whole thing blows up again. Do you follow me, Con?'

'Yes. I think so.'

'Good, because I'm going to take you into my confidence. Eamonn always said you had balls – said you didn't give an inch when you were taken in after that business at the churchyard. You know what I'm referring to? Good. I remembered that when we heard that you were held in London and I thought to myself, He won't give anything to the boys in blue. I was right, wasn't I? You told them nothing.'

'I didn't know anything to tell.'

'Ah, that's not true, is it, Con, my lad? You found something and you kept it to yourself. We both know that.'

'What makes you think so?'

'Come on, now. Stop fooling with me. You weren't shocked when I told you that Eamonn was working for us, were you? You knew he was doing something for us. You may be a clever fellow with every sort of degree in the world, but you're no actor. I'll tell you that for nothing.'

Lindow weighed up how much he should tell the man. Since talking to Tag, he'd decided that he would hand over the passport and the scrap of paper to Commander Foyle. The decision had come easily enough once he heard about the third bomb.

'So, tell me, what did you find at Eamonn's place? We know there was something there, but for obvious reasons we couldn't get at it ourselves. We knew that Eamonn had discovered something on his last trip to the States. But when we got into his place, the package was gone. The police didn't find it. We know that because they would be acting differently if they had. So we want it back. We want it all back because it's ours.'

'I don't know what you're talking about.'

The man jerked his head towards an old winch that stood about chest height on the dock. In an instant the two men holding Lindow bent him backwards against the teeth of the winding gear. They wrenched him backwards three times and slapped him about the face. He tried not to cry out, but failed when the cogs ate into his vertebrae.

'That's nothing to what we can do, is it, boys?' The man poked the embers of Lindow's fire with a stick. 'You may want to be a hero, but you're not the only one these boys can hurt.'

He turned round to face the boathouse and gave a short whistle. Two figures emerged from behind the building, one prodding the other forward with a gun. It was Tag. They came a little way up the dock, just out of earshot. She was gagged and blindfolded, and he could see that she was trembling.

'Don't fret yourself now, Con,' said the man. 'She's not been hurt. I brought her here to show you we can get to the lass any time we want. You follow me?'

He nodded.

'So about this package. What did you find in it?'

'Some money and a passport.'

'What did you do with it?'

'I left it in a safe in London – with my lawyers.' Lindow looked at him hard, hoping the lie did not show in his eyes.

'Did they know what was inside?'

'No, I didn't tell them. They didn't ask.'

'There wasn't anything else, nothing with some names written on it?'

'No, just the passport and money. The passport was in my name.'

'Does the name Rhodes mean anything to you? Or Lasseur? Have you ever heard those names, Con?'

He looked into the man's eyes. 'No, I've never heard those names.'

The man smiled and poked the fire again. 'Eamonn was on to them when he was killed. It had been a long-term interest of his, this character Rhodes. He knew what he was made of and we should've listened to him earlier. Now we need to pick up where Eamonn left off. That's where you come in. See, you're going to find them for us.'

'Why? How do you mean? I can't help you.'

'Nonsense, Con, you're the perfect fellow for the job. Eamonn told us where they were. They're in Maine, that's the state north of Boston. It won't be any problem for you to go over there. After all, we've been sending Eamonn over there under your name. Eamonn was always telling us how well connected you are. Our people over there don't have the sort of contacts we need for this. But you do. You've got plenty of influential friends and the like. He told us you know people in the FBI. Talk to them, find out where these two characters are hiding. You see, we're all on the same side now and we need to get to these men before they do any more harm.'

'Why don't you hand this information to the British police? They're desperate to find out who's responsible for the bombs.'

'You're a fine one to talk. You didn't tell them anything, did you?'

'No, but I don't know anyone in the FBI. I've never met anyone like that in my life.'

'Sure you do. What about that Varrone fellow?'

'How do you know about Varrone?' He was shocked they knew Varrone's name. 'He's a colleague – he's got nothing to do with the FBI.'

'You're forgetting Eamonn made it his business to find

out who you knew. He had to learn about your life because he was pretending to be you when he was over there. One of the things he told us was that you had a friend who was an adviser of some sort.'

'But Varrone . . .' Lindow stopped. He looked over to his sister. The wind had got up and was fanning the embers of the fire. 'Look, if you let the women go, I'll talk to you. I'll do my best to help you.'

'Okay.' The man gave a smile that said nothing. 'I'll tell you what I'll do. If you agree to help us, I'll make sure they're safe at home by the time you get there later. That's as long as you co-operate with us, Con.'

'But what if I don't find Rhodes and Lasseur?'

'By Jesus, you've got a good memory there, Con,' said the man slyly. 'I just mention those names once and they're locked away in that memory of yours. A phenomenal brain is what you've got there, Con, a phenomenal brain to be sure.' He signalled to one of the men holding Lindow, a wiry young thug in a leather jacket. He seemed to know what he was meant to do for he jogged over to where Tag was being held, took her arm and led her towards the lane. When they were out of sight the man began speaking again. 'So are you going to do this thing for us?'

Lindow nodded.

'Okay, so you'll fly out to Boston tomorrow and telephone your friend Varrone. Mind not to tell him everything. Just say that you know it's a matter of life and death that you find these men. When you've found them, go to Melly's Bar in South Boston and ask for a man named P. J. McKenna. He's the fellow that runs the place. From the moment you give him the information you'll be off the hook. You'll never see or hear from us again, and your sister will be safe. Remember this, Con, you'll be handing us your brother's killers. We'll make amends for what happened to him and, if we're quick about it, we'll stop a lot of this mess in London. It's not doing anyone any good, least of all us.'

Lindow blinked at him. 'I don't understand any of this. I mean, the bombs are being planted in London so what makes you think these people are in the States?'

'Technology,' he said. 'Technology, that's the problem these days. Too much damned technology. Now, you've got the details right in your head, have you, Con?'

Con repeated the name of the man and his bar in South Boston.

'Good, because that's the only way you can contact us. There's one other thing. I don't want you blabbing your mouth off to the police. This business is between you and me. That's the way we'll keep it. Don't try and screw around with us, Con, because we can get to that young sister of yours any time we want.' He turned, keeping his eyes fixed on Con, adjusted his hat to the back of his head and walked back down the dock. 'So I'll be hearing from you in a few days,' he said.

A minute or two later, Lindow heard two cars start up and roar off down the lane. Then he was blindfolded and pushed across the field to a third vehicle. His head was forced down behind the driver's seat and a gun was pressed to his ear. Twenty minutes or so later, the car pulled up outside the White House, he was rolled out of the door and left sprawling in the driveway. He ripped off the blindfold to see his hire car parked a few feet away, and Tag and Mary running towards him.

'Don't tell Dad,' said Tag breathlessly, flinging her arms around Lindow. 'We said you wanted to take a longer walk. He doesn't know anything about it.'

The commissioner returned Foyle's call at three thirty that afternoon.

'Yes,' said the commissioner abruptly, 'I haven't got long, so please be brief, Commander.'

'In the light of this morning's discoveries, sir, I was

wondering if you'd reconsider your decision to take me off the case. I was right about the mechanism behind these bombs and I believe I'm in a better position than anyone to develop this inquiry.'

'I'm sorry, Commander. That's out of the question. I appreciate that you introduced this new line, but I have to bear in mind that the theory came from Con Lindow. That's part of my overall concern about the way you were handling things. So, to give you a straight answer, no, I won't be reconsidering my decision.'

'But we are making a mistake, sir. We are making a profound mistake to think of this as an Irish problem. There's something else in it all, I know it.'

'I'm sorry, Commander, I don't have the time to discuss this now. We'll talk in a few weeks.'

When he'd hung up Foyle dialled Forbes and asked why the commissioner had been so unyielding. Forbes told him that there had been some new developments that pointed to Lindow's guilt. The SIM card taken from the bomb scene that morning had belonged to a telephone with the exact same number as one that had appeared three times on Con Lindow's phone log. Lindow had called on Friday morning and then twice again on Monday. All three calls had been made in the morning, during the rush hour.

'What? That's not possible,' said Foyle.

'To make matters worse, we've just got pictures of Eamonn Lindow's funeral this morning. There's one of Con Lindow talking to Rudi MacMahon. They're standing together in the funeral procession. It certainly doesn't look good. He's on record as saying that he didn't know MacMahon. That's what he told Phipps.'

'What do you think?'

'I think it looks very bad. The instant Lindow gets back here, Scarratt will have him locked up again. And this time they won't wait before charging him. It doesn't help you much, does it?'

'No. There's one other thing. You remember the girl Lindow looked after in the street after the bus explosion? What happened to her?'

'She's still alive. We tried to interview her but the hospital wouldn't allow it.'

'Do we know if Lindow actually helped her, or was that just something he told us?'

'I don't think we've established that one way or the other.'

'Have you got her name there?'

'Yes, she's called Kay Gould – single, twenty-six years of age. I don't think we ever found out what she does for a living. She's still in hospital. Why do you want to know?'

'Thought I'd see if she's able to talk,' said Foyle.

'Well,' Forbes sounded doubtful, 'I wouldn't say too much about that if I were you, sir. It's breaking every rule in the commissioner's book.'

'Thanks for the advice. Keep me in touch, eh?'

Foyle hung up and prowled about his sitting room. Everything pointed now to Lindow's guilt and, moreover, to his own colossal failure of judgement. Perhaps it was true that he wasn't fit to be a policeman any longer, which Scarratt had made brutally clear when Foyle returned to Scotland Yard after the King's Cross bomb. He'd found Scarratt sitting at his desk, leafing through his papers. 'You've brought it upon yourself, Commander. I tried to give you advice, but you wouldn't listen. You need to listen to people at this level. It's the first requirement.'

Since his unceremonious departure from New Scotland Yard a few minutes later, he'd gone over everything and concluded that he would not have acted in any other way. He'd made errors, certainly, and he regretted his feeble grasp of the higher politics at the Met but, on the essentials of the case, he had been sure of his instincts.

The news of these calls from Lindow's flat worried

him. How could Lindow's behaviour be explained? He thought through the events of the last few days. The one point that Scarratt would not appreciate was that Lindow knew he was being watched and almost certainly suspected that his telephone was being tapped. That's why he had called from a phone box on Saturday. Foyle remembered hearing the sound of traffic in the background. If he had been going to detonate the bomb in King's Cross, he would hardly have used the phone in his flat. He must have made those calls innocently, thinking he was phoning someone else. That was it! Lindow had been tricked into making those calls, just as he had been on Thursday.

Foyle picked up his coat, felt inside the pockets for the three sets of keys he would need and left the house, slamming the door with unusual force. Half an hour later he produced his police warrant card at St Luke's Reception and was given directions to where Kay Gould lay in a private room. The sister in charge was reluctant to let Foyle see her, explaining that Kay had been on the brink of death when she was brought into the hospital and was still very weak. Foyle was on the point of leaving when a short dark man in an immaculately pressed white coat appeared in the corridor. After Foyle had shown his warrant card, he introduced himself as David Peretz, Kay Gould's specialist.

Foyle asked how she was doing.

'Remarkably well. She's got a lot stronger in the last thirty-six hours. I'm especially pleased with this case. She damn nearly didn't make it.'

'What about her face? I hear she was pretty badly cut.'

'Too soon to tell. But the damage was a lot less than we expected. She's a strong girl and she's doing a lot of the work herself. She's healing fast.'

'Is there any chance I could have a word with her?'

'Sorry, she's not up to it yet. Maybe at the end of the week. I'll have to see.'

'Did you operate on her when she was brought in after the bomb?'

'Yes.'

'How long was it before she got here?'

'Something over an hour, I'd say.'

'That would mean she was in the street with Lindow for nearly all that time.'

'Lindow ... was that the man you arrested?' Foyle nodded. 'Yes, apparently he looked after her pretty well. In fact, he contributed greatly to saving her life by insisting that she receive quick treatment.'

'So he stayed with Miss Gould all that time instead of making off?'

'Yes, and I believe he called on Sunday to see how she was doing.'

Foyle prepared to leave, but Peretz seemed eager to talk.

'We couldn't stop the haemorrhaging. At first I thought it was her liver, which wasted an awful lot of time. I was giving her blood by the gallon and she was slipping away from us, going into bleed out. Then I found that her spleen had been punctured by a piece of glass and we stemmed the bleeding. It was touch-and-go for a couple of hours after that. She stopped breathing, her heart stopped, but each time we revived her. She just refused to give up.'

Foyle didn't have the stomach for extensive medical descriptions, but he was moved by the doctor's pride. 'Look,' he said, 'is there a phone I can use in private?'

Peretz showed him to an empty office and left him. Foyle closed the door, dialled international directory inquiries and asked for a listing in Ireland. Less than a minute later he was speaking to Con Lindow in Bally-hanna. 'We need to talk. Are you alone?'

'Yes, what about?'

'You heard that we had another bomb in London this morning.'

196

'Yes, but I don't know much about it.'

'Right, what you don't know is that it was wired to a telephone, as you predicted. We now have the number of that telephone. The problem is that the same number appears on the phone records for your flat.'

'What? I didn't make those calls. You must know that.'

'It doesn't matter whether I believe you any more. I'm no longer leading the investigation.'

'What happened?'

'I've been replaced by a man named Scarratt and am now enjoying a holiday, largely because I let you go. This business of your phone records simply makes everyone certain that I got you wrong.' He paused. 'Did I get you wrong, Con?'

'Of course you didn't.'

'Whatever. The important point is that you are now very likely to be arrested and charged with conspiracy to cause explosions. The case against you is very strong – overwhelming, I'd say.'

There was a silence. Then Lindow asked, 'When were the calls made?'

'On Friday and Monday during the morning rush hour, which leads them to suppose that you were aiming for the maximum number of casualties. Can you remember who else you telephoned after you were released?'

Lindow was silent, trying to recall. He told Foyle he'd phoned his sister on the evening of his release and the following morning he'd rung Imperial College, the lawyers and the police. 'Hold on. I remember now. I also phoned the agent after he left a message on my machine, saying that he'd found a flat for me. He rang early. I've got the number – hang on a minute.'

He returned and read out the number. It matched the one Foyle had been given by Forbes an hour before – 08052 289476.

'That's it! And you rang that number three times?'

'Yes, I think so. Yes, once on Friday and twice on

Monday, nothing doing each time. I didn't keep trying because there was a lot to do before Eamonn's funeral. I decided to leave it until I got back.'

Foyle thought for a moment. 'If you're telling me the truth, the man who left that message on your machine is the bomber.'

'I *am* telling you the truth.'

'Did you wipe your messages before you left London?'

'No, I don't think so.'

'Right, I'm going round to your place. We'll need to talk later by phone. Will you be on this number?'

'Yes.'

Foyle had still got Lindow's keys. When he arrived outside the house he lingered in his car, watching the street for any movement. He looked up and saw that the windows of Lindow's first-floor flat were dark. He got out of his car and made for the front door.

Once inside he didn't switch on the lights, but groped his way to the kitchen where he opened the fridge. Just enough light spilled out to enable him to find the answering-machine in the sitting room. He pressed the playback button and listened.

There were a few messages that predated Lindow's arrest, then an estate agent named Robertson came on the line to ask why Lindow had failed to turn up for an appointment the day after the first explosion. He left a number, which Foyle noted down. The last message was from a Mr Lustig, who said he was Robertson's colleague and announced in a rapid voice that he'd found Lindow a flat. Lindow was instructed to ring a number between nine and ten that morning, or at the same time on Monday. Foyle knew, without checking, that the number given at the end of the message was the same one for the telephone hooked to the bomb in King's Cross.

The messages came to an end. Foyle pressed the eject button, removed the tape from the machine and placed it in his pocket. Then he closed the fridge door and left the flat.

Instead of returning to his car, he walked round the block to a telephone booth where he put a call through to the number in Ballyhanna. Lindow answered. 'Okay, I need you to find a phone outside the house and then to call me on this number. Can you do that?'

'Sure. Is it for the same reason that you didn't call me from my flat?'

'Yes.' Foyle gave him the number and hung up.

He waited for five minutes, watching a party of children dressed in Hallowe'en costumes, progressing up the street. The phone rang.

'You're right about the tape,' said Foyle. 'I've got it with me now and I want you to listen to it again.'

'Why didn't you play it over the phone to me from the flat?'

'The phone is tapped, as you appreciate, which is the reason I wanted to talk to you on a clean line. Look, I think we need to meet. There's a lot to discuss.'

'Yes.' Lindow paused. 'Have you heard of anyone called Rhodes or Lasseur?'

'Those were the names given to Forbes by his friend in the Ministry of Defence – the soldiers at Droy. Where the hell did you hear those names?'

'It's a long story. I was paid a visit this afternoon by some people, if you know what I mean. They mentioned them.'

'Have you heard of them before?'

'No, but Eamonn knew one of them. It's really too complicated to explain over the phone and I haven't got any more change. I'll tell you everything when we see each other.'

'You can't come to London. I'll have to come to you. I'll fly to Dublin and we'll meet in the airport. Can you get yourself down there this evening?'

Lindow said he could.

'Bring a suitcase. We'll need to spend some time on this. I'll see you in the main restaurant in the departures lounge. I should be there by nine thirty.'

Foyle rang off, then called Heathrow and booked himself on the seven thirty flight. He looked at his watch. He should just make it in the fifty minutes.

Lindow tramped back to the house and told his father that he had to leave, he had some urgent business in the States. He promised that he would be back as soon as possible to spend some time with him. Then he went to break the news to Tag, who was in the kitchen being calmed down by Mary. She was still pretty shaken. When he told her, she looked at him accusingly through her tears. Mary said nothing, but Lindow noticed her expression and her flickering eyes, which seemed to betray rapid processes of deduction.

Tag pleaded with him to stay, if only for their father's sake, although it was quite clear that she was fearful for herself as well. Mary intervened. 'If Con was worried about your safety, I'm certain he would stay here with you. Isn't that right, Con?'

'Of course. I can't say much at the moment, but it's best if I keep my head down for a few weeks before trying to go back to England. In fact, you'll be a lot safer if I'm in the States. This business I have there will sort things out for all of us.'

'What do you mean?' demanded Tag, both hands gripping the back of the kitchen chair. 'What can you sort out for us all? Are you working for the Provos? Is that what it's about? For God's sake, tell me.'

He took her in his arms. 'Believe me, I'm not working for anyone, Tag. I just can't say what I'm doing. There's no other way. I've got to go.'

He went upstairs to collect his things. Mary came into the room and touched his shoulder lightly. Lindow straightened from packing his bags to face her.

'Are you sure this is all right?' she asked.

'No, I am not.' Right now, he wished she wouldn't interfere.

'Then why are you going?'

'I've got to. They've threatened to hurt Tag.'

'Christ! Why?'

'I can't explain. It's too complicated.'

'Could you use some help on this? I've got family stuff to do over there anyway and two minds are better than one. You don't have to tell me what it is. I'll just be your bag-carrier, if you like.'

Without saying anything, he knelt to do up a suitcase. She touched his shoulder again and leaned down to kiss his cheek.

'And let me tell you,' she added. 'I really know Boston. I mean Boston Boston, not Harvard Boston.'

Lindow straightened again. 'Haven't you got to get back to London? Work and all that.'

'It can wait. I am freelance, remember?'

'Look, this could be dangerous – and, frankly, I haven't the first idea what I'm going to do.'

'But you'd like me to come along, right?'

'Sure . . . er, sure. If you want to and you've got the time, I'd like it a lot.' He was surprised at himself for having agreed so readily.

'Good. I'll stay here tonight and look after Tag and your dad, then I'll get a flight tomorrow from London.'

She gave him the name of a hotel in the centre of Boston and said she'd aim to get there late the next day. Then they went downstairs. Lindow hugged his father and sister, exchanged nods with Mary and climbed into his car.

Foyle found Lindow sitting in the Silver Lining restaurant with a cup of coffee. He walked over to him and sat down, placing a duty-free bag on the table.

'You look terrible,' said Lindow.

'You don't look so good yourself,' said Foyle. He produced a new tape-recorder from the bag and fitted it with batteries.

'Now, I want you to listen to this again very carefully and tell me if you recognise the voice.'

He inserted the microcassette from Lindow's answering-machine. The voice began in a flat London accent, but near the end of the message, when the man instructed Lindow to ring him between nine and ten on either Friday or Monday, it assumed a terse note of command. Foyle remarked on it.

'It could be anyone.' Lindow sounded despairing. 'The disturbing thing is that not only was this man trying to incriminate me, he must have known about my movements before the bomb in Clarence Street. He knew I was looking for a flat.'

'Yes, he may well have listened in to your calls last week.' Foyle noticed the restaurant was filling up. 'You know, I'd rather not talk here. What do you say we book into a couple of rooms in one of the hotels near the airport and discuss this over some food?'

Twenty minutes later they had checked into a large anonymous establishment decorated with garish lithographs of rural Ireland.

Foyle said that he'd put both rooms on his credit card and told Lindow to register as J. Peters.

'I don't want any kind of audit trail,' said Foyle. 'If I'm ever asked who J. Peters is, I will say it's my girlfriend and that, for appearances' sake, she likes to take a separate room.'

Lindow smiled and went off to deposit the bags in his room, while Foyle went straight to the restaurant and chose a table beside an oblong aquarium, where he sat down and watched a small black fish with whiskers position itself in a stream of oxygen.

When Lindow rejoined him he said, 'I read somewhere that you can only put fish from the same lake in the same tank. That way they don't kill each other. But if you put a strange fish in they kill it. I'm sure there's some kind of metaphor in that, but I don't know what.'

'There isn't. Things in nature just are. They don't have to have cute lessons for humanity.'

Foyle was surprised by his tone. 'You need food. I've ordered two steaks and some wine. That should set you up. Now, tell me what happened today.'

The wine arrived and Foyle listened to Lindow's account of the funeral and being snatched that afternoon. He pressed him for the exact words used by MacMahon and then for a description of the man by the lake.

'It seems likely that you had the pleasure of meeting Raymond H. McCreath – Chickpea McCreath. He's quite a legend. He gets his name from an incident back in the seventies when he replaced the lead shot in a twelve-bore cartridge with chickpeas. That way he could make one hell of a mess of someone's body but be sure not to kill them. He was one of the IRA's chief quartermasters but he was also an enforcer. When someone was misbehaving, skimming from IRA funds, he'd be brought in to sort them out. There was talk of him coming out of retirement to help the Sinn Fein leadership. If it was him, you can assume that he was working with Rudi Mac-Mahon. MacMahon and McCreath are part of the IRA, which is an indication of your brother's loyalties. Mac-Mahon is on the political side and McCreath has been deployed as the muscle. Anyone that looks like breaking away from the republican movement is paid a visit by Chickpea and his friends and is persuaded to toe the line. They have one chance. If the dissidents persist, they're beaten or killed.

'We received an intelligence briefing from Belfast a few weeks ago, which explained that McCreath had also been put in charge of retrieving IRA supplies that had fallen into the hands of the rebel republicans. It's not a pretty business. Several of the hard men from South Armagh have turned up dead. Others have been snuffed out in their beds. Very clean, very silent. Six months ago a woman in the border country woke up in the morning to find that her husband had been shot through the head with a silencer while she slept.'

'Jesus, my countrymen!'

'McCreath knows what sort of supplies are out there and, more important, where they're likely to be hidden. That's why they pulled him back. He's a real mystery man. The authorities have no idea what he looks like. The only picture of him was taken thirty years ago. He's never been arrested. In fact, the security forces almost wondered if he was a myth, like that old joke – Eamonn Wright.'

Lindow looked puzzled. 'Sorry?'

Foyle put down his glass. 'For years the police heard about a sniper called Eamonn Wright. He was killing British soldiers by the dozen. They could never track him down although everyone talked about him on the streets. Then eventually someone got the pun – aiming right.'

'That's sick,' said Lindow. 'So what you're saying is that the IRA believe the London bombs were the work of the rebel faction. Is that why Eamonn was killed?'

'No, it's not that easy. The bombs are too sophisticated. The Explosives Unit hadn't seen a device like the King's Cross bomb before. It was connected to a telephone, a timer and two anti-handling devices. The man who made it and then left that message on your machine intended that it would explode even if you never called.'

'But I did call. Why didn't it go off?'

'It's very simple. After the bomb was driven there, some scaffolding was erected on the adjacent building plot and clad with a mesh screen. This had the effect of blocking the signal from the cell antennae. The timer would have detonated the bomb this morning, but it was set on British Summer Time, so the disposal officer just had time to grab the important parts of the telephone before the whole thing went up. It was a very near thing.'

'So where does all this leave you?'

'A better question is, where does it leave you, Con? You see, I'm just a policeman now on enforced leave. I have no responsibility for this case at all. You, on the other hand, are in this thing right up to your neck. I'm here to help you and I want to, but you've got to help me, Con. Those names they mentioned to you this afternoon. You say that Eamonn knew them.'

'Only one of them.' Lindow dug inside the breast pocket of his jacket. 'I found this hidden in Eamonn's flat last Friday. You can see it's a fake US passport in my name. You will also see that Eamonn used it to travel to the US on four occasions. He was there in the last five weeks.'

Foyle examined the passport and picked up the paper that Lindow had placed in front of him.

'These are compass bearings. Originally I thought the word Rhodes referred to the place or a ship. Then I did some work with the atlases in the library.'

'That's what you were doing there.'

'So, I *was* being watched. I thought as much. That woman – was she yours?'

'No. She was the other lot – MI5.'

Lindow shrugged and produced the photostats of the maps of Ireland and the north-east coast of America.

Foyle pushed them back to Lindow's side of the table. 'Put those away. Just talk me through it.'

Lindow looked around. 'There's no one here, surely.'

'Nevertheless, I'd prefer you to talk me through it.'

'Well, the crucial point is that the bearings on the paper were taken from two towns in Maine, not in Ireland. Coincidentally they're called Belfast and Limerick. It was the magnetic variation that put me on to it. The one stated by Eamonn is too big for Ireland. Of course, I didn't know what Rhodes meant. Then this afternoon McCreath mentioned someone called Rhodes and I realised that Eamonn had left exact instructions on how to find him and, presumably, this other man, Lasseur.

'I nearly told them. Then I thought that if they were forcing me to find this man – which they are, because they're threatening my sister – at least I've got a head start. But they must have known Eamonn was on to something because they said that they'd tried to search his flat for a missing package. I assume the information is pretty new.'

'You can also assume', said Foyle, 'that they know you've got it and will be aware of your movements in the United States – that's if you go.' Foyle drained the bottle into Lindow's glass and ordered another. 'Do you know who Rhodes and Lasseur are?'

'No, I don't.'

'They're two former British Army officers. Both of them were at Droy when the cemetery blew up.'

Lindow was incredulous. 'Are you sure?'

'On Monday a colleague of mine acquired the names of the soldiers involved in the operation. Someone was trying to stop us which was interesting in itself but, leaving that aside, it means you've got a lot of explaining to do.'

Lindow's glass was poised at his lips. 'My head is beginning to spin with all this. Are you saying that two British soldiers blew up Eamonn, then tried to implicate me in revenge for something that happened in 1983? Why have they waited so long?'

'Who knows? But I can tell you now that you weren't the only one tricked into making a call. I was too. I didn't think anything of it until you came up with your theory about detonation by telephone. You see, Blackett had been asked to call the same mobile number as me.'

'Who's Blackett?'

'Blackett's the man who interrogated you and Eamonn after the Droy explosion.'

'But, as far as I remember, there were four or five police officers who questioned us. They worked in rotation.'

'Yes, but Blackett was the man in charge. The point is that neither of us had left a message for the other, but both of us received a message to call the same number. I was the one who called it first.'

Lindow slumped back in his chair. 'What's this guy about?'

'He's playing a game, a very subtle game, which may have something to do with Ireland. Or it may simply be the product of a deranged mind – something on the lines of the Unabomber in the States. Still, it does seem to point to Ireland. With the exception of myself, the bombs have involved three people who were all connected with Droy – you and Eamonn were both suspects and Blackett was the investigating officer.'

'But where do you fit in? Why did he get you to make that call?'

'I was thinking about that on the plane. It's a kind of joke. He tricks the head of Scotland Yard's Anti-terrorist Unit into detonating a device that the hapless Commander Plod is then expected to investigate. Very neat, when you think about it.'

'So why haven't you told your colleagues?'

'As of midday today my services were no longer required. I am a non-person as far as the commissioner is concerned. And, besides, no one would believe me. But we're getting away from the main point here, aren't we? The line that runs through all these bombs is Droy. Rhodes was at Droy, you were at Droy, Eamonn was there and Blackett was the investigating officer. I need enlightening, Con.'

Foyle sensed that Lindow was wrestling with something. 'Yes, Con?'

'I wasn't there. I was nowhere near the place when it blew up. We just stopped there for Eamonn to take a piss.'

'Look, I'm not fucking around here,' said Foyle. 'I know you didn't cause any of this. But now you have to say what happened. Why has Rhodes come back? What made him flip?' He held Lindow's eyes with an intense glare, defying him to look the other way. 'You are the only person who can stop it all. The only person, do you hear?'

'I wasn't there,' Lindow repeated deliberately. 'I wasn't there.'

Chapter Ten

Lindow watched Foyle push back his chair, wipe his mouth vigorously and turn to look at the black catfish, which had come to rest on the side of the tank, its grey mouth suckered to the glass. 'For a clever fellow, Dr Lindow, you're one hell of a daft cunt.'

He said nothing.

'You don't see we're in this together,' Foyle said. He placed a finger on the glass by the catfish. 'Like I said before, we're two creatures at the bottom of the sea, trying to see their way. We need each other, but at present you need me much more than I need you. My career is strictly past tense, but you – you're up to your neck in trouble. The bomber won't be content to leave you be. He'll come after you. He's clever – cunning as hell – and he'll have you like he had Eamonn. Why you two is what I'm wondering. Tell me what he's got against you?'

'It's plain enough,' said Lindow, bridling at Foyle's manner. 'He believes that we were responsible for the explosion at Droy.'

'We – plural!' Foyle said the last word with such force that the other diners in the Kerry Carvery swivelled round to look at them. '"We" is not the word I'd use in this context. "I" is the word you're looking for, Con. You blew up that dump and killed all those soldiers and now the thing that you erased from your past has come back to besiege you. It's taken your brother's life and a good many others besides. There isn't any "we" about it, is there? It's all due to what you did seventeen years ago, and you won't even bloody well admit it to yourself. Why don't you say something? Come on, get it off your chest, man. If you tell me what happened I won't be able to do anything about it. It's all long gone. You won't be charged. It'll just be between you and me.'

'You've made your point,' said Lindow. 'Let me just say this. Droy was an accident.'

'That's it!'

'Yes. That's all there is to it.'

Lindow wasn't going to say any more. What Foyle did not know, could not know because Lindow had only just begun to see it himself, was that he had changed. The bomb, two days of interrogation, the wretchedness of Eamonn's funeral, the pummelling from the IRA and the vague but persistent guilt over Eamonn's death had come together to form a crude resolve.

He knew well that he had always let life come at him and that he used the gifts of his mind to avoid any sort of confrontation. It bothered him sometimes, and he'd once tried going to a shrink after his mother's death. The sessions had lasted only two or three months. Before he gave them up, the therapist had suggested that this lack of engagement stemmed from his mother's overpowering personality. He had simply dealt with everything else in his life the same way, deftly manipulating people to find the way of least resistance. 'Low-risk evasion strategies' was what she'd called them. She told him it was the reason he'd never fallen in love. Relationships involved too much exposure and threatened his cover.

Lindow hadn't liked what she'd said, but he conceded that the string of lab assistants and students who found their way to his bed had been selected precisely because they offered no risk and wanted little more than fleeting physical contact. The ones that had hoped for more – the girls who showed up once too often at his rambling apartment overlooking the Charles River – were quickly dumped.

As Foyle went on about the need to work together, Lindow was thinking not so much about what he should do, but about the rather astonishing fact that he was actually going to do *something*. He had no plan, no sense of how he'd get to the people who had killed Eamonn. But he'd make sure he found them and pass the information to the people who would put an end to them. It seemed unlikely that this would be the British authorities, who were lumbering several miles behind Foyle's understanding of the case. Much better to deal straight with the thugs he'd encountered that afternoon. In fact, he would do exactly as the man in the trilby had instructed. He'd make the connections and he'd try to locate the place where Rhodes was meant to be. At the same time, he'd keep the British on side in the hope that eventually he could resume his life in London. That was why he needed Foyle. He was out in the cold, but he'd be an excellent conduit if the trip to America did produce something. Foyle wanted to vindicate himself and would help.

He poured himself another glass of wine.

'So what're you going to do?' asked Foyle. 'Fly off to America then blunder about in the undergrowth of Maine? What then? It's not going to be easy for you to return to Britain, you know, not unless you want another few sessions with Phipps.'

'I'll see how things work out. I've got plenty of people I can stay with over there, and money isn't a problem.'

'Yes, but you can't just let things stand as they are. There has to be some sort of solution. Don't you see that?'

Lindow nodded slowly.

'Tell me about this girl, Mary Menihan. You mentioned she was with you when you were taken this afternoon. Was it her idea that you went for a walk? Did she suggest where you went?'

'No, to both questions. Why do you ask?'

'Just wondered. She seems to pop up at interesting times, that's all. I'm right in thinking that she called Eamonn's flat when you found the package? How did she know that you were going to be there?'

'She said she guessed. Are you implying Mary has got something to do with all this?'

'You've got to admit it does look like that from the outside. She's from Boston and she was a friend of Eamonn's, which could mean that she was working with him. She may have turned up at the flat to retrieve a package the IRA knew was there. It fits perfectly.'

'Well, if she is, I'll find out soon enough. She's meeting me over there tomorrow.'

'Christ, she's sticking to you like a sheep tick. Be a good boy and don't take her to bed, Con.'

Lindow wondered about her reasons for staying in Britain. And Foyle was right – she had turned up at the flat. It was as if she didn't want to miss anything.

'I'll remember what you say.'

'Good,' said Foyle, 'because the Provos may just be using you.'

'How?'

'They probably know a lot more than you suspect. They could be sending you over there to draw the fire. They won't give a shit what happens to you.'

'But you're using me too, aren't you? You haven't told me to come back to Britain with you tomorrow because you think there's a slender chance of me finding out things that will put you back in your command.'

'Nah,' said Foyle dismissively. 'There's not much hope of that. The thing that drives me is that I want to find the man or men who did those things to your brother and Kay Gould – and the others. When you take away the intrigue of this affair, you're left with a lot of bodies and several people with their faces missing.'

Lindow thought of Eamonn in the hospital, the look of dumb resignation that had clouded his face for ever. Foyle was right. That's what it came down to: death and mutilation. And now he was following his brother, taking up the pursuit of Rhodes where Eamonn had left off.

Before they left the restaurant for their beds, Foyle gave Lindow his home number and told him he could also be reached through Inspector Graham Forbes at New Scotland Yard. Forbes, he said, was utterly trustworthy. Meanwhile, he would see what he could find out about Rhodes and Lasseur. 'I'll be off early in the morning, Con, so I won't see you. But stay in touch, and good luck.'

Lindow woke at nine, showered quickly and rang the airport to get a seat on the next plane to Boston. Then he took out Eamonn's false passport, examined the picture and raised it against himself in the mirror. Their faces were alike and his brother's weight loss helped, but Eamonn's hair was further receded, also wirier and darker. He put down the passport and went to the hotel shop, where he bought a pair of manicure scissors, a small tub of hair wax and a sachet of wash-out dye. He returned to his room, thinking that it was indeed a bizarre task to make himself look like Eamonn who had been trying to look like him. He gingerly removed the plaster from the back of his head, then cut the hair from his forehead back to the hairline. He rinsed a quarter of the dye into his hair, rubbed some wax on to his hands and ran them through his still-wet hair. While he waited for his hair to dry, he arranged for the hire car to be picked up from Departures at the airport, then called Peter Varrone's office voice-mail and left a message to say he was arriving that afternoon and would be staying at the Omni Parker Hotel in the centre of town. He used the office number because it was still the early hours in Boston and he didn't want to risk waking Varrone at home. An hour and a half later Lindow passed into the departures lounge without a hitch and boarded the plane to Boston.

The flight was only half full and he was able to stretch out. He drifted in and out of sleep, going over the conversations he'd had with Mary. He tried to remember exactly what she'd told him about her life. He had the impression that her father ran a business in the Boston area, that her parents were divorced and that she had money of her own, but he wasn't sure about any of it. In fact, the more he thought about it, the more certain he became that Mary had told him little about herself. She handled herself well in conversation, never gave much away and was always right up to the mark, coolly anticipating the other person's thoughts. Come to think of it, she'd been damned cool after their experience at the lake.

The plane was ahead of schedule at Boston, the first of the European flights to land that morning. The lines at US Immigration were short and moving quickly. Lindow found himself in front of a young officer. His eyes flicked between the passport and Lindow's face. The man turned and hit a few keys on his computer terminal. Satisfied, he held out the passport.

Lindow hurried away to collect his bags. He was soon outside in the sharp Boston air, making plumes with his breath and looking across Boston harbour to the towers of the city's business centre. They glinted in the flawless white wintry sunlight.

He took a cab and checked into the Omni Parker. No sooner had he set his bags down in his room than the telephone rang. Varrone's voice came on the line, smooth and reassuring. 'Couldn't keep away from us, huh?'

He muttered a reply.

'I'm working at home today, writing a briefing for the White House about quantum computing. The President wants a paper to read over the Thanksgiving holiday, would you believe? Why don't you come over and release me from this insufferable grind?'

Twenty minutes later Lindow pressed the entryphone beside a pair of discreet iron gates near the crest of Beacon Hill in the centre of Boston. From the outside, Varrone's home looked like a normal-sized townhouse, but he had also bought the properties either side and knocked them through to create two huge galleries on the first and second floors. Lindow had never asked his friend how much he was worth, but he'd seen figures in the press that referred to the sale of VBSS – Varrone Business Software and Systems – for a hundred and thirty million dollars. After the sale of his company he'd returned to teaching, writing and the activity he termed envisioning. When Lindow and Varrone had first met at a conference on 'The Future', Varrone had given a paper which held that what was imaginable, but technically unfeasible, in the present would determine the development of the future. The very act of imagining laid a trail into the future. Lindow had disagreed violently with the audience, saying that each new problem required lines of reasoning that would necessarily lead to solutions that no one could predict. They'd talked afterwards and hit it off, although Varrone was nearly twenty years older than Lindow.

The gates clicked open. Lindow made his way to the front door where Varrone appeared in his familiar working gear – plaid shirt, bulky blue cardigan, beige cords and sneakers. His eyes shone through a pair of heavy tortoiseshell spectacles and his hands quivered rapidly as if he was shaking water from them.

'My God, have you joined the music industry?' he asked, with a critical squint at Lindow's hair. 'What in the hell have you done to yourself? Come in and tell me about it.'

He led Lindow into a long kitchen where the cook was placing a dish of lasagne and a salad on the table. Varrone collected beer from the fridge and gestured to Lindow to sit down and help himself. 'What's going on?' he said, when they were both seated and the cook had departed silently through a side door. 'The London police called me after the bomb. It was big news on the TV. I was worried for you. They said your brother was injured and you'd been arrested. I told the guy they were being idiots. They didn't take a bit of notice. Are you still in trouble?'

'You could say that.'

'And the hair? It's awful.'

'I was trying to look like Eamonn looking like me. It's going to take a bit of time to explain.'

Lindow told his story, pausing only when his friend needed the order of events clarified. After an hour, Lindow reached the end of his tale and leaned forward to pour himself another beer. On the plane he had taken the decision not to tell Varrone what the IRA had said about him and the FBI. It wouldn't help.

Varrone sat, chin resting on his clasped hands. His expression was unusually solemn. 'There's one thing I don't understand. What do you hope to achieve by coming here and hightailing it up to the mountains with a compass? Even if you do find these guys, you're hardly equipped to deal with them. By what you say, they're professionals. You're not trained for this kind of work.'

'What else can I do? I can't go back to Britain because I'll be arrested. I can't stay in Ireland because it would endanger Tag's life. I had to come here, if only to make contact with their people and show that I'm doing what I can to find these guys. And there's Eamonn – I realise that I won't be free of this thing unless I do something to find Eamonn's killers. This is my responsibility. I owe Eamonn.'

'I understand that – really I do. But you're out of your depth with this thing. You're going to get yourself killed, Con. Aside from anything else, you'll be depriving mankind of a superb microbiologist. This isn't you! You can't handle it.'

'I've got to. That's the way it is.'

'Well, if you're bent on this thing, I'll help you. I'm going to put you in touch with a former student of mine, Frank Mundy. Frank works at the FBI here in Boston. He's a smart kid, one of the best students I ever had. He got himself a law degree then went into the Bureau. Go talk to him. There isn't anything he doesn't know about the Irish American community here. He was wired right into the Irish crews, as he likes to call them. I'm sure he'll be able to help you locate these guys.'

They went into Varrone's long sitting room where Lindow was left to inspect a fossil of an ichthyosaur, which Varrone had placed in the middle of the room on a raised slate platform. The beast was perfectly preserved. Its flippers worked at the rock and the long serrated bill was opening to snap at a prey that had vanished forty million years ago. It was as if it had been turned to stone in mid-stroke. He walked around the room, marvelling at Varrone's eclectic taste: four works on paper by Rothko, a sheet of calculations in Einstein's hand, a minute Leonardo sketch of a man levering a boulder, and a model of Watson and Crick's double helix.

The murmur of Varrone's voice came from behind the door and Lindow couldn't make out what he was saying. After about ten minutes, his head appeared in the doorway.

'He says he'll see you tomorrow. He's still on the phone. You can make the arrangement with him now.'

Lindow went into Varrone's workroom, a vast well-lit

study with several screens and an enormous computer box. He picked up the phone and said hello.

'Hey, Dr Lindow, Frank Mundy here,' announced a vinegary Boston twang. 'The professor says you need advice. What you say we meet tomorrow outside my office at the JFK Building? You know it? Right. There's a memorial to the first transmission of sound by telephone there. Seems the appropriate place to meet, given the problems you've been having in London. See you there at ten tomorrow.'

Lindow hung up and joined Varrone in the sitting room.

'He's the perfect man for this,' said Varrone, letting himself down on to a sofa. 'I told him as much as I could – about the phones and Rhodes and Lasseur. He'd heard about Rhodes, but he wasn't sure about the other guy, so I guess he'll fix you up with some information. But he'll want something for himself. Tell him as much as you can. Leave out the stuff about you and the cemetery. He won't need that and, anyway, it's a long time ago. But don't spare any detail on the current stuff. That's what he'll want to hear about. I promised him it was going to be a two-way thing.'

'Thanks, Peter. You've been a good friend.'

'It's nothing. But, if you don't mind, I have to get back to work. I have to get this thing drafted by the end of the day and sent to the White House. Shall we do dinner tomorrow night?'

'Yes, if I'm still in Boston. Oh, by the way, I don't want anyone to know I'm here. That okay with you?'

Varrone nodded, got up and grasped Lindow by the shoulders. 'Look after yourself, Con, and use your brain. That way you'll get out of this thing alive. You'll call me after you've seen Frank, right?'

Lindow let himself out of the house and walked down to Charles Street where he hailed a cab to Harvard Square. On the flight he'd made a mental list of what he

218

would need. The first thing that had occurred to him was a proper set of maps, and he knew he'd be able to find them in the Globe Corner Book Store, which lay just off Harvard Square. After browsing through the shelf devoted to Maine, he bought a guide published by the Appalachian Mountain Club that included lists of lodgings and hotels, a highway map of the state and the *Maine Atlas and Gazetteer*, which contained forbiddingly large areas of wilderness marked simply by the numbers of the state's geographic code. The next stop was a good hiking and mountaineering shop, for which he had to return across the Charles River to the centre of Boston. He found the store and bought a compass, a torch, a pair of lightweight hiking boots, an all-weather jacket and a small pair of binoculars. He paid by credit card.

By now, night was falling and the weather had closed in on the city, shrouding the top of the taller buildings with veils of mauve cloud. Lindow made his way back to the hotel and set out his equipment on the bed. He unfolded the highway map and scrutinised it under the bedside light. He'd be able to calculate where the two bearings crossed much more precisely in daylight, but he knew he'd be within a few miles of the location. With the scarcity of any kind of development up near the Allagash River, that would be all the accuracy needed. But what would he do when he got there? He had no plans to tackle Rhodes and Lasseur. Instead he'd hide out and watch the place. The one advantage he had was that they wouldn't be expecting him. Lindow folded the map and made a note on the hotel paper to remind himself to find the best camera store in Boston. Then he lay on the bed watching CNN. If the phone hadn't rung, he would have woken the next morning in his clothes.

'Con, I have a question for you.' It was Mary.

'Where are you?'

'In the lobby. This is my question. Are we going to economise on tonight, or what?'

'What do you mean?'

'Jesus, Con, you can be awful dumb sometimes. If we're going to spend the night together I don't want to waste two hundred dollars on another room.'

He was shocked – delighted. 'Very practical,' he said, smiling into the phone. 'And also very unromantic.'

'Try me.'

He gave her his room number and, in a very short time, Mary was beaming at his door and complaining that her plane from London had been carrying a basketball display team, each one of whom had made a pass at her.

She walked in and looked at Lindow's purchases. 'What's all this? Going hiking? You weren't going to leave your lover behind, were you?'

'You aren't my lover.'

'But I will be by the time you go hiking.'

Lindow put his arms around her and smelt her hair. She pulled her head back and made a face. 'What've you done to yourself? You look like—'

'Like someone in the record industry. I know.'

'No, it's more a kind of street-junkie look. The pallor is just the right side of dead.'

She touched his cheek with her fingertips. 'Dinner first,' she said. 'I need food now – never eat in the air. I'll show you a place down near the fish pier. It's full of scary Italian garbage collectors with pinkie rings.'

Lindow kissed her, brushing her lips tentatively with his. Then they left the room, content to delay the moment when they lay in each other's arms.

The restaurant was noisy and full, but Mary got a table by giving the proprietor a wickedly suggestive look. She told him later that her father did business with the man, who'd made a fortune developing the land around his restaurant and now ran it as a social accessory.

'So what's been going on?' she said accusingly, when they were seated. 'You've gone all mysterious since that thing at the lake yesterday. Shit, you know, I thought they were going to kill us.'

'I did too.' He resented being dragged back to reality.

'Are you going to do what they told you?'

'How do you know that they told me to do something?'

'It's obvious. You take off without a word of explanation and catch the first plane here. Tag told me you knew something. She wouldn't say what it was, except that Eamonn had left you something. And then those guys by the lake – the IRA – they told you something too, didn't they? They think the men letting off the bombs are here, right? And they've told you to find them, right? So you come here to find them and either deal with the problem yourself, though I can't imagine how you would do that, or tell someone else who will deal with the problem. But you're not sharing any of it with me, Con, because you don't trust me. Is that it?'

'No, I trust you. It's just that you don't need to know what I know.'

'So you *do* know who these guys are? You've got names, right?'

'What is this? An interrogation? Look, do we need to talk about this now? I've lived it every second of the past nine days and, frankly, I'd like a break.'

Mary leaned forward, placing her hands on top of Lindow's. 'It's just that I care about you, Con. I don't know how it's happened so soon, but you're important to me. I care what happens to you. And I worry that you think you can take on these people. They've killed your brother and they'll kill you too, if they get a chance.'

Lindow was embarrassed at the suddenness of her declaration. 'That's strange,' he said, looking down. 'Someone said that to me last night.'

'Well, it's true. How do you expect to do this thing on your own?'

'All I need to do is establish where they are – nothing

221

else. I'm finding out as much as I can here, then I'll go to Maine and have a look around.'

'But it's not going to be that simple. This is serious stuff, Con, and you're an amateur.'

'And I suppose you're the pro?' He looked at her hard. He was now beginning to believe Foyle's warning about her. 'What's your interest in this, Mary? Are you here because of me, or something else?'

'I am here for you.'

'And . . . ?' He waved his fork. 'Who else? Are you working for someone?'

'Who, for Chrissakes? I'm a goddam book editor!'

'The Provisionals, for instance?'

'Fuck you, Con.' Her eyes flashed with temper. 'Fuck you.'

The meal ended quickly and in silence. They barely spoke on the way back to the hotel. Mary sat in the cab staring sullenly out of the window while Con was kept awake only by the motion of the cab bouncing over Boston's potholes. Once in the hotel room, they undressed without the slightest thought of making love. Mary showered, while Lindow collapsed into bed and straight away entered a clammy, restless sleep. An hour later he woke. Mary shifted beside him and raised her head from the pillow to peer at his face in the light that came from a crack in the curtains. He turned to her. She sat up and moved towards him. 'Don't do a thing,' she said. 'Just relax.'

She worked her way round to behind his head, lifted it and placed it in the cradle formed by her crossed legs. Lindow could feel the softness and abundant warmth of her lap. She began with his right arm, holding it up and gently working the joints, then rubbing the flesh and the muscles downwards towards his fingers where she locked her hands with his and kneaded his palm. She did the same with his left arm, taking care to avoid the weal on the biceps. He could feel the tension draining from him and gave himself completely to her touch. Then she moved her hands to his shoulders, pushing the skin up to the nape of his neck and using the base of her palms to massage the knots of muscle along the ridge of his shoulders. Her fingers splayed upwards into his hair, pausing to negotiate the scab at the back of his head, and then ran behind his ears and down to his Adam's apple. She lifted his head again, and revolved it in her hands.

After a little while she eased her legs sideways and lowered his head to the pillow. Lindow was still awake and aching for her touch. He hoped that she would not leave off yet and murmured something. She bent down to catch it. '*Acushla*,' he said again.

'What's that?' she whispered.

'It means darling in Gaelic.'

'*Acushla* – I like that.' She straddled his stomach and trickled her fingertips across his eyelids, down to his cheeks. He could feel the hair between her legs brush his stomach and her breasts graze over his chest, but he did not reach up.

Then he was asleep again.

Next morning Lindow woke to find Mary gone and a note on the pillow. 'Don't leave without me,' it ran. 'Seeing my dad – back by noon.'

There were a couple of hours yet before Lindow was due to meet Mundy so he breakfasted on some apricot juice and crackers from the minibar then unfolded the highway map of Maine. He'd need a larger ruler to work out the exact position from the bearings, but he could see that he'd have to aim for a point west of the Allagash Wilderness. He guessed it was about six or seven hours by car, perhaps more. Up in the north the roads became tracks and it would be slow going.

He left the hotel and walked the short distance to the windy plaza in front of City Hall. On his left was the John F. Kennedy Building, a twenty-two-storey block with a hundred-yard limb of low offices stretching out in its shadow. He took up position by the memorial at the front of the building and examined the bas-relief of the telephone, which looked like a small printing press. There was an inscription dedicated to the first transmission of sound by wire, in June 1875, from a building close to that spot.

'Hey there, Dr Lindow.' He turned round to see an exceptionally tall man in a long black overcoat advancing from the entrance of the building. He was in his mid-thirties with a vigorous brush of greying hair and alert, expressive blue eyes. He thrust his hand forward and gripped Lindow's. 'Special Agent Mundy – Frank Mundy. Pleased to meet you, Dr Lindow. Hey, you want some coffee? There's a Starbucks across the square.'

They sat on stools in the coffee-shop, looking out on the FBI building.

'I guess Peter told you that I'll be happy to help you, but that I want something in return. For a start, we want to know what's going on in London. Those bombs interested Washington a hell of a lot. The stuff about telephones hasn't been made public. It's the kind of gimmick that'll appeal to any number of our home-bred loony-tune militiamen. So, why don't you start by telling me about it?'

Lindow ran through everything that Foyle had told him about the wiring of the third bomb, then the circumstances of the previous explosions.

'So tell me about your brother,' said Mundy, reaching for a napkin. 'Why does this policeman – Foyle's his name, right? – why does he believe your brother was the target? A lot of people were killed on that bus.'

'It's complicated. The obvious reason is that Eamonn was working for the Provisionals. He knew who the bomber was and was killed before he could tell anyone.'

'And what's the un-obvious reason?'

'That it may have something to do with an explosion

years ago near where we lived. We were both arrested and questioned afterwards. We weren't charged.'

'And it's been suggested to you that one of the guys at the scene of the explosion came back after all these years to take his revenge on Eamonn. And this guy's name is Rhodes and he's pitched up in Maine. Right?'

'Right.'

'Okay. So why are you here? If it *is* Rhodes, he's probably in London, not here. Why don't you tell all this to the British authorities?'

'For the reason that I can't go back to London because a lot of people think I'm the bomber. The other reason is that I had an ugly encounter with some people in Ireland a couple of days back – Provisionals. They made it plain that they'd hurt my sister unless I came over to look for Rhodes.'

'I'm missing something here. Why would they think you'd know how to find him? Like the professor says, you're a scientist, Dr Lindow. What would you know about this kind of work?'

'I don't pretend to know anything.'

'Yes, but you're leaving something out, aren't you, my friend? There's something you haven't told me.'

Lindow pulled out the passport and slid it towards Mundy, who flattened it open on the bar with his palm.

'I believe I'm looking at a federal offence here, Dr Lindow.' He wasn't smiling.

'I know, but it's the only thing I could do. The British are holding my passport. I had to use this to get here.'

Mundy continued to look at the passport. 'It's a pretty good job.'

'In the back of the passport I found this scrap of paper written by my brother.' Lindow reached for his wallet where he had slipped it behind an old MIT library card. He removed it and showed it to Mundy. 'These are two compass bearings from Belfast and Limerick. Originally I thought they were in Ireland, but they're not. They're in

Maine. The magnetic variation or declination gives it away. Twenty degrees is far too large for Ireland. And here you see the name Rhodes and this odd phrase Axiom Day.'

'I know Belfast – it's on the coast,' said Mundy. 'But I haven't heard of Limerick.'

'It's in the south-west of the state, a very small town.'

'So the idea is that Rhodes, or his base or whatever, is at the place where these two bearings meet?'

'Yes.'

'Do you have any idea what Axiom Day means?'

'None at all.'

'There's another thing I don't understand,' said Mundy. 'If you had all this stuff, why didn't you hand it straight to the IRA, or the police? It would have gotten one of them off your case.'

'It was a question of timing,' said Lindow. 'I'd more or less decided to give it to Foyle at Scotland Yard. That's why I didn't tell the Provisionals about it by the lake. Then later that day I talked to Foyle in London. He told me that the number of the phone attached to the bomb corresponded with a number on my phone records. They still think that I tried to set off the bomb.'

'Jesus, what a fucking mess. Seems kind of rough on you, this whole thing.' Mundy paused to weigh up something in his head. The easy-going manner had disappeared. Lindow knew that he was being sized up and Mundy was not a person to cross. 'You're not bullshitting me, Dr Lindow? I mean, I know you're a good friend of the professor's and all, but I can't afford to be screwed around by you. So don't even dream of fucking with me.'

'I wouldn't. I need your help. That's all.'

Mundy seemed to accept this, although his eyes did not lose their menace for a few seconds more.

'Okay, so here's the deal. I tell you what I know about Rhodes, so long as you guarantee to come back to me on what you find in Maine. If he *is* hiding up there, I want to know about it the moment you find him. Is that agreed, Dr Lindow?'

He nodded.

'This isn't my area now. If it was I'd have a couple of guys go up there with you. But it's just too damned complicated – I'd have to explain this thing to too many people. So you're on your own.' He paused again. 'We heard of Rhodes a long time back. We knew he came out of the military – some kind of special forces – and worked for both British intelligence agencies.'

'Is that right? That could explain why the British want to blame me and Eamonn. It might even explain why Foyle was taken off the case.'

Mundy nodded. 'Could be. In the early nineties he went off the radar screen, but then he comes back and broadens his client base and starts making real money. He may even have helped the IRA with some supplies.'

'You mean he worked for the security services *and* the IRA?'

'That's how we came to hear of him, because of our interest in the activities of home-grown Irish republicans. But he was a cut above the other gun-runners. He had a greater range. He could get anything anyone wanted out of the East – he built relationships right across the former communist-bloc countries. He even had some kind of outfit in Moscow. The overseas stuff was CIA business, but we kept tabs on him anyway because we were interested in the way he moved money around and because we got to hear that he was operating out of Canada. Believe me, a lot of bad people hang out in the land of the moose and the maple leaf. And your man Rhodes is a bad guy. It wasn't like he was just into supply, he actually went out and did some killing himself. No one screwed around with him. People always paid up.'

Lindow took out a pen and scribbled some notes on

the corner of a newspaper. Mundy swept his hand across to knock the ballpoint from the paper's surface.

'You don't need to do that. I've got a printout here, which you can have later. Read it and then be sure to destroy it. I'm taking a big risk in giving it to you. But I owe the professor. He's helped out a huge amount with the work we're doing over there.'

'What's that?'

'We'll stick to the matter in hand, shall we? What you have to focus on, Dr Lindow, is that Rhodes and his partners are dangerous. Go up there like you're on a hiking trip, learn what you can. Then get the hell out of there and come back and tell me what you've found. I guess you've got some kind of Irish contact here. I won't embarrass you by asking who that is, but just be sure to tell me everything you tell them. Understood?'

'Understood,' said Lindow. 'Can I ask you another favour?'

'Try me,' said Mundy, draining his *caffe latte*.

'If I do find Rhodes, when the time comes would you be prepared to tell the British authorities that I've helped you?'

'I see no problem with that. Just tell me when.'

'I'll give you Foyle's number now. He'll confirm anything I've told you.'

Lindow copied the number on to the corner of the newspaper and gave it to Mundy in exchange for his card.

Mundy got up from his stool. 'So I'll be hearing from you.'

'Thanks.' Lindow rose. 'You were going to give me a printout too?'

'It's in your jacket pocket. Be careful now.' Lindow flipped a salute from his brow and slipped from the door with a predatory grin. He felt for the FBI file and transferred it to the inside of his jacket, before hurrying from the coffee shop. He had a lot to do.

First he went to a branch of the Bay State Bank, where the revenues from his protein work accrued each month from DahlTech on the West Coast. Lindow had wired $50,000 to an English bank a few months before, but the statement showed that the amount had already been made up by fresh deposits. He blinked at the total of $145,000, then arranged two payments to his credit-card companies and withdrew a further five thousand dollars.

On the way back to the hotel he bought a metal metre rule, a camera and low-light telephoto lens. He told the assistant in the camera shop that he planned to photograph wildlife in Maine and made him go over the operation of the lens and camera several times. Satisfied, he returned to the hotel with a dozen films and the camera equipment stowed in a small knapsack.

When he got into his room there was no sign of Mary, so he sat down at the table and began to read the outline of Rhodes's early life. He was born in Nairobi in 1952. He had been educated in England at two private schools, leaving the second at the age of seventeen. He joined the British Army in 1970 and was commissioned in 1972. His service record included periods in Northern Ireland, Borneo, Hong Kong, Belize, Norway and the South Atlantic. His expertise was listed as communications, ordnance disposal, languages, sabotage, undercover operations and surveillance.

It was at this point that the report became interesting, describing operations Rhodes had been connected with, his known associates and movements. Lindow skimmed the contents and decided to read it properly later. Right now he needed to check out of the hotel and hire himself a car. He packed his things, confining everything he'd need in Maine to one bag, and looked round the room. Then the phone rang. It was Mary.

'Con, I'm in the lobby,' she said brightly. 'When are you planning to leave?'

'Just about now.'

'Okay, so are you going to bring my bag down? I've hired a Jeep. It's outside.'

In moments during the morning he'd thought about Mary's behaviour during the night. It seemed to him that they were somehow still at odds. He had the impression that part of her operated independently from her corporeal self – as though she separated from her shadow and the shadow went off on its own business. He had his doubts about taking her. On the other hand, what could be more normal than a couple going on a break to Maine in the late fall?

'You there, Con?'

'Yes, I was just thinking. I'll come down now. I'll bring your bag.'

Fifteen minutes later Mary was driving them across the Tobin Bridge, going northwards to Route 95.

Chapter Eleven

'Is this a bad time?' asked Speerman, from around Kirsty Laing's door.

'Not at all, do come in.' These visits of Speerman's were becoming a habit. It was his third in a week. 'How can I help?'

'I just wondered how you were thinking about things. There's no particular problem, but I've come to like our chats. They help clear my thoughts.' His face said otherwise. She knew there was a problem. Although she was out of the loop she had learned from a junior member of A-Branch that Lindow was now in Boston. The watchers had got a line into his credit-card account and had monitored transactions involving a car hire in Dublin, a travel-book shop in Cambridge, Massachusetts, a hotel in downtown Boston and a photographic shop that morning. All of this suggested to Laing that Lindow was acting with definite purpose and probably explained why he had been looking at maps in the reference library at the beginning of the week.

'Our friend Lindow is moving rather quickly,' said Speerman. 'I gather he's now in the United States – Boston.'

'Really, what's he doing there?'

'Difficult to know. Of course, he worked there until recently.' Speerman wanted to say more but she knew he needed to be helped.

'What's on your mind, Peter?'

'It's just that we believe Rhodes had some sort of

set-up over there and it looks very much as though Lindow is on his trail. He's travelling north to Maine now.' Laing wondered how he knew this. The last credit-card transaction had been an hour or so ago at the photographic shop, which gave no clue about his movements.

'How does Lindow know about Rhodes?'

'Good question, Kirsty, which I am afraid I can't answer.'

'Maybe he learned about Rhodes from someone else?'

'We don't know. It's possible the IRA have given him some information this week. MacMahon was at the funeral and the two of them talked. We've got photographs.' He paused and looked at her with appreciation, his lips spreading into a rare smile. 'But tell me, Kirsty, what would you do in this situation?'

He was drawing her out. She had seen him use the technique before. He would appear genuinely in need of advice and then as soon as he had got what he wanted he would resume his official distance. She guessed he had learned it from David Cantor who famously let an issue unfold around him, allowing opposing sides to emerge, before revealing his own position. Speerman had told her nothing that she didn't already know, but here he was asking her to declare herself. She would play his game and say exactly what she thought.

'I believe we should come clean, as far as that's practical. The longer we continue to keep this to ourselves, the more people Rhodes will kill and the greater the potential scandal.'

'I wonder if that's true,' said Speerman. 'We think that the first bomb was aimed at Eamonn Lindow and the second and third bombs were both part of some sort of contract, issued by environmental extremists on the Continent.'

'I hadn't realised that was the case in King's Cross,' she said.

'It emerged last night that the building backing on to the alley was leased by an outfit called Worldwide Site Surveys, which acts as an agency for companies seeking to dispose of hazardous materials. There's a direct connection with the device at Interwaste. But the main point is that Rhodes may now have completed his work here. We know all three bombs were planted by last Friday morning. That's a week ago. He's probably long gone.'

'Yes, but it doesn't serve the cause of justice, does it? There *are* issues in this that are greater than simply what's good for the service.'

Speerman nodded solemnly.

She pressed home the point. 'Even looking at this solely in the context of our self-interest, we may be doing the wrong thing by keeping it to ourselves. Rhodes's involvement might emerge of its own accord – through Lindow's efforts, for instance.'

'What do you propose we should do?'

'I believe we must start preparing key people for the possibility that a former British Army officer is the bomber, playing up his long years of service in Northern Ireland and subsequent breakdown. We would distance ourselves from any involvement with Rhodes, and the MoD would be left fielding the questions about his service record. I could put the argument I've just made to the director general and persuade him that a change of overall strategy would leave the service less exposed.'

'Certainly not. He will already have thought of everything you suggest. We could review the situation on Monday, by which time there may be developments. If Lindow has genuinely good information about Rhodes and he finds him in the United States, other options will begin to open up for us.'

She nodded as if she saw the wisdom of the argument. 'Whatever you say.'

He sat in front of her for a few moments saying

nothing, his mind evidently in turmoil. Then he got up with an oddly rueful expression.

'See you on Monday,' he said. 'We'll talk then.'

Even with his currently attentive mood Speerman could not be trusted, and she knew it had been risky to talk so openly about her views. Still, she was slightly ahead of his game. The day before she had been told that a Special Branch officer had seen Commander Kenneth Foyle leaving for Dublin. Put together with Lindow's presence in Dublin at the same time – established by the return of the car early on Thursday morning – it was worth rather more. Foyle's reason for going to Dublin could only have been to see Lindow. They must be working together. Lindow's sudden departure to Boston meant that they had much more information about Ian Rhodes than anyone in the service realised. She was sure there wasn't much time.

Foyle toiled up the last few flights of stairs in a near-derelict council block in Shoreditch. He had spent the previous twenty-four hours attempting to trace Lance Corporal Christy Calvert, one of the surviving members of the undercover squad at Droy, and had eventually got Forbes to access the police national computer. Since leaving the Army in 1991, Calvert had two convictions for assault and one for possession of ecstasy. He was now said to work as a bodyguard and club doorman in the West End. Police records gave his last known address as Aberavon House, Shoreditch, East London.

He reached the landing outside Flat 42C and knocked on the door. He heard a sound of voices inside the flat, then a man called out from close behind the door. Foyle explained that he was a police officer, seeking information. The locks were drawn back and the door opened to reveal a bare chest and tattooed arms. The face was still hidden.

'Mr Calvert – Mr Christy Calvert? I'm Commander Foyle. I wonder if I could ask you a few questions.'

The man stepped forward out of the shadows and looked down the stairwell. He had a compact physique that was still in reasonably good shape, but his face told another story. There was a graze on his left cheek, his nose was livid with tiny red pustules and his eyes shied from the light.

'You by yourself? What do you want at this time of day?'

'It's gone midday, Mr Calvert,' said Foyle, 'but I'll come back in an hour or two if you prefer.'

'I work nights. Only got to bed at six. But since you're here, you'd better come in. The place is in chaos, though.'

Foyle stepped into a fetid atmosphere that smelt of cooking fat and cigarettes. Calvert showed him into a sitting room with two armchairs facing a large TV. Sports magazines were strewn across the floor and several empty beer cans stood on the table. Calvert drew back the curtains before going to his bedroom to fetch a shirt. Through the open bedroom door Foyle could see the naked shoulders of a young man on the bed.

Calvert returned. 'I won't introduce you,' he said, sniffing and smoothing his bed-ruffled hair, ''cos I don't know his name. What can I do for you?'

'I want to know about an explosion in Ulster in July 1983. You remember? You were part of an observation patrol led by Major Ian Rhodes.'

'Yeah,' said Calvert, searching for something in his trouser pocket. 'You're talking about the churchyard.'

'Yes, the one at Droy. You were watching the place for two or three weeks before the cache exploded. Do you remember much about it?'

'Course I bloody remember it. My friends were killed by the fucking Paddies. Now the Paddies are taking tea at Number Ten – running around in suits, wearing green ribbons in their lapels, like they worked for some fucking charity. And look where I am – in this fucking shithole. Course I remember it. There isn't a day goes by without me thinking about those bastards.'

'Would you mind telling me what happened, I mean *exactly* what happened, at Droy?'

'Why do you want to know after all this time?'

Foyle watched Calvert tip a quantity of tobacco from a tin and begin to roll a cigarette. 'Because it may have a bearing on some recent terrorist actions here.'

'What, you mean the bombs last week? Nah, that wasn't the Micks. Too bloody clever for them.' He lit the cigarette and took a deep drag, causing his lungs to explode in a series of tight little coughs. When the fit was over, Foyle could hear the whisper of Calvert's chest from where he was sitting.

'Bronchitis,' said Calvert, dipping his ash into a beer can. 'So ... Operation CUDGEL is what you want to know about. Well, we was there nearly three weeks. It seemed like years, but it was worth it because there was a charge fixed to the cache and we wanted to see it blow up when the Micks came to collect their stuff. Nothing too complicated, just a trip-wire that set off a five-second fuse down in the vault. We reckoned they'd be bringing the guns and explosives out when it blew up.'

'Do you remember which of you made the device?'

'Either Rhodes or Creech.' He paused. 'It might have been Lasseur. He was trained in sabotage.'

'What happened?'

'We saw this geezer a few times. Each time he gets out of his car and takes a leak. I had his dick in my sights twice – took all my training not to shoot it off. We didn't know if he was sussing the place out or if he just had a weak bladder. Then, after his last visit, someone came to the church at night. We heard him moving around but we couldn't see a fucking thing in the night scopes.'

'Can you show me where you were in relation to the church?' Foyle offered him a blank page of his notebook.

Calvert ignored it and placed his tobacco tin on the table to represent the church, then surrounded it with a ring of matches to show the graveyard wall. On the left of the tin he placed two cigarette papers to represent the road, then folded another paper to show a farm track that branched from the road and followed the line of the graveyard wall to the back of the church. 'The track was what made this the perfect place to hide the stuff,' said Calvert. 'They could unload and load without anyone seeing them from the road. There was an entrance to the graveyard at the back of the church. All very handy it was.'

'Where were you?'

'Four of us were in the trees up here.' He pointed a little to the right of the ring of matches. 'And there were a couple who covered the farm track. We were well dug in and we came and went through the woods without being seen.'

'And what happened on that night?'

'We heard someone in the churchyard. He must have made his way to the church on foot then sneaked along the inside of the wall. I remember thinking it was a fox or a badger. When you're dug in like that for a long time it's amazing how animals get used to you. Then one of the lads – I think it was Vince Creech – radioed that he'd seen a man. We thought that maybe he was checking out the place before the wagon came so we sat tight. Nothing happened for about ten minutes, except one of the lads said he saw a light from a torch. We waited and waited, and all the time the geezer was down there by the vault. Then the noise stopped and we realised he'd buggered off – vanished like a bleeding ghost, he did. Major Rhodes told four of us to see what this guy had been doing. Jimmy Pascoe and Bob McGurk moved in first from the woods, then Vince Creech and Lieutenant Lasseur left their positions near the farm track. Dawn was breaking and I saw all four of them in the churchyard. Then it went up, just like that. I couldn't hear for days. They found bits of Vince and Bob McGurk on the church roof.'

'What about the others?'

'It made a right mess of Pascoe's face. He was blinded too. The lieutenant was hurt down his left side – blast wounds on his face and neck. But when we saw the size of the crater, it was amazing anyone got out of there alive. They reckon there was a hundred pounds of Semtex in there. And that's saying nothing about the ammunition and mortar bombs.'

'Tell me about Major Rhodes.'

Calvert got up and went over to a side table, and poured himself a couple of inches of vodka. 'You want one?'

Foyle shook his head. 'No thanks.'

He returned to his chair and drank. 'Rhodes was a special kind of officer – not one of them public-school Ruperts. A real technician, a real pro. He'd done time with the signals, knew about codes and explosives, communications, sabotage, weapons, the bleeding lot. He had about a dozen languages and he could mimic anyone in the world. There wasn't anything he wouldn't do for his men. That's why he took the loss so bad – personal failure and all that. But he never showed it. And you know something? A few weeks later he was leading another op-react.'

'What's that?'

'It stands for Observation Post/React. Ambush, in your language. They had word that six Micks were planning to ram the gates of a police station with a JCB digger that was loaded up with a fertiliser bomb. So when they burst in with their digger they find Rhodes and five other soldiers. He killed two of the bastards, then went up to a third, who'd run out of ammunition, removed his glasses and shot him in the face. That wasn't the end of it. A couple of weeks later Jimmy Pascoe got this package in hospital – a pair of glasses and an unsigned postcard. Jimmy told me it freaked the nurses. They thought it was some kind of sick joke, see – him being blind and that. But Jimmy knew better. It was Rhodes saying he'd scored a Mick for him. That was the kind of man he was.'

'What happened to you all afterwards?'

'I went back to the regiment, lost touch with everyone. Then one day I saw Rhodes in the street. Must have been five, six years ago, anyway, some time after I'd left the Army. I called after him, but he never turned round. Then I heard on the grapevine, like, that he'd been in a home for nutters – lost his marbles big time. That explained why he didn't stop and have a word.'

'You said you heard it on the grapevine. Who do you know who knew Rhodes?'

'So it's the major you're interested in?'

'Maybe.'

'When I said the grapevine, I meant the security business. A lot of us went into security after the Army – bodyguards for the Sheikh of Araby, specialist driving, electronic surveillance, that sort of thing. It's all a load of crap to make the Arabs feel important, but it pays the bills. Anyway, I heard Rhodes was doing a bit of work for a company in Victoria. Cram Associates is the name, a cut above the agencies I was working for at the time, but they're in the same game which is how I come to hear about Rhodes going loop the loop.'

Foyle looked out of the window of Calvert's flat to the towers of Canary Wharf and the Millennium Dome beyond. 'Tell me, Mr Calvert, did you ever hear who might have been responsible for the explosion at Droy church? Were you given any names of suspects?'

'We knew that the Paddy with the bladder problem was arrested with his brother. Can't remember the names, but we could've got them, if we'd wanted.'

Foyle rose and thanked Calvert. 'One other thing. Did you hear anything of Lieutenant Lasseur?'

'Not much. His face was in a terrible state. Burns, blast injuries. You know the score. He had a lot of surgery then left the Army – went back to Canada, I heard.'

Foyle thanked Calvert again, said goodbye and descended the thirty-odd flights of stairs to his car, where he called Forbes on his new cellphone and asked him about Cram Associates. Forbes said that the company was run by ex-intelligence people, but he wasn't sure of which variety. 'A lot of these companies sprang up in the early nineties,' he said. 'Cram is a pretty respectable consultancy – picks up work from the government and has a couple of retired permanent secretaries on the board. It's run by a man named Archie Cram.'

'How do you know all this?' Forbes never failed to surprise him.

'Actually I read it in the newspaper. There was an article in one of the Sunday business sections about the kidnap and ransom industry. Cram is "Mr K & R".'

Forbes looked up the number for him and they arranged to meet for a drink that evening.

Half an hour later Foyle presented himself at a basement in Buckingham Gate that had been gentrified by carriage lamps and potted bay trees. A young woman with an upper-class accent showed him into a conference room and gave him an information pack that outlined the careers of Cram's consultants. He glanced through the file and noted that most of them had intelligence backgrounds. Two specified MI6 but the rest were vague, citing affiliations with various foreign agencies. He put down the folder and looked at a set of watercolours of the Middle East, hung on either side of the room.

'Interesting, aren't they?' said a voice behind him.

Foyle turned to see a tall man in a grey checked suit. He introduced himself as Archie Cram and offered Foyle a cold, tentative handshake.

'I picked them up in Cairo. They must've been done

about the turn of the century. They're unsigned and I've never been able to establish who painted them.'

The man before Foyle had thinning, gingerish hair, a freckled complexion which had not fared well in the sun, and sharp brown eyes that darted in constant appraisal.

'So, how can I help you, Commander?'

'I'm looking into the background of a man named Ian Rhodes – Major Ian Rhodes. I believe you know him.'

'Yes, of course. I know him pretty well. He did some contracts for us after he left the Army.'

'What sort of contracts?'

'I take it you know what we do?'

'Yes. Kidnap and ransom, security, that sort of thing.'

'Then you'll know what Rhodes did for us. I can't give you many details because they're confidential. But let's say that he was a valued sub-contractor. Then, of course, he became ill.'

'What sort of illness was that?'

'Its immediate cause was some kind of virus picked up in the Far East. They never discovered what it was but it was obviously debilitating and eventually it triggered other problems – a nervous condition. It all happened just after he'd completed an assignment for us. Nothing very strenuous, compared to the things he was used to.'

'What sort of assignment? Can you give me details?'

'It involved negotiating the release of a hostage – an employee of one of our clients – held in Indonesia by a group of rebels. Rhodes managed to strike up a relationship with these people and he did an exchange.'

'What kind of exchange?'

'Weapons and ammunition for the hostage – this is all very confidential. We had nothing to do with it, but naturally we were pleased to get the hostage back for our client.'

'So he used the firm's money to supply the weapons.'

'No, no, no, not our money. He used the money made available in a bank account to pay the ransom – probably made a profit over the fee he was paid. But we saw no harm in that. You see, he was an exceptional operator and deserved all the perks he got.' Cram fixed Foyle with a look of suspicion. 'I wonder, Commander, would you mind telling me exactly what it is you want? Is this official business? Normally I'd expect someone less senior than you to be asking me these questions.'

'I'm looking into the circumstances of the recent bombing campaign in London.'

'Yes, but is this official business?'

'I'm continuing an investigation that began when the first bombs went off last week.'

'I see. So this is more in the nature of an unofficial visit. But tell me, why are you asking about Rhodes? He's hardly likely to be involved.'

'Why do you say that with such certainty?'

'Because, first and foremost, Ian Rhodes is a British soldier, and deep down his loyalties and values would prevent him from doing something like that. This is to say nothing of the lack of motive.'

'Yes, but you yourself said that he had some form of nervous breakdown. It may have unbalanced him for good.'

'No, I saw him afterwards and he was quite his old self.'

Foyle had the impression of watching an opening batsman, pushing away the ball with a series of expert defensive strokes. 'What about his background, his habits, his character? Can you help with any of that?'

'I don't think he made any secret of his background. His mother was Italian. I believe she was from Northern Italy and ended up with her parents in Ethiopia during the Italian occupation. His father was originally a railway engineer from Yorkshire who played quite a part in the Abyssinian campaign. That's how they met. After the war they went to Kenya and bought a farm. This would have been in the fifties, the time of the Mau Mau.

The family farm was attacked while his parents were away in Nairobi, and he and his brother held off the Mau Mau from the roof with hunting rifles. A servant was killed in front of their eyes and then Rhodes's brother was shot before help arrived. I'm afraid I can't tell you much about his career in the Army, except that he was regarded as an extremely valuable asset, which is why we approached him. Then after his illness I gather he went into business for himself. Even had some kind of office in Moscow.'

'Doing what?'

'Well, some of the same areas of work as ourselves, but personally I never saw Rhodes as a natural businessman – not in the accepted sense. And such clients as he attracted were hardly corporate, if you know what I mean.' Cram looked at his watch to indicate that Foyle's consultation was over. 'Is there anything else you wanted to ask me?'

'Yes, do you have any idea where Rhodes might be?' Cram shook his head. 'Absolutely none.'

'I've heard that he may have a base in the States. Is that at all possible?'

Cram shook his head again. 'I really couldn't tell you.'

Foyle left Cram Associates and walked back to his car, where he sat for a good ten minutes thinking. He had little doubt that Cram had held back in their interview and it wouldn't be long before word got out that he had been to see him. Still, it hadn't been an entirely wasted effort. With Calvert's information, a picture of Rhodes was emerging.

Fifty-odd miles north of Boston, Lindow and Mary Menihan passed into the corridor of land that allows New Hampshire to claim a portion of the Atlantic coastline. A little way on they came to the great wooded state of Maine. '"Welcome to Vacationland, home of the claw and the clam",' said Mary, reading a sign beside the highway. 'Con, you do realise that this state is something in excess of the size of Ireland? Perhaps it'd be a good time to tell me exactly where we're headed.'

He reached into one of the bags in the back of the Jeep and pulled out the map he'd used to plot the bearings from Belfast on the coast and from Limerick in the south. Then he ran his finger to a point in the north, thirty miles inside the border with Canada.

'My, what's all this?' She craned her neck to look at the map. 'Where did you get this navigational stuff?'

'Never you mind and keep your eyes on the road.' Lindow let his hand come to rest on her shoulder. There was no need to explain yet.

They travelled north for just under three hours, then took the road that branched westwards, outside the town of Bangor. Soon the land began to rise and the woods closed in on the road. Occasionally they glimpsed vistas stretching in tones of grey and brown into a baleful hinterland. They stopped once for coffee and doughnuts at a clapboard diner and stamped their feet in the car park. Mary peered gloomily over the take-out coffee and said there was snow in the air. Nonsense, he told her. It was fall. He pointed to the yellow leaves of the scrub beneath the trees and a maple that was still hung with vivid red tissues. As they stood, debating the point, a stocky little deer broke from the trees on the other side of the road, thought better of crossing and trotted back to merge into the cover. Lindow took the wheel and Mary sang desultorily, misting the passenger window with her breath. Each little town they passed through seemed overwhelmed by the woods and to peter out to a few scattered tin shacks, all dedicated to the storing of winter fuel and the repair of snowcats. There wasn't a settlement where men didn't seem to be tinkering with snowcats, oiling and firing up the engines and waving the clouds of exhaust from their faces.

'I told you so. Up here they can smell snow coming,' said Mary.

She took the wheel again because Lindow wanted to look at the large-scale atlas of Maine to gauge how far they'd be able to travel before nightfall, and also to find a place to stay. To the north they saw a huge grey cloud streaked with white that reared over Spencer Mountain like a skunk tail and made the land beneath a purply blue. He reckoned there wasn't much more than an hour's light left in the sky. But he wanted to reach the area of green on the map where Eamonn's lines met. He had the rough position, marked with a cross on one of the huge nameless rectangles numbered in the state's geographic code. There wasn't a settlement within twenty miles of the place.

'Look,' said Mary, 'this is crazy. We're not going to find anything in the dark. Besides, I'm not going to sleep in this. I want a bed and a shower and something to eat. It'll be much better if we get some sleep and start looking in the morning.'

Lindow reluctantly agreed and they made for a town on the edge of Moosehead Lake. There they were directed by a slow-talking garage hand to a hiking lodge with the Indian name of Piscataquis. The light was fading quickly as they climbed the mile or two out of town, but Lindow could just make out the shapes of seaplanes tethered to the shore and the unmistakable outline of a Dakota perched on two vast floats. The aircraft gave him an idea.

They arrived at Piscataquis Lodge, a squat wood and granite building, and were shown to a cabin decorated with old snowshoes and ancient skiing paraphernalia. The cabin was already too hot from a fire lit in expectation of weekend hikers turning up unannounced. Mary opened a window on to the night and leaned from the sill, listening to the pellets of ice rattling on the dry leaves of the forest floor as though someone was throwing handfuls of rice from the sky. She held out her hands to collect the grains of ice then turned and showed them triumphantly to Lindow. He inspected her hands and pronounced that it was hail, not snow, at which Mary shrieked a protest and threw it up into his face. He slipped his hands inside her jacket, held her for a moment and ran his lips down her neck, which caused her to wriggle in his arms and nip at his chin with her teeth. He reached up behind her to close the windows and shutters then drew her towards the fire and began to undress her, in the flickering light, kissing each newly exposed area of skin as he went. She tasted salty and her hair smelt of woodsmoke and scent. He crouched to pull her jeans to the floor. She stepped out of them. Her neat, olive-skinned body rose above him utterly naked.

'I had no idea how beautiful you were. I mean you *are* quite, quite beautiful.'

'You didn't notice last night?' She smiled down at him.

'That wasn't real. More like a dream. Anyway, I couldn't see you properly.'

She bent down, undid his belt and slipped her hand inside his trousers.

'For God's sake, undress, Con. I'm getting goose-bumps.'

She pushed him on to the bed and stripped the rest of his clothes off. She was strong and agile and, as she scrambled over him, he could feel the muscles working in her shoulders. Then she rolled to one side and guided him into her, fixing him with a playful myopic gaze. They moved for a long time in the firelight. At length Mary came with a series of small shudders. She smiled again and shifted so that her legs rested across his. She gripped his temples in the vice of her palms and brought him to a slow climax. 'Christ,' he said wonderingly.

Afterwards they lay for a while and Lindow moved down to place his head on the depression of her pelvis. Far out in the early evening a freight train pushed south along the Canadian–American Railroad, its horn sounding again and again across the lake and into the muffling firs.

Lindow raised his head from her belly to look at her. A glow of pleasure had settled on her face, but as the train thundered over a crossing below them, it seemed to shake her from her reverie. She abruptly disentangled herself from his body and sprang up, saying that she was hungry and needed a shower. Lindow clutched at the air as she went.

'Look, we have to have food and we're going to need some rest tonight,' she called from the shower.

He lay on the bed for a few minutes, feeling stung. Then he remembered the file on Rhodes, which Mundy had given him that morning. He fetched it from the bag and began reading it again. There was less to it than he had thought because Mundy had mistakenly printed out the file twice. He skimmed the details that he'd read earlier and moved on to the main body of the text.

Rhodes is regarded as a top-level operator by the British Army and intelligence services. Before resigning his commission in 1988, he was seconded to the Government Communications Headquarters at Cheltenham, England. Both foreign and domestic intelligence services unsuccessfully tried to recruit him. But for reasons unknown he remained an independent operator. In the latter part of the decade he undertook occasional assignments for MI5, the British domestic intelligence service. These were outside British sovereign territory and were connected with investigations into the supply of arms to terrorist organisations in Northern Ireland. It was on this basis that Rhodes came to the attention of the Bureau and other agencies in the United States.

Between 1990 and 1992 nothing was heard of Rhodes. In 1993 it was learned that Rhodes had moved his interests to Eastern Europe to deal in arms and other materials from the former Communist bloc. He has a relationship with at least one private security agency in London – Cram Associates. On behalf of Cram Associates, he was responsible for the negotiated release of Dr Lawrence Lloyd, a geologist employed by mineral concerns in Indonesia. It is believed that Rhodes supplied arms to gain the hostage's freedom.

His current status with the British security services is unclear due to the fact that, having traced and eliminated certain supply routes, Rhodes may have taken the opportunity to become a supplier himself to the Provisional IRA. Between 1994 and 1998, Rhodes made several visits to the US, which were confirmed by Central Intelligence sources in Europe. These trips were made under other names and their purpose is not known. It was believed that Rhodes was making his operations base somewhere in the United States.

He has been implicated in the assassination of two minor arms dealers. On March 11, 1997 Jimmy L. Marcuse was killed by a car bomb in Miami. Four months later on July 10, Patrick Lyne Jnr, an Irish-American businessman, was found dead in the Grange Hotel, Chicago. Marcuse and Lyne were business associates and may have dealt with Rhodes, although his whereabouts at the times of the murders was not established and in neither investigation was the subject questioned. As of this time, both cases remain unsolved. Rhodes has personal reserves of stamina, determination and technical expertise. Little is known about his political affiliations or his personal life. His only known associate is Robert Christian Lasseur. Born 1960, Quebec. Former British Army lieutenant. Height 5 feet 9 inches. 180 pounds. Distinguishing marks: heavily scarred on left cheek and shoulder area.

Known aliases: Rhodes is believed to travel under the name of Brian Carver, precision-tools salesman, born 1955, Leicestershire, England. He has also used the name Richard Saffarello, naturalized US citizen, born 1950, Padua, Italy.

Lindow sat on the bed and read the paper again. If Rhodes had worked for the security service and then started supplying the IRA, that would explain a lot – for one thing, why Eamonn was tracking him for the Provisionals. And it was also clear that Rhodes had all the necessary logistical and technical knowledge to mount his own bombing campaign in London. But why? Who for? Not the IRA – they wanted him found as much as anyone else.

Mary called out from the shower, 'Shall I leave this running for you, Con? Why don't you come in here with me?'

Lindow slipped the papers back into his jacket and went to the shower, where he found Mary looking absurdly youthful, her hair flattened and parted in the middle by the jet of water. He got in with her.

'What were you doing? You went awful silent for a while there.'

'I was wondering why you shot off the bed like a frightened virgin.'

She kicked at him.

'Actually I was reading some stuff about our man. He sounds a pretty mean character.'

'Where were you reading about him?'

'In an FBI report.'

Mary cocked her head. 'I'm impressed. Where did you get it from?'

'The FBI.'

'Yes, but they don't just hand out files like tourist maps. You must know someone there.'

'I was put in touch with a guy. I saw him this morning. Agent Mundy, do you know him?'

'Why should I?' She left the shower, wrapped herself in one towel and took the other for her hair.

'No reason,' said Lindow, stepping under the jet and grimacing at the thought of a damp towel. 'It just occurred to me while I was reading that stuff about Rhodes that I don't know very much more about you.' He turned off the water and stood naked before her. 'You see, I'm in the odd position of imagining that I could fall in love with you, but also realising that I know nothing about you. May I have one of the towels?'

She gave him the one from her head before turning to get dressed.

'Let's go eat,' she said.

Chapter Twelve

Peter Speerman waited for Cantor to speak. He noted that his face was a little paler than usual and that his eyes were quite drained of expression, moving only to evaluate what Speerman was telling him.

'I take it we're doing all we need to?'

'I think so. We've got the best part of five hundred people looking for Rhodes and there's been no trace of him. Nothing whatsoever. Weegee is being used to full capacity. A-Branch have been tapping into conventional street surveillance systems and London Underground's cameras. We have watches on every port.'

Cantor unclasped his hands and sat down. 'Assuming he did cause these explosions, I think we should conclude that he left the country after the last device. In fact, if we hadn't got the pictures from Weegee, I'd doubt he had ever been here.'

'Yes, but we do have them. And it looks as though Rhodes may be responsible.'

'I wouldn't put it as high as that.' He touched some papers on his desk with three manicured fingers of his right hand.

Speerman decided to wait again. The conversation with Kirsty Laing earlier had persuaded him that the initiative must be seized by the service before things ran out of control. What he needed most was a hint that Cantor had developed fallback positions in case the link with Rhodes was exposed. A hint was all he needed and

Cantor would have his backing. He waited, but nothing came so he broke the silence himself.

'Have you been reading the reports of Lindow's movements in the US?'

'Yes, I've seen what Keith sent me.'

'It appears that he's gone north. We had a call from Brown Owl who said they'd hired a car and were driving somewhere in Maine.'

'Weegee, Brown Owl – for heaven's sake, who thinks of these names? Anyway, what did she have to say?'

'She believes that Lindow has been given information by the IRA that may lead him to Rhodes. As you know, both of them were snatched by McCreath's lot. It seems McCreath told Lindow to go to the States and threatened to harm his sister if he didn't. It's an improbable story, but she insists it's true. She also suspects that Lindow found something in his brother's flat, something the police missed. But she says he keeps his cards close to his chest. She's not sure when she's going to be able to get the information and call us again.'

'Menihan's her name, isn't it? What's she like?'

'Craven-Elms says she is extremely capable. We've had a relationship with her for nearly ten years. She was plugged into Eamonn Lindow for a while before his death, although not much came of her efforts. She is very patient and never loses control of a situation, which is how she managed to avoid being unmasked on a couple of occasions in the past. Keith says she'd be his first choice for a job like this.'

'Well, that's something. In the meantime the police investigation reveals not very much, I gather.'

'By that you mean the official police investigation,' said Speerman, causing Cantor's hands to seek each other's company on the top of his desk.

'Commander Foyle is proving rather tenacious. Earlier this evening I had a telephone call from Cram Associates – you remember Archie Cram? He said that Foyle was nosing round there this afternoon, asking about Rhodes's background. Cram didn't give him anything. Foyle asked whether Cram thought it possible that Rhodes was in America. This may indicate that Lindow and Foyle are working together, or have at least remained in touch. Why else would Foyle ask about America?'

'I'll have a word with the commissioner about Foyle's unofficial activity. If he persists, it might be possible to make use of that troublesome daughter of his. A little research into her life will produce many dividends, I'm certain of it.'

Cantor seemed satisfied with this and Speerman saw his attention move to the papers on his desk. He recognised this as an oblique dismissal, but he wasn't going to leave just yet. 'If Commander Foyle has anything serious about Rhodes,' he said, 'it's bound to come out. He had a lot of respect as a policeman. Just because he's been removed, it doesn't follow that he's lost all credibility among his colleagues.'

'Nevertheless,' said Cantor, with studied patience, 'it shouldn't be difficult for his superiors to ground him. I'll call the commissioner before I leave. Is there anything else?'

Speerman didn't reply immediately, but weighed up for the last time what he had been planning to say. 'I was wondering,' he began, 'how we're going to explain things if Foyle, Lindow or anyone else publicises the fact that Rhodes may've been involved. It would set things back ten years – a disaster for our relations with government, especially as half of them suspect us of keeping their files from the seventies. Might it not be prudent to admit the possibility of Rhodes's involvement and be seen to be instigating an investigation that features Rhodes as someone who has gone off the rails? Kirsty has made the point that we don't have to take responsibility for him. He wouldn't be the first British soldier to go over to the other side.'

Cantor looked up. A lethal stillness had passed into his face. 'I'm aware of Kirsty Laing's views but, Peter, I imagined you were more – how shall I say? – astute. Of course we can't have Rhodes in court, disclosing details of a highly sensitive nature. It would be unthinkable, even *in camera*.'

'Yes, but you can show that as director general you ended the service's involvement with Major Rhodes as soon as you took control – well, as near as damn it.'

'But that isn't quite true, Peter. The truth is that we have used him quite recently, more recently than you appreciate. You do understand what I'm saying to you?'

Speerman nodded. He understood perfectly. Cantor was making him complicit in the secret. He must have done the same thing with Craven-Elms, Grove, Fuller and even Brian Etheridge, the head of legal affairs, welding them into a defensive alliance around him. Speerman, however, instantly knew that he was going to have nothing to do with it. Cantor had kept him in the dark about the extent of Rhodes's work for the service and he wasn't going to accept retrospective responsibility simply to save him.

He gave no hint of his decision. 'We're already into the weekend,' he said brightly, looking out over London. 'Are you going away?'

'Yes, I shall be in Sussex, staying with some friends – shooting tomorrow.'

Speerman smiled at the idea of Cantor's social climbing. 'I have your mobile number if anything arises.'

'Good. Now, you do understand what I've just told you?'

'Perfectly.'

Cantor was already engrossed in his papers. Speerman withdrew.

Laing found Speerman sitting on a bench of dubious red velvet in the pub near where he lived. She thought he

254

looked rather cowed. She wondered what had happened.

'How kind of you,' she said, looking at the two glasses of white wine. 'But if you don't mind, I'll have a gin and tonic. It is the weekend, after all.'

Speerman went off to get it and returned to sit down beside her so that both looked out on the thinning crowd of office workers.

'What did you want to say?' she asked.

'I've just had a word with the director general. He tells me that our involvement with the subject is more recent than we've been led to believe.'

'How recent?'

'Within the last two or three years, I'd guess, though he wasn't specific.'

Laing was genuinely surprised. The one thing she had not taken into her calculations was Cantor's direct involvement with Rhodes.

'The problem', he continued, 'is that we don't have much time. I feel certain that Foyle and Lindow are working together and that they're about to make significant discoveries. This afternoon I learned that Foyle had been to see a former colleague of ours. He was before your time, but perhaps you have heard of him – Archie Cram.'

In fact, she remembered Cram and knew that he had set up the supergrass deals in Ulster twenty or so years before.

'Actually he was with the service when I joined.'

'Well, Archie runs a small consultancy now, which used our friend once or twice. I believe he paid for his treatment after he suffered some kind of breakdown. He'd been working for him at the time and picked up a bug in the Far East, which apparently precipitated the collapse. The crucial point is that Foyle knows enough to have found Archie. Moreover, his line of questioning establishes that he knows there's an American connection. This bloody Foyle is a problem because we don't have the first idea of how much he knows. I mean, how the hell did he get on to Cram? Who else has he talked to?'

Laing understood now why Speerman was looking so damned rattled. Things were moving very quickly indeed. 'Then we've got to go and talk to him,' she said, 'and find out what he's up to.'

'Yes, but then we'd be committed to a course of action without knowing how Foyle will react. I've met him. He's like a buffalo – large and, once travelling in a particular direction, difficult to stop. The director general has some notion of getting at him through his daughter, who's been arrested for public disorder offences. But that seems to me to be surprisingly crude for him.'

'Tell me, have you met Brown Owl?' Laing had only heard about Mary Menihan from her source in A-Branch that evening. Normally she would have kept to herself the fact that she knew, but now it was important to learn how good Menihan was.

His eyes acknowledged the indiscretion. 'No, I haven't met her, but I gather she's first rate. As you probably know she effected a neat transfer when Eamonn Lindow was killed, effortlessly moving to watch the younger brother for us. Only in the last few weeks did she understand that Eamonn was acting as an intelligence officer. Originally we supposed that he was a superior form of quartermaster, or a scout. Then it became clear that he was one of their top men and that he was in charge of tracking down our friend. You see, the IRA had realised that Rhodes had killed two of their people in the States. This was a couple of years back and eventually they began to suspect him. They believed he might try to supply various Protestant groups, as well as themselves. There were any number of possibilities. But the main point is that these two fellows in the United States may have been eliminated at our instigation. That's something I did not appreciate until an hour or so ago.'

Laing emptied her glass and declared that she needed another drink, although what she really needed was time to absorb everything Speerman was telling her. As he went to the bar, she was struck by the terrible clumsiness of it all. She had always had a basic faith in the wisdom of the service, but it was vanishing by the second.

'You're saying that our friend killed two IRA arms suppliers then took over their business?' she whispered on his return.

'Yes, except by that time the peace process was so well advanced that the business was worthless.'

'Christ! This is a mess. So you think he planned to kill Eamonn? How did he know that Eamonn was on to him?'

'That's a fascinating question. Eamonn Lindow and our friend came across each other once before, in the early eighties, when Lindow was used to keep an eye on a supply dump. It was probably one of the first jobs he did for the Provisionals.'

'That was the thing at the churchyard?'

'Yes.'

'So you're saying that he knew Lindow's name and killed him, after all this time, as revenge?'

'It's possible, certainly. He would have had access to the names of the suspects and, given the circumstances of the explosion, he wasn't likely to forget them. Whether the bomb that killed Eamonn last week was intended as a revenge for Droy or as a horrendously wasteful way of eliminating a threat to his current operations we'll probably never know. Either way, the Droy explosion was the thing Foyle picked up on. By luck, intuition or investigative brilliance – I'm not sure which – he's stumbled on the right route through this particular thicket.'

'You know, Peter, I'm beginning to agree with the

director general. This should never come out. It all seems so bloody amateurish.'

'You have a point.'

She knew he was on her side. 'Peter, the first thing we must do is find out how much they know. I'll speak to Foyle this weekend. The problem is going to be Brown Owl, who reports directly to Craven-Elms, which means that Cantor will get the information before us. We've got to talk to her directly. Do you remember from the credit-card records which hotel they used in Boston last night? They may return there.'

'It was a place called the Omni Parker.'

'I'll try to call her. I may have to explain a little of this to her. That'll be all right, won't it?'

'Be very circumspect.'

Kirsty Laing rose and put on her overcoat. Speerman remained seated. 'Aren't you leaving yet?'

'I'll finish this and go in a minute,' he said, gesturing to the untouched glass of wine.

Foyle lay slumped in front of his television set, watching a preview of Saturday sports fixtures and taking modest nips from a bottle of whisky. He could not have been less interested in football and rarely drank by himself. But he needed to stay awake and collect his thoughts, and he found that the cheery inanities of the two presenters acted as a kind of balm.

After seeing Cram he had driven out to Mayfield Manor, a private nursing home near Woking where Ian Rhodes had been treated for three months in 1993. Forbes had discovered this after talking to one of his contacts in the Ministry of Defence, who suggested that Rhodes might have been referred to Mayfield because of its reputation for the treatment of post-traumatic stress disorders. A lot of military personnel were sent there.

Foyle had seen the head psychiatrist, a courteous individual named Alexander Grocyn, who'd treated

Rhodes. He confessed at the outset that Ian Rhodes had baffled him. He told Foyle how Rhodes had arrived by private ambulance early in 1993, swaddled in blankets and barely capable of walking. He did not speak or show any desire to communicate with those around him. 'In some senses,' said Grocyn, 'it was like a case of autism. He was obviously very run down physically. But you could not get through – he had shut down. Then after the first week he began to cry. I've seen it many times before and it's usually the symptom of great emotional or nervous exhaustion. At the time my feeling was that rest would probably be the best cure and, indeed, after the third week, Major Rhodes showed considerable improvement. We had several sessions together and it emerged that he had no private life whatsoever. It was quite extraordinary. There was no one he could talk to – no friends, no woman, no family to speak of, no intimate contact of any sort. One might have been tempted to read this as a sign of psychopathy, but that never struck me as being the right answer. He had none of the behavioural disorders associated with the psychopath's egocentricity. In fact, he possessed a rather acute insight into other people's motives, their hopes, loves, fears and so forth. In other words, his ego did not eclipse his understanding of the world. I suppose it was rather like talking to someone who had lost their sense of taste or smell. They fully appreciate that the sense exists in other people and understand why someone would go to a good restaurant or smell a bunch of roses, it's just that they cannot enjoy these experiences themselves. That is as near as I can describe his condition. There was something missing, but I could not say what it was.'

'How did you treat him?'

'I didn't treat him. I talked to him, yes, but I didn't treat him because I couldn't reach a clear assessment of his condition in my own mind. And, anyway, he made it plain that he didn't need my help. He would do whatever had to be done alone. That was the point – alone. I've met men like him, but never seen one quite so self-reliant, quite so alone. Clearly he felt strongly about things, but he was not prepared to share them with me.'

'Did he mention his childhood in Africa? Apparently he saw his brother shot in front of him.'

'Yes, he told me about it but I could not see that as being the root cause of his problems. He was matter-of-fact about it and talked easily about the loss of his brother. He made a kind of statement to me, which he had clearly formulated long before and which embraced the proper emotional responses, but did not betray any real signs of delayed trauma. I have to say that I took him at his word, although this, of course, is not the usual practice in my profession.'

'So what happened? How did he leave here?'

'He got better, and in the last few weeks took a great deal of exercise. By the time he left, which was in the early spring of that year, he looked fit and well, as normal as any of us. There's not much else to say apart from that.'

'And you felt there was no danger of him having another episode?'

'You can never tell. But my view was that this man had decided that he would not succumb to mental illness or nervous strain. He had analysed the problem and fought it. Some people can do that. It requires immense strength of character, but it's not impossible.'

When Foyle had returned to his home in Wimbledon he found the phone ringing. It was the commissioner, who was in his car on the way to an *Any Questions* radio discussion in which he was expecting to have to defend the Anti-terrorist Unit's performance. This hadn't helped Roy Urquhart's mood and he'd told Foyle that if he persisted in getting in the way he'd be dismissed from the force and his pension rights would be jeopardised. Later Foyle had turned on his radio to listen to the programme, in which Urquhart came in for some heavy criticism from the panel.

But now he waited for a call from Con Lindow. He looked at his watch. It was six thirty p.m. in the States: he still might phone. The football programme came to an end and Foyle allowed himself to be drawn into a French film which starred Stephane Audran and seemed to be set entirely in restaurants.

A few minutes past midnight his doorbell sounded. He hitched up his suit trousers and went to the door to find an attractive woman in a dark overcoat and scarf tied loosely around her neck. 'Commander Foyle?' she said. 'It's late, I know, but could we have a word?'

Foyle looked at her and wondered wildly if someone was trying to set him up. 'By all means,' he said. 'But who are you?'

'Would you mind if I didn't give you my name? I'd prefer that this conversation took place off the record. It'll be simpler for both of us.'

Foyle shrugged and showed her into the sitting room where Audran reclined in a silk slip, having moved swiftly from a restaurant to the bedroom.

'She's good, isn't she?' said the woman.

'Yes,' said Foyle, aiming the remote at Audran in mid-pout. 'What do you want to talk to me about?'

'The investigation into the recent explosions.'

'If you've information to give, you must approach New Scotland Yard. I'm no longer leading the investigation. Assistant Commissioner Scarratt will be happy to talk to you at any time.'

The woman sighed. 'Look, Commander. I am not trying to trap you. I know you've probably been warned off by the commissioner. I also know that if you continue getting under their feet they will seek to use your daughter as a means of acquiring your compliance.'

'Ah, I see,' said Foyle, 'you're from MI5. I should have guessed it. You might as well tell me your name now.'

'That won't be necessary. I'll say it again – I haven't come here to threaten you, merely to find out whether we can help each other. That's all. I mentioned Katherine because I believe they will attempt to embarrass you with an arrest, probably for drugs, so you should tell her to be careful for the next few weeks at least.'

'For the record, my daughter, Kate, does not use any form of drugs.' Foyle felt that he sounded less than confident.

'I'm sure. Look, we both know that your investigations have led you to a man named Archie Cram.'

'I assumed Cram might alert your lot. He told me very little and I know almost nothing else. I'm out of it, as you know.'

'You're underestimating yourself, Commander. I know you went to Dublin this week to see Con Lindow, and that subsequent to that meeting Dr Lindow left for the United States with information that he believes will lead him to the individual or individuals responsible for this campaign. You are collaborating with Dr Lindow and, far from being on the margins of this investigation, as you pretend, you are at the centre of it. I would guess you have a clearer understanding than anyone else at this moment.'

'So you want to know who I'm going to talk to. Well, to tell you the truth, I have no more leads. I've reached a dead end.'

The woman shook her head, then said, with an air of self-reproach, 'Perhaps I've mishandled this. Let me explain why I'm here. I care deeply for the service and I believe it has an invaluable role in modern government. This situation threatens everything. I can't pretend that my colleagues share my view, but I'm certain that the danger is real and immediate.'

Foyle's eyes rolled to the ceiling.

'No! Hear me out, Commander. This case is not simply a minor inconvenience to us. It's much more than that. It could destroy the important – and legitimate – work that we do, to say nothing of the advances we've made over the last few years within government. There are issues of justice in this, but I confess that I now believe there is a far bigger principle at stake, and that is the survival of my department as a credible force for good in this country. What I want to know is quite simply this. How close are you to the exposure of my department?'

'You mean you've come here off your own bat, without anyone knowing?' Foyle was incredulous.

'Yes, I've been utterly straight with you, Commander. I want to go away with an idea of the timescale involved.'

Foyle studied his visitor. It was just his luck to get saddled with some bluestocking spook at the very moment he expected Lindow to call. Still, she was attractive, in a formal way, and all this business about saving the honour of the service was too bizarre to be anything but true. The main point, though, was that she confirmed his suspicions that Millbank had a very special interest in Rhodes.

'Can I give you a drink?' An echo of Christy Calvert, he thought.

She shook her head. 'No, but I'd like to smoke, if that's all right?'

'Go ahead. I'd like to be able to help you,' he said. 'But my interest in this is solely about bringing the right man to court. Your people knew that Lindow was innocent and yet Cantor moved heaven and earth to get him charged – presumably to buy you time.'

'But there are still very good reasons for charging him,' said the woman. 'His phone records indicate that he made calls to the telephone connected to the last bomb.'

'My word, you are up-to-date. Nevertheless, we both appreciate that Lindow didn't make that call knowing he was dialling a suitcase full of Semtex. We both know that the bomber was playing a game. It's my belief that this character is unhinged, and I think these games he's been playing with the telephones indicate that he's got a taste for it and will explode more devices. We can explain the last two bombs, because they were clearly commissioned by some lunatic environmental group. But in each case he added his own twist. I believe – but I cannot prove – that the second bomb at the Interwaste building was detonated by a call I made. The same method was used with Lindow. He responded to a message from a letting agent.' Foyle paused. 'So, you'll forgive me if I do not put the reputation of MI5 high on my list of priorities at the moment. My aim is simply to stop this man creating the sort of carnage he did in Clarence Street.'

'Believe me, I understand,' said the woman. 'One of our people was badly injured.'

Foyle was shocked. 'Really! I didn't know that. What was he doing there?'

'I can't say. But I can tell you this. There is evidence of Rhodes's presence near Clarence Street that evening.'

'What sort of evidence?' demanded Foyle.

She gave him a look of regret. 'Again, I can't say. But I believe there is evidence, and you will need it because all you've got so far is a lot of hunches and instincts. There's nothing hard to connect Rhodes with the bombs.'

Foyle's eyes flicked to the message cassette from Lindow's answering-machine lying on the table. That was evidence, and in all probability the bomber had no idea that the connection had been made between his message to Lindow and the third bomb.

'I am prepared to help you,' she continued, 'but you've got to help me in exchange. You've got to tell me when you're getting close.'

'We'll see. But why can't you give it to me now, this evidence you have?'

'Because I don't have it in my possession.' He had a strong suspicion that she was lying. 'It's a well-guarded secret and at this stage I simply can't get it for you. But I will, at the right moment. Then I want you to give me an undertaking that it will only be used as supporting evidence. You won't produce it in court as primary evidence for the prosecution.'

'I can't agree to conditions until I see the evidence. Anyway, it's more likely that you'll get to Rhodes before I do. You must have the whole service working on this. I'm just one person.'

'Two,' she said.

'A former suspect and a discredited detective are hardly a match for MI5.' Foyle cocked his head sceptically at her.

She ignored the remark. 'You may need to get in touch with me. Here's my pager and telephone numbers.' She tore a page from the back of her diary.

'And your name?'

'You won't need my name with these numbers. They're all personal.'

Foyle got up and put the piece of paper on the table next to the message tape. The woman also rose and made for the front door where she turned to him. 'Thank you,' she said. 'I'd be grateful if you kept this private. It'll be in both our interests, I assure you.'

He watched her walk down the path until she was out of sight behind the laurel bushes at the end of his front garden.

As dawn broke Lindow got up and went in search of the lodge owner, who had promised the evening before to find them a plane and a pilot for the day. His only doubt had been about the weather. As Lindow walked from the cabin to the main building he looked through the trees towards the light in the east. The cloud cover seemed high enough, and although there was a wintry edge to the wind, it wasn't too strong.

He found the man making up the fire in the dining room. Without looking up or saying a word, he fished in his back pocket and gave Lindow the details of Lily Bay

Aviation. Lindow called the number from a payphone at the reception desk and explained that he wanted the plane for a couple of hours to take some photographs of an area about fifty miles north of the town. The man at the other end of the line said the plane would be fuelled up and ready by eight thirty.

He returned to the cabin clutching two cups of coffee, one of which he set down beside Mary. She rolled her head on the pillow and laid a bare arm across the empty side of the bed. Then she withdrew it under the covers and moaned, 'Where've you been?'

'Never mind,' he said softly. 'There's some coffee for you on the table. I'm going to open the shutters? Is that all right?'

She didn't answer, but groped for the cup of coffee.

Lindow went to the table in front of the window and spread out the small-scale map of Maine. He wished that Eamonn had left a third compass bearing. Three would have made the triangulation pinpoint accurate. As it was, the best he could hope for was an accuracy of five to ten miles either way, which meant they might have to search an area of several hundred square miles. He noted the position of the intersection on the map, then transferred it using his new ruler to a page on the Maine atlas. He calculated that they would need to search between the longitudes of 69 degrees, 40 minutes and 69 degrees, 25 minutes and the latitudes of 46 degrees, 20 minutes and 46 degrees, 12 minutes.

While he worked, Mary got up. After showering she presented herself stunningly nude in the bathroom doorway. 'What are you doing?'

'Finding out where we're going today. You've got ten minutes to get dressed and have some breakfast before we go and find Lily Bay Aviation.'

She made a face at him. 'So you've got a plane?'

'Yep.' He turned to check the contents of his knapsack – notebook, pen, binoculars, camera, film and zoom lens.

'It's bound to be cold,' he said, examining the long-range lens. 'Take gloves and thick socks.'

'Con, quit bossing, will you? You're sounding like some kind of fucking instructor.'

He smiled, put on his jacket and shouldered the knapsack.

Fifteen minutes later they were driving down to the lake in the Jeep, Mary clutching her cup of coffee and a pastry she had lifted from the breakfast table. They found Lily Bay Aviation on the outskirts of town and pulled up outside a large corrugated-iron hangar, which sloped to the water's edge. Nearly a dozen seaplanes were tethered to a long pontoon. A man in his thirties with a weatherbeaten face came from a shed at the side of the hangar and introduced himself as Pete Tilsson, the proprietor and chief pilot of Lily Bay Aviation. He gave them each a muscular handshake. The wind whipped up from the lake, making his eyes water.

'Is the weather okay?' asked Lindow.

'As long as we don't go too far north it'll be fine.' Tilsson led them to a shed where they signed insurance forms and paid him three hundred dollars in cash. Then he turned to a wall map and eyed Lindow shrewdly.

'What is it that you're looking for?'

Lindow replied truthfully that his brother, who was now dead, had left him instructions to find a place north of Moosehead Lake where some friends of his lived. He added that it was his brother's last wish that he should find the place. By air seemed the best way. He showed Tilsson the atlas with the search area outlined in pencil.

'We're looking for somewhere that's well hidden, but probably consists of one or two buildings. I guess it'll be near a track, but that's all I can tell you.'

Tilsson looked doubtful. 'I know most of the folks up there. Can't think of too many places where I don't know the people. Still there may be some place and we'll stand more of chance of finding it with the leaves gone.'

He led them to a single-engine Cessna at the far end of the dock. He unclipped the wire that held the wing to the shore and two more that were attached to the starboard float. They all scrambled aboard and Tilsson started the motor, motioning Lindow to put on a pair of headphones. He mumbled something into the radio and steered the plane's nose out into the centre of the bay. When they were facing dead into the wind, he checked his gauges and looked along the wings one last time, then pulled back the throttle and sent the plane skidding across Moosehead Lake. A few seconds later the pounding on the floats ceased and the plane lifted clear of the waves, leaving the town behind the starboard wing.

They climbed for ten minutes, then levelled off at eight thousand feet. Out in the east, light shafted down from a sun they could not see and scores of lakes shone like slivers of silver foil. Ahead were huge black clouds, which trailed curtains of rain beneath them. Tilsson said they'd soon hit the bad weather. Lindow turned round to tell Mary who was staring from the window with a look of childlike wonder on her face. Quite suddenly hailstones began to crackle on the windscreen and roof of the cockpit. Tilsson pushed the throttle in, causing the plane to drop into a belt of cloud. A few minutes later they emerged into clear sky with the great northern woods spread out before them. Wisps of cloud hung in the forest as if clawed from the sky by the bare branches.

They passed over the Penobscot River and approached the search area. Lindow got out his binoculars and trained them along the roads and trails that snaked through the forests. They flew north, took a sharp turn westwards, leaving Allagash Mountain to their right, and looked down at the lumber roads that criss-crossed the wilderness. Tilsson turned south and later east, completing the first in a series of diminishing squares. They flew like this for forty-five minutes. Occasionally Lindow pointed down to a homestead, but each time Tilsson shook his head and shouted that he knew the people who lived there, or that it was used in the wintertime by skiers and snowcatters, or in summer by hikers.

They dropped down to two thousand feet and flew along a strip of water marked on the map as Black Finger Lake. Tilsson bellowed that he didn't know the lake well because the fishing was no good. On the south side there was a swamp, where hundreds of bleached pine trunks lay in the silt like bones. On the north side, the lake was bordered by a long shoulder of land that ended in a cliff. Behind that was an area of high ground, which sent out a ridge of rock that plummeted into the lake about a hundred yards along from the cliff. It was difficult to make out what lay between the two points because a squall had blown down from the high ground and was dumping rain along the shoreline, but as they passed the cliff Mary shouted that she had seen something – a roof by the water and a flash of wet metal glinting in the lee of the cliff. Lindow looked on the map. Nothing was shown, no trails or buildings. Tilsson flew down the lake then turned the plane to fly past the cliff again.

Now Lindow saw the buildings. There was a boat-house or hangar on the water, painted brown and dark green to blend into the terrain. A path led through the trees to a cabin, behind which was a barn and a parked vehicle. They passed over it a second time and saw a radio mast and a satellite dish. Lindow realised the place had been built to be almost completely hidden between the cliff and the ridge of rock. In fact, it could only be seen briefly from the air for a few seconds, or from a boat stationed directly in front of the cliff. Tilsson flew along the lake, losing altitude, and turned for a final pass at a few hundred feet. By this time Lindow had got out his camera and was aiming through the port window. He shot off five frames with the motor drive whirring before the buildings disappeared behind the ridge of rock.

'Wow!' said Tilsson. 'He's got a Beaver!'

'What?'

'He's got a DHC-2 Beaver – great little workhorse.' Tilsson pointed at the snub nose of a seaplane in the waterside hangar. 'Hey, you want me to put her down so you can take a closer look?'

Lindow shook his head. 'No, thanks. This must be the place,' he said, turning back to Mary. 'We'll come back in the Jeep.'

He asked Tilsson to fly north to see if there was a road that led to the buildings. They scoured the ground for several minutes before spotting a rough track that followed the shoulder of land, then disappeared into a narrow gorge, covered by pine trees. A few miles on they picked up the track where it climbed a hill to join a lumber road. Lindow looked at the map again. Nothing was marked, but he saw they'd be able to reach the lumber road via the main route to the Allagash Wilderness from the south. It shouldn't be more than an hour and a half's drive from Moosehead Lake. He signalled Tilsson to turn for home. With the wind behind them, they were soon approaching the town. They circled and for a moment the plane seemed to hang over the buildings before dropping down to the iron-grey surface of the lake, nearly clipping the trees along the shoreline.

They left Tilsson and went to buy food and a flask of coffee for the trip. Mary argued against leaving so quickly, saying that they should find out more about the people by the lake before crashing into a situation they knew nothing about. Someone was bound to have information about the place. After all, there was an aircraft that needed fuel and servicing; there were power lines running to the buildings. They would have to get gas for the vehicle that was parked by the lake.

But Lindow was adamant. If she wanted to stay behind that would be fine. Either way he was leaving. She said nothing more, but put on a pair of sunglasses and got behind the wheel.

About fifteen miles out of town the paved road ran into a wide dirt boulevard that was humped in the middle and strewn with bark. The sides had been eroded by storms, so Mary drove along the crown, swerving occasionally to miss the long coils of bark that had been shed from the lumber trucks. They saw no other cars, but passed two groups of hikers. At a place where the road dropped, giving them a rare view of the landscape, they stopped and hurriedly consumed a ham roll each and coffee. Lindow took a compass bearing from a mountain in the west, and then from Allagash Mountain, which lay hunched to the north. He estimated they'd need to go another twenty miles before they started looking for the trail to the lake.

'Con, are you sure you want to do this?'

'What choice do I have? All I need is the exact location, some pictures of the layout, maybe some shots of the people there. That ought to be enough.'

'You really think it's going to be that simple?'

He shrugged and got into the driver's seat.

They did not speak for the next half-hour. Then, as they drove through a long stretch of utterly featureless forest, she noticed an opening in the trees and shouted out. Lindow slammed on the brakes, causing the car to skid on the dirt. Thirty yards back a track joined the road at an acute angle.

'That's it.' Lindow swung the Jeep round. 'Let's go and have a look.'

It was clear that the track had been used recently. The grass between the two wheel ruts was brushed forward, and here and there was the imprint of tyres in the dirt. They moved gingerly down the hill, negotiating the pot-holes and the rivulets that ran across the track. Half a mile on, it levelled out and was smoothed with stone chippings. They passed several small ponds and a stretch of open land before the road began to rise again.

To their right, Lindow noticed a heavy electric cable

running through the trees at a height of eight feet. Every so often there was a big loop of cable fastened to a post by a plastic belt.

'What do you think that's for?' he asked.

'It's to allow for falling trees and big animals. When the cable's hit, the loop springs free so it doesn't break.'

It was clear that they were reaching the high ground behind the cabin. They decided to continue on foot. Lindow ran the Jeep on to a piece of firm ground beneath some saplings and got out with his knapsack. He fitted the long lens to the body of the camera, then turned to the back of the Jeep to see Mary checking a pistol.

'What's that?'

'A nine-millimetre Glock – model seventeen.'

'I wasn't asking what model. I was asking what you're doing with a gun.'

'A girl's got to have some protection.'

'You know, Mary, I'd really like to know who you're working for. Book editors don't carry guns.'

'Book editors that are shit-scared carry guns.'

'I mean, where the hell did you get a thing like that? You didn't have it in Ireland.' His temper was beginning to show.

'No, I didn't have it Ireland, but that episode made me think I needed some protection if you were going to haul me into the wilderness with no more than a damned pocket knife.' He could see the subject was closed.

She pocketed the gun and set off through the trees to the left of the track. Lindow stood for a moment, suddenly wondering what on earth he was doing. He cursed himself, cursed Eamonn and the Provisionals, cursed Ireland and his mother's nationalism. What he wanted was normality – his books, his lab, his early morning espresso and the quiet daily purpose of scientific inquiry. He slammed the car door, locked it and trudged after Mary, resenting her impressive pace up the hill.

It was much further than they'd expected and by the time he caught her, he'd worked up a sweat. The hill had several false summits but eventually they broke out of the trees to an area of bald black rock that rose before them like the back of a whale. They saw the lake below and stood still. The place was utterly silent: there were no bird calls and the wind had dropped so that the boughs of the pines swayed only a little. They edged round the hill and the cliff came into view followed by part of the cabin roof. Mary crouched and waved him down, patting the air beside her. She whispered that they shouldn't talk because their voices would travel. Then she gestured to some dense brush that had taken root in the cracks of the rock and slid expertly on all fours into the cover. Lindow followed her in an awkward crab walk, moving sideways and holding the camera above him. Twenty feet on she stopped and pointed through a gap in the brushwood. The whole place was laid out before them. There were two cabins set at right angles and joined by a flat tin roof, under which were piled stacks of timber, a wood trellis, two snowcats, snowshoes, chain-saws, shovels, coils of rope and chain. Across the yard a large Ford truck had been moved out into the open. Down by the lake Lindow could make out the hangar. He focused the camera and took some photographs of the radio mast and satellite dish. Mary flinched at the noise of the automatic drive and hissed that he should use the manual wind-on. Then she took the binoculars from him and swept the yard, pausing on the truck. He watched her lips move, as she memorised the licence-plate.

Lindow was looking down when the patch of rock beside him suddenly sent up a shower of splinters. Then he heard the gunshot echoing in the trees, almost like a woodpecker. Mary rolled to her right, pulling the Glock from her pocket. Nothing happened; they could see no one. They searched each other's faces. Then they heard movement some way off to their right. Mary raised her head.

'Stand up,' said a man's voice. 'And come towards me. Please don't try to escape.'

Chapter Thirteen

The voice was English, very calm and with no hint of menace. Lindow looked stupidly around him, without the faintest idea where it was coming from. Mary jabbed her gun in the direction of their Jeep. He leaned back on the cold, wet rock to see the torso of a man about fifty feet away. The figure held an assault rifle to his shoulder and pointed to their position with his other hand. 'Get up and walk over here so that I can see you both – and don't move suddenly.'

'Look, we were just hiking through here,' said Mary, getting up slowly with the gun held behind her. 'We don't want any trouble. We'll leave.'

Lindow rose also. He could see the man properly now. He was wearing black work trousers, a dark green jacket and a ski mask.

'I was waiting for you,' he said casually. 'It was your plane that flew over here this morning, wasn't it? You saved me a lot of hanging about by coming so soon.'

They got to within twenty feet of him and stopped. Lindow wondered if this was Rhodes.

'Now, you with the gun,' said the man, facing Mary, 'put it on the ground and tell me what your name is.'

She placed the Glock on a carpet of pine needles and said her name was Mary Sheaffer.

'And you,' he said to Lindow, 'what's your name?'

'Richard Lithgow. What's yours?' said Lindow, searching the eyeslit of the ski mask.

The man ignored the question and waved his rifle

towards a deer track, which curled round the hill down to the cabins. 'Go down there and no screwing around. You understand?'

'Look—' said Mary.

'Just do as I say.'

When they reached the yard, after sliding on their backsides and hands over an outcrop of rock that oozed water, he told them to go inside the far cabin and sit down on the floor. The place was larger and better lit than Lindow had expected. This was some kind of workshop. The other cabin must be where the man slept.

He ordered them to sit down back to back in the centre of the room. Lindow sat facing the window that overlooked the lake and aircraft hangar. Beneath the window was a long workbench with three lights angled over its surface. To the right of the bench some shelves held a radio scanner, a short-wave radio set and a TV screen, which was split into twelve small images of the surrounding forest. It was clear that the man had got all possible approaches to the cabin covered by cameras. In the bottom right-hand corner of the screen Lindow could see the milky image of their car. To the left were two views of the lumber road. He must have seen them pass the turning, go back and crawl down the track towards his cabin. He'd have known exactly which route they'd take through the woods. His eyes moved to the bench where there was a mass of equipment – circuit boards, a soldering iron, an ammeter, a rack of screwdrivers and many small electrical components still in their plastic wrappers. Everything was neatly ordered, marshalled for use.

'Yes, I saw you coming about forty-five minutes ago,' said the man, placing Mary's pistol on a table next to a computer. 'It's a very good little system. But it's rare that I see anyone. It's mostly animals and the odd deer-hunter from now on through the winter.' His tone was conversational. There was still no hint of menace.

He hit a key on the computer, which disengaged the screen-saver and brought up a menu. He waited, idly examining Mary's gun. Then he started typing with one hand. Lindow's eyes focused on the area below the workbench where trays containing electrical equipment were stacked. He recognised most of the components – five mobile phones, stripped of their casings, several different types of electrical switch, a digital display from a video-player and a number of electrical plugs, used by householders to turn on the lights when they're out.

One tray held an assortment of squat industrial batteries. Lying beside this was a plywood board, which might have been constructed by a schoolmaster to demonstrate a particular piece of circuitry. He concentrated on the panel. At the top of the board was a small plastic box, faced with a black concave mirror. Wires led from the box to a battery then to an electrical switch and on to what he assumed was a detonator. In an instant, he saw how it worked. The box was an infrared detector, of the type used in security systems to pick up the heat radiation of a human presence. Here it had been incorporated as a trip that caused a circuit to connect when someone approached – an ideal booby trap that relied on nothing more than the warmth of a living person.

The keys chattered for a little while, then they heard the dialling of a modem. Lindow could feel Mary straining to see what was going on, but he was concentrating on something else. He had just noticed a piece of yellow paper stuck to the side of the computer, on which was scrawled in large, untidy writing AXIOM DAY.

The man stopped typing and glanced up at the daylight in the window.

'Wind's getting up again,' he said. 'Hope we aren't going to have another storm. Nearly brought my dish and aerial down last time.'

Still staring out of the window, the man removed his jacket, tugged the ski mask from his head and turned to show his face to them. An area of puckered white scar tissue covered the left side of his face and ran down his neck to the line of his turtleneck sweater. The skin around his left eye was creased and shiny, like the permanent folds in a piece of parchment. Lindow put his age at no more than forty-eight. He was still youthful and it was obvious that he'd once been good-looking. His eyes were very blue and very still. His mouth smiled easily, but the scarred cheek did not rise with the other, giving him an odd lopsided look as he talked.

'Not very pretty, is it?' he said, challenging Lindow's gaze. 'But I've got used to it now. Causes me problems in the sun and in the cold. It's not as resilient as normal skin – hence the ski mask.'

The computer bleeped and the man returned to the screen. He read for a few seconds then turned to them. 'You have to tell me who you are,' he said, picking up the rifle. 'Are you with some kind of agency?'

'It's nothing like that,' said Lindow calmly. 'We're up here for the weekend. This place looked kind of interesting, so we thought we'd explore.'

'Yes,' said the man, his tone still even and civil. 'But why did you take pictures of my yard? Why did you fly over here three times this morning? And the lady here, does she usually go out hiking with a Glock in her pocket? This is hardly casual interest, is it? So let's stop pissing about. Tell me who you are.'

He came within a couple of paces of Lindow. He smiled, then without warning lifted the butt of his gun and brought it down on Lindow's collarbone. Lindow cried out and slumped over.

The man pulled Lindow up to a sitting position and felt inside his jacket. Finding nothing, he stepped back and poured the contents of the knapsack on to the floor.

Eamonn's passport lay between the two maps. The man held it up to the light.

'It says here you're Dr Constantine Lindow.' He looked down at Lindow and smiled his crooked smile. 'But I don't think this is your photograph. So who are you – eh?' He delivered a well-aimed kick, which cut Lindow's ear open and sent him sprawling across the floor. He boiled with rage, but he stayed put and watched the blood dripping from the cut on his ear.

The man stepped across to Mary and squatted beside her, smiling solicitously. His left knee was behind her head. The barrel of the rifle pointed across the room at Lindow's stomach.

'Perhaps you'll tell me.' He grasped Mary's jaw and examined her face roughly.

'Leave her, for God's sake,' said Lindow. 'We came to find out why my brother Eamonn was killed in London. That's all there is to it. She was just a friend of his. She's got nothing to do with this. Let her go.'

'Tell me who you are then.'

'I *am* Con Lindow, as the passport says, but it's not my picture in the passport because it's a forgery. My brother had it done. He used my name and his own picture. I found it after he was killed.'

'Really?' said the man nastily. 'Now that's very interesting. Let me show you something.' He went over to a video-player, which sat beneath the CCTV screen on the shelves, selected a tape and shoved it into the mouth of the machine. He watched for a little while then stepped back with the remote. 'Pay attention to the right-hand picture. You will see a visitor of mine making his way through the woods, just as you have today.'

A figure appeared in one of the twelve sections of the screen. The man pressed a button so that it suddenly filled the entire TV screen. Lindow gaped. The figure stumbling up a hill was Eamonn. There followed several more shots from different cameras that culminated in a sequence which showed Eamonn running across the yard, looking through the window of the cabin for a few seconds and turning rapidly towards the lake. Then he vanished.

'He heard me coming in the plane, see. He must have legged it damned quick after that and he was lucky to get away without running into one of my little surprises.' He winked grotesquely at Mary and returned to her side.

Lindow knew that he had to engage him. 'Look,' he said reasonably, 'you don't have to hurt her. She doesn't know anything.'

The man took no notice. 'So, you see, you're not the first prat to blunder up here. That was your brother, wasn't it? And you've come up here looking for his killers. Am I right?'

'Not exactly,' Lindow began. 'I was intrigued by some instructions Eamonn left in the passport. They're still there, if you look in the back.'

Lindow saw Mary's eyes implore him not to say any more.

The man examined the scrap of paper and read out the bearings. 'Very neat,' he said at length. 'This device of using towns with Irish names – that's clever.' He paused and looked down at Lindow. 'So I take it that you know who Rhodes is?'

'No, I don't know who Rhodes is.' He noticed Mary's eyes fill with concentration. It was odd. Suddenly she didn't seem frightened.

'Rhodes was in charge of the operation when your brother blew up our little group at the church. I got away lightly with this.' He touched his cheek. 'A few months of plastic surgery and I was right as rain. The others weren't so lucky. You may know about it – two killed and another lost his sight. That's why Rhodes got your brother in the end. A point of honour for the op, you see. When we realised that it was your brother who was snooping on us, he became a priority.' He cleared his throat. He obviously hadn't spoken so much in a long time. 'The beauty of it was that he didn't know that someone had sold him out on his own side, someone in Real IRA or Pure IRA, or whatever they call themselves now. That's a joke isn't it – Pure IRA? You see, we had our contacts on that side of things. Rhodes had removed a couple of their people – maybe you know about that – and become their supplier. But then the whole thing shifted and it wasn't clear who was doing what to whom. Bloody funny, when you think about it. Then they found out what had happened here and decided to come back at us. But you know how it is, we had other business and we weren't about to get involved in some fucking war with the Micks. So Rhodes knew the way to sort it out was to get rid of Eamonn Lindow. He remembered the name. Odd name, Lindow. Where's it come from?' He threw the passport down with the rest of Lindow's possessions.

'I've never found out.'

Lindow knew for certain that they'd be killed. Why else would the man be telling him all this? It was then that he decided to give Mary a chance – maybe even himself as well. Her Glock was lying on the table by the computer. If he launched himself at the man's legs, he might just be able to give her time to grab the gun and fire off a round. She saw what he was thinking. Her eyes widened to signal a definite negative.

'And you don't have any idea what Axiom Day means?'

'No.'

'And you don't even know who I am?'

'No.' Lindow shook his head.

'You mean, you *really* don't know who I am? Bloody hell, you are a couple of amateurs, aren't you? Well, I see no harm in telling you. I'm Bob Lasseur – Lassa, as in fever – formerly a commissioned officer with Her Majesty's Royal Fusiliers.' The conversational tone had returned. He walked round the cabin, looking out of the windows. He was evidently enjoying himself. 'I'm inclined to believe the story that you've told me because, if you knew who I was and what Axiom Day meant, it wouldn't be just you two up here. The place would be flooded with FBI agents in body armour.'

He returned to the keyboard and began to type. This time Lindow could see more of what he was doing. After he'd composed the message, he stored it and ran a piece of software. The message flashed on the screen briefly then disappeared in a blur. He was encoding it. Finally the modem clicked and he dialled a number that he pulled down from the computer's telephone directory. Lindow knew he must be contacting Rhodes.

'We're going to have to wait,' said Lasseur. 'He's not responding.'

'Who are you trying to contact?'

'Rhodes. He's getting bad about returning messages. Still, it's understandable. We're at the end of this thing. Partnership dissolving and all that. Money banked, leaving here, going our separate ways.' Lasseur looked distracted. 'I hate this business, you sneaking up here like this. It means I've got to do something about it.'

'No, you don't have to do anything about us,' said Mary quickly. 'If you're splitting up and leaving this place, it doesn't matter what we know.'

'Oh, but it does. It's been a very profitable partnership and all our operations have been run from this humble cabin. So we can't have the FBI crawling over the place looking for clues and working out what we've been doing or who for. No, I have to leave in my own time. This place has to be decommissioned properly, everything must be disposed of. It's going to take several flights to dump this lot in the surrounding scenery.' He gestured to the workbench. 'I don't want to be hurried.'

Lindow knew that they would be disposed of in exactly the same way. Lasseur would take them down to the hangar, shoot them and load them on to the Beaver. Then he'd weight their bodies and drop them over some distant lake. If he missed, it wouldn't matter much because there were plenty of hungry animals – bears and maybe even the odd wolf – that could be relied upon to distribute their remains through the woods. By the time spring arrived and the parties of hikers came up from Boston, there'd be nothing left of them. He had to act. Any second now, Rhodes would answer Lasseur's message with an instruction to kill them immediately.

He prepared himself by rising imperceptibly, drawing one knee to his chest and pushing himself up with his left hand. He moved his leg to get some leverage, while pretending to be concerned about his ear, dabbing at the blood with the cuff of his shirt.

He hoped Mary saw what he was doing.

'Would you mind telling me something?' she asked Lasseur, with the intelligent eagerness Lindow remembered from their first meeting. 'What is this thing – Axiom Day? What's it all mean?'

Lasseur leaned forward indulgently. His face passed into a band of light that was reflected through the window from the truck's windshield.

'That's not my business. That's Rhodes's affair. To be honest, I don't know what he's planning – I'm just the ordnance man on these things. I prepare. I make suggestions. I design equipment for the contracts. But I don't go out in the field. Too easily recognised, you see.' He brushed his cheek again.

Mary nodded sympathetically. 'Sounds like quite a lot of planning was needed.'

'Yes, it's going to be *his* statement – that's all I know about it. If there's one thing he can't stand it's disloyalty, a sell-out.'

'What do you mean – sell-out?'

'Ireland, of course. Talking to the Micks over the conference table, asking their opinions, doing deals with the bastards that killed our men, letting them out of prison. That's a sell-out in anyone's language.' He looked out of the window, seeking distraction. 'Wonderful light you get up here at this time of year.'

'Yes,' said Mary. 'Magnificent. I was thinking these forests must be very beautiful in the snow, very romantic.'

Lasseur smiled. 'Yes, it's certainly very impressive.'

Lindow let his right hand slip from his knee to rest on the floor alongside the other hand. Then he distributed his weight evenly between them, swung his bottom from the floor, bringing his legs into a sprinter's start, and aimed himself at Lasseur's chair. Mary flung herself forward also, moving fast and low across the dozen or so feet. But Lasseur was too far away for both of them. He sprang on to the balls of his feet, sending the chair hurtling backwards, and swung the stock of the rifle in a scything action at Lindow's neck. He raised it and jabbed a sharp blow to the back of Mary's head. Lindow rolled over clutching his jaw. Mary dropped at Lasseur's feet, unconscious.

Then he stepped back and aimed the rifle at Lindow. 'Get her over there,' he shouted, jerking the gun towards the workbench. 'Then both of you lie face down.'

Lindow's jaw raged with pain as he placed his arms under Mary's, locked his hands together over the top of her chest and hefted her back across the floor to the workbench. He was bleeding from two places now: there was a gash on his jaw where the metal on the rifle stock had cut into the skin, and his ear was still dripping copiously. The blood splattered on to Mary's unconscious face.

'Leave her there and get down beside her,' Lasseur commanded. He looked out of the window again, and ran his hand through his hair nervously.

Lindow laid Mary out and slid his hand down to feel her pulse. It was strong and regular.

'You shouldn't have tried that,' said Lasseur. 'I haven't decided what to do with you yet. You shouldn't have jumped me like that.'

Lindow could see that he was agitated. Lasseur was tough and very agile – there was no doubt about that – but he might not have the taste for the close-up kill. What else could explain his failure to shoot them there and then? He guessed – or, rather, prayed – that Lasseur had flinched from killing them, even in self-defence, because he couldn't. Then he reasoned that this was optimistic nonsense. Lasseur had probably been on countless operations in Ulster which required him to kill without hesitation. He wouldn't in the least mind shooting them. The only reason he hadn't was that he didn't want to mess up the cabin and then have the chore of dragging their bodies down to the lake.

But there was a hesitation. Something had stopped him. Perhaps it was Mary. As Lindow had dragged her across the room he'd seen the expression of awkward regret pass over Lasseur's face. He must try to bring her round, get her talking to Lasseur again and get him responding to her as he had before they'd rushed him. He drew the hair from her face with his left hand and blew on her cheek. Then he kneaded her shoulder. But she didn't come round. He thought of Kay Gould, lying beside him in Clarence Street.

Lasseur watched him. 'She'll come to soon enough.'

The computer bleeped. He sat down by the machine and laid the rifle across his lap. He leaned in to type a few commands and waited. Then he pulled his head from the screen, muttering, 'Have I done it? Course I haven't fucking done it! It's not that simple.'

Lindow shook Mary harder. 'Come on,' he whispered urgently. 'I need you now. Wake up, for Chrissake!'

At the other end of the room Lasseur had got up and was pacing around the computer. Then he suddenly announced, 'Rhodes says he expects I've already got rid of you. That's that. No need to discuss anything. It's all right for him. He's used to this kind of thing. I'm not.' He went to the screen and stabbed angrily at the keyboard.

Lindow glanced at the door and dismissed any idea of escape. There was no hope of making a run for it and, anyway, he'd have to leave Mary. He looked under the bench for a weapon. There was nothing. Then Lasseur marched over and pointed his rifle at them. Lindow forced himself to look up into his eyes. Lasseur must see his face – understand what he was about to do. 'Rhodes says he wants confirmation that you're dead. But I need time,' he said, with an eerie note of apology. 'I'm going to tell him you're dead. I've got to think about this.'

He strode back to the computer, typed a few words and encoded them. Then he stood, bent to the screen, waiting for a reply. Lindow thought furiously. There was nothing he could do. If he tried to tackle him again he'd make Lasseur's mind up for him. At that moment it seemed that Lasseur's anger was directed at Rhodes and that was good.

The computer bleeped again. Lasseur waited. Then he straightened up, frowning at the machine. 'What the fuck . . . ?'

He didn't finish. There was a flash. The console lifted into the air and sent a storm of glass and metal over the room. The blast hit Lasseur in the stomach, folding him like a leaf and throwing him into the wall on the other side of the cabin. Instinctively Lindow covered his head in one arm and wrapped the other round Mary. Then he looked up. The explosion had blown all the bulbs, but there was still some light coming from the windows. Lasseur was sitting crumpled against the wall looking astonished. A dark red patch had spread across his chest. A curious sputtering came from the remains of the computer. Ribbons of fire had sprung along the electric cables. Lindow jumped up and hauled Mary to a standing position. He hung her arm around his neck and dragged her at a trot through the door and out into the clean, turquoise dusk. As he laid her against the wheel of the truck she moaned. 'It's okay,' he said. 'There's been an explosion. We're going to be okay. He's badly injured. The computer blew up.'

She asked again what had happened. He said there wasn't time to explain and opened the door of Lasseur's truck to see if the keys were in the ignition. They were.

Then he heard a cry come from the cabin. Lindow rose from Mary's side and walked the few paces towards the door. Lasseur screamed again – a shriek that cracked his voice. Lindow went into the cabin and searched round for a light. The fire had moved to the wall socket and was edging along a shelf of papers and manuals.

'I'm coming.' He went over to Lasseur and found a switch above his head, which turned on a light in a corridor. He stood for a moment, looking at Lasseur. The blast had ripped the clothes from his chest and torn a hole in his stomach. His intestines were showing and, lower down, an organ had spilled out from the torn muscle. Lasseur wouldn't live much longer. Lindow squatted down beside him.

Lasseur's chest convulsed and a gobbet of blood showed at his mouth. 'I was going to kill you both. I'd made up my mind.' He sucked and revolved his tongue in his mouth, as if to rid himself of an unpleasant taste. 'Finish me with the gun. Finish me off, for Christ's sake. This is hell.'

Lindow said nothing and waited. Lasseur's pain seemed to ease and he began to speak in a hoarse whisper. 'The bastard wired the CD drive with a charge . . . When I told him you were both dead, he sent me a message with a code that activated it . . . and that fired the detonator . . . That was my fucking trick – my idea. He must have put the stuff in there weeks ago. He knew he was going to kill me . . . and I knew it too, but I thought I was safe while he was in England.' He paused and closed his eyes. Lindow noticed that the old scar tissue stood white in his face.

'That was damned clever,' he murmured. 'Damned clever, programming the computer so everything would be destroyed. He knew I'd be killed . . . I'd have to be sitting there, decoding the message. He knew the charge would go straight for my head. But I wasn't sitting. That's why it got me in the stomach.' He swallowed several times.

'Don't talk.' Lindow rested a hand on Lasseur's shoulder. 'I'll see if I can find some water.'

'Listen to me,' whispered Lasseur. 'It's all here. Records – everything. I kept it all. Backed it up on Zip disks.'

'What're you saying?' asked Lindow, bending his ear to Lasseur's mouth.

'There's a loose floorboard . . . under the workbench. The disks are in there. They'll tell you everything.'

Lindow crawled under the belt of smoke to the workbench and tore at the trays, scattering the contents behind him. He worked his way under the bench and started thumping his fist along the floorboards. Near one of the legs he felt a panel move. He hit it again and the wood flipped up. He plunged his hand inside the cavity and felt a small plastic box. Inside there were six fat one-hundred-megabyte disks. He recognised the type at once: they were used to back up research data in his laboratory. He slipped them into his jacket pockets and ran back to Lasseur, coughing. The smoke was getting worse.

'Shoot me . . . I can't take this,' moaned Lasseur. Blood issued from his mouth with each word.

'What's Rhodes planning? Tell me what he's going to do.'

Lasseur didn't answer. Instead his eyes rolled in bewilderment.

Lindow stood up mechanically and fetched the assault rifle, which was lying a few feet away. The draught from the open door was fanning the flames. It would be only a matter of minutes before the cabin reached flashpoint. He held the rifle to the side of Lasseur's head. Lasseur felt the metal of the barrel on his skin, looked up and nodded.

'Don't!' shouted Mary, who was standing in the doorway.

Lindow hesitated, then looked down again. Lasseur's head had fallen to the left. His eyes were shut, but his last lopsided smile was still there. He was dead. Lindow threw the gun down and ran to the centre of the room where the contents of the knapsack lay in a pile. He scooped up the maps, camera and passport and ran outside, hooking his free arm round Mary in mid-stride. He pushed her into the truck, started the engine and tore from the yard. She was shaky and kept on asking him what had happened – how she had come to be lying out in the yard and why he went back into the cabin. Lindow didn't reply.

Only when they'd dumped Lasseur's truck and climbed into the Jeep, and were making their way up the track to the lumber road, did he begin to hurry through the sequence of events that had ended with the computer blowing. Once on the lumber road, he gripped the wheel to stop himself trembling, and spoke deliberately, as though to bring some order to the events of the last hour. He told her that Lasseur had used the phrase Axiom Day, and about the note on the side of the computer. He didn't mention the cache of disks under the floorboard because he'd grasped their value and, besides, it was obvious to him that Mary was a lot more than a book editor. The gun and the way she had handled herself in the past hour convinced him she'd been in situations like that before.

They reached the high point of the road where, earlier in the day, Lindow had taken bearings from the mountains. Mary looked back into the darkness and spotted a pool of orange some way off to the north-west. They got out and she made him bend down into the headlight so she could see the cuts on his jaw and ear. She wetted the sleeve of her shirt using their bottled mineral water and dabbed some of the blood away.

'Someone will see the fire,' said Lindow. 'They'll look into it tomorrow and it won't take long for Tilsson to make the connection. He'll tell the police about our trip this morning. I think it would be a lot better if we just left tonight.'

'You okay to drive? I still feel pretty rough.'

'I'm fine.' Lindow got back into the Jeep and they continued towards Moosehead, eating the remainder of the food and sipping the coffee, which the flask had kept warm.

'"Out there we walked quite friendly up to death—"'

'Are you all right?' Lindow worried about the blow to her head.

She repeated the line, '"Out there we walked quite friendly up to death, sat down and ate beside him, cool and bland – Pardoned his spilling mess tins in our hand, sniffed the green thick odour of his breath."' She paused. 'It comes from "The Next War" by Wilfred Owen. Did you know Owen was killed just a week before the Armistice was signed? That's tomorrow, the fourth of November. We should drink to him and celebrate our own survival.' He saw her lift her plastic cup in the light of the dashboard and shudder. 'Jesus . . .' she said.

'You're not a book editor, are you?'

'Yes, I am – and a few other things also.'

'What other things?'

'That's for another time, Con. We're alive. That's all that matters now.'

When they got back to the lodge they went straight to their cabin rather than walking through Reception. Lindow was particularly conscious of his appearance and knew he needed to clean up before paying. In the cabin he removed his bloody shirt then sponged down his ear and jaw with warm water in front of the bathroom mirror.

The cut on his ear turned out to be surprisingly small. The injury to his jaw was nastier.

Meanwhile, Mary scrutinised the lump on the back of her head by holding up a makeup mirror to it. She found a little of Lindow's blood on her shirt collar and pulled her sweater and shirt over the bruise with care. Lindow moved behind her, cupped her breasts in his hands and looked at her in the mirror. She turned in his arms. They kissed lightly, then greedily. 'I will tell you what I do,' she said, between kisses, 'but I can't yet. You must understand, Con.'

Lindow nodded in the knowledge that he hadn't been entirely open either. They began to make love urgently, slipping on the tiles of the bathroom floor before reaching the bed. There Mary straddled Lindow, climaxed quickly and slumped forward exhausted. She returned to the sitting position and rose to the point of disengagement, whereupon she lowered herself by degrees, looking down at him with an odd, distant expression.

Twenty minutes later they checked out of the lodge, telling the owner they were heading north, to Canada, an unlikely story at that time of the evening. But he seemed happy to accept it, particularly as Lindow offered to pay for the night they wouldn't be staying and added that they would certainly return when they were less busy.

They reached Boston six hours later at one thirty a.m. Mary had slept most of the way and, on arrival at the Omni Parker, was drowsily compliant to Lindow's suggestion that they should take separate rooms. The desk clerk handed her a slip of paper, saying that there had been several phone messages for her during the day. Mary read the message and tucked it into her jeans.

'What's that?' asked Lindow.

'Nothing. I told my father he could contact me here. I thought we'd be back sooner or later.' He suspected she was lying but said nothing.

Thirty-five minutes later he was sitting with Varrone relating the events of the past twenty-four hours.

'It's ingenious,' said Varrone, after Lindow had completed his account. 'This guy Rhodes obviously programmed the computer to think that a CD had been placed in the drive when it received a certain command. Thereafter it was a simple matter to wire the drive to a detonator and pack the box with plastic explosive. When the command came, hidden in one of their messages, the drive started and, boom, Lasseur gets it in the stomach. Let's have a look at these disks and see what they tell us about Rhodes.'

They went through to his workroom where he started searching the shelves for a Zip drive. At length he located an oblong blue box, about the size of a paperback, and plugged it into the back of one of his computers. He fed one of the disks into the external drive, which began to hum. An icon appeared on the blank screen, which he opened to reveal a series of numbered files. He clicked on one with his mouse and the screen filled with a patch-work of symbols and digits, as if someone had been hitting the keys and space bar at random.

'As I expected, it's encrypted. Know anything about modern cryptography, Con?' Varrone slipped another disk into the drive. 'We're going to need some serious computing power to read all this, particularly if these six disks have different codes.' He grunted as a new cyphertext appeared on the screen. 'From what you've told me, I think we ought to bring Mundy in on this now. I'll call him at home.'

'That's fine,' said Lindow, 'as long as I can be the first to take any relevant information back to the British authorities. In fact, I'd like to call Commander Foyle now.'

'Be my guest. There are several lines in the next room,' said Varrone, without looking up.

*

It was eight thirty a.m. in Britain when Foyle moved unhurriedly from the bathroom and picked up the phone by his bed. 'Yes,' he snapped. He was conscious of a certain opacity at the front of his head, the result of a bottle of Merlot shared with Carla Pryn over a late dinner at La Bourriche.

'It's Con Lindow. I know it's early.'

'Good heavens, don't worry about that,' said Foyle, wiping the shaving foam from his neck. 'I was hoping to hear from you. What's happening?'

'You're going to have to speak up. My hearing's not so good at the moment.'

'What's happening?' boomed Foyle.

'A lot,' said Lindow. 'There's so much I don't know where to start. The first thing I need to tell you is that Rhodes plans a further bombing. I don't know when or where, but he's got some kind of crazy operation called Axiom Day. You remember – that was the phrase I found in my brother's passport.'

'Yes, do you have any idea when?'

'No. Look, how do you want to handle this? I've got a lot to tell you. Do you want me to call when you're ready?'

'No, go ahead. I've got a pen and paper here.' Foyle settled himself on the bed and pulled the bedside table from the wall so that he could write more easily.

Lindow described the plane trip and told him how they'd spotted a cabin hidden in some rough terrain about thirty miles from the Canadian border. He related how they'd driven up there later in the day and were caught observing the place by a man whom they'd later learned was Lasseur.

'So, they're working together.'

'Were. Lasseur's dead. He was killed by an explosion today – actually yesterday. Rhodes had wired Lasseur's computer so it exploded on the receipt of a coded command.'

Foyle whistled. 'What? A kind of e-mail bomb?'

'Exactly.'

'Were you in the room?'

'Yes, he had us lying on the floor by that time so we were shielded from the blast.'

'Who's we – Mary?'

'Yes.'

'So, when the time comes, she can be a witness to everything you saw and heard in that cabin.'

'Yes, but not everything because he knocked her out when we tried to overpower him. But she definitely heard him talk about Rhodes. In fact, as I recall, she asked what Axiom Day was about. Lasseur told her that he only knew it was going to be Rhodes's statement, some kind of revenge on the British government for dealing with the IRA, letting prisoners go and so on. But there's something else. After I got Mary out of the cabin I heard Lasseur cry out. I went back. He had terrible injuries, but he was still alive. He knew Rhodes had caused the explosion and he knew he was dying. He told me that he'd backed up everything on some disks. All their messages, all the details of their plans – everything.'

'Good Lord. Have you got them?'

'Yes, but they're encrypted – it's going to take some time to decipher them. I don't know how long. I'm working on them now with Peter Varrone.'

'Tell him to keep all of this to himself. I don't want anyone to hear about these disks until we've got the whole picture and we can use the information to pin down this bastard. It's crucial that none of this comes out before we're absolutely ready – crucial for both of us. What about Mary? Does she know about the disks?'

'No, she was still unconscious while all this was happening. And I decided not to tell her about them.' He went silent.

'Con?'

'Sorry, I guess I'm pretty tired.'

'Well, I can't let you go yet, I'm afraid. It's too important.'

He then asked Lindow to imagine himself in the cabin and to describe everything he'd seen. Forty minutes later he had filled half a dozen pages of the notebook with a detailed inventory of the cabin and a record of what Lasseur had said about Rhodes and their operations. Towards the end of the conversation Foyle could feel Lindow's energy flagging. He was slurring some words and not finishing his sentences. 'Okay, Con. That's enough for the moment. There's a lot to do while we're waiting for those disks to be decoded. Where are you going to be in the next few hours?'

Lindow gave him Varrone's number.

'We'll talk later then. This is looking really good, Con. You've done marvellous work. Thank God you're safe.'

Foyle put down the phone gently, then stood up and clapped his hands together.

Chapter Fourteen

After talking to Foyle, Lindow stretched out in Varrone's sitting room and slept. Three hours later he was woken by the looming figure of Mundy, proffering a cup of coffee.

'We need you, Dr Lindow. Hey!' he exclaimed. 'You should have a real doctor take a look at that jaw.'

Lindow eased himself up and drank the coffee. Varrone came into focus, sitting on the arm of the sofa opposite. 'Thank you,' he said to Mundy. He rubbed the back of his head. 'God, I've come to hate mornings.'

'That's because you're young,' Varrone told him. 'Get to my age and you'll find mornings are accompanied by purpose rather than regret.'

'I'll look forward to that,' said Lindow sourly.

'Okay,' said Mundy. 'Let's cut to the chase here, Doctor. I need to know exactly the position of this cabin you were at yesterday. Can you point it out to me on this map here?'

Lindow peered down at a map on the coffee table and silently ran his finger north of Moosehead to a tiny strip of blue, marked Bl'k F'ger Lake. 'The cabin is on the north side of the lake. You'll find a track that branches at a sharp angle from the road here. It doesn't look promising but that's where you'll find it.'

'The wolf's lair, huh?' Mundy grinned and folded the map. 'You've certainly stirred things up, Doctor. Peter told me some of what happened yesterday. I'll go through that with you later. But at the moment I want to get some of our guys choppered up to Maine. There may be quite a lot we can recover from the cabin.'

Lindow nodded.

'We've had someone make discreet inquiries with the state police. They've received no reports of a fire, but at some stage they'll hear about it and then I guess this'll become a murder investigation. You and your friend, Miss . . . ?'

'Mary Menihan.'

'You and Miss Menihan are the only witnesses, so they'll want to interview you.'

'That'll have to wait,' Lindow said sharply. He didn't want Mundy taking over. 'What matters is the material on those disks. We need to get them decrypted, then I'll take the results to London.'

Before he could finish, Mundy had risen and was making for the door. 'Look, there's no problem here. All I want is to get this information to my people.'

'I was coming to the disks,' Varrone said, when Mundy was gone. 'They're interesting because I don't know what software they were generated in. Normally a file carries a tag to ensure that the computer recognises the type of software and responds accordingly. So the first thing I've done is to copy the header from one of the files and post it on an Internet site to see if anyone can help with the software identity. No replies yet. But we can start making some assumptions. Tell me what the set-up was – the way Lasseur sent his messages and what he did when he received them.' Varrone's hands shook. It irritated Lindow, but he checked himself, realising that his lack of sleep was the problem.

'Lasseur had a standard PC with the screen mounted on the box. There was a modem and that was about all. I think he had some sort of encryption software but I don't know whether he was using the Internet.'

'I wonder if he was using a secure modem too. It works on the same principle as a telephone scrambler and would add another layer of security. I think we may be dealing with something relatively simple here – a standard compression program, which can only be unlocked with a password consisting of an eight-character combination of letters and/or digits. People make their own choice, their mother-in-law's maiden name, a distant constellation – whatever takes their fancy. The method of compression, or the algorithm that encrypts the text, remains a secret held by the software company.'

'So in theory we could ask the software company,' said Lindow, pouring more coffee.

'Yes, but we don't know who they are – and, anyway, they're unlikely to help because it would invalidate their product if they gave it out to just anyone.'

'So what other routes are there?' asked Lindow, feeling fully awake now. 'Can we attack the password?'

'If there is a password, yes. But it's going to take huge amounts of computing time. We began to set up a relay of mainframe computers while you were asleep. I've called a few favours in, and having Frank around helps. The FBI carries weight in this area now.' Varrone paced the room, glancing across the roofs to Boston Common which, in the first light, had become a study in grey. 'We can start doing some work on the password now by pooling all the information we have on Rhodes and Lasseur, looking for areas in their backgrounds that would suggest a particular type of password.'

'That sounds damned hit-and-miss to me.'

Varrone ignored him. 'If we knew that either of these parties was religious, we could easily apply all eight-letter words in the Bible to the password, even eight-letter words that have slight spelling mistakes or where one letter is substituted by a number. For example, where the "I"s in "Divinity" are replaced by the number one. It follows that we can do this with a dictionary or any other reference book. Then it becomes a matter of time. But you can't be half right – either you get a match or you don't. The main problem now is that we can't do anything until we know what sort of software generated those files. Only then can we extract the encrypted password and start a brute-force attack.'

'You mean you can find the password in the file then feed it to the program? That doesn't seem to make sense.'

'No, the fact that you possess the password file doesn't mean that you're anywhere near compromising the encryption. Passwords are encrypted one way. There is no inverse route, you simply type in a word, the computer encrypts the word and waits for a match. If there is no match, the file stays in code. There's no way of pulling a password and reversing the encryption.'

'You know quite a lot about this, Peter.'

'A little. This is Frank's line of work now. He runs a cryptanalysis operation for the Bureau. I help him out with resources and contacts – sometimes ideas.'

'Look, there's something I need to say now. If you get anything out of those disks, it's crucial that I take the information back to London with me. If the wrong people get hold of the material it might easily be destroyed. There's official resistance to anything that links Rhodes to these bombs. That's why I'm here and why Foyle was removed from the investigation. To turn that situation around, I want to give Foyle complete access to the information before anyone else. What I'm saying is that Frank can't hand it on to MI5 or the police in some kind of act of fraternal co-operation.'

'Con, I know you've been through a lot, but cool it. There's no question of Frank jumping the gun. He's utterly straight – and, besides, his views on British law-enforcement agencies are not complimentary.' Varrone held a hand up. 'Hold on, I think I heard my e-mail come up.'

They rushed to his office and Varrone brought up the

message. 'It's from some guy at Berkeley. Says the file is GenoType. Have you heard of it?'

'Yes, it's the software used by drug companies engaged in recombinant DNA technology – inventing drugs and vaccines from new combinations of genes, usually from different biological sources. In short, it means inserting a characteristic found in one organism into another.'

'Yes, yes, I'm familiar with these techniques, Con. What do we know about the software?'

'The point is that the combinations of genes have great value, so the data is stored in encrypted form to prevent theft, while the company applies for a patent and carries out more research. GenoType is a software that performs this task very quickly. But it's odd that Lasseur got hold of it. I wouldn't have thought he'd know where to find it. It's not exactly Windows.'

'It's not a problem with a software directory. He was probably just looking for an obscure encryption program. It's fast and relatively simple and, if used in conjunction with a secure modem, it would offer acceptable levels of privacy. Do you know anyone who uses it?'

'I guess I could find someone,' Lindow replied. 'But it's not going to be easy on the weekend – and, anyway, I doubt if they'd know much about the actual software.'

'True. I wonder if this individual here knows anything,' said Varrone, pointing to the e-mail still on his screen. 'I'll try him again.'

Varrone began typing a message. Lindow returned to the sitting room, helped himself to more coffee and took one of the pastries from a basket laid out by Varrone's cook.

Varrone joined him shortly. 'My Californian night owl is still awake. He's going to send me something in a few minutes.' No sooner had he finished speaking than a ping came from the computer mailbox next door.

The e-mail from California was quite specific. The password was to be found near the top of the encrypted file in a special cache. Varrone immediately located and isolated the code, then copied it into a separate file on his own system. He repeated the process with each disk, collecting six strands of code. Since there was no way of telling whether the passwords were the same he numbered the new files from one to six, and pencilled a number on the case of each corresponding disk.

'This man at Berkeley seems to know a lot about the software,' he said. 'I wonder if he's connected with the company that made it. I'll ask him later. But what we need now is to raise your friend Foyle and ask him to tell us everything he knows about the two men. I'll set up a conference call next door.'

In a few minutes Lindow, Varrone and Frank Mundy, who had returned from seeing off the helicopter mission, sat waiting for Foyle to answer his phone. At length Foyle came on. Lindow smiled. 'Hello, it's Con. We've made a little headway with these disks, but Peter Varrone, who's here with me, believes that you can help with your knowledge of Rhodes. I am also sitting here with Special Agent Frank Mundy from the FBI.'

'Is he trustworthy?'

'We're on a conference phone, Commander. This is Peter Varrone speaking. You can take my word for it that Mr Mundy has unimpeachable credentials.'

'Good.' Foyle betrayed no sign of embarrassment.

'Good morning, Commander,' said Mundy coolly, turning to a fresh page in his notebook.

'The position is this,' said Varrone. 'We have these files and possibly six passwords, which we'll need to break before decryption is possible. I have set up a relay of computers that can mount a brute-force attack, but it would be useful to narrow down the area of search. Anything you know might be helpful. We just don't know what it is.'

Foyle began with Rhodes's early years and went right through to his time as a freelance operator. Mundy wrote it all down. Lindow noticed him occasionally underlining words and phrases that might have been used. Nothing seemed to stand out and after nearly thirty minutes Foyle ran dry.

'Commander,' said Mundy, 'we shouldn't forget about the guy this end, Robert Lasseur. He was the desk man in this outfit. According to Con, he looked after the technical side of their operations, arranged supplies, kept the business records. It could be that he set the passwords.'

'I agree,' said Foyle. 'But Con met Lasseur.'

'I spent an hour in his company. The circumstances were not conducive to gaining a lot of information. But there were a couple of things I noticed. The first is that his designs incorporated devices normally associated with safety. In London they packed fire extinguishers with explosive. Up at the cabin I saw an arrangement that used an infrared detector from a burglar-alarm system. I'm certain that was a prototype booby trap. The other thing is the obsession with revenge. Lasseur mentioned Rhodes's final operation – this thing he called Axiom Day. He said something about the British government ignoring the sacrifice made by soldiers in Ulster – how the only people that were consulted were terrorists.'

'This ties in with what I've been hearing,' said Foyle. 'I'm going to have another word with Christy Calvert. He's the only other member of the Droy group still to be walking around. That's what I ought to be doing now, unless there's something else you need.'

The call ended and Mundy and Varrone went into a huddle around his computer to draw up a plan of action. Mundy already had a list of hackers and mainframe operators, who had been contacted by his office at the FBI that morning. Each one was now sent an e-mail with the encrypted passwords attached. He and Mundy divided the dictionary into eighteen sections, giving each operator one part. The Bible was divided into three sections and distributed between five large computers that used the UNIX operating system. Then Mundy got on the phone to his department and instructed a young programmer, who'd been hauled out of bed, to write the scripts that would search several smaller reference books, including a register of international radio-call signs and a history of twentieth-century military codewords. Mundy's hunch was that Rhodes and Lasseur had chosen words that had been used before in a military context.

Within two hours, some thirty people across the United States were engaged in the task of decrypting the six passwords. None had any idea of what the passwords would unlock – they just accepted Varrone's assertion that this might be a matter of life or death. He told them that when and if the situation allowed he'd make sure they all knew how important their contribution had been.

Mundy then left for his office to keep in touch with the team in Maine. Lindow grabbed a couple of hours' extra sleep, then also left, saying that he had to do something the other side of town. As he waited outside in the street for a cab, he wondered why he had kept to himself the knowledge that Eamonn had been caught on Lasseur's surveillance system. He had come close to telling Foyle during their first conversation, but had held back at the last moment. He wanted time to think about it. He hailed a cab and told the driver to take him to Kineally Street, the address of Melly's Bar, which he'd found in Varrone's Boston telephone directory.

The traffic was thin and the cab moved quickly from the city's financial district, through an area part waste-land and part hopeful regeneration, into Southey, the Irish enclave in South Boston, where the roads narrowed. They passed along several streets of identical clinker-built houses until they reached an intersection. On the far side stood Melly's Bar, a low, uninviting, red-brick block with grilles over the windows and a neon shamrock leaf advertising Budweiser beer.

It was late morning and the intersection was busy. Youths were hanging out by the local grocery store and bulky men stood about in groups, wrapped against the damp sea air that rolled up from Old Harbor. Lindow paid off the driver and entered Melly's, where a dead Saturday evening still lingered. A dozen drinkers were ranged along the bar, their upturned faces lit by the emerald green of a TV sportscast. He walked to the far end and spoke to the bartender, a young man with a stud in his ear and eyes that shifted resentfully between the action on the football field and Lindow. He ordered a beer and asked to speak to P. J. McKenna.

'Who are you?' asked the man.

'You're meant to say, "Who wants him?"' said Lindow, sliding Eamonn's passport across the bar. The man opened it then looked up. 'Are you McKenna?' asked Lindow.

The man nodded.

'My message concerns two men. One's called Rhodes, the other Lasseur. Lasseur is dead. Rhodes is presently in England. He's planning something big. The British authorities will shortly be made aware of this. They will learn that he is working on his own account.'

'And how did the other party come to be deceased?' asked the man, with a leer.

'He was killed by an explosion late yesterday afternoon. The FBI know about it and will contact the British police independently. The situation is now clarified. There is no longer any doubt about who's responsible for recent events in London. The authorities there will learn that it is Rhodes and no one else. Have you got that?'

The man nodded and started towards the TV set.

'I haven't finished, damn it.' Lindow's temper snapped and his hand moved to grip the bartender's sleeve. The man wheeled around, but something in Lindow's eyes made him lower his fist. 'You tell Chickpea, or whatever his damned name is, that my part of the deal has been

304

completed. I expect him to leave me and my family alone now. He knows what my brother risked to help our friends. If he doesn't lay off, I will bring the entire force of the British security establishment down on him.' The last part was bullshit, but he saw that McKenna believed him. He turned and left the bar without looking back.

Outside, the street was still busy but there were no cabs in sight. Lindow swore for letting his go and began to walk in the direction of L Street. Then he spotted a cab coming from the west along Kineally Street. It slowed as it approached the intersection and, instead of crossing, came to a halt outside Melly's Bar. Somebody was about to get out. Lindow turned to run back and flag down the cab when it became free but then he saw a figure emerge, an attractive woman in a black jacket and scarf, who caused the knot of men on the other side of the street to turn their heads in unison. Lindow was seventy or eighty yards away, yet there was no mistaking Mary. He saw her bend down and say something to the driver, then enter Melly's Bar. She'd told the cab to wait.

He backed into a slight recess and watched the entrance to the bar, holding the collar of his jacket up to his face. No more than ten minutes elapsed before he saw her walk quickly from the door, look left and right, grimace at the group of men and climb into the cab. The driver did a U-turn and sped off westwards, with Mary sunk low in the back seat. She did not see Lindow.

He watched the cab disappear, blinking with anger. There was only one explanation for her sudden arrival at Melly's. She must be working for the IRA and using the same contact to send a message to them. Now everything made sense, like a problem that had been exposed to the correct formula. He'd half suspected her all along, but he cursed his stupidity none the less. It was so obvious. The IRA had used him to find the place where Rhodes and Lasseur ran their operations and they'd sent Mary along to keep track of him. They couldn't have done it without

305

his help because they didn't possess the information that Eamonn had left. Yet they must have known that it existed. That's why Mary had come to the flat the day after he was released. But when she had found him there she had made up the bullshit story about hoping to catch him. Smart of her to ring the doorbell, instead of breaking in or using her own keys. She had turned it to her advantage and moved in on him, attending the funeral, going with him to the lake. She must have set him up. She knew that he'd be beaten and that Tag would be threatened in front of him. The whole point was to start him running, to make him use the information he'd got from Eamonn. It didn't matter that they didn't have it for themselves. As long as Mary was with him every second of the day, they'd know where he was.

And then there was the gun. Where does a book editor get a professional weapon like a Glock, if not from the back room of somewhere like Melly's Bar? That first morning in Boston she must have caught a cab out here, picked up the gun, then hired the Jeep and presented herself at the hotel with that cute smile. What an idiot he'd been, suspecting her all the time but never quite facing it. He'd been simple-minded about her from the start.

Then, as he tramped up the last rise before L Street, he began to think the situation wasn't so bad after all. For one thing, Mary must have confirmed his story about Lasseur to McKenna. The IRA would therefore know that he had told the truth. He had not wavered and they'd got everything they wanted from him or, at least, everything they could hope to get. So there was now no reason for them to continue to threaten Tag. That was the outcome and the only thing that had been hurt in all this was his pride. He could live with that, although in one way he knew that Mary was the best thing that had ever happened to him. Still, that was over now and he'd just have to live without it.

He walked on for a while, then spotted a bus going to the North End. He climbed aboard and, in a very short while, arrived at the hotel where he paid the bill and collected his things from his room.

Before he left he wondered if he should leave Mary a note. Part of him wanted to, but he couldn't think what to say.

Kirsty Laing tried all Sunday to get hold of Speerman, eventually raising him at six in the evening. He seemed mildly irritated to hear her voice.

'I hope you don't mind me ringing you at home,' she said, 'but I felt you would want to be kept abreast of things.'

Now it was her keeping him in touch, her telling him the score. It felt good to her.

'Yes?' he said.

'I had a long talk with Brown Owl earlier today. She and Lindow have been north and what they've found out is going to have grave implications for the service.'

'Does she know about Rhodes – about his past association with us?'

'Yes, she was in on it. Then Lasseur, who served with Rhodes in Northern Ireland, confirmed it. Before he was killed – I'll come to that later – he told Lindow that Rhodes was planning something big in London. That's the important point. A big operation that he called Axiom Day. God knows what it is, but she was definitely under the impression that it's imminent and well planned. So it makes Rhodes an absolute priority.'

'He already is.' Kirsty felt Speerman's manner stiffen at the other end. 'A huge proportion of the service's permanent staff of two thousand are in some way deployed to look for him.'

'And that means it will leak out eventually, however security conscious we are. But it isn't getting us any-where, and all the time the service is being plunged deeper into the mire. Rhodes's name and our involvement with him are now bound to come out. The more we delay, the greater the risk to the general public. That's what matters now – not the politics, not the Millbank power games. It's the threat Rhodes poses to public safety. The wisest course must be to bring the police and the Home Office in on this. That way we distribute the responsibility.' She paused and took a breath for effect. 'If something goes wrong while this man is still at large and we haven't informed the police, we will take all the blame. All the blame, Peter, because our relationship with Rhodes is bound to come out. Foyle probably already knows what I know – maybe more.'

'You were going to tell me what happened in Maine,' said Speerman.

'Lasseur took both of them prisoner. It was clear he was planning to kill them because he talked openly about his and Rhodes's operations. He made no attempt to pretend otherwise. He told them that Rhodes and he were winding up their partnership. There was this one last unfinished piece of business to see to.'

'Then what happened?'

'Lasseur received some kind of coded message from Rhodes and his computer blew up. Brown Owl didn't see any of this. She was knocked out by Lasseur when they tried to disarm him. Lasseur died later. I gather the cabin was destroyed in the fire caused by the explosion.'

'Completely destroyed?'

'She said they saw the cabin still burning twenty miles away.'

'That's something, at least. But I take your point that the Americans are likely to comb through the place.'

'Yes. We must assume that Lindow has already told the FBI. Apparently a friend put him in touch and they showed him their file on Rhodes.'

'Is there no honour in our community these days?'

Pompous fool, thought Kirsty. 'Tell me how the computer blew up. They don't just explode of their own accord.'

She knew he was stalling her, but she was prepared to humour him. 'The computer had been programmed to act on a hidden code – I believe it's called a TSR, terminator stays resident, a very apt description in this case. It triggered the explosion when a signal was received through the modem. Look, Peter, there's a TSR in this affair. The whole thing is ready to blow up. Are you with me or not?'

'Of course, of course,' he said.

'Does that mean yes?'

'Apart from a few minor reservations, yes.'

'Then you'll come with me to the Home Secretary tomorrow morning. It will greatly help to have you there because your rank will add weight. But, to be frank, what's going to happen is going to happen, whether you come or not.'

'Do Craven-Elms and Fuller know about the developments in the States?' he asked.

Kirsty understood that Speerman wasn't just playing for time now: he was assessing the risk involved. If the watchers section and Domestic Terrorism had heard from Brown Owl, it would only be a short time before Cantor was informed. All the advantage would be lost and the director's defence would begin in earnest. She knew enough about Cantor to appreciate that in a fight for his survival there was nothing he wouldn't do.

'I don't know whether she has made her report yet.' She kept her voice neutral. 'She could wait until tomorrow, or she might already have been in touch. My purpose in talking to her was not to persuade her to follow a particular course. It was to find out what the situation was.'

This was a direct lie. She had pleaded with Mary Menihan not to call Craven-Elms before eight a.m., East

Coast time, on the following day. That meant no one would know about the events of the weekend before one p.m. in Britain. She lied because she saw no reason to make it simple for Speerman. He had to show that he wasn't merely looking after himself.

'Kirsty,' he said, in the mandarin manner that was beginning to get on her nerves, 'I'd like to sleep on this. You understand it's a very big step going straight to the Home Secretary. As far as I know, it's never been done before.'

'We've never been in such a mess before.'

'Yes, but the disloyalty entailed is very great and needs to be carefully considered.'

'Then hold your nose, Peter. When you've reached your decision you know where to contact me tomorrow.'

She realised she was on her own. Speerman hadn't even asked for the time of the appointment. He had no intention of going with her.

'Foyle's pulled it off, Con,' said Varrone, flying down the stairs. 'He's found the needle in a billion haystacks.'

Lindow put his bags down in the hallway. 'He's got all six passwords?'

'No, just two, but it was brilliant work. He interviewed a guy named Calvert, who was in the original group of soldiers, and got him to talk about Army slang and the nicknames they used for each other.' Varrone referred to a yellow legal pad. 'Two of the original group, Vincent Creech and Robert McGurk, are dead. Creech was called Muffhound or Lunchbox. Muffhound was too many letters so I tried Lunchbox, and bingo – we hit the jackpot. The encryption matched perfectly. Without Foyle's information we'd never have got it. Lunchbox is not in Webster's dictionary, so we might never have found it. By the way, why in hell would anyone be called Lunchbox?'

Lindow smiled. 'It's slang for the male genitalia,

specifically in the context of athletics when the guy's shorts leave little to the imagination. They suggest a package containing lunch . . . Forget it.'

'Damn British humour. But if that's obscure, listen to this one. McGurk was called Disney. You've got to use a Scotch accent to hear the joke – he *diz nay* work. It rhymes. "Robert McGurk diz nay work" – see?'

Varrone's Scots accent was poor, but Lindow got the point.

'So,' continued Varrone, 'I tried Disney with every possible combination of letters and numbers. Eventually I came up with DISNEYWK. And, hey presto, we got ourselves a fully decrypted file.'

'That's incredible,' said Lindow. 'So what's on the files?'

'I haven't opened them. You risked your life to get them, so I thought you'd like to be the first to read what's there.'

'Thanks.'

'But, before you do, I want you to look at something else for me.' They began to walk up the curved staircase. Varrone put a paternal arm round Lindow's shoulder. 'We didn't have any success in this brute-force attack, so a couple of hours ago I e-mailed the guy in California. Somehow I guessed he'd be waiting for me, and I was right. He was still awake. So I asked him outright whether he wrote the software. He wasn't going to answer that, but I pressed him and he sent me an intriguing little puzzle. I'm certain this guy wrote the program, but he's trying not to give too much away. Maybe he's a little scared. He wants to help, but can't.'

They reached the workroom. 'You know next to nothing about cryptology – right?'

'Not much.' Lindow bridled. However much he admired Varrone, the assumption that Varrone knew more than he did about any given subject grated with him.

'Well, in certain government-endorsed cryptosystems there are rumoured to be "trap-doors" – weaknesses that have been built into the program so that law-enforcement agencies can access the vast flow of digital traffic without using brute-force attacks. The idea is the cryptanalyst drops in on a particular communication, performs a rapid decryption using the trap-door, then moves on. It's a way of keeping an eye on a lot of different stuff – money-laundering operations, that sort of thing. I can't say whether these official trap-doors exist, but it wouldn't surprise me. Now, the point is that a lot of software writers out there have had the same idea. They write the program and build in a trap-door without their company ever knowing. Mostly they're just having a little fun, showing off to their peer group. Other times it's got a more sinister purpose. They include their own personal key to unlock the encryption so that at some future date they can rip off whatever's been encoded in that software. Let's say this guy out on the West Coast wrote the program and built in a trap-door that only he knows is there. It'd mean that he could read any file stored in the program – and if that happened to be research data on some new kind of disease-resistant potato or an all-purpose flu vaccine, or whatever, he would be in possession of something of real value. He could steal what he wanted without anyone suspecting, right?'

Lindow nodded.

'Say this guy has made a trap-door,' continued Varrone, 'but he can't say what it is, either because he'd be liable to a suit from the software company or he'd be laying himself open to criminal prosecution. He wants to help and he understands the urgency of the situation, but he just can't do it.' He picked up a printout of the e-mail. 'I know you want to read these files, but absorb this for a moment and see what you think. Let it marinate, Con, let it sink in and see if you can come up with anything.'

Lindow looked at the e-mail. There were two separate blocks of numbers, each arranged in two rows.

$$3\ 2\ 2\ 7\ 7\ 5$$
$$5\ 7\ 7\ 2\ 2\ 3$$

$$2\ 2\ 3\ 5\ 7\ 7$$
$$7\ 7\ 5\ 3\ 2\ 2$$

'It doesn't mean anything to me,' he said, 'except that both blocks can be read either way – they're symmetrically arranged and the groups are combinations of the first four prime numbers.'

'Yes, but there must be something else to them. I've got a couple of kids from the math department seeing if they can spot any special properties. Anyway, let's have a look at the files.'

Lindow folded the printout of the numbers and put it in his wallet. Varrone typed in LUNCHBOX with a flourish. The screen filled with several dozen icons, each representing a separate document.

He clicked on an icon at the top left of the screen. It opened and they began to read.

Lake to Scalper: Collection of supplies underway by Shrodinger. Rendezvous at Pizek due sth of Pilszen 23.00 hours / 23. 3. Casmar Brath has sent $US 20K for payment to usual destination.

Scalper to Lake: Nothing doing. He didn't show. Is this man reliable? I've taken contract so cannot disappoint. Sincerely hope he produces necessary goods by Monday (26.3). Will wait for him at previous rendezvous. No fuck-ups this time. Has transfer gone through? $US60K sent to BA no 3476/78949276 acc 2. Confirm receipt.

Scalper to Lake: Supplies received and stored. Will

move in due course. Two CCs needed in name of Richard K. Holmes. Expedite without delay.

Scalper to Lake: Closure. Contract completed. Final payment routed through Korean Bank. Should be in Melbourne (Account 42751684/04SZ). Retrieve asap. Parties satisfied. More contracts on offer – one v. hazardous with price tag of US$150K. Negotiate up by 50K – two-thirds to be deposited in Georgia State Agro on acceptance. Information needed on cellphone set-up in Hungary. CCs not here yet. Get a grip.

Varrone frowned. 'Foyle told me that Scalper is Rhodes's nickname. Lake presumably refers to Lasseur. Does the rest mean anything to you?'

'Yes,' said Lindow, feeling a rare, nervous excitement. 'It could be very important. There were two explosions in Eastern Europe which were thought to be terrorist actions but turned out to be assassinations, each aimed at one individual. A cellphone was used in both cases. That's why the last lines are important. They might be crucial in linking Rhodes with the technique used in London.'

Varrone began to print out the documents so that Lindow could read them on paper. In all there were forty-one documents in the LUNCHBOX disk. Most were brief, telegraphic communications between Rhodes and Lasseur, conducted in the commercial language of a shipping agent. The pattern seemed to be that Rhodes would go out and find the business while Lasseur was left to arrange the details and delivery of any special equipment needed. Their field of operations extended through Eastern Europe and Turkey. Occasionally Scalper's rovings would take him back to the British Isles, though for what purpose was unclear. He occasionally made terse remarks about England – 'Fucking bad weather. Dripping noses and crap food. Leave Saturday,' was one that made Lindow smile. But, in general, a hectoring note pervaded Scalper's communications – he was a martinet, endlessly complaining that equipment wasn't good enough, or that it had arrived late. By contrast, Lasseur seemed amenable and compliant, making suggestions rather than issuing instructions. Both showed an acute interest in the financial side of the operations. One document appeared to be a kind of profit-and-loss account. After expenses, money held in fourteen different bank accounts totalled US$367,000. On receipt of this information, Rhodes had apparently queried the division of spoils, arguing that a one-third/two-thirds split was unjust. He claimed that a one-quarter/three-quarters division better reflected the effort he put into the 'marketing and sales operation'. Lasseur agreed without complaint and transferred Rhodes's share ($275,250) to a bank in Buenos Aires, routed through Antigua. He attached a warning that Rhodes should lose no time in distributing the funds to other bank accounts or investing in securities.

Lindow read the forty or so sheets again, trying to work out a chronology. The messages were undated, but it was possible to place them in a rough sequence by using internal evidence. Judging from Rhodes's movements and the amount of business transacted, the period covered by the LUNCHBOX disk might be anything up to two years.

The DISNEYWK disk was altogether less interesting, but Lindow knew that what seemed dull to the casual eye might prove exceptionally interesting to Foyle. In one message Lasseur described taking delivery of the plane and the arrangements made for a regular fuel stop over the Canadian border. He had had a bad winter, with an emergency generator breaking down and constant problems with the plane's ignition system. Evidence that the pair had accumulated a great deal of money was shown in the figure of US$747,000 that appeared in a message to Rhodes, which didn't satisfy him: he repeated in several different messages that they needed to put the business on a firmer footing, and rely less on one-off contracts. Lindow assumed that these were 'hits'. At any rate, it was clear that Lasseur had taken this to heart. There were records of the companies he had set up, the names of lawyers and banks that had been used and a list of company names, with the ostensible trading purpose entered alongside each one. Lakeside Electronics operated out of Chicago and was a retailer of electrical components. Ridgeway Hyde Inc was based in Alabama and had interests in British Columbia. Dix Metal Salvage, operating in Philadelphia, specialised in the recycling of valuable alloys. Invoice numbers were listed, along with payment receipts, bank statements, consignment numbers, the dates of their arrival and dispatch. In some cases, the original paperwork appeared on the screen, copied into the computer's memory by a portable scanner.

Lasseur had undeniable talents as an accountant and bookkeeper. Lindow imagined him out there in the wilderness, diligently constructing the network of cover operations and bank accounts, then moving to the workbench to design some new device for Rhodes. He was a kind of Jeeves, the terrorist's gentleman who anticipated his master's every need and was locked into service by the unalterable fact of that scarred face.

Then a couple of lines in one of Rhodes's messages caught Lindow's attention. He read them again.

Have agreed to take on two jobs in US for Millbank boys. Will not make us rich, but may provide opportunities in the future for bigger deals. Also good to keep up contacts with Millbank. Jobs do not require special equipment. Will need to collect papers and CCs in name of R. C. Cannon within two–three weeks from friends in Baltimore.

'I may have something really important here,' Lindow told Varrone, who was also engrossed in a mass of messages. 'I'm going to call Foyle. Did you tell him that the nicknames got us into two of the files?'

'Christ, I forgot.' Varrone slapped his head.

'It doesn't matter – I'll tell him.'

Foyle answered on the second ring.

'We've got the Crown Jewels – or whatever the equivalent is in police terminology. Two of the nicknames worked as passwords. The two dead men from Droy, LUNCHBOX and DISNEY.'

'That's marvellous. What's in the files?'

'Pretty much everything – a complete and detailed record of all their activities. Well, not all because there are still four disks to unlock. We're missing four out of six passwords.'

'Give me a summary of what you've got so far.'

'Rhodes seems to have had some contact with the security service, and quite recently – there are references to Millbank and the Millbank boys. You used that phrase. Millbank is MI5, right?'

'Yes, it is. This is exactly what I needed. Well done.'

'You did it with the nicknames.'

'What else have you got? Any mention of Axiom?'

'No, but there's a lot of detail – bank accounts, cover operations, supply lines, messages between Rhodes and Lasseur. And there's the other four disks still to come.' Lindow became aware of Foyle talking to someone in the background. 'Did you hear that?'

'Yes, yes. We've just been discussing when you should come back. I think we need you back here as soon as possible – by tomorrow morning. Meantime can you fax everything you've got to me at home?' He gave the fax number from June Foyle's machine.

'Yep, that's okay. I'll come tonight. I expect I'll have to catch the shuttle from Boston to New York and get the last flight from JFK.'

'Let me know which airline and I'll pick you up first thing in the morning. That should avoid any problems you might have with that duff passport of yours. Oh, by the way, have you got any cash?'

'Yes, a lot.'

'Then pay for your ticket with it, just in case someone's looking at your credit-card transactions.'

Lindow put the phone down. 'He wants me to go tonight. What shall we do about the rest of it?'

'Nobody's been in touch, so I guess we'll have to chip at it through the week. You never know, the kids working with the number blocks may come up with something, or we could get lucky with the computer search – there are a lot of people out there working on this problem. I'll copy the disks on to my system and make some more copies to be on the safe side. You should take the original set, plus a printout. And you've got that copy of the e-mail with the number blocks.'

Lindow nodded. 'Should we give this to Frank Mundy now?'

'Sure. Give him everything now, just so long as he agrees not to release it to the Brits before you get to London. You can make a trade so he tells you what they find up in the cabin. Sounds to me as if you're going to need everything you can lay your hands on to catch this guy.'

Lindow called all the airlines and eventually got a reservation on the overnight flight from New York to London. Then he prepared to leave the house. He put the e-mail from the West Coast in his pocket, then slipped the disks and printout into his hand luggage. Varrone saw him off at his gate. Lindow was not usually demonstrative, but now he was overwhelmed with gratitude and clasped Varrone to his chest. 'You've been a real friend, Peter. I thank you from the bottom of my heart.'

Varrone looked more than a little taken aback, and as Lindow climbed into the cab he noticed the other man's hands go into their water-shaking spasm.

Chapter Fifteen

By the time the first sheets from Boston began to unfurl from the fax, six people were gathered in Kenneth Foyle's living room. A little over an hour earlier he'd summoned Graham Forbes, Sergeant Pennel, WPC Nancy Longmore and Detective Constable Kepple. With varying degrees of reluctance and scepticism, they made their way to Wimbledon, bearing the lap-top computers and mobile phones he'd urged them to bring. Finally Katherine Foyle burst through the front door of the family home, having been told by her father a little earlier in the day to come from Bristol to help with some urgent typing. The expressions of Stephen Pennel and Jim Kepple lightened somewhat with the appearance of Foyle's striking offspring.

He handed each of them a drink, then told them of the extraordinary developments in the States. He took the story at a gallop, without bothering to deploy his usual layers of supporting detail. For this was no theory – not even a wild version of the facts – but the truth. Con Lindow had located the hideout of two former British Army officers. One of them, Lieutenant Robert Lasseur, who was now dead, had admitted to Lindow that his old Army colleague, Ian Valentine Rhodes, was responsible for the three explosions. The first had been designed specifically to kill Eamonn Lindow, who was a senior member of the IRA's intelligence section. The other two were contract bombs. Rhodes was believed to be planning another spectacular attack, codenamed Axiom Day.

Foyle set up one of the lap-tops and continued his story. 'By last week it was plain that Rhodes had no further use for Lasseur. Their partnership was at an end so he arranged for Lasseur's death by sending a signal to a computer that had been primed to blow up.' Foyle made a key stroke on the lap-top. 'In other words, he e-mailed the command to the bomb. Lasseur died soon afterwards from injuries to his stomach. This happened last night about ten.' He paused and straightened from the computer. The expressions around the room were grave. Katherine looked at her father with new eyes. 'That's the sort of man we're dealing with. He is probably the most dangerous assassin at large in the world today. Rhodes is resourceful, cunning, highly trained and imaginative. So far he's made fools of us. But now we have an advantage. We know that he is planning a dramatic outrage in Britain. But more important is that, unknown to Rhodes, Lasseur kept computer records of their dealings. Before he died he was able to tell Con Lindow where six encrypted disks were concealed. Lindow took them from Lasseur's base in Maine and they are presently being decrypted in Boston.'

Right on cue, Lindow's call came through, telling Foyle that two disks had yielded their secrets and that there were vague references to MI5. While they spoke, the first file from the LUNCHBOX disk shuddered out of the fax machine.

'That was Lindow,' said Foyle, turning from the phone to look down at the fax. 'There is another aspect to this, which I have known about since Friday evening and which is now established in these files. Ian Rhodes worked for the security service, which in part accounts for the difficulty we've had investigating this case. The files will show the extent of their association. These details must remain secret, which is why I have chosen each of you to help me sort through the evidence that will come from Boston over the next few hours. I know I can rely on you not to talk about what you read tonight. So, let's get to it.'

Katherine suggested that she make copies of the fax at the late-night grocery around the corner. She set up a run between Foyle's house and the shop, which was persuaded to stay open by the production of Pennel's warrant card. At length each person had a complete set of the seventy-eight-page fax. Then the group assembled around Foyle's dining table and began sifting through the files and separating the information into three broad categories: operating methods, evidence of past crimes and intelligence about future actions.

There was little of the last category but plenty of the first two. After an order of pizzas had been delivered and consumed, Katherine and Nancy Longmore began to type up the first coherent accounts of the activities of Rhodes and Lasseur. Katherine's document consisted of several tables: a roll-call of contacts referred to in the communications between Rhodes and Lasseur, a list of banks and account numbers mentioned, and a roster of suppliers who furnished them with explosives, timers, detonators and other equipment. To this Graham Forbes added a rough chronology that he'd distilled from Lasseur's electronic correspondence with various banks. Their patterns of business, the way they'd cultivated their client list and Rhodes's remarkable operating range were all suddenly brought into focus.

Nancy Longmore's draft co-ordinated all references to Rhodes's use of explosives and the clues about the way he planned and researched his jobs. There was evidence of the meticulous care he took to equip himself with a new identity for each operation and important hints about the way they marketed themselves on the Internet. Each observation was cross-referenced with a page number from the original fax so that when the members of SO 13 came to read the papers next morning, as Foyle fully intended, they would be able to get a quick grasp of the new information.

At two thirty a.m they broke for coffee, made by Katherine. As she brought the tray into the sitting room, the phone rang. Foyle answered a call from a friend of his daughter in Bristol. She listened, then replaced the handset. 'We've just been raided by the police.' She was looking at her father aghast. 'The drugs squad in Bristol. They only searched my room. Nowhere else. Just my room!'

Foyle laid an arm on her shoulder. 'Don't worry. I was expecting it, which is half the reason I wanted you up here.' Everyone except Forbes looked baffled. 'It's fine. Just someone's fun and games. Now we've got all this I'm afraid they're going to have to call it a day.'

He sat down again at the head of the dining table and momentarily considered the strangeness of the situation. Four of the people in the room had not reached thirty. Only Forbes and himself had seen their fortieth year. And yet it fell to this group to unravel one of the greatest scandals in British public life, a very great secret, which in a matter of hours would hurtle through Whitehall.

He drained his coffee and started to write a complete review of the case, leading off with the evidence that had come from America and describing how it fitted with the results of his own informal inquiries. Then came the revelation of Rhodes's past association with MI5, which he stated as a matter of unassailable fact, backing it up with three further references to the security service that had been found in the decrypted files. Foyle cited the payment of nine thousand dollars received by one bank, and placed this against Rhodes's report of 'closure'. The word closure appeared many times, and in most cases it meant that a person had been executed. This was the probable outcome of Rhodes's meeting with two American citizens who had supplied arms to the IRA. There was good reason to believe that members of the security service were aware of Rhodes's involvement in these deaths. They were also fully aware of his presence in Britain and of his possible involvement with the bombings. The motives were clear to the security service, yet they had withheld this evidence.

He moved on to the danger now presented by Rhodes, who was evidently planning an attack in the near future, probably in London. The events in the USA suggested that he intended Axiom, as he called it, to be a final horrific gesture. When the remaining files were decoded there might be more to go on, but Lasseur had told Lindow that he knew only that it was to be Rhodes's 'statement'. Plainly the two had not discussed Axiom.

The review ran over seven pages and ended by recommending an immediate concentration of police and MI5 resources in the hunt for Ian Rhodes; a publicity campaign in which the country was made aware of Rhodes's appearance, using pictures from Army files; a survey of the cellphone networks in London and other major cities that would determine the ability to shut down particular networks at short notice; a news blackout on the events in the USA so that Lindow's survival and the existence of the disks remained secret; and a thorough psychological profile of Rhodes, to be undertaken immediately. Foyle had many more minor recommendations, but that would do for the present.

By now it was four thirty a.m. Foyle checked what he had written, then asked Forbes to go through it.

'It's very powerful and persuasive,' Forbes concluded. 'The only point I'd argue with is where you say that MI5 intentionally suppressed evidence.'

'I was paid a visit late on Friday evening by a curious woman who refused to give me her name. She was plainly from Millbank, though I'm certain she came on her own behalf. She was concerned about what Lindow might discover in the United States and asked me to let her know when I was close to exposing Rhodes. She said that she wanted to avoid meltdown in the security service – that wasn't her phrase but it was what she meant. She gave me a bloody lecture about the good work that would be lost to the nation if the service was discredited. But the important point, apart from her inadvertently confirming practically everything I suspected, was that Millbank had gathered evidence that Rhodes was in the vicinity of the first bomb.'

'What was she up to?'

'It was all very bizarre, but I believe she was genuinely concerned about the ability of the service to operate if all this came out.'

Forbes thought for a moment. 'I'd take it out if I were you. It's the only part that isn't backed by hard evidence. It means that you've got a card you can play later.'

Foyle deleted the sentences. Then he signed and dated the paper as it juddered from the printer and placed it in a large brown envelope with a copy of the original and the two memoranda typed up by Katherine and Nancy Longmore.

'Right, this is what happens now.' He rose from his place at the table to address his little team. 'You leave all the copies of the decrypted files and your notes with Graham Forbes. When you see these papers again, you may notice certain deletions. For instance, the references to the security service may disappear. This is for a good reason. I am not in the business of revelation for its own sake. I simply want this investigation to get under way as soon as possible. No purpose will be served by their humiliation. The fact that they will shortly understand the extent of our knowledge will be enough for us to get what we want. Our job is to catch this lunatic, not act as some kind of government ombudsman. So I want an assurance from each one of you that nothing will pass your lips on the subject of Rhodes or Millbank. This is very important. The second point is that you must keep

Lindow out of all discussions until you hear otherwise. Is that all understood?'

The group nodded in unison.

'Okay. Pennel, Kepple and I are going to Heathrow to collect Lindow, who'll be arriving in a couple of hours' time.' He held up the envelope. 'Inspector Forbes will deliver this to Sir Derek Crystal at the Cabinet Office. Graham, if he isn't available, find out where Adam Durie is and give it to him. Don't take no for an answer. Say it's a matter of national security and make sure you stay there until it's been read. Then tell them I'm coming in with the chief witness. I should be at the Cabinet Office by eight thirty a.m. Nancy, I want you to go into the department as normal and dream up ways of explaining the absence of Forbes, Kepple and Pennel. Not a word about anything, mind. Just lie through your teeth.' He stretched, raising his arms like the Angel of the North. 'So I'll see you all in a few hours.'

Lindow tried to sleep on the flight from New York, but couldn't keep his mind still. The last few days had merged into one long day that was still nowhere near ending, and now his body was so high on adrenaline that he simply couldn't rest. It was as if he had become trapped in the action of a clumsy dream sequence, in which, as part observer and part player, he stumbled through a series of ultra-vivid setpieces.

An hour out from Heathrow breakfast was served. Lindow drank his coffee and pondered the e-mail from Varrone's Californian night owl, the man they were sure had designed the GenoType software. His neighbour, a middle-aged Englishwoman with a leathery tan and spectacles on a gold chain, let her curiosity get the better of her. 'Do you mind me asking what in heaven's name that is?' she said, wafting a heavy scent towards Lindow. 'You've been staring at it for half an hour now.'

'It's a palindrome,' Lindow told her, without thinking.

'You know – when something reads the same forwards as it does backwards. It's like one of those phrases "Madam, I'm Adam" or "Live not on evil".'

'But why?' she persisted.

'It's part of a scientific problem I'm working on.'

'Oh, I see,' she said, no wiser, and returned to her breakfast.

Lindow looked at the numbers again.

```
3 2 2 7 7 5
5 7 7 2 2 3

2 2 3 5 7 7
7 7 5 3 2 2
```

The blocks were all palindromes. There were only four elements to each block – the numbers 2, 3, 5 and 7. They were prime numbers, but maybe that wasn't important. Palindromes occurred somewhere else in nature along the sequences of DNA. He borrowed a small gold diary pencil from his neighbour and wrote:

$$A = 2$$
$$C = 3$$
$$G = 5$$
$$T = 7$$

Then, using this key, he matched the numbers to letters which he wrote above and below the rows of numbers.

```
C A A T T G
3 2 2 7 7 5
5 7 7 2 2 3
G T T A A C

A A C G T T
2 2 3 5 7 7
7 7 5 3 2 2
T T G C A A
```

He studied it for a while, trying to seize hold of the thing that was flitting about in his memory.

Then the seat-belt sign came on. Within a few minutes the 747 had slipped from the darkness and lined up over the illuminated circuit boards of London, heading for Heathrow. They landed and taxied to the terminal. But there was a problem. The captain asked everyone to remain seated until a party had boarded the plane and made an inspection. Lindow looked towards the front of the plane to club class. Several businessmen, who had grabbed their coats and luggage, were being told firmly to sit down. A lot of interest was being directed at the three men making their way through the cabin. Eventually Lindow saw the unmistakable bulk of Kenneth Foyle.

'Ah, here he is,' boomed Foyle. 'I'm afraid we must ask you to come with us, sir.'

Lindow blushed, climbed over his neighbour and searched for his bags in the overhead locker.

'Just point them out to us,' said Foyle formally. 'We'll bring them for you.'

They left the plane and walked to Immigration. 'I'm sorry about this.' Foyle broke into a smile. 'Bloody Special Branch started kicking up, so I pulled rank and told them it was a matter of national importance that I make an arrest. Now, give me your passport. Pennel is going to put some handcuffs on you for the benefit of Immigration and HM Customs. Just look guilty.'

Foyle flashed the passport and his identity at one of the duty officers, who waved them through. There was no sign of anyone at Customs and they walked briskly out of the terminal to the car, where Pennel released Lindow from the handcuffs.

Forty minutes later they reached Whitehall. The time was eight five a.m. Foyle told Lindow that the papers had been delivered to Sir Derek Crystal's office earlier that morning. He should have digested them by now. They were shown into a small anteroom by a bustling young man. Lindow noticed the flicker of alarm that entered his small blue eyes as he stared at Lindow's hiking boots, which still bore the traces of dirt from a hillside in Maine.

Foyle must have noticed it too. 'Is there some kind of problem?' he asked.

'No, no!'

'Good. This gentleman hasn't been to bed for at least two days. So perhaps Her Majesty's Government might see its way to providing a pot of coffee.'

The young man retreated, saying he'd see what he could do.

'You look bloody rough, Con,' said Foyle. 'How did you get that bruise on your jaw – Lasseur?'

'Yes, but it's not a problem.'

'What about Mary? Where's she?'

'That's another story. I guess she must be still in Boston. We haven't seen each other since yesterday.'

Foyle frowned quizzically.

Outside in the corridor they heard secretaries and civil servants arriving for work. The door opened and Sir Derek Crystal entered, looking worried. The cleft in his forehead was long and deep.

Foyle introduced Lindow, then Forbes.

'This is an extremely serious, not to say complex, situation,' said Sir Derek, closing the door behind him. 'I've sent a copy of your remarkable document to Number Ten for the Prime Minister's immediate attention. I'd like you to come to my office. We can discuss it there.'

Lindow and Foyle followed him, while Forbes made his excuses and slipped away. As they passed along the corridors, Lindow attracted one or two strange looks but took no notice. He was still pursuing the train of thought that had come to him on the plane.

They reached Sir Derek's office, a large, airy room that

overlooked Horse Guards Parade and St James's Park. Sir Derek gestured to a tray of coffee and biscuits.

'When I started reading this document I expected that there would be much that was unreliable or lacked evidence. But I find I cannot argue with your evidence, your logic or your conclusions. It is clear that this man Rhodes has got to be found as a matter of national urgency. It is also clear that there has been a grave attempt to divert the proper course of this investigation. That's why we owe you both a debt of gratitude. That should be said before anything else.'

Lindow hardly noticed his remarks. He knew he had approached the threshold of a solution. He had the sensation that something was fixing itself in his mind, like a photograph in a developing tray. He pulled out his wallet and unfolded the number blocks to stare at them once more. 'I think I've got it,' he said slowly. 'In fact I'm certain I have. Do you mind if I use your phone?'

Sir Derek looked at Foyle. 'What have you got, Dr Lindow?' he said.

'I think I know how we can unlock those other four disks. Can I use your phone?'

He was on his feet and requesting the dialling code before Sir Derek had time to nod. He dialled Boston and waited, looking at Foyle. 'There may be another way into the disks without using passwords.' He began speaking into the phone. 'Peter, it's Con here, I think I know what those numbers are. They're recognition sites. Hold on a moment. I'm with some people here – do you mind if they listen in on this?'

Sir Derek moved to his desk and pressed a button. Lindow put the receiver down and continued talking. 'Have those kids had any luck with the number blocks?'

'No,' said Varrone. 'I'd heard nothing by the time I went to bed a couple of hours ago.'

'There's a good reason for that. It's not a math problem – well not strictly. What I think he has given us

330

are recognition sites. You can think of them as gateways, or docking points, which appear periodically along human DNA. In most cases the enzyme recognises the gateway because it is a palindrome – the base pairs of DNA read the same way forwards as backwards.'

'Where does that get us? We've got numbers, not letters.'

'The guy in California expects us to replace the numbers with letters. All we have to do is substitute the numbers 2, 3, 5 and 7 with the letters A, C, G and T which, as you know, stand for the chemicals that make up DNA – adenine, cytosine, guanine and thymine. We don't know yet which letters substitute which numbers, but you understand the general principle?'

'Yes, I'm there.'

'Good.' Lindow darted an encouraging smile at Foyle and Sir Derek, who both looked mystified. 'The man who wrote that software obviously knew something about genetics. When he built his trap-door in the software's encryption system he used the idea of these gateways. A basic one would be A C G T T G C A. There are others which involve ten letters. Each palindrome attracts an enzyme, produced by a particular bacteria. That is the crucial point. Are you with me?'

'Yes,' said Varrone, his voice rising in the still air of Sir Derek's office. 'You think the first part of the decryption is based on these gateways and the second part utilises the chemical make-up of the enzyme which enters via the gateway.'

'Exactly, exactly,' said Lindow. 'If we can work out which numbers should be replaced by A, C, G and T, it will be simply a matter of looking up the recognition site in the standard reference books.'

'Then we'll know which bugs it attracts.'

'Yes, yes.'

'I'll make a start now. Where're you going to be?'

'I don't know – I'll call you in a couple of hours.'
Lindow hung up.

He looked up at Foyle and Sir Derek and saw they
were still struggling. He reached across the desk for a
piece of paper then drew a diagram.

```
A C G T C G
G C T G C A    <    Protein sequence of enzyme

T G C A A G
G A A C G T    <    Protein sequence of enzyme
```

'On the left,' he said, 'there are two blocks of letters.
These are the gateways I've been talking about. Sequences like these occur along the three billion units of human
DNA and they're special because they attract the enzymes
made by certain bacteria. What we have to do is work
out which gateways we have been given. That will tell us
which enzymes they attract. Then we feed the whole lot
to the encrypted software.'

'When you say "feed", what do you mean?' asked
Foyle.

'We'll input the blocks of letters on the left here. This
will alert the program that another set of letters is about
to be presented.'

'I'm not sure I understand,' said Foyle.

'Look, it's simple,' said Lindow with a flash of
impatience. 'We're building a gateway in each encrypted
disk, through which we're going to pour hundreds of
letters. Then the file will simply unscramble itself.'

'Good, I'm glad you think it's so promising. Now,' Sir
Derek turned to Foyle, 'what I have to tell you,
Commander, is that the Prime Minister has already
decided that you will be reinstated at SO 13 – that is to
say, your enforced leave has ended as from this moment.
The commissioner is being informed by the Home
Secretary, who I gather had some hint of this affair. Early
this morning he had a meeting with a high-ranking

officer in the security service. She gave him an outline of the affair that you have told us about in your briefing, although her version was naturally nothing like as detailed and included none of the intelligence from the United States.'

Foyle smiled.

'You were aware of this dissent in the security service, Commander?'

'Yes, I had a curious approach from a woman on Friday evening. She wanted to know how close I was getting to Rhodes.'

'Well, it was undoubtedly the same person who talked to the Home Secretary. It was admirably principled of her – and timely, too, because it meant that the Prime Minister had confirmation of the main allegations in your briefing without having to instigate an investigation. That means that we can move now. At eleven thirty there will be a full meeting of the Joint Intelligence Committee, which you will address. It would be helpful if you were to play down the connection between Rhodes and the security service. Everyone in the room will guess or know anyway. Our purpose must now be to move forward in a united effort to apprehend Rhodes.'

'Does this mean there won't be any sort of inquiry into their behaviour?' asked Foyle. 'I mean, it amounts to a criminal conspiracy, to say nothing of the commission of criminal acts on foreign soil.'

'Yes, yes, Commander, I have already indicated that the Prime Minister takes this very seriously indeed, and you can be assured that action will follow. But, as I say, we must put this aside until Rhodes is behind bars. MI5 is still a formidable intelligence service, and over the coming days you will need its resources.' He paused. 'However, I would say that, given your unequalled understanding of the case, it would be wise for them to comply with your wishes and offer you every assistance.'

'I'll believe it when I see it.'

'By mid-morning there will be no doubt in their minds as to who's running this investigation,' he said, rising and buttoning his jacket. 'So, we'll meet in a couple of hours, Commander. Dr Lindow, it has been a great pleasure. Thank you for all your efforts.'

They left the building and passed into Whitehall. 'That was our moment of triumph, believe it or not,' said Foyle, waving to Pennel, who was parked a little way up the street. 'It never gets better than that, so don't hold your breath for the victory parade. Look, I'm afraid I'm going to need your help on these final disks. I hope you won't mind coming with me now.'

Lindow nodded. He was anxious to get to another screen.

'I have some more bad news,' Foyle continued. 'We're going to have to keep you under guard in a hotel. I can't risk Rhodes hearing that you're still alive. He knows your telephone number. It follows that he also knows your address.'

The moment Speerman entered Cantor's office he knew something had gone terribly wrong. Keith Craven-Elms and Angus Grove were there, both looking appalled.

'Why haven't we heard from Brown Owl?' Cantor demanded, in an accusatory hiss. 'Where the hell's her report? You told me she was glued to Lindow – he couldn't move without us knowing about it. But now he's miraculously back in Britain along with a complete record of Rhodes's activities. Did she know about these disks? If so, why did she not inform us? Where is she? Keith?'

'We thought she was out of contact. There was no way of getting hold of her over the weekend. She was with Lindow all the time and wasn't expected to make contact until this morning.'

'Well, find her, damn it. You must all realise how important she is to us now.'

Speerman immediately saw Cantor's escape route. He was going to use Brown Owl's assignment to show that the security service, far from wishing to suppress information about Rhodes, was active in his pursuit. That Lindow had suddenly returned to Britain with information he'd kept from Brown Owl could not – and should not – be used to discredit the service's motives.

The case would take some building, but it was not beyond Cantor. His survival would now depend on two things: the extent to which the security service was implicated by the disks and his ability to demonstrate that MI5 had no knowledge of Rhodes's presence in London during the bombings. The second would be easy enough: the secret film taken by one of Weegee's cameras two weeks ago had almost certainly hit the incinerator, although there were probably some stills hanging around. The disks were a bigger problem. He would have to find out exactly what was on them and prepare his defence accordingly. Speerman concluded that the odds were marginally in Cantor's favour. While Rhodes was free, there was no question of any action being taken against him and that meant there was everything to fight for.

The meeting broke up with the director general urging Grove to use every contact he possessed to acquire a copy of Lindow's disks.

Kirsty Laing was sitting in her office running through the conversation she'd had over breakfast with the Home Secretary when Speerman entered.

'Well, it's broken. The Prime Minister and the Home Secretary have spoken to the director general already. Lindow has brought some important material back from that place in Maine, some computer disks, apparently. These enabled Foyle to produce a briefing overnight, which was delivered to the Cabinet Secretary this morning.'

'Really?' Kirsty Laing licked cappuccino froth from her finger.

'It means that your plan to talk to the Home Secretary has been overtaken by events. The cat is very much out of the bag. The government knows everything they need to know and you don't have a lever any longer.'

'I see.' She tried to look anxious. 'Well, that's that, then. As you know, I've only been concerned that we don't put our interest before the public's safety. Clearly that will not be allowed to happen now.'

'A small piece of advice, Kirsty.' Speerman's manner made her think that 'threat' would have been a better word. 'Don't put money on the director general going. If I were you, I'd do everything in my power to secure the information on those disks.'

'I'll do whatever I can.'

Speerman departed abruptly. Laing saw exactly the way he was playing it. If Cantor fell, Speerman would be sufficiently remote from the involvement with Rhodes to be considered his natural successor. If, on the other hand, Cantor survived, Speerman's loyalty during the crisis could never be doubted.

She looked out of her window on to the car park below and allowed herself a smile. The timing was perfect. The appearance of Lindow had occurred at exactly the right moment. Everything would be blamed on him and no one in the service would have the slightest idea about her *tête-à-tête* with the Home Secretary.

She picked up the phone and dialled the number of the new hotel, the one to which Brown Owl had moved instead of flying straight back to London.

'I'm going, I'm going,' said Scarratt petulantly as Foyle opened the door. Foyle knew that the assistant commissioner had only received the news of his reinstatement a few minutes earlier, but he wanted him out straight away.

'Where're my pictures?' he demanded, looking at the bare walls.

'They're down there, by the filing cabinet,' said Scarratt. 'I found them distracting. Everything else should be as you left it.'

'Good.'

'I wish someone would tell me what's going on.' Scarratt gathered a dozen files into his arms. 'This is no way to conduct a proper investigation.'

'You're quite right. We've lost a week because of you and your friends down at Millbank. Now, if you don't mind, I've got a lot to do.'

Scarratt tucked the files under his arm and marched stiffly from the office.

'Bloody fool,' murmured Foyle, bending down to pick up one of his watercolours.

Lindow was put in the adjacent room, where Foyle's video and TV were kept – the very place in which Foyle had first set eyes on him, caught in the murky footage from the Clarence Street security camera. Pennel came in bearing a computer, connected it to a phone line, then left him to his own devices.

Half an hour later, having gone through his plans with Forbes, Foyle walked to the briefing room to address his staff. The room was packed and humming. He moved to the front, nodding to one or two of the officers, then waited for the talk to die down. He was guilty, perhaps, of waiting just a bit longer than he needed. He coughed once. 'As I was saying,' he began.

The room exploded with laughter. Foyle waved for silence.

'Thank you,' he said, the brief smile vanishing quickly. 'As I was saying . . . a week ago, we have a serious problem with a terrorist bomber. We now know his name to be Ian Valentine Rhodes. He has planted three devices in London already and information brought from America last night indicates that he's planning at least one further attack. I believe we have very little time. But we've got an advantage – we now know a great deal more about Rhodes than he suspects. Even he is unaware that the information now in our possession exists, and we must keep it that way. Two disks from a computer at his American base were decrypted last night and they provide us with remarkable insights into his working methods, his contacts and his psychological state. The remaining files will, I hope, be unscrambled today.'

Foyle signalled to an officer at the back of the room, who dimmed the lights and turned on a projector. The screen behind Foyle was filled with a picture of a young soldier in regimental uniform with a cap tucked formally under his arm. He possessed a cautious smile and small dark eyes that gave nothing away. His blond, possibly light red, hair showed the beginnings of baldness.

'This is Rhodes aged twenty-two,' said Foyle. 'The photograph was supplied by the MoD this morning, as were these shots.'

The room was silent as three further photographs were flashed on the screen in quick sequence. In the first two Rhodes wore the same neutral smile. The last picture showed a group of four soldiers in fatigues, carrying a selection of unorthodox weapons. Rhodes was second from the right, the only member of the group without a beret. His left thumb was tucked into his belt, his right hand supported an Armalite rifle. Strapped across his body was the belt of another weapon that looked like a long-barrelled sniper's rifle. A tuft of hair glinted in the slanting sun. Rhodes didn't smile along with the others.

'This was taken in the late summer of 1982 for a military publication. Rhodes was about thirty. He had just returned from the Falklands – or, rather, Argentina,' said Foyle. 'At the time the SAS and fourteen Intelligence Company, of which Rhodes was a member, were very active in Northern Ireland. This picture shows four of the six members of the close observation post at Droy cemetery. On the right of Rhodes is Christy Calvert, who is still alive and is available to help us – I've spoken to him twice but he needs exhaustive interviewing. The two on the left are Sergeant Jimmy Pascoe and Robert McGurk – "Disney", as he was called by his mates. Pascoe was blinded at Droy, McGurk was killed. Pascoe is probably in some kind of home. We need to trace him and interview him today.

'These pictures will be released to the press in due course. But I want them circulated to police and ports first, also to second-hand car dealers and every phone shop in the Metropolitan area. Then we'll hit the press. But we need to think about this carefully. If Rhodes sees his face in the evening paper, he won't hang around for people to recognise him on the TV news later that evening. The first scent of trouble and he'll be off. So we need maximum simultaneous coverage. Inspector Forbes will handle the release strategy and is setting up the free telephone lines.'

In fact, Forbes was already handling a number of issues connected with the MoD's picture file. Copies of the photographs had been sent for computer analysis to see if Rhodes's face could be matched to any of those that had appeared fleetingly in the salvaged video from the bus. He had also arranged for a computer graphics firm in Soho, which specialised in image manipulation, to age Rhodes's face. His hair would be thinned and receded, the skin under his eyes darkened a little, the line of the jaw and neck slightly altered. Then the result would be released to the press with the original picture.

Foyle spoke without pause for fifty minutes. Even the seen-it-all-before brigade at the back of the room had to admit that, in five days of enforced leave, he had produced an incredible amount of material. Foyle took the narrative from Rhodes's childhood in Kenya, and his beating off the Mau Mau with a hunting rifle, through the disastrous undercover operation at Droy and his nervous collapse to his subsequent emergence as an assassin, arms dealer and terrorist with a beady eye for profit and loss. There was also the trajectory described by the life of Eamonn Lindow, the deceptively amiable elder brother of Con Lindow, who had moved to London after the Droy affair to become a librarian and one of the IRA's most successful intelligence operatives.

Eventually their paths had collided. Eamonn had been deployed by the IRA to track down Rhodes, but Rhodes had heard somehow of his assignment and struck first, killing Eamonn with a bomb that was intended to look like an IRA action. The next two devices had also seemed, on the surface, consistent with an IRA attack, although they were probably the result of a contract. That was part of Rhodes's illusionism: he enjoyed making one thing appear to be another. Thus a fire-extinguisher left at Interwaste became a bomb; a burglar alarm, as Lindow had reported from Maine, was converted to a trigger device; and a seemingly innocent phone message became the instruction that would kill and maim scores of people. That's why Rhodes had ignored the risk of leaving a recording of his voice on Lindow's ansaphone. He was arrogant enough to assume that he could get away with the joke. As a result, said Foyle, holding up the microcassette from Lindow's flat, they could now put a voice as well as a face to the name Ian Valentine Rhodes. The recording would be released to the media once Christy Calvert had confirmed that the voice belonged to Rhodes.

Foyle said little about the role of the security service, only mentioning in an aside, which few in the room seemed to pick up, that Rhodes was briefly considered as material for the service. No formal arrangement had been reached, though he may have done some odd bits of work in the past. It was hardly the whole truth, but it wasn't a lie either. He congratulated himself that he had at last found some political nous. He caught the eye of Forbes, who'd just walked into the briefing, and smiled.

Foyle moved back a pace or two towards the image of Rhodes on the wall and gazed up. The light from the projector was in his eyes as he turned to his audience. He shifted sideways to avoid it. 'We see the whole picture now,' he said. 'We understand how it all fits together. We've got a suspect. We've got evidence coming out of our ears. We can build a case and present it in court tomorrow to prove who killed those people in Clarence Street. What remains is the man-hunt. Everything must be focused on the capture of this man, whom we know to be planning a final, dreadful act of terrorism – the thing he refers to as Axiom.' He paused and looked grimly down at his audience. There was not a sound from them.

'So,' he continued, 'only two questions remain about Ian Rhodes. Where is he and what the hell is he planning? Ladies and gentlemen, we have very little time.'

Foyle returned to his office and looked into the adjoining room to find Con Lindow asleep, chin down, hands folded across his chest like a dead man. He closed the door and hurried out of New Scotland Yard for the Cabinet Office. He decided to walk, but instead of going through St James's Park he took the shorter route along Tothill Street through Parliament Square and Whitehall.

As with the first meeting, nearly a fortnight before, he had no papers. There was really no need: he possessed the answers to all the questions that would come his way – except, of course, those concerning the whereabouts and intentions of Ian Valentine Rhodes.

Chapter Sixteen

Lindow snapped awake with the first shake of Pennel's hand.

'You've got a call, sir.' Pennel noted Lindow's pallor. 'From FBI headquarters in Boston. Agent Mundy is on the line. Says to tell you that he's with Varrone. They've got some letter combinations for you and he wants to know how to send them.'

Lindow sighed. 'You must have an e-mail address – why not use that?'

'As long as that's all right with you, sir.' Pennel hesitated. 'I wonder . . . could you speak to him anyway? The commander wants to know what was found up at that place in Maine. He'll probably tell you more, seeing as you were there.'

Lindow watched as Pennel cradled the phone and had the call put through, while simultaneously logging on to his computer. 'Here you are,' he said, handing him the phone. 'I'll write the e-mail address down here while you're talking.'

'Hey, Lindow.' Mundy's voice grated in his ear, not helping an incipient headache. 'Christ, you must have the stamina of a horse. Look, Peter's had some success with those number blocks. He's pretty sure your instinct is right and that each of the numbers represents letters in the genetic alphabet. I'll talk to you in a second about what's going on up at the cabin.'

'Tell me now, if you want.'

'Well, nobody saw the fire, that's the first thing, so

there hasn't been any kind of publicity. We'll keep it that way for as long as we can. There was every kind of nasty waiting in the woods – anti-personnel mines, booby traps. It was a miracle you weren't blown up before you got to the cabin. You were lucky to get out of there alive.' So was Eamonn, thought Lindow. 'So we have to move pretty slow. I'll hand you over to Peter and we'll talk later. Is this Commander Foyle's direct line?'

Without thinking, Lindow replied that it was. Then Varrone came on the line and told him the letters A, C, G and T could be 2, 3, 5 and 7. Lindow retrieved the crumpled e-mail from his wallet and wrote out the message again, substituting letters for numbers.

G A A T T C
C T T A A G

A A G C T T
T T C G A A

Lindow's mind focused. He was almost certain that he knew the first configuration. There was an aptness and beauty about it. 'I think the first group is the recognition site for an enzyme isolated from a nasty bacteria named *E. coli*,' he said.

'The food-poisoning bug?'

'Yeah,' said Lindow. 'But it's not the bug we're interested in. It's the enzyme produced by the bug and this is the DNA sequence that it cleaves to – the gateway.'

'I think I'm with you.'

'What's important is that we have the first part of the lock. We need to identify the second sequence and make a couple of calls to find out the amino acid sequence. I believe we're nearly home and dry, Peter. I've got the disks here. I can load them on to the computer in front of me, and then we can work in parallel. I'll call you when I've identified the second recognition site. Then it'll be a matter of minutes before we find the key.'

*

As he approached the Cabinet Office, Foyle slowed his pace. He wanted to arrive a minute or two later than the others. Perhaps he was guilty of relishing the moment a little too much. He strolled past a couple of policemen and a man loading a ladder on to a van, took a deep breath and walked inside.

The room was a good deal fuller than it had been for the two previous meetings. He guessed between twenty and thirty faces turned towards him as he entered. The commissioner of the Metropolitan Police walked over with the Home Secretary and effected a quick introduction, then took the opportunity himself to shake Foyle's hand. Adam Durie, the head of the Joint Intelligence Committee, looked up from a conversation with Derek Crystal and nodded. Robin Teckman, the chief of MI6, did likewise, although with more understanding in his expression. Foyle's eyes moved round the room as the table came to order. At the far end was David Cantor, seemingly engrossed in some documents. He alone remained apparently unaware of Foyle's entrance.

Sir Derek began, 'You know most of us, Commander. We've been joined by Giles Levington and Sarah Turville from the Northern Ireland Office, Ann Cumber from Number Ten and Linus Tabor from the MoD. Before you start I thought I'd offer a general view of the situation so we know exactly how we stand and we don't waste your time.

'It is clear that we know we are dealing with a homebred terrorist who is, for his own reasons, bent on destroying the Ulster Accord and all that the people of Northern Ireland voted for. He believes he is vindicating the actions of the British security forces in Ulster over the last twenty years. All sides now understand that this man is a maverick, rather than belonging to any of the loyalist or republican factions. Most of you know that the advances in the case have been made by Dr Lindow and Commander Foyle here. We are also receiving help in this area from personal contacts of Dr Lindow's. The FBI is aware of the situation and we can expect news of the events in Maine to reach the highest American circles within the day. I mention this ahead of what Commander Foyle has to say because we must assume that this knowledge will soon leak to other countries, in particular the Irish Republic, which has close connections with the staff of the White House. So, Commander, tell us how you see things.'

Foyle began to speak about the disks and the manner of the decryption. As with his own staff, he made no mention of the relationship between Rhodes and MI5. He assumed that most people in the room had an inkling of it anyway. He outlined the severity and urgency of the problem facing them all. He had their complete attention. Occasionally one or other of the officials around the table made a note or glanced meaningfully at a colleague, but they didn't interrupt. Foyle was aware of the commissioner looking on with an attitude that suggested headmasterly pride. He forbore to smile.

'The first step must be to strengthen the security arrangements for all big public occasions over the next few weeks.' He paused. 'Even though all the Northern Ireland parties will be made aware that this man is a maverick, and almost certainly mad, there could be no more devastating way of harming the Peace Accord than by repeating the IRA's action at Enniskillen on the eighth of November 1987. Given this man's hostility to the current situation in Northern Ireland, and to the Army in general, we shouldn't rule it out. We have a crisis, ladies and gentlemen, and I'm here with a wish list of what I need from you.'

He bent down and took a sip of water.

'First, I want the Ministry of Defence to make available to my department all the files concerning Rhodes's career, no matter how secret. We are especially interested in this man's mental state so any psychologist's report would also be appreciated. Second, my officers will have to acquaint themselves thoroughly with the sort of training Rhodes has received. We want to know how he will react in certain situations – his escape strategies, his knowledge of anti-surveillance techniques, his training in urban warfare and so forth.' The defence official wrote rapidly as he spoke. 'The best possible option would be for you to let us have a couple of your people from the SAS regiment at Hereford, probably instructors. I want them on hand from this afternoon to tell me what sorts of things will be going through his head once he knows we're closing in. For the moment that's all the help that we require from the military. I'm anxious that this remains a police operation to the end because this man's motives and his methods are acutely interesting to us. We need to know what he's done and what he's planning. If my thinking changes, I will of course let you know.'

Foyle turned to the Home Secretary. 'From the Home Office and the Department of Trade and Industry we need permission to switch off the cellular phone networks in any part of the country at a moment's notice. As we know, sir, Rhodes uses cellphones to detonate his bombs. There are twelve million phone sets in circulation and, frankly, we are unlikely to pinpoint the numbers he plans to use – although we will be trying. So circumstances may arise in which we know about a particular device but cannot get to it in time. We need both departments to approach the five big companies and tell them this must be done. We will then agree a procedure for rapid shut-down with them.'

The Home Secretary nodded and signalled to an official.

'Moving to our own efforts, we plan to co-operate closely with the security service on this investigation. Given the misunderstandings of the past few weeks – the overlaps of effort and the information that has slipped between us – this is essential. I believe we should open a direct line of communication, placing officers in each other's buildings.' He looked at Cantor, who gazed at him unblinkingly. 'The communication will be two-way. So there won't be any confusion in either camp about what we're both doing.' Foyle's tone was almost placid, but nobody in the room mistook what had just happened. He'd challenged the director general of the security service and was now telling him exactly how things would be in the future.

He inhaled deeply and folded his hands on the conference table. 'That, for the moment, ladies and gentlemen, is all I have to say. I will keep you informed as things develop. If there is anything you want to know over the coming days, please don't hesitate to contact me.'

There was a murmur from the far end of the room. Cantor was leaning forward in his chair, poised to speak. All eyes turned to him.

'I wonder, Commander,' he began, smoothing the papers in front of him, 'when you're going to share the results of Dr Lindow's expedition. You see, we have a fair interest in those disks – almost as if we'd brought them back ourselves. You may not know this, but we were also on Rhodes's trail. Our operative accompanied Dr Lindow at every stage of his journey, having already monitored the activities of his brother Eamonn for us. So you will understand that we're most anxious to see the results of that investment of time. Indeed, I'm bound to say that we're a little surprised, in this new era of co-operation, that you haven't yet chosen to show them to us. Could I now therefore formally request sight of the material, both decrypted and still-encrypted disks? We have our own expert cryptologists, and I'm certain we'll be able to make some headway with them.'

His eyes moved between Foyle and the commissioner. Urquhart looked uneasy. Nobody in the room imagined that Cantor would come out of his corner fighting so effectively. If the security service had been after Rhodes all the time, it certainly put a better complexion on their behaviour.

'Dr Lindow and I were aware that Mary Menihan was working for someone,' said Foyle. 'He believed that it might be the security service or the IRA – he didn't know which. In any event, he was unwilling to disclose the existence of the disks to Miss Menihan and this, I am also bound to say, turned out to be exactly the right decision because the information contained in them is very sensitive.' He let that last sentiment hang in the air, then continued. 'However, once we have all the disks decrypted, we'll be happy to let you – and anyone in this room – have copies of the material.'

There was neither concession nor belligerence in Foyle's expression, just a trace of admiration. He knew Cantor wanted the disks badly, but more urgent was his need to put on record that the security service had been actively pursuing Rhodes. He'd done this with his usual efficiency and the seed of doubt had now been successfully sown around the table. He might well extricate himself yet.

At that moment Foyle was aware of the muffled ring of a mobile phone. He looked round and realised it was his own. He apologised to Sir Derek, took it from his pocket and answered the call. It was Pennel.

'Sorry to bother you,' he said. 'Thought you'd want to know the disks have been decrypted. They look pretty good to me.'

'Right,' said Foyle softly. 'I'll be back in a few minutes.'

He returned it to his pocket. 'Unless there's anything else, sir,' he said to Sir Derek, 'I think I should be going. The last four disks have been successfully decrypted and apparently contain very useful information.'

*

348

Lindow had loaded Pennel's computer with the encrypted disks then phoned Professor Sethe Sharma at Imperial College. He found Sharma in his usual vague form and barely aware that Lindow was still absent from his department. Sharma identified the second group of letters as the recognition site for the enzyme produced by *Haemophilus influenzae*, a bacteria that causes pneumonia, ear infections and meningitis. He hung up, saying that he would e-mail the amino acid sequences for both enzymes produced by *E. coli* and *Haemophilus influenzae*. Ten minutes later the e-mail came with two attachments from a database named Swissprotein, which included the sequences of amino acids. Lindow printed it out. On the left of the long columns of letters he wrote the original palindromes.

E. coli

(Recognition site
or gateway)   (Enzyme sequence)

	SNKKQSNRLT	EQHKLSQGVI	GIFGDYAKAH	DLAVGEVSKL	VKKALSNEYP	QLSFRYRDSI
G A A T T C	KKTEINEALK	KIDPDLGGTL	FVSNSSIKPD	GGIVEVKDDY	GEWRVVLVAE	AKHQGKDIIN
	IRNGLLVGKR	GDQDLMAAGN	AIERSHKNIS	EIANFMLSES	HFPYVLFLEG	SNFLTENISI
C T T A A G	TRPDGRVVVNL	EYNSGILNRL	DRLTAANYGMPINSNLCINK	FVNHKDKSIM	LQAASIYTQG	
	DGREWDSKIMFEIMFDISTT	SLRVLGRDLF	EQLTSK			

Haemophilus influenzae

(Recognition site
or gateway)   (Enzyme sequence)

	MKKSALEKLL	SLIENLTNQE	FKQATNSLIS	FIYKLNRNEV	IELVRSIGIL	PEAIKPSSTQ
A A G C T T	EKLFSKAGDI	VLAKAFQLLN	LNSKPLEQRG	NAGDVIALSK	EFNYGLVADA	KSFRLSRTAK
	NQKDFKVKAL	SEWREDKDYA	VLTAPFFQYP	TKSQIFKQS	LDENVLLFSW	EHLAILLQLD
T T C G A A	LEETNIFSFE	QLWNFPKKQS	KKTSVSDAEN	NFMRDFNKYF	MDLFKIDKDT	LNQLLQKEIN
	FIEERSLIEK	EYWKKQINII	KNFTREEAIE	ALLKDINMSS	KIETIDSFIK	GIKSNDRLYL

'All we have to do now is type this lot in.'
'May I make a suggestion?' said Pennel, who had grasped the principles of the decryption far quicker than Foyle or Sir Derek. 'Why don't you try it out with one of

the files that have already been decrypted? Use the encrypted version to see if it works.'

Lindow agreed. He loaded the encrypted form of the LUNCHBOX disk and typed in the first palindrome followed laboriously by the sequence of 300-odd letters that he had got from Professor Sharma. He repeated the process for the second palindrome. On the last keystroke the screen clouded in a blizzard of characters.

'Christ,' said Lindow, 'the damned thing's destroyed itself. Call Varrone and tell him we've got the right letter combinations but that, if they're not entered in the correct order, the file self-destructs. I'll make copies so we can try a different sequence.'

He thought for a moment, then entered the original palindromes because something told him it would make more sense to fit the gateways before introducing the stream of letters denoting the amino acid sequences. After typing furiously for a few minutes he waited. Nothing happened. The computer seemed to be mulling it over. Suddenly a page of plain text appeared on the screen.

Lindow yelped. 'I've got it. It's going to work.'

Within ten minutes he had repeated the procedure and all four disks were decrypted and stored on the computer's hard disk.

Pennel rushed off to find a printer for the computer and to tell Forbes. Meanwhile Lindow, hardly less jubilant, tried to make sense of the material. The first three disks contained 194 separate documents, some only a few words long. The last disk was a rambling and intermittent journal, started twenty months before by Lasseur when the cabin had been apparently cut off from the outside world by an ice storm. Lindow skimmed the journal, which was written in an odd, staccato style, but soon realised that Lasseur's existential crises offered little of immediate interest. He moved on to the other disks, scrolling through the documents at random and occasionally dipping in to read. There was enough to fill several books, an immense amount of fresh detail that would be invaluable to Foyle. It was just as Lindow was beginning to feel that he really had pulled off something and that he might now have made a real contribution to the arrest of Eamonn's killer when his eye latched almost subconsciously on to his own name. He read from the beginning of the message.

Money not here. Also need det cord from usual supplier. Other supplies arrived on time. Quaid says a man named Lindow is being used by the Paddies to find me. Will trace him and deal with him before attempting German contract.

Lindow shuddered, then went back through the documents to see if there were any other mentions of Eamonn. In one message he recognised the name of Jimmy Marcuse, the businessman suspected by the FBI of selling arms to the IRA, who had been killed in a car bomb in Miami. There was a message from Rhodes, which reported setting up a business meeting with Marcuse, after which he had followed him to a parking lot where he found Marcuse's reserved space. It was a simple matter to return and attach a device to the car. Next came Patrick Lyne, another name that 'interests our friends in London', and which Lindow remembered from the FBI's file. Lyne died in his bed in a hotel room. Rhodes did not say how, but the result was that a full payment came from London – and Rhodes stepped into the vacuum left by the two men's deaths.

The laconic style of the messages often made the thread hard to follow, but Lindow worked out that a man referred to as J. Quaid was the IRA's North American scout. He'd bought from Marcuse and Lyne. Rhodes reported making contact with Quaid, whose confidence he gained with one or two small deals. But these 'stuck in my craw'. If he was going to sell to anyone in Ireland, it would be to the 'Prods'. A deal followed through unstated avenues. Lasseur and Rhodes banked thirty thousand pounds as a result of the connection. Then came the message that had caught Lindow's eye. He read on.

Scalper to Lake: Remember Lindows? Not a name I will forget. They were the Mick brothers arrested after Droy OP. They weren't charged. RUC fuck-up by a man named Blackett.

Lake to Scalper: Of course. Lindow may have been up here two weeks ago. Caught someone on CCTV. Further inquiries established that a Dr Lindow of MIT stayed local. Checked with MIT switchboard, which has a Dr Lindow. Are both brothers involved or one using other's cover? One must have our location.

Scalper to Lake: News here bad. Everyone crawling to kiss Irish arse. Killers all gone free. AXIOM, my special goodbye, will remind them what it was really about. Final arrangements made. Traced Eamonn Lindow to S. London. Will effect closure when time is right.

Scalper to Lake: Breakfasted with friend Lindow a table away. Reads the *Guardian*. Phone tap in place and heard from his own lips about the arrival of brother here – moved last week from Boston to London. Possible both in on this thing. Could bag two Micks with one shot. Closure this week/early next. Then German contract closure and AXIOM. Money not in bank here yet. What are you playing at? J. Miles on bread line.

Scalper to Lake: Lindow's account closed. Brother arrested – not bad result for the veterans of Droy. Tomorrow German contract closure. Tell them. Then AXIOM. Money arrived. You must leave within two weeks. Leave nothing there.

Lake to Scalper: May take more than two weeks. Much to dismantle and dispose of. Final accounts squared. Your share routed to agreed destinations.

Scalper to Lake: Let me know soonest about arrangements at lake. Need to hear moment you're through. Doctor has been released. That's twice he's got away. Not a third time. Got his address/number. Will deal with him in time.

Lindow sank back in his chair, shocked by the bald description of Eamonn's death, but oddly unaffected by the revelation that Rhodes knew where he lived. There was no longer any point in concealing Eamonn's presence in Maine.

Foyle burst through the door and gripped Lindow's shoulders. 'Con, you have performed a miracle. What's the material like? Is it good?'

He leaned over Lindow and read what was on the screen. 'Is it all this detailed?'

Lindow explained that there was one disk that contained a journal, but that the rest seemed full of valuable operational information.

'Excellent! Forbes, we'll print one copy of this and then divide it between yourself, Kepple, Longmore and Pennel – the old team. Mark up the passages concerning MI5. Aside from that we're only interested in material that will lead us to Rhodes – look for names he might be using, patterns of behaviour, any place-names, associates. Once you've weeded it for mentions of Millbank you can distribute it throughout the department. Again, the same conditions pertain. Not a word of this must leave the floor. No chats with the press. Nothing to go to other departments in the building.'

'Why are you removing the stuff about MI5?' asked Lindow, when Forbes had left to round up the others.

'Because there's no point in detonating a ruddy great

mine under them now. We need them and there'll be time enough for that later.'

'Yes, but—'

'But nothing,' said Foyle. 'Why don't you start reading these disks? Go through the one with the journal – you'll probably make the most sense of it. Just say the moment you want to go. We'll get a room across the road in the St James's Hotel.'

Pennel arrived with the printer, followed by the other members of the reading team. Foyle left to tour the department, moving from one office to another, harrying and chivvying, pulling suggestions from the air and convening impromptu meetings. He appointed two officers to liaise with the FBI over the investigation at the cabin and told them to get an inventory of everything that had survived the fire. The most urgent task was to extract the records for the telephone in the cabin, which he knew would yield the numbers most recently dialled from Lasseur's computer. Then it would be a simple matter of using the reverse directory held by every police station to find the addresses used by Rhodes.

Foyle had formed the definite opinion that the capital would be exposed to the maximum danger that weekend. However, he'd arranged for security to be stepped up immediately on all targets, especially public figures. Every uniformed policeman was now searching for the face that looked out of the Ministry of Defence photograph with such disturbing self-possession. The picture was being distributed to all outlying police stations in the Metropolitan area with an instruction from the commissioner himself that the individual should not be approached and that under no circumstances was the media to be informed. The release of the pictures to the media would go ahead on the following afternoon. In the meantime, Foyle reckoned that Rhodes would be unaware of the desperate efforts to find him. He was exposed to a window of vulnerability and Foyle wanted

354

to keep it that way. With the help of Frank Mundy in Boston, a story was released through the international news agencies about a fire in Maine. The bulletin stated that three bodies had been recovered, one of which was found to be carrying a British passport. This also made it into the evening paper, appearing under the headline BRITISH BACKPACKERS DIE IN MYSTERY FIRE, and was featured on the mid-afternoon radio news with the detail that the campers were burned beyond recognition and that two of them had died in each other's arms – a lurid touch added by Mundy.

Some eighty police officers were sent out with the photograph to cover the sources that so often provided information about terrorists. London car auctioneers were visited and the managers of storage units and warehouses were asked to stay on site until they had been shown the photograph. Local police stations were requested as a matter of urgency to work through the lists of rented garages or lock-ups that each police station keeps for such an occasion. Foyle wanted to hear about any unusual activity or recent lets to a well-spoken Englishman with thinning sandy hair.

A separate team telephoned estate agents specialising in short-term lets above a certain value. Foyle felt sure that Rhodes had chosen an upmarket property. Perhaps he was posing as a respectable businessman who needed easy access to the motorway network and, of course, to Gatwick and Heathrow airports. He drew a crescent stretching from Bexley to the east of London, to Slough in the west, and told the team to check all the estate agents within that arc. One officer doubted whether it would be possible before the deadline of four p.m. the next day.

'Contact all the head offices,' Foyle said roughly. 'Get the home numbers for their managers. Then start phoning them. Don't stop until you've finished.'

He placed his greatest hopes in the operation to

contact the hundred or so dealers in Central London who sold or hired out mobile phones. Here, the police had a distinct advantage. Rhodes still had no idea that his use of cellphones to detonate the bombs had been tumbled. In each case he would be confident that the bombs had pulverised their secret on detonation. He would not know what had happened to the King's Cross device – from which Legs Lafferty had torn the SIM card.

The tiny plastic chip had enabled the police to discover where and when the phone had been purchased. Two months before, a Mr Keith N. Stephen had bought the set and network service from a shop in Holborn. He had paid £30.99 for the Japanese-made set with a 100-hour battery life and a further £130 for the service. He had settled the account using an American Express card, which turned out to have a billing address in Philadelphia.

First thing that morning two police officers had returned to the store and asked the manager and assistants if they could identify the man in the picture. Nobody remembered seeing him. Still, there was a lot to be learned from the purchase. Stephen had taken care to choose the network service that asked least about the financial state of its new customers. A credit card and an address were all the company required. Naturally the address given by Stephen was false, but there was no reason for this to be discovered. The credit card was debited with the charges each month – and, anyway, the phone had not been used to make calls. This was not a rare occurrence, the manager explained. Tens of thousands of cellphones remained operationally virgin because they were mislaid or were forgotten while their owners were abroad.

Foyle surmised that Rhodes was likely to follow a pattern of buying the same model of phone and signing up with the same undemanding network. It narrowed the field considerably. The phone companies were asked to run through their records and provide lists of all the people who had bought similar combinations of phone and service in the last six months.

It was too much to hope that Stephen had used his credit card again, but Foyle was sure that there would be other significant information on the card's expenditure records. He assumed that the card company would have been contacted in his absence, but found that no action had been taken.

'You mean this vital line was ignored?' he shouted incredulously, at a young inspector named Aylmer.

'Yes, sir, it must have slipped through the net during the handover to Mr Scarratt.'

'Incredible,' said Foyle. 'Lafferty risked his bloody neck to get that information.'

Aylmer busied himself in getting a fax of the expenditure record, which was confined in all but one case to the United States. At the bottom of the list Keith N. Stephen was listed as buying fuel at a motorway service area north of Milton Keynes on 19 September.

'Phone the garage,' said Foyle. 'Ask them if they keep security video from that far back. If they do, find out what time Stephen was there. That will be in their cash records for the day. Then wind back the video to the time of his visit. We're looking for the registration number of the car he was using that day.'

By early afternoon the reading group had reported back to Foyle. As Lindow had said, there was a vast amount of detail, and all of it useful in proving the case against Rhodes. But the journal was almost without value. Lindow had skimmed it and concluded that Lasseur's character didn't improve with scrutiny. There were flashes of paranoia and the whole document reeked of self-pity. On one page he would speak of his finer feelings and on the next he described using a small charge to blow up a moose that had come to the lake for water.

The most useful discoveries concerned the new identities that Lasseur had recently put together for Rhodes. There were another four, including J. Miles which appeared in the passage about the Lindows. Documents and credit cards had also been issued in the names of Jeremy Edward Capon, an insurance executive, and John Larson and Edward Lydd-Taylor, both described as company directors.

'Have it distributed to everyone,' said Foyle, handing the paper back to Forbes, 'particularly the officers chasing up estate agents and phone dealerships. If this continues, we'll have the bastard before the day's out.'

'You might just be right about that,' said Forbes, sliding another piece of paper across Foyle's desk. 'I found this a couple of minutes ago. There's an account been opened for Miles by Lasseur at one of the high-street banks, which has the branch address of Crossways. Here's the sort code number. It won't take a moment to identify the bank.'

'Good,' said Foyle, levitating from his chair and seizing Lindow. 'Now, Con,' he said, steering him towards the door, 'I want you to go and get some sleep. You're booked in across the road. You'll be under guard. I'm afraid that, for the time being, there's no going back to your flat or your department at Imperial. By now Rhodes may believe you're burned to a crisp, but I don't want any mistakes.'

Lindow smiled at him weakly.

Only when the vivid blooms of Bonfire Night burst in the sky did Foyle register that night had passed from daylight into darkness. During a brief moment in his office, alone with a cup of coffee, he looked out of his window at the displays and thought of the archetypal terrorist, Guy Fawkes, and his end, now being celebrated in the burning of effigies all over London. He remembered the letter from King James authorising the torture of the Catholic hero. The phrases had stuck in his mind after he had used them in a lecture on anti-terrorist operations at the police training college. 'The gentler tortures are to be first used unto him and so by degrees proceeding to the worst – and so God speed your good work.'

God speed your good work. He put it from his mind and surveyed the chaos of his desk. Then he thought of Katherine and phoned Peter Speerman at MI5.

'I was hoping you were still there. It's about my daughter. Last night her place was raided by the police in Bristol, who were acting on a tip-off that she was in possession of a large amount of drugs.'

'What's that got to do with me?'

'Let's put it this way,' said Foyle. 'If my daughter is harassed in any way over the coming weeks, with or without your encouragement, I will simply brief the crime correspondent of the *Guardian* with some of the choicer extracts from these disks. In fact, I'm seeing him for lunch at Simpson's next week.'

Speerman attempted to interrupt.

'No, Mr Speerman, listen to me. I'm certain that there was an operation to plant drugs on her, and that if she had not been with me at the time she would now be facing a charge for possession. Any more crap like that, and I'll have the whole lot of you hanged from Lambeth Bridge. Is that understood? Good. Then go and see to it, Mr Speerman.'

He hung up and phoned Katherine. 'Okay, you can go back to Bristol now. Look, Katherine—'

'Kate!'

'Oh, for God's sake, then, *Kate*, I wanted to thank you for your help last night. Truly, you were brilliant. I was really proud of the way you worked. But remember it's all very hush-hush. Not a word to your lunatic friends.'

'You sure I'm not going to be raided again?'

'Yes, that's in hand. There won't be any problem.

When this is over let's go and do something, eh? You, me and Mum?'

'Yes, that would be great.'

He hung up and turned to see Forbes at the door.

'The men from Hereford are here, sir. Where should I put them?'

'How many of them are there?'

'Just two. They're instructors with the Regiment. Do you want to speak to them now?'

'Show them in.'

A short, wiry soldier in his late forties came in, followed by a younger version of the first, who was also wearing trainers and an anorak.

'What we want to know', said Foyle, without waiting for them to introduce themselves, 'is what sort of training our man's received and what he's going to do when he knows we're on to him.'

The older of the two men spoke. 'I understand we're dealing with Ian Rhodes. As it happens, I've met him. He was never in the Regiment, but we were on the same exercise in Norway years ago. He's a tough nut, no doubt about it. To answer your question, there isn't a course that he didn't qualify on. He knows the job and he's very good at it too. Is he working with anyone else?'

'Not now,' said Foyle. 'He had someone in America – a fixer. But he's dead. Rhodes killed him.'

'So he's by himself. That won't be a problem for him. Probably prefers working that way.'

'Yes, but what's he thinking? Where will he hide?'

'Two questions there,' said the older man. 'One, if he's planning some kind of operation for the near future, it'll be well under way by now. He won't stay to watch the fun. He'll be gone. Two, he's probably got several bolt-holes. He'll use them in rotation. Maybe another place where he hides his supplies. That way he's never caught short. Have you got any dates on this? Any likely targets?'

'No, our only information is that he is planning a big operation, which he has codenamed Axiom Day. Could be anything.'

'What makes you think he's definitely planning something?'

'We've got hard information from the States. Before his partner died, he told someone about Axiom and said it was imminent.'

'Then I'm certain he will already have planted the explosives,' said the older officer. The younger man nodded in agreement. 'It stands to reason. If he isn't a complete head case, he's not going to hang about.'

Foyle felt depressed. 'All right. What if we do find him? Are we going to be able to take him in?'

The younger man gave a brief smile. 'No, sir. There won't be a moment when he doesn't believe there's some way of getting out of the situation. He'll fight, and then he'll move very quickly to a pre-planned escape route. I'm not talking about you catching him in the street now. Let's imagine you've got him in a house and he's surrounded and the situation looks hopeless. He'll still be thinking he can get away. He'll go for it.'

'How dangerous is he?' asked Foyle.

'If he's got the weapons and the circumstances are right – lethal,' said the younger man, who spoke with a slight Scottish accent. 'He could start using grenades. You see, he's not a terrorist, sir. He's a professional and he's been trained in exfiltration techniques – trained to think himself out of these situations. That's the point you've got to remember. He won't give up. He'll go for it and he'll kill a good number of people, if he has to.'

'I'm getting the message. The long and short of it is that I'm unlikely to be able to bring this man to justice. Is that what you're saying? We're going to have to kill or disable him?'

The two men nodded in unison.

'Thanks for the advice,' said Foyle wryly, signalling to

Forbes, who had been looking increasingly amazed through the exchange. 'I'd be grateful if you could be on hand over the next couple of days. Various officers may want to talk to you. Please help them as much as you can. Forbes will find you desks and telephones.'

Forbes left with the two men, then returned with his head cocked sideways and his eyes raised to the ceiling. 'I've put Bill and Ben, the killer men, in the briefing room, sir,' he said. 'Perhaps we should go home and leave the whole thing to them.'

'I know what you mean. Where do they get these people? A few hundred years ago they'd be breaking men on the rack. By the way, is there any news from the shrinks? I want the psychological profile as soon as possible.'

Forbes said that it would be ready in the morning.

At ten fifty-five p.m. the first break came. A woman police sergeant, recently transferred from Criminal Intelligence, had been sent to south-west London to visit the district offices of several large estate agents. She had interviewed most of the employees involved in letting properties. By seven p.m. only one company, Romney-Brand, remained, a small outfit run by two partners in Kingston upon Thames. She had traced the home address of one of the partners and waited until she arrived back from an evening out. The agent immediately recognised Rhodes – or, as she knew him, Mr Capon. In August she'd let him a property, at £470 per week, just outside Kingston. She knew the address by heart as she'd had Ash View in Palmer Road on her books for six months before Mr Capon came along.

A surveillance unit was dispatched to stake out the house, a detached thirties villa hidden behind a screen of *leylandii* trees. The local police were asked to keep a low profile while a second team of thirty-five plain-clothes officers spread through the area at a half-mile distance from the house. By twelve fifteen a.m. Foyle was satisfied that they had the place covered.

Five hours passed. No movement or light was spotted in the house. It was clear that it was empty. Foyle said he was going to snatch an hour or two's sleep and left instructions that he should be woken at the first sign of any activity. He dozed a little, but spent most of the time agonising about whether he should order the house to be searched. At six a.m. he woke and authorised the insertion of small microphones but then remembered the booby traps Lindow had described seeing in Maine. The men were called back before they reached the house.

Just before first light, a red Nissan saloon emerged from one of the winding suburban streets that led to Palmer Road. The surveillance team assumed that it was a local man going to work, but the Nissan slowed as it approached the house and turned into the drive. The car stopped and idled on the gravel driveway for no more than ten seconds, its lights flooding across the lawn. Then it calmly reversed out of the drive and returned the way it had come, moving without haste into the maze of suburban streets. The ring of mobile units was ordered to stop and apprehend the driver, but the car vanished.

A few minutes later Foyle spoke to the head of the surveillance unit from the operations room. 'What happened?'

'He must have seen the footprints on the lawn. There's a heavy dew this morning. The officer with the listening equipment left some pretty obvious tracks.'

'Damn,' said Foyle quietly. 'Did he see anything else? Was he aware the place was being watched?'

'I can't be sure, but I don't think so, sir.'

'Look, I want you to stay there. Don't approach the house again. He may have rigged it with explosives.'

He hung up. 'Damn! Damn! Damn! We could've had him.'

'They got the car's number, sir,' said a woman officer

on the operations desk. 'It's registered to John Larson of number thirteen, The Maltings, Sutton. The previous owner was a Mr Craig Meon of Leatherhead, Surrey.'

'Get both checked out. Nothing obvious with the address. The odds are that it doesn't exist. Trace Mr Meon and find out when and where he sold his car. Now, remind me where we are with the bank. We know it's a NatWest branch in Croydon. Any more news on that? Have we interviewed the manager?'

'Not yet, sir,' said another officer on the desk. 'He's due back from holiday today. But we do know that the account was opened in the name of Jonathan Kemp Miles in June, with an initial sum of three thousand pounds. There were references from two banks in the US. A further fifteen grand was deposited in early October. A little under ten was withdrawn immediately, but no one remembers what Mr Miles looked like. They've been going through the bank's video overnight.'

'Good,' said Foyle. 'That reminds me. What about the motorway service station at Milton Keynes? Any joy with the video recording for the day he filled up his car?'

'No, sir, the film was destroyed last week. They only keep records for six or seven weeks. We just missed it.'

Foyle looked at his watch. It was eight a.m., Tuesday 6 November. He left to get some breakfast in the canteen. As he went, he called over his shoulder to Forbes, 'Today's the day when we put this bastard behind bars.'

'The position this morning is this,' said Speerman. 'Our man over there has copies of all the material from the disks. There's nothing that connects us to the subject. However, he suspects that the material may have been edited.'

Speerman was standing in his own office, speaking to Cantor on the phone, which was why he was being guarded. He waited for a response from the other end but nothing came, so he continued, 'Apparently they just missed him near Kingston upon Thames. They've found a house they believe he's using, but he seems to have been scared off. They've got a registration number and some promising leads from the disks. I'd say they're getting very close.'

'Yes, it does sound like that,' said Cantor slowly. 'I think we must open up one or two lines of communication elsewhere. I'll be in within the hour.'

There was a click as the director general hung up. Speerman stood with the receiver in his hand, wondering what was in Cantor's mind. It was all very well to use Brown Owl's intelligence reports on the Lindow brothers to prove that the service had been pursuing Rhodes, but the situation would change dramatically if Rhodes was arrested and started talking. So the 'other option' that Cantor had spoken of a fortnight before was now his only possible course: Rhodes would have to be killed before he could talk.

Speerman replaced the receiver gently and took a turn round his office. He knew that he must act immediately. He had either to throw in his lot with Cantor and risk his entire career to save Cantor's, or he must oppose the elimination of Rhodes. That could be ugly and dangerous. There would be no third way. Cantor would make sure of that by informing him of the arrangement in advance so that he would not be able to protest his innocence.

Speerman left his office and made his way to Kirsty Laing's. She was sure to be there by now.

Laing looked up without pleasure from a file as Speerman entered. 'After you said our discussions had been overtaken by events I did not imagine you'd be back so soon.' She did not invite him to sit down.

Speerman looked pained, as if he had been the victim of a terrible misunderstanding. 'I've come to value your directness, Kirsty. It's a great asset in a situation like this.

You're right, everything has changed – and I wanted to take the opportunity of talking things over with you before we're pitched headlong into the day. It promises to be an unusually gruelling one.'

'What's on your mind?'

'Well, actually I was wondering what was on yours. I think it's fair to say that we both share the view that the service should not put its interests before the safety of the public. But, in a way, that concern is no longer relevant. By the end of the day Rhodes's name will be known in every household in Britain. The public will be alerted to the danger he presents. At the same time, the threat he poses to the service is far greater than it was before. If he's arrested, he may well expose our association. How would you feel about that?'

'I'd be extremely concerned.'

'Then would you mind if I asked you how far you'd be prepared to go to protect the service?'

She thought for a long time. 'What you're asking me is whether I would support action to eliminate the threat to us. I'd have to think very carefully about it, but my instinctive response is that I would not.'

He searched her face. 'Why?'

'It's simple – and perhaps it seems ridiculously pious, Peter. But I'll say it anyway. If we don't stand for justice and the rule of law, we are nothing. We simply become another corrupt, suspicious bureaucracy motivated by self-interest.'

'Yes, I see,' he said. 'You've been most helpful. Forgive me for dropping in on you like this again. I just wanted your take on things.'

He slipped away, leaving Kirsty Laing with considerably more knowledge of the situation than she had possessed ten minutes before.

She didn't need to think what to do next. She unlocked her filing cabinet and removed a scanned version of the Rhodes surveillance photograph from a folder marked the 'Security Service and Public Perception'. She folded the paper into four, slid it into the box of tampons in her handbag then left the building by the main entrance.

Foyle's call to the FBI headquarters in Boston went through at nine thirty a.m. Without ceremony he began to pump one of Mundy's colleagues about the phone line from the cabin.

'The trouble we're having here, sir, is that the phone company hasn't got any kind of record,' said the man.

'But that can't be,' protested Foyle, running his hand through his hair. 'We know he used one.'

'Yeah, that's right,' said the voice, which was less than a hundred per cent alert.

'But there must be some kind of phone cable running up to the cabin.'

'No, sir, and there's nothing inside. It's pretty much burned out. There's no way to fix a phone to the cable and get the number that way.'

'Why don't you get the phone company and ask them to run a search of the subscribers in that area and see which of them has recently been making a lot of calls to Britain?'

'We've tried that too. Nothing showed up.'

'Well, let me know if you get anything on this. I can't stress the urgency too much.'

Foyle slammed down the phone and marched off to the operations room, where he commandeered a large board and wrote the names of the five aliases Rhodes had used recently, and beside each the use to which he had put them. Keith N. Stephen had bought petrol at Milton Keynes and was in possession of at least one credit card. J. Miles banked at the NatWest, Croydon. Jeremy Edward Capon had rented a house in Kingston upon Thames, and John Larson owned a red Nissan. The police had not yet heard anything of Edward Lydd-

Taylor, but Foyle had no doubt that they would by the end of the day.

Earlier on, a promising lead had been produced by two detectives who'd traced the previous owner of the red Nissan. He told them that he'd sold his car through Albion car auctions. They visited the auctioneers on the south side of Wandsworth Bridge. The owner looked up the Nissan in his records and found that it had been knocked down for £1,950 on 23 September and sold to a man named Larson. They showed him a picture of Rhodes. He remembered the face. The man had been several times to the Monday-evening auctions. After he bought the Nissan he came back again. He seemed to be looking for another car with special features.

The auctioneer went back over the records for the last six auctions. Then he recalled a grey Vauxhall van with thirty-five thousand miles on the clock, a decent little motor which he'd thought might do for a friend of his. It went for too much, though. The man in the picture had paid over four grand for it. The auctioneer said he seemed a fussy sort of bloke. He'd checked the tax disc several times and inquired about spare parts. He wanted to know where he could get hold of a set of bulbs for all the van's lights.

This piece of information was of particular interest to Foyle. Terrorists and other criminals, who wanted to avoid attracting the attention of the police by committing a minor traffic offence, such as driving with a faulty brake-light, paid exemplary attention to a car's road-worthiness. They also took care to see that the tax disc was up to date.

The auctioneer found the car entered for sale on the page for Monday 15 October, noting that it was taxed until August the following year and had been sold for £4,150. Then he remembered it wasn't Larson who had bought the car. According to his records, the new owner was a Mr J. Capon.

The detectives took the registration number.

A couple of minutes later the number was checked with the Driver and Vehicle Licensing Authority at Swansea. The car's owner was indeed registered as J. Capon of 13 The Maltings, Sutton.

Foyle was wrong about the address: 13 The Maltings did exist, after all, and it was now being watched by undercover officers. The signs weren't promising, however. An officer posing as a postman had been to the door of the small terraced house. One look through the window had told him that the place was unoccupied. Foyle concluded that Rhodes must be using it as a postbox and probably no longer needed to go there. Nevertheless, the house was kept under surveillance.

A distinct South London bias was emerging. Foyle traced a line between Croydon, where Rhodes banked, and the two addresses in the south-western outskirts of the capital. Somewhere along that corridor he believed there'd be another house, and also, possibly, a lock-up or a garage, even an old barn where Rhodes could work undisturbed on his devices.

At ten thirty a.m. Foyle held a briefing, in which he instructed his staff to go through the larger data banks searching for any of the five names. He was convinced that, sooner or later, another clue would turn up. Somewhere there'd be a card billing address for one of the names, another car-registration number, a passport application or a parking permit issued by one of London's boroughs.

He left the briefing before it was over and rang the commissioner to give him an update before they attended the meeting at the Cabinet Office.

'Have you any idea yet what Axiom Day means?' asked the commissioner. Foyle guessed that this would be the only thing that interested Sir Derek Crystal's committee.

'No, sir. Not as yet. But I have high hopes of catching this man. We're within a whisker.'

They went in separate cars to the meeting. Foyle grabbed the disks from the locked drawer in his desk then told Nancy Longmore to accompany him so that he could arrange the next few hours in his diary.

When he got to Whitehall he found fewer officials than there had been the day before, but Robin Teckman, Adam Durie and David Cantor were all there. Cantor was displaying a new composure, directing confident smiles around the table.

At breakneck speed Foyle took them through the previous twenty-four hours, ending with the discoveries about the cars and the two addresses. He played down the failure of his officers to arrest or even follow the driver of the red Nissan, saying that his men had been only just in place when the car appeared.

'What are your hopes for today?' asked Sir Derek. 'If this man isn't caught soon, we really are going to have to think about making some changes to the weekend. What's your view?'

'I'm confident we'll catch him, sir.'

'Not on this morning's form,' shot Cantor. In an instant Foyle realised that the director general's people must have been listening to the radio traffic between New Scotland Yard and the surveillance teams. 'I understand that there were no members of the Tactical Firearms Unit at the house. If there had been, this affair might well be at an end.'

Foyle took a deep breath, aware that his temper was about to snap. 'With respect, sir, in just under forty hours, we've taken this investigation from a standing start to the point where we know all the addresses he uses, the cars, the aliases and the bank accounts he holds. We will get our man, I assure you.'

'But you haven't yet, and that is the problem, Commander. Not only is he still at large, but you may have lost the element of surprise, in which case he is likely to bring his plans forward. And if I may say so, I think you're slightly underestimating the time your officers were outside that house in Kingston. How are we to know that mistakes like last night's will not be repeated?'

Foyle let the question pass with a philosophical shrug. He turned to Sir Derek and asked if there was anything else, as he'd like to get back to the Yard. The Cabinet Secretary's eyes traversed the table.

Cantor spoke again. 'Could we establish the media policy? When do you plan to release the story to the press?'

'We haven't yet decided, sir. I hope to be talking over the decision with the commissioner this afternoon. But we will keep you informed.'

Foyle rose with the rest of the table, but instead of leaving, waited for Robin Teckman to reach him. 'I wonder if I could have a word,' he said.

'Certainly,' said the director of MI6. 'Let's find a quiet spot, shall we?'

They went to the anteroom where Foyle had waited with Lindow.

'It's rather a shot in the dark,' Foyle said. 'We have had difficulty tracing the number from which Lasseur made his calls in the US. We need it to work out which number he was calling most frequently in the UK.' He pulled the disks from his pocket and handed them to Teckman. 'These are the original disks that Con Lindow brought from Maine. They contain the encrypted and decrypted versions of the files, most of which are messages sent by the standard phone lines across the Atlantic via a scrambling device. Lasseur and Rhodes had belt-and-braces security – the messages were encrypted by GenoType software, then scrambled by a modem.' He paused, conscious of Teckman's shrewd eyes.

'I don't want to put you on the spot about the work of

GCHQ, sir. But it occurred to me that if GCHQ made a habit of recording such traffic it might be possible to find a match between the material on the disk and the signals picked up out of the air. Do you see what I mean?'

'If, indeed, there was such a practice,' replied Teckman, 'yes, it might, in theory, be possible, although it would be essential to know the dates and the times of the transmissions. It would also be essential to know the type of scrambler being used.'

Foyle handed him a four-page analysis of the disks. 'We've narrowed down a few recent messages on the disks to within about twelve hours. And I think in an hour or so I might be able to get you the type of modem they used.'

'Then it may be possible. I must say I think it's ingenious of you, Commander. We'll talk when you've got some news about the modem.'

Foyle knew perfectly well that MI6 wouldn't confine itself to matching the signals. They'd read everything on the disks, including the details of Cantor's involvement in operations on foreign soil – which, of course, was the ferociously guarded territory of MI6.

He returned to his office with a number of decisions under his belt. He phoned the commissioner to tell him that he was going to postpone the media campaign until the next day. While he spoke, he glanced through the psychologists' report on his desk and saw that it told him nothing new. He already knew the stuff about Rhodes's traumatic childhood and his exaggerated feelings of responsibility, so he told Forbes to get rid of the two men who'd prepared the report.

Then Frank Mundy was called in Boston. 'Have you got anything on the phone line?'

'No, it's a goddam mystery,' rasped Mundy. 'Things weren't helped by an early snowstorm up there yesterday. The area is totally shut down.'

'Okay. I've two favours to ask you, Frank. The first is

that we need to use our combined brains to work out what Axiom Day means. I didn't want to call Varrone at this hour, but I wonder if you could have a word and see if he can't put his mind to it. We may be overlooking something in the word itself – another code. The second thing is that we need to know the type of modem attached to Lasseur's computer.'

'Sure thing. We've got that information right here.'

Mundy returned and told Foyle that parts of an IRE Model HS Remote Encryptor had been found in the cabin. Its lead was still plugged into the back of the wreckage of Lasseur's computer.

Foyle thanked him and called the headquarters of MI6 with the information.

Then he phoned Lindow at the St James's Hotel and said he was coming over to take a shower and a nap. He had a feeling that he wouldn't see a bed again for at least another twenty-four hours.

'Okay,' said Lindow. 'What do I do with my guards?'

'Take them on an improving tour of the National Gallery for a couple of hours, and while you're there you can be thinking about Axiom Day. We need to know what it means, Con. I'm sure you'll come up with something.'

At three p.m. Kirsty Laing found a pretext for dropping into Peter Speerman's office.

Speerman's secretary, a large woman with a permanently anxious expression, informed her that the deputy director wasn't in. Prompted by Laing's concern, she spilled out her worries. 'He left me a note saying he'd gone with his wife to the clinic this morning. Then he telephoned to say he wouldn't be in at all. Said he was going to the Wallace Collection then out to lunch. Well, when the director heard that he was very cross. Told me himself to send someone round to the gallery and find Mr Speerman. But they'd left. I do hope everything's all right.

It's really most unlike him to take off like that – specially when there's such an important meeting on.'

Laing agreed that it was indeed most unlike the deputy director.

She returned to her own office, where two or three casual inquiries established that a meeting involving the heads of Counter-terrorism, Domestic Terrorism and Domestic Surveillance had begun in the director general's suite at two p.m. and was still in progress. She smiled at the idea of Peter Speerman skulking among the displays of Sèvres porcelain to avoid Cantor. She put him from her mind and thought about the evening ahead, and the restaurant she should choose for her first meeting with Brown Owl.

Chapter Seventeen

'You'd better get back here quick, sir. Things are warming up.' It was Forbes on the mobile. Foyle dragged himself from a profound sleep and forced himself upright. 'We've got one sighting of the Nissan in the area south of Croydon, which ties in with some information from a shop manageress in Croydon itself.'

'I'll be there in a few minutes.' He bathed his face, hurried fifty yards from the hotel to New Scotland Yard and went straight to the operations room.

Forbes came towards him, speaking rapidly. 'The car was spotted by a policeman on the beat in Banstead. He didn't get a clear look at the driver, but he knew that we were after the car. He made a note of the number then checked with his station. It looks as though Rhodes has got a place somewhere in that area and that he wasn't just passing through. Ten minutes ago we interviewed a woman in Croydon who manages a shop called the Personal Phone Company. She met Rhodes four weeks ago. He didn't buy a phone but he spent a lot of time in the shop asking about various phone services. The point is, this woman took a fancy to our friend. She remembered him and noticed him a couple more times in the area, once in the street in Croydon and once waiting at a set of traffic-lights. The sightings were within a few miles of each other over a period of a fortnight. The local police are looking for the Vauxhall and the Nissan now.'

'Tell me about the phone shop. What did he want to buy?'

'She said he was interested in a mobile with a 165-hour stand-by time – that's almost a week. He wanted to connect this phone to the pay-as-you-go service. You pay up front now for talk-time, no questions asked.'

'So we can't trace the telephones.'

'When we do find him we're going to have to consider shutting down all the cellphone networks in the Croydon area, although of course it wouldn't stop him making a call via a conventional line. And if he's moving about in a car that's not going to bloody well work. I can talk to the phone companies anyway, sir.'

'Do that. I'm going to have a word with the commissioner. Meantime, get Dick Cubbit from Tactical Firearms up here. I have a feeling we're going to need the services of SO 19 tonight. Explain the situation to him – especially about those phones.'

Foyle went back to his office to call the commissioner, but before he could pick up the handset his phone rang.

It was Robin Teckman. 'You were right, Commander. Unusual traffic of coded signals was noted. Our people have just made a match between one of the items on the disks and some archive material at Cheltenham. They located the subscriber's number for you. It's 01737 5544744.'

'Thank you,' said Foyle, scribbling it down. 'Thank you a thousand times. I believe you've cracked it for us.'

He hung up and rushed to the operations room, where he almost forcibly removed a detective constable from a computer with access to the reverse directory. He keyed in the telephone number. Within seconds the name and address of the subscriber was on the screen: G. Castermayne, Pope's Farm House, Upton Pond Road, Nr Caterham, Surrey. He scribbled the address, checked it and straightened up.

'Pay attention, everyone,' he said, moving to a map of the Metropolitan area. 'We have an address a few miles south of Croydon.'

'Where from?' asked Forbes.

'That's between me and my clairvoyant. Who've we got down in Croydon?'

'About thirty officers at present.'

'This place can't be more than a ten-minute drive.' He handed Forbes the paper with the address on it. 'I want a unit to recce this house. They're not to approach it or do anything that gives rise to suspicion. Tell them to drive by slowly, get the lie of the land and look out for signs of life. Meanwhile, get some maps of the area up on the screen. And get hold of the local police. See if anyone knows anything about the property.' As he spoke, officers peeled away and picked up telephones.

Foyle continued to work through the list he'd been assembling in his mind over the previous twenty-four hours. 'Get hold of all the cellphone companies and give them the exact location of this house. I want one person here – Inspector Alymer – to co-ordinate a shut-down of the cells in the immediate area. This is not to happen until I give the word. But all four digital and the two analog services must go down at the same time. Give this bastard an opportunity and he'll take it. Also we need at least one helicopter on stand-by, maybe two. It's rush hour, and the traffic won't ease for another hour and a bit. I want an aerial surveillance team deployed on this job, but no flying over the house yet. I'll be in my office for the next ten minutes. Let me know the moment we hear anything from the officers outside the house.'

Foyle returned to his office, and phoned the commissioner with the news.

'I'll come back to you,' Urquhart said. 'The Home Secretary will want to be informed.'

Fifteen minutes passed.

Then a sergeant in the car that had been sent to cruise past Pope's Farm House rang into New Scotland Yard from a phone box, explaining that he didn't want to use a radio in the vicinity of the house in case Rhodes had a scanner. The property stood in a swathe of countryside just outside the Greater London area. There were no signs of life that he could make out from the road. Foyle pondered this information while the sergeant remained on the line.

He turned to the officer holding the phone. 'Okay, tell him to stay put. Get the other units discreetly covering all the exits to the farm. Then have the local police prepare to put up road-blocks at a distance of half a mile on all roads leading to the farm. And tell the sergeant that he can use the radio. I'm not having this operation run from a bloody phone box. If he's worried about a scanner, he can refer to the farm as "the Factory" and Rhodes as "Mandy".'

As Foyle spoke, he became aware that the commissioner had entered the operations room. He turned to see him beckoning.

'What's your thinking, Kenneth?' Urquhart asked, when they were in the corridor.

'It depends if he's there. But he must have a phone, which will complicate things.'

'So he's doubly dangerous. Not only is he likely to shoot my officers, he can also arrange for bombs to explode in the capital, or anywhere else, for that matter.'

Foyle could see the way the conversation was going.

'I've been talking to the Home Secretary. It's his opinion, and also the Prime Minister's, that the Regiment should be used.'

'The arrest record of the SAS is not good, sir. Rhodes will almost certainly be killed and we need him. God knows what else he's already deployed.'

'Yes, but I have to weigh that against almost certain loss of life in the force.'

'I appreciate what you're saying, sir, but we have to move quickly. The SAS is in Hereford. It's going to take a couple of hours at least to get them from Hereford to Croydon.'

'They're already here in force, Kenneth. There's a team at Chelsea Barracks ready to take off as soon as they receive word. They came up last night with the advisers who have been here.'

'So, the decision was made yesterday.'

'No, but we thought it best to be on the safe side. You, above all people, appreciate how dangerous this man is.'

'Who's going to be running this operation?'

'You are, but when the time comes you'll consult with Major Jackson, who's in command of the SAS team. You'll need to work closely with him.'

There was a knock at Foyle's door. Forbes came in. 'Someone's been seen in the house. A man moving about on the ground floor. They don't know if it's Rhodes.'

Foyle wheeled round to face Forbes. 'Get the road-blocks up at a good distance from the farm. No flashing lights, no sirens. Just shut down the area quietly.' Pennel, who had been standing behind Forbes, went off to make the arrangements.

'What about the cellphone networks?' Foyle continued to Forbes. 'Are they ready to help us?'

'Richard Aylmer says that they hope to effect a blackout of the area, but it's going to be difficult. They're reluctant to blank out whole areas of the country for long periods. They need a time.'

'We will give it to them, but tell them they've damned well got to comply.'

The commissioner started towards the door. 'I'll leave you to it, then. Good luck, Kenneth. Let's hope we get our man.'

'I'm sure we will,' said Foyle quietly, to the commissioner's retreating back.

'What's going on?' asked Forbes, puzzled by his tone.

'What's going on? I'll tell you. The Home Secretary has taken the view that the SAS should be used rather than SO 19. I don't have to explain to you what that means. It means one dead body and no answers.'

'Can't you say that to them?'

'I'd be wasting my time. The Prime Minister was involved in the decision. The SAS have been standing by at Chelsea since yesterday so everyone's known that they would be used as soon as we found him.' He reached to a peg on the side of his bookcase and took down a dark blue raincoat, a pair of racing binoculars and a large-brimmed waterproof hat. 'In fact, I wouldn't be at all surprised if Cantor has had something to do with this. The last thing he wants is Rhodes alive.'

'Hasn't he been discredited by everything that's come out of the disks?'

'No, not really.' Foyle tugged at the mackintosh belt. 'It's embarrassing for MI5, yes, but there's no evidence that they impeded our investigation. The civil servants, the politicians – they already know that it's a dirty job and they'd prefer to forget the whole thing.' He braced himself. 'Let's get on with it, shall we?'

He looked at his watch – seven thirty-five p.m. Two weeks to the minute since a number 147 bus had turned into Clarence Street and seemingly blown up of its own accord.

Fifteen minutes later Foyle took off for some playing fields a couple of miles west of Pope's Farm House. He knew that teams from the forensics and explosives sections of the Anti-terrorist Unit were following by road, a route having been cleared through the thinning rush-hour traffic. He had ordered similar teams to make for Sutton and Kingston upon Thames.

Kirsty Laing rose from her chair and turned as Brown Owl was shown to the table in the Aphrodite Taverna. They shook hands and sat down. Brown Owl bent to stow a bulging leather shoulder-bag under the banquette, then glanced round the restaurant, giving each table a quick, professional appraisal.

Habits of survival, thought Laing. 'They're mostly

tourists,' she said. 'Except the man over there with the escort.'

'How do you know she's an escort?'

'Because he's too awful for any woman to consider without being paid for it. He won't hear us – he's too busy negotiating her price for the rest of the evening. Mary – I can call you that? – what would you like to drink?'

'I'll have some retsina and a large bottle of water.'

The waiter came over, full of effusive charm, but then retreated rapidly to fetch the wine when the faces of the women failed to light up.

'I've ordered *mezze*,' said Laing. 'I hope that's all right. I thought it'd be simpler – it's very good here.'

Mary Menihan took a radish from the bowl of crudités and dipped it in salt. 'So, what exactly do you need from me now?' she asked, taking the first bite from the radish. 'I delayed calling in when you explained the situation to me and I guess I'm in the shit for that. What more do you want?'

'That won't be a problem,' said Laing. 'They're obsessed with Rhodes. They've got a man holed up in an address somewhere in the south. They think it's him.'

Mary Menihan arched her eyebrows. 'No kidding. How did they come by the information so quick?'

'I'm not certain – I'm out of the loop. But obviously the disks had a lot to do with it.'

'Yes.' Mary took another radish. 'It was extremely uncute of Con not to mention what he found. Made me look such an asshole with Craven-Elms. Anyway, it doesn't matter now – in fact, I'm glad the whole damned thing is over.'

Laing watched her guest closely, trying to ignore her beauty and gauge how Mary Menihan would react to her proposal.

'You probably don't fully appreciate how your work with Eamonn Lindow and your efforts over the last two weeks with his brother will help them. It means they can make out that you were on Rhodes's case all that time – that you were using the Lindows to get to Rhodes.'

'Yes, you said that on the phone. And it's true.'

'It's true, but they only wanted to silence him. Did anyone tell you to kill him if you got the chance?'

'Not in so many words, but they couldn't have seriously imagined that I'd do it. I've had some training – self-defence, and I know how to use a gun – but I'm not up to that kind of stuff.'

'But that doesn't invalidate the point. They obstructed the police investigation by suppressing everything they knew about Rhodes. You agree on that?'

'So?'

'So, it meant that they – we – exposed the public to a terrible danger.'

'You said all this before. What's new?'

'Well, there's a principle at stake. And I want you to help me fight for it.'

Mary's eyes widened. 'When did anyone talk about principles in this line of work? I mean, please, be real, Kirsty.' She said it with gentle mockery, her eyes glinting with a smile that caused Laing to lose concentration for a moment.

'It's just part of the game,' continued Mary. 'I happen to have got sick of the game and I plan to leave, as I told you. That's because the game doesn't change. It can't.'

'How long have you been with us, Mary?'

'On and off, ten years this fall.'

'And you were recruited how?'

'I thought everyone knew this story.' She looked out of the restaurant windows at the rain pounding the cars in the street. 'I was the lover of a man named Devlin – Richie Devlin. He was a bastard, but I didn't know that until some people came and told me what he did when he was away from me . . . the beatings, the killings, the torture of young men. They asked me to keep them informed about his friends and tell them about his movements. It was simple stuff. It didn't cause me any problem, once I knew what Richie did to his victims. Hell, I was living with a psychopath. It was the ultimate deception and I was happy to do something to get back at him. I endured it for that reason.'

'And this was in Ireland?'

'We met when I was doing my master's at Harvard. Then we moved to Ireland. That's when they came to see me. Two years later he was shot by the UVF. No one knew for sure who did it but that's what the police said. He was at a pay-phone ten miles south of the border. Anyway, this kind of worked for me. I was the grieving girlfriend and it established my credentials with the republicans. They trusted me and because I was American – or that's what they thought – it didn't seem odd that I moved back and forth and held down a publishing job in London. In fact, it suited them.'

'But you *are* American, aren't you?'

'Kind of. My father was Irish, although he was a British citizen. My mother was Jewish American, originally from Hungary. My parents didn't exchange a word for twenty years. My father died – oh – fourteen years back. Never got to know him properly.'

'What happened after Devlin was killed?'

'It was very casual – I never pushed it. I built a circle of friends in Ireland and became accepted. Occasionally they asked me to run a message to a guy in London, bring some money over, nothing big. Each time I told Craven-Elms what was going on and that's how things developed.'

'And you met Eamonn Lindow through these friends in Ireland?'

'No, we had to work harder on that. I put myself in his way. When he found we knew people in common he relaxed. We became friends on a certain level, but I never saw the real Eamonn, the other Eamonn, because he was too damned good at his job. He never gave a hint of what he was doing for the IRA. He was really something – so secretive.'

'What about his brother? How do you feel about him?'

Mary looked away but Laing caught a flash of hurt passing through her eyes. 'I liked him. But the way he took off . . .'

'Tell me something. To all intents and purposes you're an American. You look American, you sound it. Why're you working for us? This isn't your fight. In fact, most Americans sympathise with the republicans, particularly the ones with Irish blood like yourself.'

Menihan toyed with a cube of grilled cheese. 'Okay. It's like this. I was appalled – shocked – by the things that Devlin did. You know, he liked to kill people in front of their wives and girlfriends. He made them beg, then killed them anyway. And I slept with this guy every night because they needed me to stay with him. I used to lie there, trying to understand how he did these things, why he did these things. Eventually I just took a decision that I was prepared to do anything to stop him – stop men like that because they weren't in the game for an ideal. They liked the killing. They did it, no matter what effect it had, no matter who it hurt, no matter what it did to the children.' She stopped speaking as more dishes of *mezze* arrived. 'And you know something? Devlin and Rhodes, they're exactly the same people. They were just on different sides.'

'So that's why you were in touch with the republicans while you were over in the States?'

'Sure, Craven-Elms knew all about it. We had to move very fast, make it up as we went along because it all developed so quickly. Actually, that side of the last few days didn't work so badly.'

'What did the IRA want you to do? Did they want you to kill Rhodes?'

'No, they've got more sense. They just told me to find

out what Con knew and how he knew it. I guess they were going to make their own arrangements. But you've got to understand there was no way I could get out of any of this. It was a shitty position – no back-up, no support, no contact with anyone. Just some garage hand in Boston who supplied the gun.'

'You must've had your hands full, watching the same man for opposing sides.'

'You could say that. And I had to go along with it all and play the dim companion. Never again, I tell you, never! But Con's a helluva sweet man, and pretty smart too.' She drank some wine. 'Look, we've got off the point here. How do you want me to help you?'

'I want you to back my story that we knew two weeks ago that Rhodes was responsible for the bombs. You're the one person who can testify to that.'

'What's the point?'

'I told you, it's the principle of the thing.'

'But you say they're about to arrest Rhodes. What does it matter now? It's just about over – unless he gets away. Then, if he does, they just put his face all over the papers and he won't be able to move.'

'It matters that we were using a paid assassin.'

Menihan frowned incredulously. 'Everyone uses paid assassins, for Chrissakes!'

'The British don't – generally.'

'Give me a break. What was the SAS doing in Ulster? You know about the executions.'

'They were defensive actions, not executions.'

'Defensive actions that wound up as executions. Every one of those IRA gunmen died from a shot to the head, usually a bullet from a Browning handgun, as I recall. Doesn't make such a mess. But you know what? They could never find a hole in the balaclavas that the gunmen wore. And why was that? It was because the SAS soldiers removed the balaclava, took a good look at the guy,

385

finished him off then replaced the balaclava. That wasn't terribly bright, was it?'

'You're talking like a Provisional, Mary.'

'And that's part of the problem. This thing has got to me so I can empathise with both sides. But I belong to neither. That's why I was good at it, but that's why it's also time to go. I'm tired of other people's arguments, of all the bullshit. I have to find my own argument.'

She broke off to look at a party of large, beery German tourists making a commotion at a table near the door. One of the men saw her looking and waved her over with a plump hand. Mary stared at him until he turned away. 'Tell me,' she asked Kirsty, 'you've got an angle on this, haven't you? You want to go higher, maybe right to the top. Am I right?'

'I want the service to be something else. I know this is going to sound sanctimonious to you, but I believe intelligence work has a valuable role to play in a democracy. It's there to serve the system, not deceive it. We're licensed to operate in secrecy, but when we abuse that secrecy we betray a profound trust.'

'Do you really believe that, or is it just the pitch?'

'Both. I want you to help me.'

'Oh, what the hell! I'll help you if I can. I'm leaving anyway, not that I even had a permanent job with you. What do you need me to say?'

'Tell me the facts of the last two weeks. I won't say where I got them. I'll certainly never let Craven-Elms know. I'd just like to be in a position to set things right.'

'Okay.' Mary smiled and waved the empty retsina bottle at the waiter. 'I'm all yours.'

Foyle landed on the rain-sodden playing fields a few minutes after three Army Lynx helicopters had disgorged a dozen SAS troopers and six military technicians, who were now heaving a large crate from one of the aircraft to the tailgate of a Land-Rover.

386

Foyle hurried from underneath the rotors of the helicopter to where a sergeant from SO 13 stood by a car. As they moved off, the sergeant gave him the latest news. A man – possibly Rhodes – had been spotted moving around in one of the rooms upstairs: lights were on and curtains had been drawn on the ground floor. The house was completely surrounded, but police activity had been kept to a minimum. An operations centre had been set up in a church hall about two miles from the house – the mobile communications vehicle was on its way. The sergeant asked if Foyle wanted to go straight to the church hall.

'No, I'd prefer a look at the place myself,' he replied. 'Just tell the officers who are watching the farm.'

They passed along several narrow lanes bordered by high hedges, and climbed a hill to a wooded chalk plateau where Pope's Farm House stood. Foyle could see why Rhodes had chosen the place. The suburbs of London were only a few miles away, yet here, in this surprisingly rural spot, there would be no problem with prying neighbours. The three or four tracks that led to the farmhouse meant he could slip in and out of the property by a different route each time. And there was another advantage, which Foyle had noted as the helicopter came in to land: Pope's Farm House was no more than ten minutes' drive from Reigate Hill interchange on the M25 motorway.

Foyle told the sergeant to slow down as they reached the main entrance where a sign read 'No Salesmen'. It was difficult to make out much through the streaming windows but it was immediately obvious that Rhodes would see a car approaching from a long way off.

They made a wide arc through the lanes so as not to pass the house twice and arrived at the church hall, a long brick building painted cream. Inside, the one bleak chamber echoed with the sound of soldiers working the actions of their machine-guns. Maps and a crude layout of the house were spread out on a horseshoe of three trestle tables, in the middle of which stood a large uniformed superintendent fussing about which way the maps should face. Foyle remembered the man from his days in the Drugs Squad, a nit-picker who saw any spark of talent in his juniors as a rebuke to his own prestige.

He shook hands with him and said curtly that the tables should be placed in a block in the centre of the room and the plan of the house should be fixed to the end wall for the briefing. The current outline was nowhere near good enough. Foyle insisted that rooms on both floors had to be identified on separate plans, and that the passages, doorways and exits from the house should also be marked. When the superintendent tried to talk strategy, Foyle told him to concentrate on keeping the roads clear, fobbing off the media and putting the local fire service and hospital on an unspecified alert.

A young man in a one-piece black battle-suit detached himself from a group of soldiers and walked over to Foyle.

'Major Jackson,' he said, in a soft public-school accent. He was in his mid-thirties with keen eyes and the pinched look of the fitness fanatic. 'I may be able to help you with the layout of the house.' He gestured to the crate that had been unloaded outside and was just visible through the door of the church hall.

'What's that?' asked Foyle.

He followed Jackson into the car park to find a round object, which looked like a hybrid of an extractor fan and a flying saucer, standing on three supports. The machine measured about three and a half feet across and consisted of a circular fuselage with two rigid rotors fixed in the centre, one above the other. A couple of cameras were mounted at diametric positions on the outside of the fuselage.

'We call it a doughnut – it's a pilotless Sikorsky. It'll recce the farmhouse for us and send back pictures. It's fitted with conventional and infrared cameras that can be linked up to a light machine-gun. But we prefer to rely on our own skills in that department.' He smiled humourlessly.

'I'll bet,' said Foyle. This was Rhodes fifteen years ago.

The major ignored him. 'Once the cameras have been checked, she's ready to go. She'll stay airborne for two and a half hours so we can take a good long peep through those windows.'

'What about the noise?'

'Virtually silent, and in this weather he won't hear a thing. We'll send her off in a few minutes, if that's all right with you, sir. Meantime I suggest I get some of my men round the house.'

'Not yet. We'll have a briefing first. Major, perhaps this is a good moment to get things straight. I want an arrest out of this, not a body. Have I got your clear understanding on that?'

The major nodded. 'Of course.'

'Good, so we're going to take things quietly and make a judgement about the best time to move. I would guess the early hours of tomorrow morning. But we'll see. For the moment the primary objective is not to give the slightest hint of our presence. If you can guarantee that he won't hear that machine, prepare to launch it.'

He went back into the hall to find Pennel, who had produced four locals who knew the layout of the house. As they spoke, the information was added to the ground- and first-floor plans that were being drawn up. A retired farm-worker gave a detailed account of the out-buildings to the south of the house and a large barn in the west. When one of Foyle's officers produced an aerial photograph of the area that had been hanging in the local pub, the old man was able to point out two paths that ran from the back of the barn down a wooded hill to the west.

Jackson joined Foyle as this information was placed in

red marker on the large-scale map. 'If he gets out of there, it's not going to be easy to find him, particularly if he's on foot. He knows how to hide himself and he's easily as good as my men.'

Foyle was thinking the same. They had to pray that nothing would alert Rhodes before he went to bed. That way they stood a reasonable chance of taking him without bloodshed. But he had to be on the safe side. He picked up the phone to Forbes, who was still at New Scotland Yard.

'I want thirty officers from Tactical Firearms down here within the hour. In fact, get as many as you can rustle up. Tell Urquhart that because of the topography here we're going to have difficulty in covering every avenue of escape. Make it clear that they will be used as back-up only. Then get yourself down here. I need someone to organise things.'

'I'll hitch a ride with the commissioner. He's been on the phone every bloody minute and now he's threatening to join you.'

'Oh, Christ.' Foyle hung up and returned to the map of the farm.

An hour sped past, during which Foyle listened to Jackson and the SAS sergeant thrash out a plan of attack. Three of their men had already been inserted into the grounds and were reporting back over their radios. As yet they had no positive sighting of Rhodes, but they confirmed that someone was moving about the house. Shadows had been seen on the downstairs curtains. Foyle told Jackson to keep his men outside a fifty-yard radius and to watch for booby traps. Then he went to the end of the hall and called for attention. 'We have a man in a house. We do not yet know that this is Rhodes, but it's been confirmed that the place was let to an individual named Edward Lydd-Taylor, an alias we know he has used. We're pretty sure it is him. Our main concern is that he does not leave the property. At present we plan to move in at three a.m., by which time we hope he will be asleep. We may be forced to change this, according to what's going on in there. At the same time as we move on the farmhouse, officers will break into the properties that Rhodes has been using in Kingston and Sutton.'

He placed a finger on the elevation of Pope's Farm House. 'Major Jackson's men will go in at two points. Four men will move with assault ladders to the north side and break in through this first-floor window. Three will go through the front door. The remaining members of his team will position themselves around the house to cover all the exits. Beyond them we will have a ring of armed police officers and road-blocks, which are already in place. There are tracker dogs and a surveillance helicopter on stand-by.' He turned to face the room, which now included Forbes, who had slipped through the far door. Foyle looked past him and through the door to see two Army Range Rovers pull up outside. He waited for the noise to die down.

'The difficulty we face is that Rhodes may have rigged up all sorts of surprises to foil this kind of operation. Given what we know about him, we should work on the assumption that there will be various booby traps and, if he has warning of the attack, he may well try to use a cellphone to set off devices. The phone companies have agreed to effect a blackout of the area for an hour starting at two thirty a.m., but remember, this house has a commanding position and it's possible that a signal will get through to a distant beacon. It is imperative that Rhodes is not allowed to use a phone. Just because this appears to be an isolated property, don't be deluded that we have isolated the target. There may be many more lives at stake than we imagine.' He paused and looked at Jackson, who nodded. 'However, I stress that what we want out of this operation is an arrest. Rhodes is infinitely more valuable to us alive than dead. Tomorrow

I want him in an interview room, not on a slab. Just in case any of you have doubts, remember this. On September the fifteenth 1984 Patrick Magee checked into the Grand Hotel in Brighton. On September the seventeenth he planted twenty pounds of high explosive in room 629. The detonator was wired into a video timer. The device was primed for a full twenty-six days before it exploded under Mrs Thatcher and the rest of her government.

'Right, that's it for the moment. There'll be another briefing in an hour or so, by which time we'll know more about what's going on in that house. Two of Major Jackson's men are preparing to move forward and insert microphones into the house. It's going to be risky, but we believe it's crucial to know what's going on in there. Oh, by the way, we shall continue to refer to the farm as "the Factory" and Rhodes as "Mandy". The signal to go will be the word Sundowner.'

The meeting dispersed. Foyle walked over to Forbes. 'So, you managed to leave the commissioner behind?'

'Yes, I told him he'd have a long wait before anything happened. He's coming later.'

Foyle's eyes drifted to the remaining members of the SAS team, who were bent over the map, listening to Jackson. They were in full gear with assault hoods and masks dangling from their arms. Most of them carried Heckler and Koch 9-mm machine-guns, which were fitted with torches and infrared sights. From their belts hung a variety of sidearms, ammunition clips and G.60 stun grenades. One of them was carrying a shotgun with a clip of cartridges attached to the barrel.

Foyle sniffed. 'Somebody's going to be injured once this lot move in. We'll need a couple of ambulances, also a fire appliance. In the event of anything going wrong, the ambulances should approach the house from the north, the fire appliance from the west. But I don't want them racing round the countryside before we're ready, so get them to report here before they go to their positions.'

At ten thirty p.m. Foyle sanctioned the launch of the flying camera, which lifted into the darkness with a low, frantic whurr. The craft found its mark quickly but there was some difficulty in keeping it steady in the wind, and the camera wasn't focusing properly. He left the technician's side and went over to listen to the radio contact with one of Jackson's men. A microphone had been inserted through a French window on the east of the house. They were waiting to establish where Rhodes was before trying to place another device in the ventilator of the kitchen window. The first was transmitting well and, with the aid of a booster in the field, was sending a clear signal to the headphones of the SAS backup man.

Foyle heard the man operating the Sikorsky call out, 'I've got him. He's upstairs.'

He tore over and saw an illuminated window dance on the screen.

'Can't you steady it?'

'I could bring her down out of the wind, but I don't want the fuselage to catch the light from that window. He might just see us.'

The operator moved the joystick forward a fraction, and then used the keyboard of a lap-top to extend the Sikorsky's camera to maximum zoom. As the craft drew nearer to the house, Foyle saw a man move slowly across the room, pass the bedroom window and leave through a door.

'Oh, Christ,' he murmured.

'What, sir?' asked the operator.

'Nothing. Keep the craft in its present position.' He beckoned to Forbes. 'We've got a problem. I want you to keep it to yourself. There are a couple of bags on the bed. Looks like he's going somewhere. Get Pennel to check the airlines for all the aliases he's been using. And find a car for me.'

He went over to Jackson, who was holding a hand to an earpiece and staring down intently. 'You'd better listen to this, sir,' said Jackson quietly. 'It's one of my men on the south side of the house. He says a light's been switched on outside.'

Foyle picked up some headphones. 'Mandy's coming out,' said the voice. 'No. He's in the garage. There must be a connecting door to the house. There's a car – looks like a family estate. He's in the car. Fuck, he's going. No. Hold on. He's moved the car out of the garage. He's parked and he's got out. It's him, no doubt about that. Now he's gone back into the house.'

'I think we'd better get down there,' Jackson told Foyle. Then he spoke to his men. 'You lot, join the others in the vehicles. I don't think we're going to need the ladders but take them anyway. I want two men on the deck of each vehicle. I'll be out in a moment.'

'He can't be going yet. He's got to pick up some bags in the house. So may have some time, Major.'

'Right,' said Jackson, 'but we'd better get down there just in case. One team will take the western approach. I'll be with the other vehicle at the head of the main drive in the north. You can refer to us as Blue and Red teams respectively. That's Red coming from the west and Blue from the north.'

'It still leaves the track to the east,' said Foyle.

'The men on the ground will cover that.'

'Okay, but you'll wait for my order to deploy.'

Jackson grimaced and went outside to the Range Rovers.

Foyle picked up the headphones again. He could hear a man's breathing. 'I've got a better view now. I can see that he's moved a bike out of the garage – a trail bike. The back of the car is open. He could be going to put the bike in the car.'

Foyle heard Jackson's voice. 'Okay. We'll be coming on the track from the west and the drive from the north.

You three position yourselves on the eastern road. Did you read that, base?'

'Who the hell is base?' demanded Foyle.

One of the technicians looked up to him. 'He's talking to Hereford, sir. They'll be listening to everything. Standard procedure on an operation like this.'

'Jesus Christ.' He looked over to Forbes, who was watching the pictures from the Sikorsky. 'Can you see anything?'

'Not much. He's turned on a light downstairs – that's all. God knows what he's doing.'

Foyle felt that the operation was slipping from his hands. He called his officers together for a rapid briefing. 'Rhodes looks like he's going to do a runner. We need to alert the armed officers now. If he does start moving and he gets away from the house, we'll need to know immediately which route he's taking. The surveillance helicopter should be ready for immediate take-off. The ambulances are to move only when they hear the word. I will be in the car with Forbes and Kepple on the lane that runs past the easterly side of the farmhouse. We'll pick up one of the armed officers on the way and park fifty yards from the entrance. Sergeant, you'll be responsible for keeping me informed about what's happening in the house. Anything seen by that camera, I want to hear about it. Right, I think we'd better be going.'

'What about the phone companies?' asked Forbes. 'Can we get a shut-down of the network in time?'

'Get Aylmer to push for an immediate shut-down.'

Foyle went outside and walked over to the two matt black Range Rovers, each of which was fitted with a platform and a huge, looped radio antenna. He leaned in to Jackson's window. 'Don't go in until I give the command. You've got that?'

The major nodded. The two Range Rovers sped off to take up their positions to the west and north of Pope's Farm House. Foyle drove to one of the road-blocks where a group of armed officers was being deployed. He recognised a marksman called Silk, who carried an automatic weapon and a side-arm, and told him to get into the car. He drove on up the hill to Pope's Farm House, stopped the car by a gap in the hedge and trained his binoculars across the fields. He could see very little. The rain was coming down hard and the windows were misting up.

Pennel's voice was on the radio. 'Commander, he's booked on a flight to Bangkok under the name of Larson. It leaves Gatwick in just under three hours' time. There's a stop-over at Frankfurt.'

'What about the phone companies?'

'Nothing doing. Trying but they can't achieve a total shut-down in the time.'

'Did you hear all that, Major?' said Foyle.

'Yes.' The voice was lazy and relaxed. Foyle heard the sound of the Range Rover's engine straining, as though someone was labouring the clutch. 'We've got to go soon, Commander. Otherwise this bird is going to fly.'

Another voice came on the radio. It was the soldier outside the farmhouse, who was being patched through to Foyle by the mobile control centre at the village hall. 'He's in the garage again. I think he's doing something with the bike. He's bending down.'

Foyle picked up the handset. 'Ask him if he's brought his bags out of the house.'

No answer came. Either the soldier couldn't see, or he didn't think it was important. The silence from the SAS made Foyle nervous. He drummed his fingers on the steering-wheel, convinced that something was happening without his knowledge.

'Look, I want to see what's going on.' He started the car and crept forward to the gateway of the eastern drive without using his lights. He got out and leaned on the roof to look through the binoculars. Despite the rain, the murky orange glow of London's lights was evident in the northern sky. He swept the binoculars down to the house, then back again up to the top of the main drive. Suddenly he saw something moving against the skyline – an unlit vehicle was making its way steadily down towards the house.

'What the ...? It's bloody Jackson. He's going in now.' He knew exactly what must be in Jackson's mind. Once the soldier had told him that Rhodes was in the garage, Jackson had decided to push his luck and approach the house from the blind side. In this weather he could be pretty sure that Rhodes wouldn't hear. Foyle switched the binoculars to the light coming from the garage. There were some bushes in the way so he had to move a few paces to the right. He saw the car and the silhouette of the bike against the garage light. There was no sign of Rhodes.

'Christ, he's gone. Forbes, warn Jackson that Rhodes has left the garage. He's in the house, in which case he may hear them coming.'

It was too late. Jackson was shouting, 'SUN-DOWNER! GO, GO, GO!' Foyle saw the beams from the second Range Rover stab through the trees at the back of the house. There was just time for him to curse before the explosions came – three distinct flashes that pulsed across his vision. He dived down beside the car as the blasts rumbled through the landscape. A couple of seconds passed, then Forbes, Kepple and Silk sprang from the car, shouting. Foyle took no notice. He straightened up and looked towards the farm. There had been three explosions, he knew that – one at the back of the house, another right in front of him and a third where Jackson's vehicle had been. He raised his binoculars. A twister of white smoke was being ripped by wind from the spot to reveal the burning wreck of the Range Rover.

'He mined all the fucking approaches to the house,' Foyle shouted to Forbes. 'He mined the fucking roads!'

He threw himself in the car. The others followed. All

hell was breaking loose on the radio. No one knew what was going on or where Rhodes was. Foyle shouted Jackson's name several times. There was no answer. He called Pennel. 'Alert the outer ring that Rhodes is on the move. Get the helicopter over to the farm now.'

He rammed the car into gear and steered down the track towards the house.

'What are you going to do?' asked Forbes.

'We're going to find out what the hell's happening. Those men will need help.'

'You think that's wise?' Forbes shouted.

Foyle took no notice. The wheels of the police saloon were spinning in two deep ruts made by farm vehicles. He wrestled with the steering-wheel and managed to push the car up the grass bank, where it gained some traction. About sixty yards from the house the track ended in a steaming crater made by one of the explosions. There was no way through to the yard. Foyle got out and beckoned Silk forward with him. They struggled around the crater by clinging to the boughs of a blackthorn hedge and walked on. The house was dark now and the lights in the garage had been extinguished.

'He's gone,' whispered Forbes, who had followed them. 'He must have left on foot.'

They waited and watched. Then, as the wind died in the branches of the hedge, they became aware of a man's groans. Forbes plunged through a patch of dead grass to a ditch where the sound was coming from. Foyle and Silk got down to watch the yard ahead of them.

'There's a man injured here,' Forbes called out. 'One of the soldiers.'

'How badly?' hissed Foyle.

'He says he can hang on. Leg injuries.'

'Then bring his gun.'

Forbes slithered back across the grass and crouched down beside them with the gun.

'You know how to use that weapon, Graham?'

'I've used one before in the Army.'

'Right, if you see him, aim low.'

Above them, on the main drive to the house, the wrecked Range Rover had caught light properly, causing a strange popping noise. Silk said it was the ammunition exploding. Foyle waved his hand to shut him up. A noise was coming from the woods behind the house – an angry whine that went first one way, then the other. Suddenly there was a stutter of gunfire and a liquid stream of tracer bullets arced over the yard in front of the house.

'He must have been waiting to make a break for it but they've cut him off in the woods. He may come this way.'

'I can't see a damned thing,' Forbes shouted.

Foyle glanced round and saw the lights of a surveillance helicopter closing on them from the east. The noise of the engine was borne away from them by the wind and they could barely hear it until it was directly above the crater, whereupon a column of light sprang from its belly and swept up the track. He turned back to the house and at that moment saw the bike burst into the yard. The rider ran straight into the beam of the light.

Forbes and Silk opened fire. The rider skidded to his left and lost the bike, which slewed across the gravel in a flurry of sparks. The man was down. He was hit and lying on the ground. Foyle waved and shouted for them to stop shooting. The man had struggled up and was standing in the light, making not the slightest attempt to escape. Foyle whipped up his binoculars. It was Rhodes. He let them drop and started forward at a jog, his drenched mackintosh flapping in the downdraught from the helicopter. Forbes and Silk followed. There wasn't more than forty yards to cover before they reached Rhodes.

But now he was moving too, dragging himself towards the house.

'Stay there!' Foyle yelled, over the noise of the

helicopter, which was hovering five hundred feet above the yard.

Rhodes was holding something in his hand which he had taken from his pocket. Foyle could see it wasn't a gun. What the hell was it? A thick, slow-moving incredulity clogged his mind. Then he understood. He stopped and held his arms out to prevent Forbes and Silk running forward. Rhodes was lifting a phone to his face. He was speaking. He was talking to someone and he was smiling.

'Get down!' shouted Foyle. 'Get down!'

They flung themselves into the mud. Nothing happened. Foyle lifted his head and watched with one eye, as Rhodes lowered the phone and looked out towards them. Then Pope's Farm House seemed to inflate and its windows flashed orange like the eyes of a Hallowe'en pumpkin. The blast penetrated every part of Foyle's being and as the storm of bricks rained down on him, he clawed and ate into the mud, praying for his life. His legs jerked involuntarily to his chest and he felt his lungs let out a single gasp of terror. A long way outside him he heard the explosion thunder into the world. He looked up. The house had disappeared in a billowing taffeta of smoke and dust.

Rhodes had, quite simply, vanished.

Chapter Eighteen

'I don't know what it is about you, Kenneth,' said the commissioner, looking with exasperation at Foyle, who was slumped in the chair facing his desk. 'You've always got to go against the grain. You've pulled off this investigation against insuperable odds and, I have to admit, at times without my full support, but you still have to kick up some damnable fuss. Others would enjoy this triumph – and deservedly so – but you, Commander, you want to start an investigation into the SAS's behaviour.'

Foyle let the speech wash over him.

'For goodness' sake, man, forget this nonsense. They lost two men and three others are badly injured in hospital. If it makes it any easier, I'll tell you formally now. This isn't going to stick. There'll be no investigation because the Army discharged its duty with courage and honour, and so did you.'

'Yes, but they went before the order was given. Had they waited, we might well have been able to take Rhodes without the loss of life.'

'Oh, come on, Commander. Rhodes was about to escape. We all know that. No one had any choice in the matter.'

'But someone was giving orders to the SAS independently of me and those orders were to kill him, come what may. Rhodes is dead and there can be no embarrassing investigation into the director general of the security service. He will escape scot-free.'

'These are not matters for you, Commander.'

'But they do concern us. Because the security service suppressed information that would have enabled us to track down Rhodes earlier. Their actions had a direct bearing on the conduct of our investigation.'

The commissioner looked at him with despair. 'Foyle, you're a bloody pain in the neck. This is going nowhere, do you understand me? You can't prosecute the security service. Look, the Prime Minister's office has already called to congratulate us on your work. Next week he plans to thank you personally. It doesn't get any better than that for a policeman. Now go and get some sleep. You look dreadful.'

Foyle was not leaving just yet. 'There's a lot to do, sir. We still don't know what Axiom Day means. We don't know what Rhodes was planning. I have to work on the assumption that if he was flying out last night, he must have completed all the preparations for Axiom Day.'

The commissioner shifted uncomfortably, but Foyle saw he had accepted the logic.

'What's emerged overnight?' he asked eventually.

'It's clear he used the place at Kingston to make the devices. There are a lot of high-explosive residues in the garage. The van at the farmhouse was barely touched by the explosions and this, too, carries evidence of Semtex. There was nothing at the flat in Sutton. He used the place as a postal address.'

'What about bomb-making equipment?'

'Nothing so far. He must've got rid of it all, or deployed it in other devices.'

'What about the other car?'

'Forensic are going over every inch of it now. He was working to a very careful schedule. We think he disposed of the Nissan some time yesterday and planned to destroy the van on his way to the airport last night. There was a computer in the front. He'd already been at the hard drive with a hammer and blow-torch.'

402

'Any news about the people who contracted him to plant the two other devices?'

'Not as yet,' said Foyle. 'MI6 are using the information from Lasseur's disks to trace the origin of the payments made to Rhodes and Lasseur. They're certain that the bombs were inspired and paid for by a Continental group, but until they trace the banking route there won't be any proof. I believe they're working with the German authorities on the problem. We're not yet sure what the legal situation will be. I mean, it's thought that these people are linked up on the Net – they're based in different jurisdictions, they don't know each other.'

Urquhart looked at his watch, smiled and moved to his door. 'You've done well. You were very fortunate to be unhurt but you must take things quietly for a few days. An explosion like that at such close quarters does something to a person – it's a shock to the system. In the meantime I accept what you say about the need to be alert and I agree we should keep the heightened security arrangements in place. But, Commander, let's forget about taking on the SAS and the security service.'

Foyle got up stiffly and left.

With a day's growth of beard and a mud-splattered suit that had been worn for over forty-eight hours, Foyle knew he made a far from impressive sight as he trudged back to his office. Ordinarily he would have gone home to change, but he was determined to remain in his office until that evening. There was, indeed, a lot to be done.

He entered his department, where things were quieter than usual. The mood of celebration that had momentarily spread among his officers when news of Rhodes's death came through had evaporated when it was learned that two soldiers had lost their lives.

Foyle went to his office and shut the door behind him. On his desk were the final editions of the morning newspapers, each with its own ecstatic, garbled version of the events at the farmhouse, which were variously presented as a 'Dramatic SAS Raid', 'Raging Gun Battle' and 'Master Bomber Gunned Down At Farm'. One tabloid described Rhodes in his final moments drawing a gun and being mown down by 'masked SAS siege-busters'. At least he knew how the MoD was going to spin the story. Still, it was probably better that the newspapers didn't dwell on why Rhodes had a telephone in his hand.

He swept the newspapers into his bin and sat down to think of the problem he now faced, which was acutely more challenging than finding Rhodes. He'd have to go back through the evidence, searching for clues about Axiom Day. Everything that was known about Rhodes's psychological state, his methodical planning and his use of surprise had to be sifted and weighed again. Lasseur's disks, which had been only skimmed for clues about Rhodes's whereabouts, had to be exposed to a much deeper analysis. And then there was the physical evidence, the things Rhodes had left behind, which contained meanings that Foyle couldn't guess at – the van, the bike, the houses he had used. Every choice he'd made was a clue.

The task made him feel weak, but it had to be faced for there was one overwhelmingly important fact. Rhodes had remained in the Metropolitan area for a full twelve days after planting his last device. Then he'd packed for good, cleaned everything meticulously and arranged his departure. That had a meaning – it had vast significance – and it puzzled Foyle that no one else could see it. Even Urquhart, a fine detective in his time, had had to be pushed into recognising its importance.

Foyle's mind ran over the last twelve hours, scrutinising his own actions. He was furious with himself for allowing the SAS to take control. It was damned naïve of him to imagine they'd help him effect an arrest. Rhodes was always going to be killed. MI5 had seen to that, although he could only guess at the way the argument for his execution had been sinuously elaborated through many intermediaries so that when it reached the top, death was the only available wisdom. Another victory for Cantor's powers of suggestion by proxy.

He kept on returning to the scene outside the farmhouse. He saw Rhodes in the shaft of light, his left arm hanging limp, dragging his wounded leg towards the house. By then he knew there was nothing he could have done to stop him issuing the one-word command to the cellphone. No one had foreseen the use of the voice-recognition technology. One word – that was all that was needed to prompt the speed dial to send out a call that triggered the explosions as Jackson's men surrounded him. Another word and another number must have been reserved for the bomb that detonated in the house.

When his burned and crushed body was removed from the rubble the police could not even be sure that it was Rhodes. But Foyle knew for certain. Only Rhodes was capable of such deliberate violence against himself. As he looked down on the hideous remains, he had had the sharp impression that Rhodes had beaten him. There was nothing he could discover from him now: the investigation had suffered a final act of sabotage.

Angrily Foyle booted a desk drawer shut and stood up. But this wasn't the moment for self-pity. He had to go on and find out what Rhodes had intended. One thing he realised now was how Rhodes had planned to dispose of all the evidence at the house: he would simply have dialled the same number from abroad so that the house suddenly and mysteriously blew apart. Meanwhile, the properties in Kingston and Sutton would yield nothing to hurt him and eventually the leases would have lapsed.

The grey Vauxhall van was a different matter. It was plain that Rhodes had planned to destroy it on the way to the airport then continue his journey on the bike. That was why he had been leaving earlier than was necessary. But there was something about the van that had stuck in

Foyle's mind. The light from the fire had caught the side of it and shown up areas where some adhesive had been applied to the metal indicating that the van may recently have carried a sign. This was odd because he was certain that the van had been bought without any distinguishing marks. In all aspects – age, model and colour – the Vauxhall was perfectly inconspicuous. Rhodes must have added the sign to give him cover on one of the jobs. It wasn't much, but it would get Foyle started again.

He picked up the phone. 'Nancy, find me some officers. I need something checked.'

When they arrived a few minutes later Foyle spilled out his instructions. 'Get Forensic to look at areas on the side of the van. I want to know how recent those marks are. It looks as if someone has tried to wipe off the remains of glue. Find all the sign-writers in South London and ask them if they've worked recently on a grey Vauxhall van. I want to know the exact date and also the details of the lettering. Two of you go to Floodgate Street and show the picture of the van around. See if anyone remembers it from the afternoon of October the twenty-fifth. Now, off you go.'

He called Nancy Longmore again. 'Where's Inspector Forbes?'

'Just got in. He's on his way to you now. By the way, sir, it's no longer inspector. He's been made chief inspector. The promotion came through yesterday. It's on your desk, sir.'

Forbes came in looking drawn.

'This is marvellous news,' said Foyle. 'My heartiest congratulations.' He raised his eyebrows. 'What's up, Chief Inspector?'

'Nothing – just lack of sleep, I expect.'

'We had a rough time of it last night, Graham. Everyone did.'

Forbes nodded.

'But we're not out of the woods yet. I'm convinced

there's one big device somewhere out there. That's what he's been doing all this time.'

Forbes looked unenthusiastic.

'Tell you what,' said Foyle, revolving his chair to look out of the window. 'Let's go and have a bite to eat. We'll talk it through.'

Before leaving, he phoned Nancy Longmore once more. 'Can you find Dr Lindow? He must have checked out of the hotel this morning. He may be at Imperial College by now. Ask him when he's free for a chat.'

Kirsty Laing looked around her office before leaving, conscious that she might not see it again. She had little choice. There had been a meeting in the director general's suite that morning, a rally for his supporters of which there were now many. During the past two days one or two had questioned his wisdom, tactically placing tokens of doubt on the table as the wheel spun, but few had seriously worried about his ability to survive the Rhodes problem. With Rhodes dead, all that was forgotten. David Cantor had survived and a flush of confidence now lit his cheeks.

The relief was not expressed explicitly. Her colleagues were never so crass. But she saw it in the body language of the department heads, heard it in the eager questions about future policy, all of them encoded with signals of fealty. She also noted how few people looked at her during the meeting and that no one spoke to her on the way out. Even Speerman did not once glance up at her. That was an important sign in a room of cowards. Her opposition had been subliminally noted and soon it would be acknowledged openly. She was finished, as far as they were concerned.

On leaving the building, she walked first to a friend's flat where she collected the photograph she'd left there two days before. Then she went to a call-box and rang Mary Menihan.

'Is it all right still?' she asked. 'I won't use it if you tell me not to.'

'Yes,' said Mary, sounding altogether more optimistic than she had been at dinner. 'Go ahead. I've sent my letter of resignation round by messenger to Craven-Elms. Actually, it's not so much a resignation as a withdrawal because I'm not employed by them. Anyway, I've withdrawn on a matter of principle.'

'Do you want me to deliver any message to Lindow through Commander Foyle, or are you going to contact him yourself?'

'I don't know. I feel we should talk, but I'm not sure whether either of us is ready.'

'Fine, I'll leave it to you then. Be seeing you.'

'Yes, I'd like that.'

Fifteen minutes later she was shown up to SO 13's offices after the front desk at New Scotland Yard had phoned ahead to Foyle's office. Foyle came to meet her at the security door. 'I assumed it would be you,' he said. 'Are you going to tell me your name this time?'

'Kirsty Laing,' she said, smiling. 'We have some unfinished business, Commander.'

They went to his office where, without a word, she placed the dated picture of Rhodes on Foyle's desk.

Foyle looked up at her. 'What is it? I know it's Rhodes, but where's it come from?'

'I told you we had proof that Ian Rhodes had been sighted in the area of the bomb on October the twenty-third. As you see, the picture is dated and timed. It comes from our visual-recognition system. We call it Weegee. That photograph of Rhodes was in our possession within a few hours of the explosion in Clarence Street. We knew Rhodes was in the vicinity and we knew that he had been taking an interest in Eamonn Lindow. This information was suppressed because of our association. The picture is on file and was also lodged in the computer's memory, although that may have been erased in the last few days.'

Then she drew Mary's two-page statement from an envelope. 'You don't have to rely on my word or, indeed, on the evidence of the photograph. This is Mary Menihan's recollection of what she was told by senior figures in the service. She confirms that she had been instructed to prevent information reaching you from Con Lindow in the United States. Fortunately Dr Lindow did not tell her about the disks, but if he had she'd have done her utmost to stop you seeing them.'

'Why are you giving this to me?'

'If you have no use for the material, I will make sure that the Home Secretary sees it. But I'd rather not take that route again.'

'You misunderstand me, Ms Laing. I understand its value, but why are you doing this?'

'Because I don't want them to get away with it. Last night's operation stinks. You can't be happy about it. I mean, it creates a huge problem for you, doesn't it? Ian Rhodes didn't hang around Croydon to be shot by the SAS. He stayed for a reason.'

'I agree, but I've had great difficulty persuading anyone else to think like that.'

'So, you'll use this as you see fit, but I believe there's enough here for you to make a serious case against my lords and masters. This can't be ignored. Will you let me know when you plan to use it? You've got my number from last time, haven't you?'

'Yes, but I will also need to speak to Mary Menihan. This is going to drop you both in it and I think I should talk to her beforehand.'

'Certainly, but you don't have to be too specific in this. I accept that I'll come in for some flak, but the very existence of the photograph should be enough to do the trick. If possible, I'd like to keep Mary out of it. She's an exceptionally brave woman. She spent years working under cover in the IRA, and she's been put under immense pressure over the last fortnight – nothing that she couldn't handle, but I would hate to see her suffer in any way.'

'I understand. Does Lindow know about Mary – about her role?'

'Not the whole story, but I think you should give him some idea of her position. They were close. It'd be a shame if they weren't reconciled after all this.'

'I never thought to hear a senior member of MI5 play Cupid.'

'Didn't anyone tell you that's what we do? Undercover Match-making and Covert Reconciliation is our speciality.' She gave him a smile and turned to the door. 'I wish you luck, Commander . . . and you can wish me some too.'

'I do, Ms Laing,' he said. 'I do.'

At four p.m. Foyle gave a press conference in which he selectively set the record straight. He would not speculate on Rhodes's motives or state of mind and he referred all questions about the man's past and the SAS operation of the previous evening to the Ministry of Defence. He then made an appeal, asking the public to come forward with information about Rhodes. The police were still anxious to trace his movements over the last month and wanted to hear from anyone who had seen him buying electrical equipment. He didn't enlarge on this or refer directly to telephones, but he did say that certain equipment remained unaccounted for and that there was an outside chance that Rhodes had been planning another outrage when he was killed. Finally, he paid tribute to the unspecified help given by members of the public, by which he meant Con Lindow. Only one or two reporters noticed that the standard pleasantries about co-operation with the security service were missing.

He hurried out of the press room and back to his office, where he made calls to Frank Mundy and Peter Varrone to thank them, and also to plead for more help, insisting that the disks and the cabin might yet offer up clues about Axiom. Varrone sounded distracted, but said that he would put his mind to it. Mundy was altogether more enthusiastic and told Foyle that the mystery of Lasseur's telephone line had finally been solved.

'We made the bad assumption that he was using an ordinary phone line,' he said. 'Then yesterday, when the ice began to melt, we traced a line leading up to a hilltop and found a specially adapted cellphone positioned in direct line of sight to the phone company's antenna. The cabin was wired into three separate installations, which allowed the guy to make calls through three different routes. Consequently no pattern of calls showed up for a particular number – kind of brilliant. We've got a list of the numbers called, but I guess that's not as urgent as it was.'

Foyle thanked him again and hung up.

It was nearing six p.m. and the light had faded from Foyle's window without him noticing. He dragged himself to the second briefing of the day. The first had been a desultory affair, but now he had a clearer idea of the way he would direct the rest of the inquiry. His conversation with Mundy had reinforced his instinct that cellphones still lay at the heart of the investigation. He increased the number of officers visiting phone stores and spread the net wider to take in the Home Counties. He assigned another dozen officers to track down the remainder of the explosives. Finally he detailed six officers under Aylmer to sift through all the evidence and come up with a list of possible targets.

The last information that he was to remember from the day was that the glue on the van was, indeed, only one or two days old. And he was right: the van had been auctioned without markings. But by now his reserves of stamina were giving out. He jerked in his chair, having almost drifted off. Forbes came forward with a piece of paper as if to give him an urgent message.

'You must get some rest,' he said, touching Foyle's shoulder.

Foyle slurred a protest but did not resist. As Forbes guided him to the door, a faint ripple of applause spread through the ranks of the Anti-terrorist Unit.

Next day he woke at ten thirty a.m. feeling no better. He remembered that June had been there when he'd got in the night before. She was standing in the hallway, holding her unopened mail. She brushed his cheek with the back of her fingers, kissed him and ran him a bath. She barely said a word, but he recalled that she looked different. She'd lost quite a lot of weight and she seemed to have slipped from middle age back into her thirties.

It hadn't been a hallucination. He could hear the radio from the kitchen now. He got up for a pee. When he returned, she was in the bedroom with a cup of tea. He sat sipping it on the side of the bed.

'How have you been?' she asked brightly.

'Work.' It was his condition, not his occupation.

'Have you got to go in today?'

Foyle nodded. 'What time did you get back?' The atmosphere was strained, as it always was when they'd been apart for any length of time. Their marriage worked on regular, if not prolonged, contact. Once they were away from each other they lost the habits of concession.

'Six thirty, yesterday evening. Have you really got to go in? I hoped we'd be able to talk.'

Foyle caught the note in her voice and examined her face. 'What about?'

'About us, Ken. About us. This isn't a good time. I know you're very busy – I saw you on the news last night.' She paused. 'Look, I think we ought to try a separation.'

'We just have,' he said. 'Nearly three months.'

'Yes, but this is different.'

He looked at her, knowing what she was going to say.

The loss of weight, the bloom of happiness in her face, had already told him that she'd fallen for someone.

'I'm in love.'

'Oh, Christ. That's all I need. Who with?'

'It's hit me so suddenly, I don't know what to make of it. I don't feel any less love for you. I don't respect you less. It's just that I need time to work it out. I've lost my bearings.'

'Who with?' He was angry now, but with himself – for not seeing the way things were going, for not taking steps to stop it.

'Dr Hussan.'

'The archaeologist – the man you introduced me to?'

'Yes, but things only developed in the last few weeks. I wasn't looking for it, Ken. It's just that you're so . . . so involved with your work. I thought I needed to find something for myself when Katherine went away. Then, when this happened, I realised what I'd been missing – affection, companionship. God, if only you knew how lonely I've been with you, Ken. Your work is a mistress and I can't compete.'

Foyle drank his tea, reflecting that every scene from every marriage was played out in the same bloody stupid language, each person uttering commonplaces with the conviction that they'd never been said before. 'Have you told Katherine?'

'No, I thought we both ought to do that. We could go down to see her on Saturday and explain things – you know.'

'No, I don't know. What things?'

'Well, that it's not just me running off. There's a history to this. I want her to understand that we've had some difficulties and that we're going to try living apart for a while and that it's not necessarily a permanent arrangement.'

'She won't believe that. And nor do I, come to think of it.'

'But I do,' said June, levelling him a look of resolution. 'I'm working things out. I just wasn't going to do that thing of not telling you. I wanted to be straight.'

'So you're sleeping with him.'

'Yes,' she said defiantly. 'We have slept together.'

'Then it is bloody well over. That's it.'

'Oh, for God's sake, don't be such a child, Ken.'

The phone rang. 'Leave it,' he said.

She reached to the side of the bed and answered it. 'It's Graham Forbes.'

'Not now,' said Foyle.

'Come on, don't be stupid, Ken. It may be important.' She handed him the phone.

'Yes,' he snapped.

'Bad moment? I'm sorry. I thought you'd want to know there's a meeting at the Cabinet Office at twelve thirty. Do you want me to make your excuses? I'm sure they'll understand.'

'No, I'll be there. Can you get a car sent? Thanks.'

She took the receiver from him and replaced it.

'I *do* have to go,' he said.

'I'm used to it.' She got up from the bed with a sigh. 'We'll talk about this over the weekend.'

'You're not going to be here tonight?'

'No, it's better that way. I'll stay with some friends.'

'You mean Hussan.'

'No. He's not even in the country. Look, we'll see each other on Saturday and drive down to Katherine. They must at least let you have the weekend off.'

She went downstairs. Foyle bathed and shaved, without being aware of what he was doing.

June's matter-of-fact briefing on the state of their marriage did not metabolise in Foyle's emotions until an hour or so later when his car was creeping along the Chelsea Embankment. He suddenly remembered Dr Hussan's ingratiating smile and slammed the *Daily Telegraph*

414

down on the back seat. The sound startled Alex, who looked in the mirror and proclaimed defensively that there was nothing he could do about the traffic.

They reached New Scotland Yard a quarter of an hour later, which gave Foyle just twenty minutes to collect himself and make some calls. He closed the door of his office and dialled the number in Pimlico that Kirsty Laing had given him the day before. There was no answer from Mary Menihan's phone. Then he phoned Con Lindow, who picked up on the second ring. 'How're you fixed today, Con?'

'Busy,' said Lindow.

'Tonight?'

'No good. I've got a work thing.'

They agreed to meet the following evening.

Then Foyle unlocked his bottom drawer, took out the photograph and statement that Laing had given him the day before and slipped them in his inside pocket. As yet he did not know how he would use them, but if Cantor came back at him again he would certainly consider it.

When Foyle arrived at the Cabinet Office he found that he was the appendix to another meeting about the proliferation of biological weapons. Sir Derek looked up and swept off his glasses when he entered and sat down at his usual place. 'Welcome, Commander Foyle. I learn from the commissioner that you have some outstanding anxieties, which is why I've asked you here this morning. But first I think it appropriate that we should convey our thanks to you. The deaths of two soldiers were tragic but our sorrow should not let us obscure the debt we owe you.' He smiled at Foyle, and, with a glance round the table, prompted the others to follow suit. 'Now, what is it you have to tell us, Commander?'

While Sir Derek spoke, Foyle focused on a point a little to the left of Cantor at the far end of the table. It was already plain to him that there were no rifts in the room and that the position of the director general of the security service was not remotely threatened. No doubt he had lost some ground in the Whitehall battleground. Perhaps he'd even received a ticking-off from the Prime Minister. The payments to Rhodes for the elimination of two arms dealers would certainly be frowned upon, but they weren't grounds enough to sack him, particularly as Cantor had so adroitly made the case that Rhodes had been the target of their investigation all along. Nothing would change. Cantor had returned to his old silky form and was looking as imperturbably in control as he had the first day Foyle set eyes on him.

Foyle rose. 'Thank you, sir. In return I'd like to pay tribute to the invaluable help we received from MI6 in tracing Rhodes. Without it, I believe we might still be looking for him.'

Robin Teckman gave a nod of appreciation.

'But I take little satisfaction from the operation on Tuesday. Instead of a live suspect, we've got a body in the mortuary and a question we can't answer. The question is this. Why did he stay here nearly a fortnight beyond the time he could have left? We simply don't have a satisfactory explanation. Yet we do know that the phrase Axiom Day had great significance for him. Everything we've learned about this man leads me to believe that he was preparing to leave the country having already executed his plans. We could be months or hours away from a devastating attack, which he timed to occur after he had gone. We've got a stack of evidence that hasn't yet suggested an answer to this problem, but we're looking in the right direction, tracking his movements over the last few weeks, which is easier now that his appearance and the aliases he used are public knowledge. More important is the identification of targets – the targets that would attract Rhodes's peculiar form of homicidal narcissism, which is the way one of the psychologists described it. Of course, as soon as we have anything on this we'll make it available to you. The problem, gentlemen, is that we're not only dealing with an exceptionally clever maniac, but also a dead one.' He sat down.

'The commissioner intimated that these were your worries,' said Sir Derek. He looked at David Cantor. 'What's your assessment of the situation? Is it as forbidding as Commander Foyle's?'

Foyle could no longer contain himself at the idea of Cantor being asked his view, and emitted a growl of disbelief.

'I couldn't be more at odds with it. We have no intelligence whatsoever to support the commander's statement.'

'I wasn't talking about intelligence,' Foyle fired back. 'I was talking about evidence – the solid fact that there are telephone sets not yet accounted for, explosives not found, motives still unidentified.'

'These surely aren't facts in the accepted meaning of the word,' replied Cantor. 'They're simply gaps in your knowledge, which is hardly the same thing. There are many acceptable explanations for his delayed departure, one being that any assassin or terrorist worth his salt does not flee the country once a bomb has gone off. He lies low for a few days then makes a move without hurry. We know that Rhodes used this time to tidy things up, making sure that he left as little behind as possible.' Cantor's tone eased to a conciliatory note. 'I'm certain, however, that Commander Foyle is right to keep us on our toes – that is the policeman's duty – but we should not allow him to persuade us that Rhodes is capable of operating from beyond the grave. As we've learned this morning, there are many other threats to the security of this country. These, unfortunately, are a clear and present danger. As the commander pointed out, Rhodes is dead.'

He ended with a small, self-satisfied smile. That was the thing that made Foyle rise to his feet again. He fixed

Cantor with a cold stare, checked his temper, then began to speak. 'You'll forgive me, sir,' he said slowly, to Sir Derek, 'if I don't pay too much attention to what the director general has to say on matters of security. He knows very well that for an entire fortnight he did everything in his power to prevent the name of Rhodes entering the police investigation. Not only that, he pressed for Dr Lindow's continued detention, arguing that he was guilty. You were all here when he made that case. In fact, he was so persuasive that I remember almost agreeing with him myself. But all the while he knew Rhodes was in the vicinity of the first explosion and that he was probably responsible for subsequent bombings.'

'You're straying into areas of defamation, Commander. You have no proof of that.'

'But I do, you see,' said Foyle, producing the picture from his breast pocket and unfolding it. 'This photograph of Ian Rhodes is one of half a dozen copies made on the night of October the twenty-third by technicians at Millbank. It was distributed among the senior staff at a meeting that evening, a few hours after the bomb exploded.'

He held it up to the room, which was by now electrified with interest. Adam Durie and Robin Teckman rose from their seats to get a better look at the photograph. 'Although it is timed and dated to that evening, this picture was never offered to us as a possible lead. You can imagine for yourselves where we'd be today if we had been able to begin our hunt for Rhodes on that Wednesday. We might have prevented two further explosions and there would have been no question of Rhodes carrying out his Axiom threat – whereas now, of course, I believe there is still that possibility, even though he is dead.'

Cantor stood up too, his fingers splayed out on the surface of the table. 'These are operational matters,

418

Commander. You have no business with that photograph, which I hasten to add is classified intelligence material.'

'Wrong, sir! It's evidence, and you suppressed it because of your association with Ian Rhodes.'

The blood had drained from Cantor's face and a lock of hair had fallen across his forehead. 'It is on record that the security service has been pursuing this man for many months. Naturally we had his picture on file and clearly we would have pulled it from our system on the night of the bomb. That's what the date and time indicate – the time the file was retrieved from our system.'

'Good try,' said Foyle. 'I might have believed you, but for three details, each of which I'm sure will comply with your scrupulous definition of a fact. First, this picture comes from the Weegee secret surveillance system that automatically recognises and tracks a suspect in a crowded street. Some of the people around this table will know about your tailor-made system, which is officially known as ARTS. This photograph was taken within a few minutes of the Clarence Street bomb – that's what the date/time line indicates. You knew Rhodes was close enough to be implicated and that it was probable he had just alighted from the bus, having carried the bomb on board and stowed it behind Eamonn Lindow's seat. Second, I have two witnesses who'll say that your senior staff suspected Rhodes's involvement and were intent on hiding this from the police. There's a statement in my pocket to that effect, and I'm in a position to take another at any time I choose. Third, I have here a recording of Rhodes's voice. This message tape was retrieved from Dr Lindow's flat in Notting Hill.' He placed the tape on the table in front of him. 'On it you can hear Rhodes pretending to be a letting agent and instructing Dr Lindow to call a number in connection with his search for a flat. The number turned out to be connected to the King's Cross bomb. It was Rhodes's way of incriminating Lindow. Now, this is the point, gentlemen. MI5 were monitoring Dr Lindow's calls. Mr Cantor's people knew about this call and yet they said nothing when the police released the number to them. In other words, there was a deliberate suppression of the evidence.'

Sir Derek tried to cut him short with a motion of the hand, but Foyle's voice had risen. 'What this amounts to, sir, is that you and your colleagues are liable to charges under Section 18 of the Prevention of Terrorism Act (Temporary Provisions), which specifically makes it an offence to withhold information, knowing or believing that it might be material in the detection of a terrorist.'

'That's enough.' Sir Derek made himself heard. 'You've made your point, Commander. I'm not having this committee turned into a court. I'm certain the security service has adequate explanations for all this. In the meantime, I take your point that there is still a certain level of threat and will advise accordingly. That'll be all. Thank you.'

Foyle was aware of the clock ticking on the mantel-piece. He'd never noticed it before, but that was because the room had never been so silent. He glanced round the tableau of shocked expressions. Sir Derek had buried himself in his papers; Adam Durie held his brow with one hand and shook his head; and the man from the Northern Ireland Office had spotted an interesting insect on the ceiling. Only Robin Teckman looked unembar-rassed. He sat, examining Cantor, with his right index finger pressed to his lips. As Foyle turned to the door, Teckman removed his glasses and gave him another nod.

By the time he reached the main entrance to the Cabinet Office, Foyle realised he'd gone too far. He would be deemed guilty of inappropriate behaviour, however obvious Cantor's crimes. It was a question of table manners in Whitehall. Assassins were permitted, as long as they held their knives properly.

Outside, the car was nowhere to be seen so he began to walk. As he reached Parliament Square, he thought of the photograph in his pocket and reminded himself to find out where it had been taken. He was sure Laing had told him and he'd forgotten. But there were a thousand other things to remember. For that moment Foyle forgot them. He marched into the wind, which blew across Parliament Square like a sea breeze, soft and damp with the promise of more rain. It made him feel better – a lot better.

Friday 9 November began early for Peter Speerman. He couldn't sleep, so he rose before dawn and went for a walk with his wife's dachshund, an animal he heartily detested but which threatened to wake up the house if it was left behind.

He had a vague but piercing sense of anxiety as he trudged through the empty streets towards Kensington Gardens with the damned dog winding its lead round every possible obstacle. He knew things had gone badly wrong at the Cabinet Office the day before, but was unable to find out what had happened. This in itself was worrying, for it meant that he had been left out of things. All Cantor would say on his return was that a grave breach of security had been committed. Circumstances led him to believe that Kirsty Laing was the source and that she would be suspended, pending further investigations. Cantor made it plain that he held Speerman responsible for Laing's advancement and thus her treachery.

'Well, find out what she's been doing,' he snapped, in answer to Speerman's protestations, before dismissing him from the room with a flick of his hand.

He had tried to find Laing, but she was out of the office and her home phone number was permanently engaged. No one knew where she was, although a lot of people were eager to speak to her. Rory Fuller and then Angus Grove rang him, each in a state of blind fury.

'Why should I know where she is?' he replied defensively to Grove.

'Because that fucking frigid dyke bureaucrat is your creature, Peter. You made her and now she's doing her damnedest to destroy the service and all of us with it.'

Speerman was particularly worried that he had no clear idea of what Laing had done, but he certainly wasn't going to ask Grove or Fuller. It was disturbing that he'd apparently read so much the wrong way. From the moment Rhodes was killed, Cantor had appeared to become fireproof again. The revelations from the disks had been swept under the carpet in the general jubilation and Cantor had smoothed any remaining doubts about the service's behaviour by arguing that it was sometimes regrettably necessary to get close to an individual like Rhodes. That was the very essence of intelligence work.

But now everything had changed. What the hell had happened? Why hadn't she involved him? And what had she got that was so devastating for Cantor?

He walked on past Kensington Church Street, towards the gardens, thinking back over the meetings of that week. It had been his suggestion to get Kirsty involved. Despite her seniority, he remembered regretting it. She seemed utterly out of her depth. She didn't even know enough to keep quiet when Rhodes was discussed. Cantor had been angry and told him to bring her up to speed. Oh, Christ! That was it. He'd given her the file with the picture of Rhodes – the dated picture of Rhodes. Laing had squirrelled it away then dropped it in the lap of Foyle or someone at the Home Office.

Speerman had to find out for sure. He dragged the dog to the nearest call-box, and dialled Laing's number. The number rang.

'Ah, Peter,' she said, without surprise.

'What's happened, Kirsty? Everyone was looking for you yesterday. Where the hell were you?'

'At the Home Office.'

'At the Home Office? Why?'

'I can't speak on the phone.'

'Can we see each other?' He knew he sounded desperate. 'Look, I'm out walking the dog. Why don't we have a cup of coffee somewhere?'

'Can't this wait?'

'No, it can't. I want to know what's going on. Everything's in such a state of confusion.'

'I've got a car picking me up in half an hour. We'll meet at eight in the Pret à Manger near Marble Arch tube.'

Speerman hurried home, propelled the dachshund through the door and hailed a cab to Marble Arch. Laing was already there, standing at one of the shelf tables along the window. She looked taller to him, and altogether more tailored and polished. He didn't bother buying coffee for himself, but perched on a stool beside her.

'Good morning,' he said, trying to strike a note of conspiratorial bonhomie. 'I hope you're going to tell me what's been going on.'

Laing put down her coffee and studied him. 'In due course. But I'm glad of this chance to talk. I want you to stay on, Peter, but not as deputy director. Andreas Guthrie from D-Branch has agreed to be my deputy. Meanwhile I want you to develop a new role, with special responsibilities for government liaison. After this, we're going to need to win back people's confidence and you are by far the best person for that. But it will mean taking a slightly higher profile. I want you to be our public face, Peter. In relation to me I see you assuming the position of special counsellor.'

'I don't understand,' he stammered.

Laing smiled. 'Oh! I am sorry. I had assumed David Cantor would have told you by now. He resigned yesterday evening – or, rather, he decided that he was taking early retirement. It was for the best. It'll be announced to the press next week, but naturally the news will be circulated at Millbank today. So, if that's all, I've rather a lot to do. There are going to be some changes, Peter. We need to start behaving like a responsible department.'

She drained the last of her cappuccino. 'Oh, I nearly forgot. How's Mrs Speerman? I take it she's better.'

'Eh . . . ? Oh, yes, of course, she's fine now. Well . . . I suppose . . . I suppose I should say congratulations.'

'Thank you, Peter. I know I can look forward to receiving your full support.'

Chapter Nineteen

All Friday Foyle struggled to keep SO 13 focused on the case, but there was little for his officers to bite on. No trace had been found of Rhodes's explosives and it was proving impossible to identify cellphones he might have bought. Foyle insisted again and again, as much for his own benefit as anyone else's, that the body lying in the mortuary in Croydon still presented a very real threat. By now the commissioner had accepted this and agreed to increase security for the two parades over the weekend. Barely an officer in southern England would be allowed off for Remembrance Day and the City police were already running heightened security checks along the route of the Lord Mayor's Parade, monitoring the cars, passing through the ring of steel and searching empty buildings.

After Foyle's eruption in the Cabinet Office, relations with the top floor had again cooled dramatically. In the early afternoon he'd been summoned to the commissioner's office to be told of Cantor's departure and then given a dressing-down by Urquhart. Foyle played doggo, as the commissioner paced in front of him, and thought of June and their visit to Bristol the next day – a trip that filled him with much greater dread than Urquhart could inspire. Eventually he was dismissed, having assured the commissioner that the information about Cantor's obstruction would have reached the Home Secretary and Prime Minister by at least one other route that he knew of.

Later in the afternoon, Sergeant Pennel entered Foyle's office bearing a small wooden crate. 'You've got a fan, sir. Feels like a bottle to me.'

'Well, don't shake it, man. What drink improves with shaking?'

'A martini, sir. By the way, Con Lindow's on his way up.'

'Ask him to make his statement about the business in Maine before I see him. The FBI need to calm down the local police force.'

'What about Miss Menihan? Couldn't we wait and do them together?'

'No, she's not due until after seven. You get Dr Lindow's under way and then show him in here. It shouldn't take more than an hour. And, Pennel, don't tell either of them that the other is here. Is that understood?'

The sergeant nodded and left Foyle to open the crate. Inside lay a magnum of champagne, with a note that read, 'Here's to a new era of co-operation. Yours, with best wishes and thanks, K. L.'

Foyle smiled – chiefly because the bottle was chilled.

Three thousand miles away another law-enforcement officer, Special Agent Ralph Cartergue, scrambled to the bald, windswept summit of a nameless hill in Maine. The hike from the cabin, only a mile away as the crow flies, had taken him through half a dozen small bogs and numerous thickets of scrub on the leeward side of the hill. The trip wasn't necessary, but Cartergue welcomed the air and he wanted to see one of the telephone installations for himself. The other two had been located and dismantled earlier in the week.

At the top of the hill the cable he'd been following broke out of some thornbushes and ran across the rock to a small wooden construction about the size of a bedside cabinet. On the top was a solar panel, which he realised acted as the backup supply in case of power failure.

Beside it was fixed a four-foot plastic-coated antenna. He walked round, peering through cracks in the wood. The box was plainly designed to be mistaken for an automatic weather station of the type used to transmit data from inaccessible locations. Cartergue gave it a thorough check for booby traps, then broke open the side with a long hunting knife.

Inside, the phone was set in a cradle of polystyrene insulation. It was still switched on. Without disturbing the wires that sprouted from the back, he peered more closely at it. The phone's display indicated there had been several unanswered calls. Cartergue was familiar with the model, so he went through the steps to recover the numbers. Each time, the display showed INT'L, meaning that the calls were from abroad and the numbers were not registered by the phone set. However, it did tell him the date and time of each call. The first had been made at 7.01 a.m. on Wednesday 7 November and the others had followed on the hour, at 8.01 a.m. and 9.01 a.m. and so on throughout the morning.

Having noted down the times, he radioed to his colleagues at the cabin and asked them to retrieve the numbers from the phone company's computer. He took some pictures of the inside and outside of the box, then removed the wires from the back of the phone, cut the copper strip leading to the outside aerial and placed the phone in his pocket.

By the time he reached the cabin the phone company had responded to the FBI's request. The same London number had called Lasseur three times. Cartergue was intrigued. By Wednesday morning Lasseur had been dead for over three days while his partner had been killed some time during the night before. So who had made the calls from London? It might have been a misdial – perhaps a fax machine stubbornly redialling the wrong number. But, in that circumstance, the calls would have been made and logged in quick succession, not at hourly intervals. What else could explain the precise timing of the calls? It probably meant nothing, but he'd ask Mundy when they next spoke.

Lindow finished giving his statement to Pennel and was taken to Foyle's office where other members of Foyle's Sunday squad – Forbes, Kepple, Longmore and Hardwood – had assembled for the opening of the champagne.

Foyle popped the cork inexpertly, filled the odd collection of glasses that had been scavenged by Nancy Longmore and proposed a toast. 'We drink first to Con Lindow – the most valuable and co-operative suspect this department has ever had the good fortune to detain. Also to Graham Forbes, who, as you all know, has won promotion this week. This is to all of you.' He lifted his glass to his lips. 'Sterling work, ladies and gentlemen, sterling work.'

There was an embarrassed pause. Foyle shuffled his feet and took some more champagne, swilling it briefly in his cheeks. 'But we're not home and dry yet. Rhodes is still with us – I'm sure of it.'

The remark extinguished the tentative mood of celebration and soon the three junior officers made their excuses, leaving Lindow, Forbes and Foyle standing in an awkward frieze.

'You must be relieved to be back at work,' Foyle mumbled to Lindow.

'Yes, it's surprising how quickly you lose the habits of the mind.'

There was another pause. Foyle looked down at his desk, then glanced at Forbes with a cocked eyebrow.

Forbes took the hint. 'Well, I think I'll leave you to it. I need to remind myself what my wife looks like.'

When he had gone, Foyle helped them both to more champagne then crashed down on the sofa. Lindow took the chair opposite.

'So you didn't get the arrest you wanted,' began Lindow.

'You can say that again. I was naïve – bloody naïve. And now I'm left with this unnerving mystery. What the hell did Axiom Day mean to Rhodes? Am I missing something here, Con? I don't suppose you've come up with anything?'

'Nothing. I'm no good at word games. But surely there's only a limited number of targets he could pick to make his big gesture?'

'Yes, we've got it all covered – Parliament, the Cabinet, the main ministries, prestige buildings and the Royal Family. You name it and it's covered.'

They talked on. Lindow drank a good deal more than he meant to, which was why he didn't notice the acute watchfulness enter the policeman's expression. But Foyle was also busy masking his attention with a succession of expansive gestures.

Then he struck.

'So . . . are you going to tell me now, Con?'

'Tell you what?'

'Are you going to tell me what happened at the churchyard in Droy? I mean, what really happened.'

Lindow threw himself back in the chair and looked away. 'So that's what this is about,' he said indignantly.

'You don't have to tell me, of course. But I'd like to know because everything leads back to Droy. It set you all on different courses. Each of you, Rhodes, Lasseur, Eamonn and yourself. You all dispersed from that incident with your lives changed for ever. Then, years later, fate contrives to bring you together again. And now you are the only one who is still alive.'

Lindow revolved the glass in his hand and watched the centrifuge of bubbles. Without looking up, he began to speak.

'At first I didn't suspect anything, but Eamonn kept on stopping by that church. I knew there had to be a reason why he was taking the longer route home every time. Then a couple of things happened. I saw Eamonn sitting in a parked car with Rudi MacMahon. They'd hated each other at school but there they were in that car like the best of friends. I didn't understand it. A few days later I heard my mother and Eamonn talking. They didn't know I was in the house. She was going on about MacMahon and how Eamonn was helping him. She was saying that it was a fine and brave thing he was doing and that his forebears would be proud of him. Well, that meant only one thing – she'd got him working for the Provos. You see, he'd had years of that crap about his sacred duty and he just didn't have the will to resist her. So, if you're looking for culprits, one of them is Ma.

'Anyway, we went fishing one more time and we had a row. I asked him outright what he was doing at the church. I said I knew he was watching something for MacMahon. I said I thought the police would be interested to hear about it. He denied it all, but it was obvious he was lying. So I decided to find out for myself. I was worried for him, you see. I felt I had to protect him because only I knew the pressure he was under from our mother. I knew he'd got himself in too far and wouldn't be able to handle the Provos. At any rate, that's what I thought then. Little did I know . . .

'I had a small bike at the time, a Honda. The night after our argument I left home about two or three in the morning and set off for the church. I didn't know what I was going to do. If I found something in the churchyard, I thought I might tell the RUC by using the informer's line, or maybe just confront Eamonn with it. I didn't want to get him into trouble.'

Lindow paused. Foyle knew enough not to prompt him. He waited in silence, fascinated by Lindow's sudden lapse into a pure Northern Irish accent. Phipps had noticed the same thing in the interrogation.

'About three miles from the church I left the Honda

and went across the fields on foot. I'd put on some waterproof trousers. I was worried because they made a rustle when I walked. I got to the church and waited on the other side of the lane, watching. I thought someone might be there, but of course I didn't think of the Army.

'It was dead quiet. I s'pose I was a bit scared – being in a cemetery at night and all that. I was also kind of excited. You know how it is when you're that age. Anyway, I slipped over the road and crawled along the inside of the cemetery wall. There was a lot of dew on the ground so I was glad of the trousers. I got to the spot that Eamonn had shown so much interest in and turned on this little flashlight. It was like a pen – we used it to tie on fishing flies when it got too dark to see. I put it between my teeth and groped around a bit. I was very close to the ground, which is how I came to notice that some earth round the top of a vault had been disturbed. People had been working there, but you could only have seen it when you were right down on the ground, like I was.

'I knew that I'd found something. I should've left the cemetery then but I didn't. I wanted to know for sure. I felt around the top of the vault some more and realised that turf had been laid over some wooden planking. It was an old door. I pulled the turf aside and lifted the end of the door a few inches, jacking it up with a brick so I could feel under the wood. About halfway along, in the middle, I touched a piece of wire hanging from a metal eye, which had been screwed into the underside of the door. One end was fastened to something below in the vault. The other end ran through the eye and was tied round a big iron shackle.'

He paused and looked round Foyle's office, then his eyes returned to Foyle. 'If you lend me your tie, I'll show you how it worked.' Foyle undid his tie and handed it to Lindow, who then made a knot in one end.

'When the door was lifted the wire ran free until the shackle snagged in the eye.' He tugged the tie so that the knot jammed in a hole made by his thumb and forefinger. 'At that point, anyone lifting the door away from the entrance would be pulling directly on the other end of the wire down in the vault, which must have been fixed to detonator and charge. It was a cunning arrangement because the few feet of free wire meant you wouldn't feel any resistance until the door was clear of the opening. I suppose it could have been attached to a hand grenade, in which case there would have been a longer delay.

'I hadn't any idea that it was a booby trap. I unscrewed the eye and laid it with the wire and shackle out on the ground. The other end of the wire was still attached down in the vault. I lifted the door a few inches and pointed the torch into the vault. There was a lot of stuff down there. Most of it was covered, but I saw these gun muzzles poking out of some sacking. It looked as though mice had eaten away at the sacking. There was a strange smell down there too – like engine oil or something. I still remember it now.

'So I knew exactly what Eamonn'd been doing. I just lay there, shocked to pieces. I couldn't think what I was going to do. Then, suddenly, there was this damned noise over my head – very close. It was an owl swooping down into the churchyard. I panicked and just took to my heels back along the wall, leaving everything sticking out of the vault. I don't know how they set it off, but it must have acted as a trip-wire when they went to check it.'

'What happened next?' asked Foyle.

'I was about half a mile from home when the explosion came. They said people twenty miles away heard it. My problem was I had to get in the house, undress and pretend I'd been woken by the noise. It wasn't long before the police came and arrested us. Someone must have noted down Eamonn's car number when we stopped there. As they were taking us away one of the policemen put his hand on the engine of the bike. Before I had time to think of an excuse, Eamonn told them that he'd been out with a girlfriend. That was a joke. Eamonn didn't have girlfriends. Anyway, they rang her and it checked out. You see, he'd got a permanent alibi fixed up. There was an agreement that if the police called she'd say that he had been there for the night. He was in a lot deeper than I ever knew.'

'Did you know how the dump exploded?'

'No, they never told me and I only got to working it out in the cells. At first I couldn't believe they'd set off their own damned booby trap. They must have known someone'd been down there.'

'They did,' said Foyle. 'They were waiting to see what you were going to do. Then you vanished and four of them went to look and, as you say, one of them must have tripped or pulled on the wire. Did you ever tell Eamonn what happened? He must've suspected you'd been up to something when he told the lie about the bike.'

'He never so much as mentioned the bike. But I did tell him – a couple of years ago when Ma died. We had a long talk about things, my mother, what she stood for – the damned cause and all that. It came up then.'

'What did he say?'

'Not much, but he suspected I'd been fooling around in the churchyard. He said it was all in the past and it had been a lesson to him because he might have lost me in the explosion. He told me he never had anything else to do with MacMahon after that, which wasn't true. They must've kept in touch all those years. Now I find it hard to know what to think. I mean, when we talked after my mother's funeral, he told me he was glad that I'd got out of it – gone away. He was proud of me and all that. I believed him, and still do, even though he used my identity, what I had become in the States, to help the IRA.'

The phone rang. Foyle ignored it and poured more champagne. 'Why didn't you tell anyone else?'

'With my mother's background? You can't be serious! She took us on civil-rights marches from the year dot. We were a "republican" family, with a cousin that'd killed a policeman. There's no way anyone would've listened to my story and believed it. I would have been accused of rigging the arms cache myself and killing those soldiers. Then what? Twenty years in the Maze? That's why I didn't tell them the truth. That's why I didn't tell Phipps.'

'He got a pretty fair idea about it. He felt it still preyed on your mind. Does it?'

'Look, I know those men died because of me. But I didn't put the booby trap there. They did. They wanted to kill – not me. I wanted to help Eamonn, that's all.'

The two men were silent. Foyle felt secretly elated by Lindow's account. He'd already guessed most of the details, but he'd been determined to hear the whole truth from Lindow himself. If asked why he'd pressed him now, he would have put it down to curiosity, the thing that made him a good detective. Yet at a deeper level he knew he was driven by the more powerful need for vindication.

'So you think Rhodes was changed by what happened at the cemetery?' asked Lindow, fingering the bruise on his jaw.

'No. He was on his way to the person he became long before that. His brother was killed in front of him when he was a child – that must've had a vast effect. But a hell of a lot of it was in the blood. His old man was a loner and a real bastard, by all accounts. So you can't blame yourself for what Rhodes became. And the interesting thing is that I don't believe he had any notion of finding your brother and killing him when this whole thing started. He was an opportunist, and when he discovered Eamonn was working for the IRA in London he decided

434

to settle the old score. Then you arrived and he thought he'd have some fun setting you up.'

'But he couldn't have known I was here. Eamonn and I hadn't seen each other.'

'Yes, that puzzled me too. Then I realised he must've tapped your brother's phone. It's easy to attach a caller display unit to the line. He would've known exactly who was calling Eamonn without having to monitor the phone. After that, it was no trouble finding you. He bugged your phone. That's how he knew you were looking for a flat and why he left a message, pretending to be an estate agent.'

'What was the point?'

'I don't know if there was one, except he got you to make the call to the phone connected to the bomb. If something went wrong with the device on the bomb and it didn't explode, it would lead back to you. I suppose he also appreciated that the cellphone companies can recover the position of a mobile user on any single call. That might have given us an idea of his movements. So by getting you and me to make the calls, he put himself at one remove. Course, he could have dialled the bombs from a phone-box, but it wouldn't have been so much fun.'

'But why you? Why did he get you to make the call?'

'It wasn't just me. Remember, he left a similar message with Blackett. He must have laughed at the idea of both of us dialling that number. Why me? My name is in the papers the whole time and, as I said, the idea of having the head of the Anti-terrorist Unit detonate a bomb must have been irresistible. This prankster aspect is what worries me now. There are any number of scenarios that Rhodes might have dreamed up that work after his death, although I appreciate he didn't expect to die. For example, he could use the classified-advertisement section of a newspaper. All he'd need to do is place a suitably enticing advertisement with a phone number to appear days – maybe weeks – later and the timer would be set. Whatever happened to him, wherever he was, he'd know that on the day the paper was published some sucker would respond to the ad and dial the number that would detonate a bomb. That's why I don't think this is over. But where do I look? How do I find this thing? Apart from shutting down the cellphone networks for the next month, there's absolutely bugger all I can do. Rhodes didn't leave much behind him.'

Foyle heaved himself out of the sofa and went to the window, where he looked down at the traffic streaming along Victoria Street.

'It could be anywhere. We could be sitting on it, for all I know. Frankly, I haven't the first idea what I should be doing, and that really worries me.'

'Then why are you going away tomorrow? Pennel told me you were going down to the West Country. Couldn't you put the trip off for a few days?'

'I've got to go. My wife has left me, or is in the process of leaving me – I'm not sure which – and I've agreed to go and see Katherine with her to explain things. There's a point when you've got to put the job second and I've reached it. If I don't go, it will be a clear signal to June that I don't care – to say nothing of hurting Katherine's feelings. And I do care very much about both of them, Con. Of course, if we had something more to go on then I could persuade June to let it wait. But there's nothing. Not a damned thing.'

The phone rang again. Foyle picked it up. 'Yes . . . fine. That'll be okay.'

He hung up and looked at Lindow. 'I want to thank you for telling me about Droy. I know it was difficult and, in case you're interested, I don't hold you responsible for any of this. It's just that you bloody well should've told me before – I'd have believed you, you know.'

Lindow shrugged sceptically, put down his glass and rose to go.

'You can't leave yet,' said Foyle, his expression brightening. 'I've got a surprise for you.'

The door opened and Pennel came in, followed by Mary Menihan.

Con involuntarily started towards her, then something stopped him, a notion that he might be rebuffed.

'Leave me in Boston, would you, Con Lindow?' she said, coming into the room, her hand outstretched to meet Foyle's.

When they had introduced themselves, she turned back to Lindow. 'Sneaky old Con. Didn't tell me anything, did you?' Her eyes danced over his face mischievously.

'That makes two of us,' said Lindow humourlessly.

'Don't be so pompous, Con.' She laughed. 'I was only kidding.'

'We were just having a drink,' said Foyle, anxious to head off any kind of scene. 'Perhaps you'd like to join us?'

'Certainly. But then I've got a dinner engagement – I take it you're free, Con?'

Lindow found himself smiling. She looked wonderful – hair glistening like a crow's wing, eyes liquid and warm. Lindow knew he'd never desire anyone more completely. Mary Menihan was it: the thing he'd never dared to look for.

'Good,' she said, reading his slightly dazed expression as acceptance. 'There's a great Lebanese restaurant near my place. We'll go there and confess to each other. Is that okay with you, Doctor?'

Lindow nodded. 'More than okay.'

They got up to leave Foyle's office half an hour later, during which time Lindow came to realise he was seeing the real Mary for the first time. She began by asking Foyle about the steps that had directed the police to Pope's Farm House. Her questions tumbled out in quick, logical succession, until she pinned Foyle down on the way the match had been achieved between the information on the disks and calls from a number in Croydon. No one else had thought to ask him exactly how he had got the telephone number that led to Pope's Farm House, but within a few minutes Mary had prised the information from him. Lindow saw that the commander was taken aback and, having himself just surrendered to Foyle's interrogation skills, enjoyed the spectacle of the big policeman struggling to return Mary's baseline volleys.

As they left, Mary shook the policeman's hand with a kind of coquettish modesty. Lindow thought she looked very slight beside him. Then Foyle remembered something, and removed a brown envelope from his desk. 'This is yours.'

'What's that?'

'The statement you made for a friend of ours.'

'I shan't be needing it any longer. I've left all that. Listen, why don't you just destroy it?'

Outside New Scotland Yard, Mary said she'd prefer to walk so they made their way across Parliament Square towards Victoria Tower Gardens. They bent their heads to the wind as they went, grabbing at each other as they slipped on the pavement of wet leaves. In the gardens a bonfire smouldered, which filled the air with a smell of burned humus. At the point near Lambeth Bridge where the gardens tapered, they stopped and looked down at the river.

'You know that piece by Auden?' Mary asked. Without waiting for a reply, she began to recite:

> And down by the brimming river
> I heard a lover sing
> Under an arch of the railway:
> 'Love has no ending.
> I'll love you, dear, I'll love you
> Till China and Africa meet,

438

And the river jumps over the mountain
And the salmon sing in the street—

She broke off. 'I don't remember the rest, except there's something about loving your neighbour's crooked heart.' She squeezed his arm with both her hands and darted a girlish kiss to his cheek. 'Will you love my crooked heart, Con?'

'Yes, if you stop quoting goddam English poetry at me.' He looked down again and shuddered at the thought of the river's waters.

They walked on past Millbank and the Tate Gallery, then cut up into Pimlico to find Mary's restaurant, a discreet place with booths separated by panels of intricate latticework. Mary told him all about what she'd done for the security service, running messages between Ireland and England, and how, when sitting on the floor in Lasseur's cabin, she had sworn she'd leave the business, if she got out alive. 'I lost my nerve a while back,' she said, her eyes swivelling from Lindow across the room to a party of thickset Arabs, wearing big rings and horizontally striped ties. 'At first I kind of got a kick out of playing dumb yet knowing all the moves. Then I got sick of having to watch myself, having to watch everything I said – the long, long lie that became a kind of parallel life.' She sighed. 'One time in Dublin, about three or four years ago, I was taken for a drink by a republican named Jerry Crane – only it wasn't a drink. Before I knew it, this guy had driven me out of the city to some kind of trailer-park. It was like a vacation place by the sea. There were three other men there. Do you know what the IRA call them? A nut squad. That's because they nut people – kill them. They interrogated me all goddam night. It was like a security vetting. There was one man who said nothing. He sat a little way away from the others, playing with this pointed piece of wood. He kept on working at it with a knife then holding it up to the light. I got a pretty good

439

idea what he'd do with that wood if I started to forget my story. He was the one they'd let loose on me if my story cracked. And these people aren't stupid. They're really smart and cunning and I knew they'd get to me soon enough. So I feigned outrage and told them I'd inform the people at the American Embassy about their treatment of me. They weren't sure enough of their ground to go the whole way and start hurting me because then they'd have to finish the job. And they couldn't do that because I'd made sure that people knew I was with Jerry Crane. So I ranted on about my friendship with the ambassador. They knew it might be true, because their people had seen me at an embassy reception in Dublin. So finally they apologised and let me go. That arsehole Jerry drove me back to the city, giving me a whole lot of bull about security. You want to know something? I threw up for a straight two days after that night.'

'So they didn't have anything to go on – no evidence against you?'

'Nothing. I was involved with them and they thought they'd better check me out. But that wasn't the only thing. There's a certain type of man that gets a thrill out of a woman's terror.'

She looked at him and a shudder rose through her shoulders. He touched her chin and held it until the warmth returned to her eyes.

'It's okay.' She kissed the palm of his hand. 'God, I want you. You see, I'm not a heroine. I spent a lot of the last ten years scared shitless.'

'You were pretty cool at the cabin and before that at the lake. Or was that a set-up? Did you plan it all with them?'

'Christ, no. I had an idea that something would happen. They were just so damned desperate about the bombs. I didn't plan it and I didn't know they were going to use your sister. What could I do? I couldn't blow my own cover. I had to wait to see what they wanted you to

440

do. Then I was locked into the crazy attempt to find Rhodes.'

She put down her napkin, slipped round the table and placed her hand on Lindow's thigh. She kissed his neck and squirmed beside him.

'We have to go now – I need you,' she said.

'Before that I want to know one thing. Did you know that Eamonn had been to Maine? Was that why MI5 put so much effort into having Eamonn watched by you?'

'No, it wasn't like that. I had no idea where he had been. You see, we didn't know much. We knew Eamonn was important and even after the peace accord was signed we got the feeling he was still very active. Craven-Elms told me to search his place and for this I needed to get closer to him and find out where he would hide things.'

'Would you have slept with him?'

She looked at him and he saw something happen behind her eyes. 'Yes.'

'Jesus!' He threw down his napkin.

'Oh, Con, it's over now. I've quit. And you're all I want. I implore you to believe me.'

He said nothing but signalled for the bill. 'It's okay,' he said, as he gave the waiter his credit card. 'I guessed as much. All I can say is that he would have been lucky to have you.'

Mary led him the few hundred yards back to her flat, a sparsely decorated place on two floors, much of which was given over to neatly stacked piles of manuscripts. They rushed to her bed, as though running out of the rain, and there Lindow began to make love to her. This time she submitted, smiling as he ran his lips over her body, leaving a snail-trail of dampness that made her shiver and giggle. Then they joined together and moved slowly, noiselessly, in the half-lit room. When it was over she held his head with greedy hands and kissed him hotly.

Lindow rolled on to his back and looked up through the skylight at the clouds tearing over the city catching the orange light from below. 'Do you feel like sleeping yet?'

'Yes,' she said softly. 'We've got all tomorrow and then the day after that and the day after that and the day after that. It's endless.'

He pulled the covers up around them.

'Let's get a dog,' she said. 'We need a dog in our life.'

And they slept.

Later, Lindow returned to the churchyard at Droy. He was crawling between the gravestones on his belly, slithering like an eel across the damp, damp dew. Someone was with him, but he didn't know who. He reached the opening of the vault and peered down into the chamber. Eamonn was stretched out on the sacking, Mary curled up beside him, her hands tucked under her cheek. Both were quite, quite asleep and, however much he shouted, they couldn't be woken. Then Foyle came and dragged Lindow away through the damp, damp grass. An owl swooped down upon them.

Foyle left London with his wife at one thirty p.m., having satisfied himself that the Lord Mayor's Parade had passed off without incident. The journey was spent discussing exactly what they would tell Katherine, who had already sensed that something was wrong when June called her the day before. Foyle watched his wife from the corner of his eye as he drove past Heathrow and out into Berkshire. There was a lightness in her manner, a kind of youthful flippancy he found difficult to deal with. He could remember seeing her like this only once before – when they'd just been married. It was obvious that she was in love with the Arab bone-hunter, as he thought of Dr Hussan, and that his marriage was over. He said this gently, arguing that they should be completely straight with Katherine. If there was no chance of them staying

442

together, they shouldn't offer hope. Now it was June who refused to accept the inevitable, and during the two-and-a-half-hour journey she repeated over and over that all she needed was time to work things out. Eventually Foyle retreated into himself, occasionally murmuring a response, but for the most part he thought about the Rhodes investigation and wondered what he'd missed. What did Axiom Day mean?

Lindow and Mary rose late and drifted out to breakfast at a coffee-house in Sloane Square. Mary clung to his arm as they walked, teasing him that he had an almost English fear of showing affection in public. He denied it furiously, then wrapped his right arm around her shoulder and looked ahead of them self-consciously.

In the coffee shop she held up a huge cup of *caffe latte* and looked over it with a glint in her eye. 'Our problem is that we don't have a history, you and I. We don't know anyone in common, we don't have anything in common. I mean you're a scientist and I'm a book editor.'

'And a spy.'

'I'm a book editor and former spy,' she corrected. 'Look, the point is that we've never done anything together, never been to a movie or a play or a gallery together. We've never bought anything together, never looked around old shops together, never fought over a newspaper, argued about politics, read the same book. I mean, we're like strangers. So what I want to know, Constantine Lindow, is how are we expected to stay married?'

Most of her face remained obscured by the cup, but he saw her eyebrows arch with expectation and a serious look enter her eyes.

'Are you joking, or what? I never know with you. I mean, this is serious stuff, Mary. I mean serious.'

'Answer my question,' she demanded. 'How're we meant to stay married?'

'Before we decided to get married,' he said, now smiling broadly, 'we would have to put ourselves through a kind of rapid induction, just to make sure we had something in common. I suppose we'd try to do it all very quickly – go to a lot of movies, plays, galleries, antique shops, football matches.'

'No sports,' she said. 'I don't watch sports.'

'Okay, no sports. But we'd do all these things in rapid succession and see if we were compatible.'

'So, what are we waiting for? It's just two weeks and one day since we met. But I want you. I want to become the dull wife of a dull scientist and get a dull little dog. That's what I want, Con. It's all I want.'

'So this *is* a proposal?'

She sipped again, then glanced away shyly. 'Kind of.'

Con put his hand out and turned her face to his. 'Is it okay if I give you my answer at the end of the day, when we've been through our cultural initiation? But there's one condition – you have to stop quoting poetry at me.'

'That's a big sacrifice. I'll work on it.'

They left the coffee-house and went shopping, an occupation that Lindow heartily loathed. She bought a short black overcoat and insisted that he buy two dark shirts in the same store. He went along with the suggestion, anxious to show they had some of the same taste, though he disliked them. Then they wandered through London, diving into bookshops, trailing through antique markets and talking.

Eventually, in the late afternoon, they reached Imperial College, where he showed her a mass spectrometer and then a gallery containing some false-colour images of resistant bacteria strains. He told her how the genes of a certain strain of a bacterium called *Staphylococcus aureus* produced a protein that shielded it against antibiotics.

'Will it wipe us all out?' she asked.

'Not yet. But it's poised and, with a few modifications in its genetic code, it might.'

Night had fallen by the time they left the college and took a cab to the Gate cinema in Notting Hill, a favourite place of Mary's because she said the people hanging around outside always reminded her of movie lines in the States. They watched an obscure art-house film, which bored both of them, but neither said anything. Then they ate at an Indian restaurant and snapped poppadoms together. Towards the end of the evening she suggested that they stay at Lindow's flat because she'd never been there. 'You may live like a pig and I couldn't endure that.'

In less than twenty minutes Lindow unlocked the door to his flat in Homer Road.

'Hey, look,' said Mary. 'You've got a message. Your machine is flashing.'

'No tape,' said Lindow. 'Foyle took the message cassette and I haven't replaced it. It means that people hear the greeting tape but don't know that they're not being recorded.'

'Yes, but you can dial the recall service and find out who called you.'

Lindow dialled the four-digit number, feeling that Mary was being a little bossy. 'No number.' He put down the phone and took her in his arms.

'I guess it's safe,' she said slyly. 'No one's watching.'

'Does the state of my establishment meet with my lady's exacting standards?'

'Yep, just about.'

'Good. Would she like to hear my answer to the question she put to me this morning?'

'Yep.'

'It's yes. I guess we could make it together, even with a dull little dog.'

They fell into Lindow's ill-sprung double bed and made love easily, as if they'd known each other for years.

Mary went to asleep in Lindow's arms, her breasts against his chest. He could feel the beat of her heart and remembered what *acushla* meant literally in Gaelic – pulse.

A clock chimed in the distance and 10 November became 11 November. Remembrance Day.

A little after eight a.m. Lindow received a telephone call. He woke as the bell ceased to sound and a voice spoke into the ansaphone.

'Con, are you there? This is important. Answer your goddam phone, for God's sake. I know what Axiom means. Pick up for God's sake. Damn you, Con.'

He recognised Varrone's voice, sprang from the bed and ran to the sitting room. He dived for the phone but Varrone had gone.

It must be important if he was calling from Boston in the middle of the night. He dialled Varrone's number and got the answer-machine. 'I'm away for a couple of days. Leave a message and I'll get back to you.'

He must be at the beach-house, thought Con. He looked up Varrone's weekend number in his address book, dialled and got another ansaphone. This time Varrone's voice told the caller to leave a message or try his Boston number. Lindow left a message saying that he was in London and waiting for Varrone to call.

Twenty minutes later the phone rang again. Lindow got there in time.

'Peter! Is that you?'

'Where've you been?' Varrone sounded irritated. 'I left three messages for you. Don't you return calls any more?'

'The ansaphone isn't working. No message-tape. Hey, it's late for you,' said Lindow, looking at his watch. It was three thirty a.m. in Boston.

'I'm in Seattle for the quantum computing conference. It's only half past midnight here. I came out here with Frank. Look, this is important. I believe I've figured out what Axiom Day means. It's a kind of acronym, which is why we couldn't crack it with normal decryption programs. You said this guy Rhodes was half Italian, right? He had an Italian mother, right? So this is the way I think it works. The A means 'At' in Italian, the X and the I stand for eleven in Roman numerals, the O stands for *ora*, which means hour in Italian, and the M stands for *mese*, which means month in Italian.'

'So?' said Lindow.

'You don't see it, do you? With the word "day" it precisely describes today's date. As near as damn it, it means "at the eleventh hour of the eleventh day of the eleventh month" – the day the Armistice was signed in 1918, Veterans' Day in the States and Remembrance Day over there.'

Lindow scribbled Axiom Day on the pad by the phone, spacing the letters out. Then he saw how it worked. 'I'll call Foyle,' he said.

'I already tried that earlier. He isn't at his home number.'

'Yes, I remember him saying he was going away,' said Lindow.

'I also spoke to New Scotland Yard a couple of hours back. I tried to explain it to a duty officer but he thought I was a lunatic. He didn't understand what the hell I was talking about.'

'Okay, I'll call them now. We'll talk later.'

Lindow hung up without saying goodbye, then cursed that he hadn't taken Varrone's number in Seattle.

He dialled New Scotland Yard and was put through to the duty officer at the Anti-terrorist Unit. A laconic, know-it-all voice came on the line. Yes, said the police officer, someone had spoken to Dr Varrone and he'd left a note for the commander that explained Dr Varrone's observations. The commander was due in, but he couldn't say when and he didn't know Foyle's mobile number.

Lindow saw he was getting nowhere and left a message for Foyle to call him urgently. Then he tried Foyle's home number and let the phone ring for a couple of minutes. Foyle must be in Bristol still.

Just as he got back into bed the phone rang again. He hopped into the living room and snatched up the receiver.

'Commander?' he said.

'No, it's me again,' said Varrone. 'What's with you? You hung up before I finished. Look, Mundy's just got in from dinner. He's got some information from a man up at the cabin. It may be nothing but they have faxed it to New Scotland Yard. He says a London number has been dialling one of Lasseur's phones in Maine. The number called several times on Wednesday morning, each time at a minute past the hour, one call an hour. The crucial point is that by Wednesday your friend Rhodes was dead. Mundy's man traced it through the phone company to London.'

'Could be a misdial.'

'Sure, that's what Mundy thinks. Here's the number. It's 0171 701 7972. You should have someone check it out.'

Lindow wrote it down on the notepad beside the words 'Axiom Day'. He thanked Varrone, then dialled New Scotland Yard. The officer still had no idea where the commander was and assured Lindow, in a heavily condescending manner, that he would pass on his message.

It was twenty to one on the west coast of the United States and eight forty a.m. in London. Lindow returned to bed, clutching the piece of paper he'd written on, and slipped in beside Mary's warm, curled-up body. She stirred and drew his arm around her.

'You're cold,' she said.

'Sorry.'

He kissed her on the nape of her neck. He would wait half an hour, then try Foyle again at New Scotland Yard.

*

448

Foyle had intended to leave Bristol the previous evening, but the way things turned out it had not been possible. Katherine had taken the news of the impending separation badly and set about trying to reconcile them over dinner, pointing out that neither could live with anyone else. Foyle had waited for June to say something about her new interest, as she referred to her lover, but she hadn't. This he had dared to read as a good sign. He decided to leave it as late as possible before driving back, but by the end of dinner he knew he'd drunk too much and he checked into a small hotel near Katherine's flat. June stayed with Katherine.

Now he was making good time and was able to stop for a much-needed cup of coffee at a service area. He reached London by nine twenty a.m. but then got caught on Chelsea Embankment behind a convoy of coaches, carrying British Legion veterans to Whitehall. Eventually he lost patience and pulled out of the line of coaches, waving his warrant card through the window at the traffic police.

It was nine forty-five by the time he arrived at New Scotland Yard and parked his car in a side-street. As he stepped out he looked up. The sky was sombre and a steady wind tugged the still-green leaves of the plane trees. To the east he could see two police helicopters hovering over Horse Guards Parade, where thousands of veterans, wearing their campaign medals, bowler hats and old service berets, would now be assembling. Foyle thought of his own father, a paratrooper and Arnhem veteran who, in the last weeks of his life, suddenly attended the parade, having resolutely refused to think or talk about the war for thirty years. Foyle had been one of the uniformed officers lining the route and had caught sight of him marching along, chin thrust out and eyes watering with pride. He saw him only once more. Two weeks later he was dead of a heart attack.

He hesitated for a moment to catch the sound of the

bagpipers and buglers practising a few hundred yards away in the Wellington Barracks. Then he hurried across the street to the main entrance and took the lift up to his department. It didn't matter that he'd missed the briefing as he had no direct responsibility for the security operation and, anyway, he was familiar with the arrangements – the numbers of officers from the Tactical Firearms Unit on the rooftops overlooking Whitehall, the increased force of plain-clothes officers mingling with the crowds, and the position of Bomb Squad Range Rovers. Lafferty had put most of his explosives officers into the Westminster area, and, on the way, Foyle had seen some probing man-hole covers and unscrewing the service plates of the traffic signals and street-lights along the southern end of Victoria Street. Below ground other officers would be wading through sewage ducts, checking every recess for unusual devices.

SO 13 was practically deserted, most of its officers having been drafted into the security operation. Foyle found Pennel in the corridor outside his office, clutching a folder containing overnight messages, one or two faxes, the latest copy of the security briefing and some outstanding reports from officers involved in the Rhodes investigation. Pennel said that Chief Inspector Forbes had intended to look through it, but he had been called into the operations room. Foyle said that was fine. He would join Forbes there and go through it himself while waiting for the parade to get under way.

He went into his office to dial Katherine's number in Bristol and asked how things were going. She was guarded. Foyle could hear June in the background talking to one of Katherine's flatmates. He made a point of sending his love to her and said he would call Katherine later.

It was nine fifty-nine a.m.

*

Lindow had entered another deep sleep and it was not until twenty minutes past nine that he was woken by Mary.

'Shit. What's the time?' he said, reaching for his watch.

'Was someone calling earlier?' she asked.

'Look, it's late. I've got to try Foyle.'

'Who called?' she persisted.

'Peter Varrone – you know, my friend from Boston. He's got a theory about the meaning of Axiom Day. He thinks it's code for today's date.'

'Yes?' she said, interested. 'How did he figure that?'

'It's not exact,' he said, 'but it's convincing.' He swung his legs from the bed and pulled his arm out from under her to hold the piece of notepaper in front of her. 'Here, see how it works.'

'That's neat,' she said. 'It's like a crossword answer.' She propped herself up and scrutinised the paper again, pulling her head back to focus on it. 'Con, why have you got Eamonn's number written down here?'

'It's not Eamonn's number. Varrone just gave it to me. The FBI retrieved it from one of the phone sets at the lake. Apparently that number rang one of Lasseur's phones several times on Wednesday morning.'

Mary shot upright and took the paper from Con's hand. 'No, you don't understand, Con. This *is* Eamonn's number. I know it by heart. Don't you know your own brother's number?'

'No. I only called him there a couple of times. Are you sure?'

'Tell me exactly what Varrone told you.'

'He told me that when one of the phone installations had been checked in Maine it was found that a number had been calling Lasseur. He said the number had rung several times on Wednesday morning, a minute past the hour each time. They traced the number and it turned out to be this one. I'll check it in my book.'

'He said Wednesday, right?'

'Yes, by which time Rhodes was dead.' He went into the sitting room and returned with the book. 'Jesus, you're right.'

'What's it mean, Con?'

'I don't know but I think the fact that those calls were made on Wednesday is really significant.'

'Why?'

'Because Rhodes had a schedule. By Wednesday morning – that's to say Wednesday morning East Coast time – he would have been in the Far East. Perhaps he programmed the computer to send a coded message to Lasseur's computer, once he was safely out of the way.'

'He'd already done that. We saw what happened to Lasseur.'

'Yes, but perhaps these were fail-safe calls, programmed into a computer well before we went to Maine.' He paused and momentarily absorbed the beauty of her body on the bed. 'Look, we'd better get dressed. I'll find us some coffee.'

By the time Lindow returned with two cups of Nescafé she had pulled on her jeans and sweater and was drying her face. As he searched around for his own clothes, his mind tore at the problem.

'The fail-safe must have been the original plan for killing Lasseur and destroying everything that was important in the cabin. Then he decided Lasseur was becoming a liability. You remember how strung out he was? Rhodes must have sensed that and decided to get rid of him right then. Once he thought we'd been killed, he had no further use for him and sent the message that detonated the explosives in Lasseur's computer.'

'But that doesn't make sense,' she protested. 'Why would he program the computer to make those calls when he knew Lasseur was already dead?'

'I don't know, but I think we should go over there and take a look. I've got to use the bathroom. You try Foyle and tell him we're going over there.'

She dashed into the sitting room. As Lindow urinated, he heard her shouting at someone at New Scotland Yard.

'Well, find him now! Tell him we'll be at fifty-six Jasmine Road, Peckham. That's fifty-six! Yes! Say we're going there now. It's important. Say we'll call him on the way. Our names? I told you, for Chrissake – Mary Menihan, Con Lindow.'

She slammed down the receiver and came back into the bedroom.

'They're not even sure he's in the building. They're going to get a message to him. Christ knows how long that'll take.'

Lindow snatched up his jacket, felt for his wallet and took Eamonn's keys from a bowl near the telephone.

As they left the flat he glanced at his watch. It was nine fifty-five a.m. Another ten minutes passed before they found a cab.

Chapter Twenty

Foyle stood in the operations room with a folder under his arm, sipping at a Styrofoam beaker and skim-reading an account of the death of Ian Rhodes in one of the Sunday papers. Towards the end of the two-page spread there were vague references to David Cantor's expected retirement, which were phrased in such a way as to imply that the director general was being blamed for the failure to capture Rhodes. A sidebar devoted to Rhodes's mental state was particularly well sourced and included information from the psychological profiles, drawn up for Foyle at the beginning of the week. This and the material on Rhodes's childhood could only have come from the police or the Home Office – probably the latter since the Home Secretary emerged from the main article with a greatly enhanced reputation for decisiveness.

Foyle sat down and concentrated on the magnified image of Rhodes. The eyes gave nothing away, but prompted a dull anxiety to move in his stomach. There was no sense in obsessing about Rhodes, he thought. He was an unreadable blank, an aberration. He glanced from the paper to the banks of television monitors. Each screen showed evidence of the huge police presence. He watched a feed from a helicopter, positioned high above the Cenotaph, then another from a military camera, which showed the final inspections of the bands in front of the Guards. A third camera was trained along the first storey of the Foreign and Commonwealth Office where the blue drapery of the royal balconies was trembling in the wind.

From street level to rooftops, scores of cameras panned, zoomed and observed as Whitehall readied itself to honour the Glorious Dead, the 1,694,999 men and women from Britain and the colonies who lost their lives in two world wars. Foyle reasoned with himself that the operation being played out on the screens in front of him was impressive, a perfectly timed piece of choreography that allowed for more or less every conceivable eventuality. Even some of the phone networks had been shut down for the morning, although it was impossible to screen off an area in the heart of London where scores of small repeaters enabled signals to penetrate every nook and cranny of the street layout.

He drained the beaker, feeling the jip of the caffeine, and looked again at a monitor showing the faces of the people moving through one of the checks in the south. They smiled with good-natured deference as police officers frisked them and handed out service sheets. Soon the pavements, which stretched the two hundred yards from Parliament Square to the Cenotaph, would swell and the thoroughfare itself would fill with ranks of servicemen, military bands and clerics, making an odd, curiously human pageant of British life. Before the hour was up, the Prime Minister, members of the Cabinet, the leaders of the main political parties, three or four ex-prime ministers, the chiefs of the General Staff and up to fifty-three high commissioners would file from the Foreign Office and form up around Sir Edwin Lutyens's austere Portland stone monument. Finally the parade would be called to attention and the Queen and three princes, encumbered like turn-of-the-century generals with great-coats and ceremonial swords, would move stiffly to their position north of the Cenotaph. The service would begin, a moment of national homage to the fallen, in which the entire establishment stood clustered within a few square yards, more vulnerable than at any other time of the year.

Foyle folded the image of Rhodes into four and placed the newspaper deliberately on the floor against the leg of his chair.

'Everything seems to be going pretty well, like clockwork.' It was Forbes who had come up behind him.

'Yes, for the moment it is. But I'll be happier when this damn parade is over.' Foyle thought of Remembrance Sunday in Enniskillen when the IRA had killed eleven people.

Forbes drifted back to the desk where he'd been sitting.

Left alone, Foyle opened the folder of messages and read through the security schedule for the morning. For a few minutes he concentrated on a diagram giving the exact position of each VIP during the service. Overleaf was a chart showing the protection arrangements before and after the ceremony. He moved on through the folder and paused at a report from Sevenoaks Police, which had been faxed over that morning by an officer named Andrew Gresham who was leading the investigation into the murder of one James Hallwell. Foyle assumed that there had been some sort of error but on the first page of the report was a yellow sticker, indicating that Gresham had called that morning to make sure that the report would reach him. He read the first sheet, which described the unremarkable slaying of a small-time drugs dealer, then he flipped through the remaining two sheets. On the third Gresham had circled a passage concerning a grey Vauxhall van and written, 'Could this be your man's vehicle?'

A grey Vauxhall van had been seen in Hallwell's workshop the previous week. Sevenoaks Police had no record of the registration number of the van but they were anxious to trace the owner. Foyle went back to the beginning of the report and began to read carefully.

James Hallwell had been murdered the previous week-end. At first an overdose had been suspected. The body was found slumped on an old car seat in the workshop and a syringe, containing a mixture of heroin and cocaine, was lying by his right hand. Gresham noticed that this didn't tally with the nicotine stains on the victim's left index finger. He confirmed that Hallwell was left-handed and, after finding no other needle marks on the body, concluded that Hallwell had not administered the dose himself. A search of the premises gave no clue as to why he had been murdered, but it did turn up some vinyl strips from which letters had been individually peeled and, according to a neighbour living opposite the workshop, applied to either side of the van. There were eight strips, which had been output from different machines – an indication, perhaps, that the owner of the van had something to hide. Using the remains of the vinyl strips Gresham worked out that the van bore the words 'Jefferton Brothers 24-hour CCTV Repair and Service'. There was no trace of any such firm in the area.

Foyle sat back in his chair, furiously trying to make the connections that he knew were waiting for him. Then he realised there was more to it than just the van. According to Gresham's report, at the time of his death Hallwell was working on a special job, which he had not wanted to discuss with friends or his neighbour opposite. All anyone knew was that it involved the production of aluminium boxes. Filings and shavings consistent with this were found on the floor of the workshop and almost certainly indicated that he had just finished the work at the time of his death. There was no sign of these boxes, but by measuring the gaps in two vices, Gresham had estimated that the boxes were between eight and ten inches wide.

Foyle's mind was on the point of crystallising a conclusion when an ashen-faced Sergeant Pennel burst into the operations room.

'This is important, sir. There was a message last night – several, in fact – from Peter Varrone. The overnight man wrote it down for you on the system, but didn't print it out at the end of his shift. Varrone's cracked Axiom Day. He thinks it means November the eleventh. It's code for "at the eleventh hour of the eleventh day of the eleventh month".'

'For God's sake, slow down, Sergeant,' snapped Foyle. 'Tell me what Varrone said – exactly.'

The operations room had fallen silent and some of the officers had swivelled their chairs. Pennel explained how the word Axiom could be read as an acronym. Added to the word Day, it was a clear indication that Rhodes had been planning something for Remembrance Day. He went on to say Miss Menihan had phoned. 'Her message wasn't clear but the officer who spoke to her said she was desperate to get in touch with you. She and Lindow are on their way to Eamonn Lindow's address in Peckham.'

Foyle was silent for a moment. His eyes went to a large clock on the wall. It was ten twenty-seven a.m. The second hand was moving with incredible speed around the clock face.

'Get me Kirsty Laing on the phone now,' he shouted to Forbes. 'And the minute Menihan or Lindow phone, put them through to me. Get some officers to Eamonn Lindow's address in Peckham. Find out what the hell's happening. I want Lafferty up here.'

The superintendent in charge of the operations room came over. 'What's going on?'

'Wait there, and I'll tell you what to do.'

Foyle had guessed right. Kirsty Laing was in her office. 'Tell me where that first photograph of Rhodes was taken,' he demanded. 'You know, the one you gave me. Where was it taken?'

She hesitated. 'In Whitehall, I think.'

'You've got Weegee operating there the whole time?'

'Yes, why?'

'Find out if there were any more sightings. Get your people to work out exactly where he was in the first photograph. There's very little time.' He gave her his extension number and hung up.

'We've got a problem,' he said to the superintendent. 'There may be a device in Whitehall.'

'There can't be,' the officer protested. 'Every square inch of the street and buildings has been searched. And not just once, several times.'

'Believe me – I'm serious. We've got to evacuate Whitehall immediately. There could be more than one bomb.'

'What evidence have you got? I can't abort the whole damned thing without some convincing evidence that there's a device down there.'

Foyle had no time to reply. He was suddenly aware that the commissioner and Martin Scarratt had entered the operations room. One of the officers on the main operations desk must have alerted them.

'What's happening here?' asked Urquhart.

'The commander says there may be a device in Whitehall, sir.'

'What reason do you have for believing that, Commander?'

Foyle was silenced. What reason did he have? Apart from Varrone's solution to the phrase Axiom Day and some circumstantial evidence concerning the activities of a small-time crook in Sevenoaks, there wasn't much to go on – nothing firm, nothing that was going to convince the commissioner. He hastily explained the inquiry into the murder of James Hallwell, pointing to the ringed passages in Gresham's report. Then he moved to MI5's surveillance photographs, saying there was evidence that Rhodes had been in Whitehall on 23 October.

Urquhart looked at him despairingly.

'Yes, but where are these bombs?' he said. 'Who's

going to set them off? I mean, we've got to have more than this, Foyle.'

Lindow and Mary's cab was stuck behind a line of vehicles, waiting at some emergency gas repairs, near Clapham Common. They looked ahead of them nervously.

'Jesus,' he said, clapping his forehead. 'I know what it all means.'

'What?' asked Mary.

'Those calls came from a computer in Eamonn's flat. Rhodes must have set it up there. He must have programmed it to call Lasseur's number and send the message to explode his computer and kill him.'

'We've been over this,' said Mary. 'It doesn't make sense to program a computer after he knew that Lasseur was already dead.'

'No – that's the point. He'd already set it up in Eamonn's place. He probably did it some time before last weekend. But he kept all the same software – and the same code – on a lap-top he carried around with him. We know he had more than one base, why not more than one computer? Do you see? It means that he probably sent the coded message to kill Lasseur from his lap-top, although the other computer at Eamonn's had already been primed to do the same on Wednesday morning.'

'So what're you saying?'

'What I'm saying is there's a computer hooked up in Eamonn's flat that was programmed to send the message on Wednesday after Rhodes had left the country. It kept on calling the number that morning – right? If it was capable of sending a stream of calls to a telephone in the US on Wednesday, it's capable of performing the same task in London today. Mary, it's still sitting there and it's operational.'

'God, I hope you're not right.' She looked out at the

traffic in front of them, swore and slipped from the back seat to perch on one of the fold-downs behind the driver.

'Can you get us out of this jam?' she said to the driver, proffering a twenty-pound note through the partition window. 'It could be a matter of life and death.'

'Certainly, madam.' He took the money.

They swung round out of the line of traffic, went back up the road they'd been waiting in and dived into some side-streets, which took them through Brixton. Mary looked down through the partition. 'Hey, is that cell-phone working? Can I borrow it for another twenty?' She snapped her fingers at Lindow for the money.

'For another twenty I'll tap-dance on the roof,' said the driver. 'How long do you need it for?'

'About an hour. Can I make a call now?'

The driver passed the phone over his shoulder. As the cab stopped to join the flow of traffic going up Denmark Hill, Mary dialled New Scotland Yard and handed it to Lindow.

'It's Lindow, sir,' said Pennel. 'He's on a mobile.'

Foyle took the phone. 'Con, where are you?'

'I'm with Mary. We're five minutes from Eamonn's flat – maybe less. I believe there's a computer there which is primed to send out signals. Did you talk to Varrone?'

'No, but I got a message. I know about Axiom. What did you say about a computer?' Foyle heard the engine of the cab revving. Lindow's voice rose over the noise.

'One of Lasseur's phones recorded several calls received from Eamonn's number the day after Rhodes was killed. The FBI traced the calls. Mundy faxed you last night. You should have had the information by now. The point is that the computer was most likely pro-grammed to make the call to Lasseur after Rhodes had left England. Do you see? He set up a system to dial Lasseur's number about midday our time, in advance. That was when he originally planned to kill him. Then

461

we arrived and he decided to do it immediately, but the other computer was still set to send out the signal. If it can do that on Wednesday, it can do it today at eleven o'clock.'

'Now listen to me very carefully,' said Foyle. 'I don't want you blundering into the flat. I'm sending officers and I'll be in direct contact with them. The Explosives Unit are on their way too. Now, I'm going to put you on a speaker. I want you to keep this line open and tell me where you are at every stage. You are not to go in. If you're right about this computer, the place is likely to be booby-trapped. Do you understand, Con? You're breaking up, Con? Con? Can you hear me?'

The line went dead. Foyle brought his fist down on the desk. Then Forbes shouted that Kirsty Laing was on the line. Foyle reached over to another phone, picked up the receiver and pressed the button next to the flashing light.

'Yes.'

'He was at the northern end of the street, about fifty yards south of the Whitehall Theatre,' she said, without preliminaries. 'And there was an unconfirmed sighting this week – on Monday. The picture wasn't good and there'd been several false alarms.'

'Where was he then?'

'In Whitehall again, lower down, near Parliament Square. We weren't sure it was him. It might've been a camera repairman. The man was in white overalls and was driving a grey van. He was carrying out some repairs.'

'Christ! Oh, Christ!' Foyle turned to the room and met Forbes's eyes. 'You say a grey van?'

'Yes.'

Foyle dropped the phone. 'It's in a bloody camera!' he shouted at the commissioner, who was at the other end of the room talking to Scarratt. 'The bomb's in a security camera. It's got to be. That's his pattern – turning a safety device into a bomb. That's what he was doing in

Sevenoaks – building something which looks like a camera. Sir, you've got to stop the ceremony.'

Urquhart nodded. 'Right. Evacuate immediately! Get the place cleared and the damned royals out of Whitehall now and all the rest of them – the Cabinet and diplomats. Now! By God, I hope you're not right, Foyle.'

Foyle didn't reply. For some reason, his eyes came to rest on a big jolly-faced woman with an ample bosom, who was standing directly in the line of the street-level cameras. She dabbed at an eye as she watched the massed bands strike up 'Men of Harlech'.

At the bottom of the screen a digital display recorded the time as ten hours, forty minutes and twenty-four seconds.

Apart from a disconsolate young man plodding back from the newsagent's with a carton of milk and the newspapers, Jasmine Road was deserted. A flock of pigeons pecked furiously at some breadcrumbs under the watchful eye of a cat, sitting on a wall about twenty feet away.

Lindow and Mary got out of the cab and stood in the road. It was beginning to spot with rain.

He dialled Foyle and was put through almost immediately. 'We're outside the flat now,' he said. 'There's no sign of any policemen. What should we do?'

'Hang on. They should be there any moment. Let me give you my extension number in case you get cut off.'

He wrote it down then looked up at the building. Nothing had changed, except that the vines had shed a few more leaves, exposing the cracked plaster. There was no sign of life in any of the windows and the curtains were still drawn in the ground-floor flat.

Mary walked the few steps to the garden wall and looked up, then returned to Lindow's side, hands thrust forward in the pockets of the coat they'd bought together. 'Where're the police?' she demanded.

'God knows.' Lindow looked up and down the road. 'Give me the keys. I'm going to take a look.'

Lindow was listening to the voices coming over the phone from the operations room. 'Hey, shut up for a second, will you? Something's going on. I think they've stopped the parade.'

Mary pointed to her watch. 'Have you seen the time, Con? We've got to see what's in there.'

Foyle heard her. 'Don't let her go, Con.'

'They say we've got to wait,' Lindow said to Mary sharply. 'So just stay here, will you?'

The cab driver chimed in, 'So what do you want me to do? My meter's going here. I'll have to charge you waiting time, as well.'

Neither of them took any notice.

Within six minutes of the evacuation order being given, three suspect cameras had been identified in Whitehall by police marksmen, using binoculars and rifle scopes. The helicopter spotted a further two in the side-streets leading down to Victoria Embankment. All five devices were fixed at a height of about fifteen feet by means of brackets bolted to the masonry walls of the buildings. Inspector Lafferty, who had been rushed the few hundred yards from the corner of Parliament Square to New Scotland Yard in a police Range Rover, estimated that the two-feet-long camera housings might contain as much as twelve pounds of explosives each – enough to bring down the sides of the buildings. Pointing to a map of the area, he addressed the commissioner and a knot of senior officers gathered round Foyle.

'These boxes are almost certainly packed with nails and bolts, which will act like shrapnel. They're probably timed to go off in a relay, the devices nearest the Cenotaph exploding first, followed by the ones in the side-streets. They'll catch the people escaping from the first explosions.'

464

'And there's no hope of disarming them?' said the commissioner.

'Not in the quarter of an hour we believe is available. We're examining one of them in Whitehall – here.' He tapped the map at a point on the south-east side of the street. 'There's no way we can lift our equipment up to the boxes, and we certainly can't tackle five at once. There may be all sorts of anti-handling devices attached to them.'

The head of Tactical Firearms suggested that it might be possible for his officers to shoot off the rubberised antennae that could be seen protruding from at least two of the silver casings. But Lafferty dismissed the idea, saying that a stray bullet might detonate the explosives. Then he left the group to radio the men who were examining one of the devices from a window on the east side of the street.

'The only sensible course is to get the people out of the area as soon as possible,' said Urquhart. 'How're we doing on the Royal Family?'

The operations-room superintendent replied that the balcony outside Room 238 in the Foreign Office was being cleared at that moment and the remaining members of the Royal Family, the Prime Minister, members of the Cabinet, diplomats and chiefs of the Defence Staff were being rushed from the area. The main problem was the vast number of people still in Whitehall.

In unison the group turned to the screens. To the north of the Cenotaph well over a thousand veterans, a good number of them blind or in wheelchairs, were mustered in the centre of Whitehall, ready for the march-past. On either side crowds were held back by crush barriers. The obvious escape routes lay to the west, through the arch to Horse Guards Parade or over the open ground in front of the Ministry of Defence. The latter route, however, would bring them too close to the suspected device in the east. And in the north there was another device, with a

465

blast range that meant the street to Trafalgar Square was effectively cut off. The only solution was to send them back through the arch.

An order was sent out to turn the veterans back and funnel them through to Horse Guards Parade, but the monitors showed that the police on the ground were having difficulty communicating this to the leaders of the various sections, particularly those in the middle of the mass of servicemen patiently waiting for the service to begin.

To the south the only solution was to get the people out into the centre of the street and down to the square. That would remove them from the immediate killing zone. But things were already going badly wrong. Gaps had not been made in the crush barriers and people were either attempting to climb over them or pressing back along the pavements towards the security gates at the southern end of the street. On both sides monitors showed the police trying to pull the high wire fences aside to release the pressure of the crowd.

But the chaos was not yet universal. In some places along Whitehall, the crowds seemed unaware of the danger. What they did notice, however, was that it was beginning to rain. Umbrellas appeared, which meant that people's view was obscured and for a few seconds longer they remained ignorant of what was going on. But word was spreading quickly along the pavements. Soon the umbrellas were dancing as the crowds shifted first one way, then the other. As they realised that they were trapped between the buildings and the barriers, their eyes widened and their mouths opened. Waves of panic and disbelief rippled across their faces.

In the midst of the calamity there were some bizarre sights. Without orders, many of the servicemen seemed unwilling to break the formations around the Cenotaph. The twelve ranks of the massed bands were still intact, and detachments from the Household Cavalry and Welsh

Guards stood at ease demonstrating either bone-headed stupidity or a suicidal sangfroid.

Others were quicker to react. An officer from the Green Jackets regiment could be seen organising his men to move aside the crush barriers and herd the crowd towards Parliament Square. Beside him, a BBC cameraman was filming, and around the street nine other crews relayed the unfolding scenes to the world.

The commissioner grasped the situation quickly and barked a stream of orders to the officers in front of the monitors. Most of them repeated the instructions already radioed to the ground, but the controllers went ahead and reissued them nevertheless. It was clear that response time was slowing as every minute passed. What had been an exemplary reflex between the command of the operations room and response on the ground had atrophied.

Foyle listened with one ear, but the majority of his attention was devoted to the speaker-phone over which he could hear Lindow and Mary Menihan talking in the street outside Eamonn's flat. He looked at the clock. It was ten forty-seven and there was still no sign of police in Jasmine Road.

Then Lafferty was at his side. 'We know what's in them. One of my officers has been lowered on a rope out of the window. You can see him on the far monitor over there. He's just unclipped the lid of the device on the south-east side. He's telling us there's a cartload of explosives in there. The detonator is hooked up to a telephone and has anti-handling circuits. It's a wonder he got the damned top off without blowing himself up.'

'Power supply?' asked Foyle.

'Batteries,' replied Lafferty.

'There's got to be a command device in Eamonn Lindow's flat. Are your people anywhere near there?'

'About five to seven minutes away, I'd guess, maybe more.'

Foyle looked at his watch and shouted across the

room. 'Pennel, anything from the networks? We need the area shut down now.'

Pennel was gesturing as he spoke into his phone and did not reply immediately. 'They're doing their best, but there's still a chance a call will get through. We always knew that it was going to be impossible to seal off the whole area.'

'Well, tell them to do everything they can,' Foyle bellowed. 'Thousands of people are still out there.' Then he turned to the speaker-phone. 'You still there, Con? What's your brother's phone number? We need to have it cut off immediately.'

Lindow told him. This time he didn't have to think about it.

Mary looked at her watch again. 'Give me the goddam keys, for Chrissake. There's twelve minutes left. We've got to find out what's in there. Come on. I'm going in.'

'Don't let her go,' barked Foyle in Lindow's ear.

'You can't,' said Lindow. 'Stay here.'

She plunged her hand in his jacket pocket and pulled out the ring of keys. Lindow was holding the phone in his right hand and tried to snatch at her with his left. But she was too quick, escaping from his grasp and bounding up the steps.

'She's going,' he yelled to Foyle. 'She's got the keys. I'm going after her.'

He glanced from Mary to the cab driver, then back at Mary. 'I'm coming too.' He lowered the phone to silence Foyle's protests.

'Hold on there!' said the driver, getting out of the cab. 'How do I know you're not going to run off?'

Lindow turned to see Mary open the door. She glanced back at him and disappeared inside. He started forward, but his right foot slipped sideways on the damp, greasy pavement. He recovered his balance and tore up the steps after her.

'No,' cried Foyle several times, but his voice was lost in Lindow's clenched fist.

He pounded through the empty hallway and up the stairs. Mary reached the corner of the landing and grabbed at the banister to pull herself up the six stairs to Eamonn's door. Lindow was halfway up the first flight when she inserted a key into the top lock, then tried the lower one, pushing at the door with her knee. He saw the blur of Mary's form and her dark hair flying as she vanished through the doorway.

'Ma—!' he shouted, but the rest was lost in the blast.

Before he fell, he saw a flash and something being propelled out of the disintegrating door frame. Then he was slammed backwards by the shockwave. His face smashed into the dado rail and he was thrown down the stairs in a storm of splintered wood and brickwork. He came to rest at the bottom of the stairs. The house roared as if in the grip of some demonic possession. All around him was the soot-fall of plasterwork and the sound of breaking glass. He opened his eyes. The flash was imprinted on his retina. He blinked and blinked to rid himself of it. He knew he was cut somewhere on his face. Blood streamed backwards into his hair from a gash just above his right eye.

Some time later – how long he didn't know – he heard the tiny muffled voice in his fist. He had kept hold of the phone and, miraculously, the line was still open. Foyle was there. 'Con? Con! Con, are you all right?'

'There's been a bomb,' he whispered, and then the terrible knowledge of what had happened formed itself into words. 'Mary's hurt. Get someone here fast.'

He shifted on to his side and swung his legs backwards so that he could get up, and began to drag himself up the stairs. It was very dark and the stairway was dense with ugly black smoke. He climbed to the first landing, where he could see better. The explosion had blown the glass from the windows and smoke was pouring out into the street. Way off, there were voices. People screaming. Below, the cab driver was shouting through the front door.

Then he saw Mary's crumpled body curled up against the wall. He leaped up the remaining stairs and pulled the debris from her. There was blood everywhere. The wall was sprayed with tiny droplets.

'Con,' she groaned. 'Is that you? I can't see.'

'You've been blinded by the flash,' he said. 'It won't last. You're going to be okay.' He concentrated on her face, on her eyes, because he dared not look down at her injuries. He knew the full force of the blast must have driven up into her abdomen and thighs.

'Don't lie. I know I'm not.' Her voice was a whisper, fading.

'Yes, you are,' he said. He drew the hair from her face and smiled at her. 'Hold on there, my love. For God's sake, hold on.'

He glanced inside the flat. He couldn't see much, except that some of the furnishings had caught light and were producing an almost liquid smoke that was flowing down through the hole in the floor. The charge must have been set four or five feet inside the door, he thought. It had blown right through to the flat below, splintering the joists into matchsticks. An electricity cable was fizzing and a water-pipe had been blown apart. Somewhere there was the sound of a cistern filling.

He knew he must move Mary. In a few minutes the building would be burning. He placed the phone on the floor beside her head, shifted from his knees to a crouching position and slipped his left arm under her shoulder.

'You're going to be fine, my love, I promise.' He touched her cheek with the fingertips of his free hand and smiled again. She looked up at him.

'You were right. I can see now.' She smiled faintly then

470

her eyes settled on something behind him. Lindow looked up.

'What is it?' he asked, and then he understood.

'No, you can't do that! No! . . . Mary! . . . No!'

He gripped her by the shoulders, as if to stop her falling asleep and shouted her name over and over again, but she was light in his hands – empty and limp. He looked down at her wounds for the first time and sank back, appalled. Nothing could be done for her. She'd had enough. She'd taken flight from her bloodied, ripped-up body and left him with it. He let her down to the floor gently, a part of him feeling a terrible repugnance – not for Mary, but for the ordinary human frailty that had taken her. It was death that made him recoil.

Then he heard Foyle's voice. Still looking at her face, he slowly lifted the phone to his ear.

Until the explosion in Peckham, all attention in the operations room had been focused on some juddering pictures from a video camera, held from the window above the bomb nearest to the Cenotaph. The explosives officer who had lowered himself on a rope could be seen attempting to unscrew the antenna from the phone without disturbing the anti-handling circuitry.

Then Foyle's cry to Lindow had thundered around the room, stopping everyone in mid-sentence. Officers rose from their screens and looked over to him. Others pulled their headsets aside, straining to hear the speaker of Foyle's phone.

'They're not going in!' Lafferty shouted with alarm. 'He's bound to have rigged something up.'

The words were barely out of his mouth when the unmistakable noise of the blast tore through the speaker. The line crackled and then seemed to fade, but it came back again. There was a roar and a sound of clattering, followed by a dreadful silence. Foyle thought both of them must have been killed. He rose from his chair, shouting their names into the speaker. Then he broke off, wild-eyed, to demand where the explosives team were. Eamonn's flat was the priority. Whitehall would never be cleared in time and the fate of all those people was now controlled by a device – a very well-protected device – in 56 Jasmine Road.

'Has that phone been cut off yet?' he shouted to the room. 'Get that damned phone cut off.' He turned to Lafferty. 'How was that set off?'

'It must've been wired into a burglar alarm – a movement or a heat sensor. There are any number of ways. Christ knows what else is in there.'

Then Lindow's voice, hoarse and uncomprehending, came over the speaker. They heard him climb the stairs and find Mary. He was coughing a lot but from the way he was talking to her they knew she was badly hurt. She began to speak but her voice was weak and seemed to grow distant. A few seconds later came Lindow's cry of agony.

Foyle winced and shook his head. He looked at the clock. There were only seven minutes left. He shot a glance at Lafferty and the commissioner. The commissioner nodded. They couldn't wait any longer. They had to tell Lindow to go into the flat and find the command device.

'Con, Con – answer me! Is anyone with you?'

'No . . . there's no one here,' came the reply. 'Mary's gone.'

'Hold on, lad, we're going to get people to you. But now we have to find out what's in there. Can you do that for us? Are you up for it? There's no time.' Foyle was now very calm. Lindow mumbled something. Foyle repeated the question.

'Yes,' replied Lindow more clearly. 'I'm here. I'll do it.'

'Good, I've got the head of the Explosives Unit with me – Colin Lafferty. Colin's going to talk you through

472

the next few minutes. Tell him exactly what you see. Okay? I'm here too.'

Lindow got up. He felt nauseous and had the sense of floating in unreality. He straightened himself, flicking blood from his cut eyebrow to the wall, and waggled a finger in each ear to stop the ringing.

Foyle was talking to him, but there were also noises downstairs – other voices, other cries. Someone had been hurt in the flat below. A man had ventured halfway up the stairs and was calling to him.

'Are you police?' shouted Lindow.

'No . . . they're coming,' replied the man.

'Then stay back – it's dangerous.'

He turned to go into his brother's home, holding the phone to his left ear.

'Where are you?' asked Foyle.

'I'm going in now. There's a lot of smoke.' As he spoke he edged around the hole in the floor, testing the floorboards with one foot to check they'd take his weight. He picked up a rug and beat at the fire on the upturned sofa. The flames disappeared quickly. He looked around. The place was unrecognisable. The TV set had been shattered and hurled into the bookcase. Books had tumbled to the floor and were covered in chunks of plaster. Every pane of glass in the flat was broken and the curtains were torn and catching on the jagged edges of glass as they flapped in the wind.

'What am I looking for?' he shouted.

'The telephone line,' said Lafferty calmly. 'The number is being taken out of service. But let's start with it anyway.'

Lindow searched the room, coughing up plaster dust from his lungs as he went. He found a telephone and traced the lead to a socket on the wall. He kicked aside the debris and bent down. 'There's no wire,' he said. 'The

473

telephone is plugged in, but there's no wire leading from the socket.'

'He must've laid it somewhere else,' said Lafferty. 'Can you look outside the window? There should be some kind of junction box. Follow the wires from that.'

Lindow threw up the shattered window and scanned the wall. A crowd of onlookers had gathered in the street.

'Is anyone hurt up there?' a man shouted.

He took no notice. He leaned down and examined a small square of unweathered paint just below the window. He reported this to Lafferty.

'It means he moved the junction box too. We need to know why. You're going to have to look for it. He's probably put it at the back of the house.'

Lindow began hunting along the skirting-boards, pulling bits of furniture aside. The sofa was beginning to flame up again, but he ignored it and stumbled towards the kitchen to take a quick look around and then to lean out of the window.

'Got it. There's a box outside the kitchen window at the back. It's out of reach – a lot of wires are coming from it. More than one line.'

'He may have wired in the telephones from the other flats,' said Lafferty. 'It means we have to find the device. A call may still get through.'

'What are you doing now?' asked Foyle.

'I'm moving to the bedroom. One wire leads to the bedroom window. Hold on, something's different. The desk's been moved.'

He looked hard and tried to remember the room as he'd left it. The desk that had contained the secret compartment had been shifted a few feet towards the window.

He bent down to look at the skirting-board behind it. Then he heard two things. First Foyle's voice came rasping through the handset. 'British Telecom have confirmed that they have cut the telephone.'

474

'Shut up!' said Lindow. He strained to hear and recognised the hum of a computer.

'It's in the desk,' he shouted.

'Where?' said Lafferty.

'One of the drawers.'

'Which drawer? It's very important you tell me before doing anything.'

Lindow put his ear to the desk. 'It's the middle drawer.'

'Don't open it. Take out the drawer above. You may be able to see from there.'

Lindow already knew that the desk had no partitions between the drawers. He removed the drawer above and found himself looking through the gap to a folded lap-top computer and a confusion of wires.

'I've got it,' he said. 'It's here in front of me.'

'What do you see?'

'There are a lot of wires. Two or three are coming from the direction of the junction box. Then there are another two that are attached to copper strips at the side. One strip is fixed to the body of the desk, the other is on the drawer itself. They're about an inch apart.'

'That's the booby trap. If you pull open the drawer, you'll connect up the circuit and it'll blow. Somewhere in there will be a detonator and a charge.'

'I think it's under the computer. It seems to be resting on something . . .' Lindow broke off as his lungs choked on the dense smoke. 'It's resting on something about the size of a book,' he said.

'What's happening with the computer?' Lafferty demanded. 'You've got to open it up and find out what it's doing.'

'Hold on, I can see the power supply. Should I unplug it?'

'No!' said Lafferty. 'That'll be rigged too. Find out what the computer's doing.'

'Okay! Okay!' said Lindow. His eyes were streaming

from the smoke. 'I've got to put the phone down for a moment.'

He wiped his eyes, then worked his hand into the drawer. He slipped the catch on the front of the computer so that he could ease the screen up. He grabbed the phone from the top of the desk.

'There are six numbers on the screen,' he shouted. 'It's preparing to dial out.'

He heard Foyle yell to the operators, 'Tell everyone on the ground to take cover.'

Then Lindow remembered Droy and the booby trap and how a simple tug had sent the whole lot up.

He put the phone in his pocket, rushed to Eamonn's wardrobe, flung the door open and saw what he was looking for. He grabbed a clump of ties that were hanging on a rail inside the door and started furiously knotting them together. When he had a length of four, he ran to the desk and fastened one end to the handle of the middle drawer. He went back to add ties to the other end. He was out of the bedroom when he tied his sixth knot.

He took the phone from his pocket and shouted, 'I'm going to deal with this fucker once and for all.'

He tugged at the rope of ties. Nothing happened. One of the knots was snagging on the bedroom-door frame. As he manoeuvred into a line of sight with the desk to free the knot, he heard the rapid music of the modem dialling out. He yanked again, and as he did so he turned his back to the bedroom and rolled towards the floor. The drawer shot forward, causing the copper contacts to meet for a split second and send a current to the detonator. The detonator fired a shockwave through the block of Semtex, shattering its fragile chemical bonds and setting off a rapid expansion of gases, which moved from the bedroom with satanic fury, throwing everything before them at the speed of sound.

Lindow had not hit the floor before the blast reached him and blotted out his consciousness.

Forty-five seconds later, the firemen and police officers who had arrived outside fifty-six Jasmine Road just before the explosion picked themselves up from the pavement and made for the building. They'd been told that a man was in there, but they didn't rate his chances of survival. Two firemen with breathing apparatus went in first, followed by the policemen who wouldn't heed their warnings about the smoke. On the landing outside the flat they found the woman. One officer knelt down, confirmed that she was dead and prepared to drag her body from the stairway. The firemen plunged on into the flat, feeling ahead of them in the smoke with axe handles. They found the man at the front of the sitting room, just under the window. He was lying on his back on a pile of books. They wiped the plaster dust from his face and felt for a pulse. It was good and strong. They took hold of him by the arms and legs, lifted him up and bore him from the building, leaving the tattered pages of what had once been Eamonn Lindow's library of Irish history to the flames.

Epilogue

Lindow waited in his wheelchair for Foyle at the hospital reception. A nurse fussed round him. His left arm was in plaster from the wrist to the elbow, and his left eye and cheek were covered with a cushion of bandages. He had been told that he might lose the sight of that eye and that he would need plastic surgery to his cheek. That was why the doctors had been reluctant to allow him out so soon. But Lindow had been adamant and he had phoned Foyle the day before to ask for a lift to his flat so that he could change for the funeral.

When Foyle appeared at Reception, Lindow climbed out of the wheelchair and greeted him in a low, cracked voice. Foyle touched his shoulder, took hold of his right arm and led him down some steps to where Alex was waiting in the car with the engine running. He moved slowly: the lacerations to his legs and torso were nowhere near healed and the two cracked ribs on his right side hurt as he inhaled the cold, sharp air.

Foyle helped him into the back seat then got in beside Alex.

'You know what day . . . ?' said Lindow. He cleared his voice. 'You know what day it is today?'

'What do you mean?' asked Foyle gently.

'It's my damned birthday. Course, I'd forgotten. Tag just called to remind me. She was planning to come over, but she can't leave my father. He's not well.'

'I'm sorry to hear that,' said Foyle, turning in his seat to face Lindow. 'I don't know what to say – I mean,

478

about your birthday.' He turned back and stabbed at the window button with irritation. 'For Pete's sake, Alex, why do you keep the car so damned hot? I can barely breathe in here.'

Alex gave Lindow a look of uncomplaining resignation.

'Okay, let's be off. We haven't got all bloody day,' said Foyle.

Outside Lindow's flat a lone press photographer was waiting. Since Sunday the newspapers had not ceased writing about Mary and Lindow. The shot of him being escorted from the hospital three weeks before had been used over and over again. To his regret no one had unearthed any photographs of Mary, which served only to increase the interest in the 'mystery MI5 heroine' who had given her life to save the people in Whitehall.

As Foyle's car drew up, the photographer raised his camera and advanced towards them. Foyle leaped out, put his hands up to the camera, then wrapped a huge arm around the photographer's shoulder and led him away down the street. After a few moments of forlorn resistance, the photographer packed his things into the boot of a car and left.

'I gave him the address of a church in South London,' Foyle said, on his return. 'That should keep him well away from Chiswick this morning.'

Nobody had been in the flat since Sunday. It was as though they had only just left. The bed was unmade and Mary's coffee cup still stood where she had left it by the phone. The green scarf she had worn by the lake in Ireland, and which she had taken off when she bought her new coat, was hanging on the back of the chair. Con folded it with his good hand and lifted it to his face.

'You know that you two are national heroes,' said Foyle, looking slightly embarrassed. 'That isn't going to go away, I'm afraid. They've been trying everything to get a shot of you together. They've even asked the security service for their file pictures of Mary.'

'Have they got any?' asked Lindow, with interest. 'I'd like one.'

'I don't know. I can find out for you.'

Lindow changed slowly into the suit he had worn for Eamonn's funeral, which had travelled with him to America and back, crushed in one of his bags.

'It doesn't look very good, does it?' he said, as Foyle draped the jacket round his shoulders.

'It's fine,' said Foyle. 'I find creases tend to fall out once you've worn it a bit.'

The mist was lifting off the Thames as they drove westwards, and by the time they reached the little church on the outskirts of London the sun had broken through the autumn haze. There were several official cars outside the church and a number of police and security service personnel, but no press. Before they climbed out, Foyle explained that, at the request of Mary's mother, the funeral had been arranged by the security service. The vicar, an MI5 man from the Cold War era who had been ordained ten years before, had found a plot for Mary in the churchyard and waived the usual requirements about the deceased being a parishioner.

'I thought her mother was Jewish,' said Lindow to Foyle, as Alex helped him out of the car. 'And what about her father?'

'Her father died a long time ago,' said Foyle. 'Didn't she tell you?'

'No, there was a lot she didn't have time to tell me.'

'You're right about her mother. Apparently she is Jewish but she felt that Mary tended towards Christian beliefs.'

'She didn't have beliefs,' said Lindow. 'Not of that sort, anyway.'

Inside the church Mary's coffin lay covered in flowers on a low catafalque. Lindow could not bring himself to acknowledge its presence and passed to the front pew, looking fixedly beyond to the altar. A short middle-aged woman in a dark blue coat and pill-box hat turned when he entered the pew and smiled at him with Mary's eyes. Foyle introduced her as Mrs Jessie Harkovitz – Mary's mother – then indicated a tall woman named Laing and mumbled that she was the new director general of the security service. Across the aisle Lindow recognised only Stephen Pennel and the Cabinet Secretary, Sir Derek Crystal, who, Foyle explained, was representing the Prime Minister. He whispered the names of Peter Speerman, Keith Craven-Elms, Adam Durie, Angus Grove, Rory Fuller, saying that most of them were Mary's colleagues. They meant nothing to Lindow.

The service began with an address by the vicar, a slight man with tufted grey sideburns brushed back over the top of his ears. As he spoke he looked down at Lindow and Mary's mother. For most of the proceedings Lindow was numb. He listened, as though from a great distance, to the lesson read by Sir Derek Crystal who also made a short address about Mary's bravery and her long service in the fight against terrorism. Lindow remembered her reading Yeats at Eamonn's funeral and thought, with a stab of grief, that it was probably the moment he had fallen in love with her.

There was another reading, this time from Kirsty Laing, and then a hymn, during which Foyle's voice reverberated around the church. But by this time Lindow had removed himself altogether, returning only to wonder about the couple who had arrived late and were now sitting at the back of the church. His bandages did not allow him to see them properly.

Then Mary's coffin was taken from the church. Lindow and Mrs Harkovitz followed the pall-bearers into the graveyard, where small patches of frost lay in the shadows of the old gravestones. As Mary was lowered into the ground the priest's words registered with

Lindow. 'For as much as it hath pleased Almighty God of his great mercy to take unto himself the soul of our dear sister here departed we therefore commit her body to the ground; earth to earth, ashes to ashes, dust to dust . . .'

Lindow stepped forward and laid a bunch of flowers, handed to him by Foyle, which bore a card inscribed with the word *acushla*. In due course, he would have it cut into Mary's headstone.

The mourners stood for a little while, each lost in thought. Foyle held his hands clasped in front of him and considered the terrible aptness that the train of events which had begun in a churchyard so many years before should now reach its conclusion in another graveyard.

As they turned and moved away from the graveside, Lindow saw the couple who had arrived late and now stood at a little distance on the gravel path. Like him, the woman wore bandages over her face. It was evident that she needed the support of the man beside her. One or two MI5 people went up to exchange words with her, then Kirsty Laing walked over, touched her arm and asked how she was. The woman acknowledged them all with nods, but her gaze did not leave Lindow. She seemed familiar, but he couldn't think why.

'Oh, yes, Con,' said Foyle, composing himself and guiding Lindow towards the couple. 'You never met properly, did you? This is Kay Gould, the woman you helped in Clarence Street. You remember?'

'Yes . . . of course I remember,' said Lindow hesitantly. He offered her his good hand. 'But why are you here?'

'Because I worked with Mary,' she said.